P9-BYS-365

Praise for

ANY BITTER THING

"Wood deals movingly with the larger themes of faith, loss, trust, fatherhood, and renewal."
—beliefnet.com, (one of the ten best spiritual books of 2005)

"If you liked *The Secret Life of Bees* . . . try *Any Bitter Thing* by Monica Wood." —*Glamour*

"A quiet, cunning novel . . . full of well-observed grace notes and observations about grief and marriage that brings you up short with a grateful shiver of recognition."
—DAVID KIPPEN, NPR's *Talk of the Nation*

"Wood illuminates the grace in the average and everyday, the miracles that lie within the ordinary life . . . [an] intimate exploration of love and faith, betrayal and penance."
—*San Francisco Chronicle*

"Prose as fresh and lovely as a Maine summer evening . . . Wood employs a sophisticated, layered architecture, circling from present to past to reveal shocking truths. . . . Wood's story unassumingly builds in power, right up to its moving final page."
—*Publishers Weekly*

"Wood's stirring domestic drama is full of surprises as it explores the weighty themes of religion, perceived innocence, and the corrosive quality of best intentions." —*Booklist*

"Polished . . . A quiet tale with epic repercussions."
—*Kirkus Reviews*

"*Any Bitter Thing* is exquisite, a soul-satisfying novel of hearts broken seemingly beyond repair and healed in the utter unlikeliness of grace. Monica Wood writes beautifully, passionately. . . . This is a gorgeous novel, by an immensely gifted writer."
—TIM FARRINGTON, author of
The Monk Downstairs and *Lizzie's War*

"Monica Wood's moving new novel [is a] story of desertions, trust, faith and forgiveness."   —*Hartford Courant*

"Beautifully written . . . Wood's characters show depth and complexity, and unexpected twists continually defy expectations. Wood's take on the modern-day suspicions of Catholic priests is new and enthralling. She circles from past to present in a richly layered plot that builds upon themes of spirituality, innocence and the question of best intentions.
—*Deseret Morning News*

"A major work of Maine literature that will find an admiring readership, and deservedly so."   —*Down East* magazine

"More than a good summer read . . . It deserves a place on the shelf with modern classics such as John Irving's *A Prayer for Owen Meany* and Richard Russo's *Empire Falls*."
—*Maine Sunday Telegram*

"[An] intimate exploration of faith and love, betrayal and penance."   —*San Francisco Chronicle*

"Opens with a bang."   —*The Washington Post*

"Rarely in the past few years has a novel stood out as something truly genuine, and genuinely different . . . Wood's masterful style, composed of complex characters, rich language and intricate plot [is] a mix that is rarely achieved. . . . It's truly a literary masterpiece."   —Milwaukee *Shepherd Express Weekly*

"This wonderful Maine writer has done it again [with] *Any Bitter Thing*. . . . The layered story, gorgeous descriptions, and moving characters make this novel one you'll not soon forget . . . This novel highlights an author in full command of her craft. It deserves to be a bestseller.   —*Maine Lawyers Review*

"Monica Wood's new novel is astonishing. The subtle architecture and trajectory belie its complexity, embracing the reader in the warmth of the narrator's voice and the insistence of her desires. You cannot guess what will happen, and what 'happens' is never forced, though it is inevitable. You will be transported."
—SANDRA SCOFIELD, author of
Occasions of Sin: A Memoir and *Plain Seeing*

"The intense, uniquely used language of *Any Bitter Thing* is perhaps its most outstanding feature."   —Clarksville *Leaf-Chronicle*

"A timely, gripping, and compassionate tale of family, faith, and deeply hidden truths. Monica Wood has written an intimate and emotionally expansive novel full of understanding and hope."
—Lewiston *Sun Journal*

Also by Monica Wood

Secret Language
My Only Story
Ernie's Ark: Stories

ANY

Bitter

THING

ANY
Bitter
THING

A NOVEL

MONICA WOOD

BALLANTINE BOOKS NEW YORK

2006 Ballantine Books Trade Paperback Edition

Copyright © 2005 by Monica Wood
Reading group guide copyright © 2006 by
Random House, Inc.

Published in the United States by Ballantine Books,
an imprint of The Random House Publishing Group,
a division of Random House, Inc., New York.

BALLANTINE and colophon are registered trademarks
of Random House, Inc.

READER'S CIRCLE and colophon are trademarks
of Random House, Inc.

Originally published in hardcover by Chronicle Books
in San Francisco, California, in 2005.

Library of Congress Cataloging-in-Publication Data
Wood, Monica.
Any bitter thing : a novel / Monica Wood.
p. cm.
ISBN 0-345-47768-5
1. Traffic accident victims—Fiction.   2. Child sexual abuse—Fiction.
3. Married women—Fiction.   4. Catholics—Fiction.   5. Orphans—
Fiction.   6. Clergy—Fiction.   7. Uncles—Fiction.   8. Psychological
fiction.   9. Domestic fiction.   I. Title.
PS3573.O5948A84 2006
126—dc22   2005055478

Printed in the United States of America

www.thereaderscircle.com

9 8 7 6 5 4 3 2 1

Text design by Jay Peter Salvas

in loving memory of Father Bob

The full soul tramples upon the honeycomb,
but to the hungry soul, any bitter thing tastes sweet.

– Proverbs 27:7

INVITATORY

ONE

Despite its abrupt arrival, my accident felt anticipated after the fact, like a long-delayed package arriving as a *thwup* on the doorstep. *Finally*, I thought, as I spun through the air and thudded back to earth, delivered.

I tell this with the authority of memory.

I'm wearing dark clothes on a moonless night. A moonless night in late March, a night scrimmed with the fine, soft rain that falls in spring, the road's muddy shoulder too slick to run upon, the wet, bare asphalt making for better purchase. Through the misty dark, a carload of joyriding teenagers makes its oblivious way toward me.

My breathing settles, the road turns, my running shoes slop against the pavement. Then: hit and run. A brief flight through the murk. A bone-rattle landing.

I hear a girl scream, then the scream of the car—a stolen Neon that will be pulled over within the hour. The jig is up for the fourteen-year-old from New York City, AWOL from a wilderness-experience program in Maine, showing off for her hick boyfriend and his three sidekicks. She tells the cop she thought she hit a deer. She tells her parents she thought she hit a deer. She tells the judge she thought she hit a deer.

Eventually, I guess, she thought she hit a deer.

⤜⤛

I land directly on the yellow line — lined up neatly, head to toe — and rattle loose. The road feels forgiving and cool. Something breaks inside me, not only bones. I am thirty years old, with a husband and a good job and a best friend and students who need me and a hole in my life that I fall straight through.

⤜⤛

Impossibly, I hear it all. The fading trail of the escaping Neon. The silence of my body laid upon the yellow stripe, waiting not to be revived but resurrected. Prone, waiting, in the middle of the road. The panicked engine sound weakens with distance, and I wait.

Another rumbling, logy and low, the geriatric throat-clearing of a Buick Skylark, another set of headlights coming around the bend. The brakes are bad — a long, anguished whinny. Some spitting gravel. A car door hitching open, the sound of boots quivering across the road.

Goddammit! Jesus on a stick! Of all the! Of all the!

Hard running, the ping of a cell phone, a few frantic directives, the car door hitching open again, and he's back. Stay with her, they've instructed him, but he doesn't.

Before he takes off, he moves me to the filthy shoulder, struggling under my negligible weight, great clogged breaths gurgling out. *Goddammit! Of all the Jeezly! Of all the Christly!* He lays me down. Hand on my cheek. Not an unkind hand. Also not the type you hope for when you are moments from dying.

4 | MONICA WOOD

His breath on my face arrives as an airy, whitish sifting, like an hourglass being cracked open and left to drain. It is a moment of confusing intimacy.

Then, he bolts.

Sorry sorry sorry!

Boot heels flinting on asphalt. Car door, again. A consumptive stutter as the Skylark pulls away, and away.

Now I hear everything: a branch leafing out. A sleeping bird.

The gate opens. Back I go.

TWO

My parents were among the passengers on Flight 2 8 6, Boston to Las Vegas, when the jet tottered in a wind shear, killing all on board. This is the first fact of my life. I was two and a half years old, staying at the rectory in the care of my uncle, Father Mike, my mother's only sibling. It was Father Mike who had paid for their trip, the honeymoon they always wanted. The news arrived as a blur of activity, side-of-the-eye glimpses of chairs being whisked aside to make room for the hastening friends.

My uncle's poor shaved face, damp and pink, pleats with grief. He melts into that vinyl chair in his office off the front hall, two of his cats draped over the desk like outsized paperweights. His face drops into the well of his hands. He knows my step, and says to me, "Men cry sometimes, Lizzy. Is that all right?" I nod, aware of the straight hem of my hair brushing my chin. He can't see me but I think he can. "Yes?" I ask him, granting permission.

It is possible I've attached these images to the wrong day in my desire to remember something of my parents, if only the reverberation caused by news of their death. The human craving is for story, not truth. Memory, I believe, embraces its errors, until what is, and what is remembered, become one.

Father Mike did nothing to dispel the widely accepted notion that I had nowhere else to go. I can't imagine what he must have been thinking, filing requests and petitions, the paperwork strewn over our supper table among plates of leftover spaghetti and a cat nosing up from a chair. There was a meeting with some priests from surrounding parishes, and a call to the bishop, and finally a trip to the Chancery Office in Portland. It's a comforting notion, all these lonely, childless men blessing my two-year-old head. Finally they let him have me, though by the time official permission arrived, my red coat with the gold buttons had landed in its permanent spot on the coat rack in the hall.

His was a lie of omission. Several priests visited back and forth in those first aftermath days—not his friends, but church officials whom he called Father and Monsignor instead of Larry or Bert. He referred to himself in their presence as "Lizzy's only uncle," which made me feel extravagantly wanted. And it was true, he was my only uncle, and my grandparents were dead. He neglected to mention, however, that I had an aunt, my father's older sister, Celie, who lived in Providence, Rhode Island, a world away from our western-Maine town of Hinton and our rectory home on the banks of the Hinton River. Celie and my father had not been close, too far apart in age and, apparently, sensibility. Celie, unmoved by the notion of aunthood, had her own family to tend, five awful boys. She would have taken me, though, being a Catholic woman well acquainted with obligation.

Aunt Celie and Father Mike discussed my care only once that I know of, on the day of my parents' funeral. His eyes must have been nearly swollen shut from weeping, for it became a story in the parish, how hard he wept while performing his offices, flicking holy water on their twin coffins. I imagine Celie stiffened into a back pew, stoic and solemn, as invisible as possible, fearing to be saddled with a sixth child. They met after the service. He must have pulled himself together, taken her coat, offered her coffee in his office. It was a smallish room with two doors, one opening onto the parlor, the other into a hall that nobody used except parishioners, who entered by the front door. The one beautiful feature of Father Mike's office was a lamp my mother had given him in celebration of his pastorship. She had often given him gifts—he still wore the tiger's-eye ring she bought for his college graduation, a ring I also came to love, that amber flash of cat. Big and sphere-shaped, it looked like the ring of a high-stakes gambler when in truth it belonged to a man who kept a piggy bank on a kitchen shelf.

He and my mother spent lots of time in that office, he liked to tell me. She always entered hesitantly, as if she were a parishioner with a problem of faith, and then they would get to laughing, ruffling the rectory's quiet with the sound of their boisterous kinship. Aside from some furniture and jewelry and a box of photographs, it is all I have of my mother, those painted scenes, a pretty woman joshing with her only surviving brother, her baby brother, the priest. My father appears in these stories, too, but not as the star.

Probably I forgot my father first.

Aunt Celie did not fill that office as my mother had, I'm guessing. There they sit, Father Mike behind a desk speckled with ink and paper clips, the cats banished to the basement on account of Celie's allergies. She takes one of the two straight-back chairs that face him. She leaves her gloves on. There could not have been much negotiation. *I want her,* he says. Her shoulders drop in relief. *Be my guest. I've got a houseful of kids already.*

I spent seven years as Father Mike's child, a time delicate and fossilized, sweet as a paw print encased in amber, telling as a line on a cave wall. Of course I mourned my parents, but that became his hardship to remember, not mine, for I have no recollection of teetering from room to room in search of them, as surely I must have done. My parents, smiling out at me from a silver frame at my bedside, took on the pleasant properties of an oft-told tale, their picture as dear and distant to me as the cover of a beloved book, one I had read many times, then reluctantly outgrown.

I learned my prayers and said them without urgency — they were just one more open flower in the garden I had been delivered into. For seven years, God adored us. I lost touch altogether with Aunt Celie, so thoroughly that when the time came that I had to go live with her after all, she was nothing to me, a stranger.

☙ ❧

St. Bart's, tucked into a few acres of woods just off the Random Road, was a small, poorly endowed parish with no school. At the turnoff stood a sign that read ST. BARTHOLOMEW'S CATHOLIC CHURCH — ALL SOULS WELCOME in blue paint that we refreshed once a year. Coming down the long gravel drive, the first building you passed was the white church hall, long and low-slung, reminiscent of a bowling alley. In winter its roof required vigilant shoveling, often by Father Mike himself. Just beyond the church hall, the trees opened into a clearing and the sky warmed down on the church itself, a modest wooden structure with a steep metal roof. The rectory appeared a few hundred feet later, a white clapboard Cape Cod with black trim and a back porch that faced a slow-moving sparkle of river.

It looked like the home of an ordinary family, a place where you would not feel rude dropping by unannounced. From all sides unrolled a carpet of lawn on which Father Mike set up croquet games, a grill that he used year-round, and a hammock with a waterproof cushion employed mainly by the cats — Fatty, Mittens, and Boo, three fussy males. We called them the bachelors. The east lawn draped down to the river; the south lawn ended abruptly at a screen of pines. A shortcut through those trees — a former animal path that we tramped into an alley over the years — revealed a straight shot to the slope-shouldered farmhouse of the Blanchards, our only neighbors.

Ray Blanchard spoke French, mostly, though his English was more than passable. He worked as a deep-sea boathand, leaving for two weeks at a time. We were far enough inland that his profession was regarded as an anomaly, a baffling mistake, or a flat-out insult to the other fathers, who labored close to home, running machines in the area paper mills or working with dyes and leather at the shoe shop. Mr. Blanchard, with his cut-up hands and sculpted, wind-bitten face, seemed mildly enchanting by contrast. Not as enchanting as Father Mike, who strode across the sacristy every Sunday morning in silver-threaded vestments, the stained-glass crucifixion affording him an operatic backlighting that never failed to thrill me.

Still, I liked Mr. Blanchard, and Mrs. Blanchard. I liked their brimming house. Their daughter, Mariette, was my best friend (two little boys would come later), so I slept there sometimes, Mariette and I wedged into her narrow bed beneath an attic gable. On special occasions — birthdays, Fourth of July — Mariette slept with me at the rectory. We whispered and cackled and got in and out of bed, fetching water or crackers or one of the struggling cats as Father Mike paced the hall. What if we fell downstairs? What if Mariette forgot where she was and mistook the window for a door? He worried like this over his cats, too, sick with anxiety if one of them didn't appear on the porch at bedtime. Every ten minutes I'd hear the screen door creak open until the last prodigal had finally scooted in for the night. "Oh, you act like the old men!" Mrs. Blanchard liked to say, though he was only thirty-one when he took me in. He agreed, smiling, that he'd been born old and wasn't getting younger. I loved that he stayed in the hallway, pacing, angling ways to keep me from harm.

He installed me upstairs in three connected rooms originally intended for the housekeeper: bedroom, sitting room, bath. I don't remember my first days there except in pieces, spangled with light. His own grief must have been unspeakable. His father succumbed at forty to the faulty Murphy heart, his uncle James at the age of thirty-eight. His little brother, Bobby, died of pneumonia during the winter of their mother's cancer, a run of bad luck so preposterous it seemed like a message from a wrathful God. When my twenty-year-old mother left their Prince Edward Island farm to try her luck in the Maine mills, my uncle, a fourteen-year-old with no other family, went with her. It was my parents who sent Father Mike to college, who took his emerging taste for classical music and fine reading, his studied vocabulary, his longing for a life of the mind, as evidence of the calling he had declared at the age of twelve. They sent him to Notre Dame and then to Grand Séminaire in Montreal, where he studied Latin and learned the ways of the Church and, according to him, felt complete for the first time in his life. When he was returned to the Diocese of Maine, he and my mother, together again, lit a votive for each of their buried loved ones.

When I arrived at the rectory with my teddy bears and ruffly ankle socks and my mother's store of dishes, some of the parishioners welcomed the idea of a child. But not all of them. Priests, especially then, in the early seventies, were expected to behave like the statues in church, their unmarked faces listing chastely heavenward, their palms turned up: *Your wish is my command.* They came to him at all hours, and the phone rang so often the cats moved nary a whisker at the sound, but now he had a kid to get to bed just like everybody else. A toddler with sleep problems. The parish council retained the longtime housekeeper, Mrs. Hanson, to get meals and watch the baby.

Still, Father Mike was a real father now. Some people didn't like this.

I wonder sometimes if he counted: his mother and father, Bobby, and Uncle James; and then my mother, his beloved Elizabeth; and his brother-in-law, Bill Finneran, my first father. He must have counted them up. Who wouldn't? It would be no mark against God to count up the bodies. I suppose he must have expected some ill to befall me. He must have waited every day for signs: rash, headache, a swollen this or reddened that. He patrolled the streets wherever we walked, his eyes sweeping side to side, scanning for hidden drives, fallen phone lines, unpredictable dogs.

He read to me at night from the novels of Lucy Maud Montgomery, fusty books that lived with the glassware in my mother's breakfront. I see us there, nestled in the only comfortable chair, an amber glow falling across our faces from a donated floor lamp. How grateful we were, being there together, he in a plain cotton shirt and black pants and shiny shoes, his day's work finished; I in a nightgown and fleecy slippers, willing him to turn the pages faster, even when I didn't fully understand the words; the bachelors collapsed on our laps like socks we'd forgotten to darn. His voice—that satiny tenor—filled the parlor with the story of Anne's grand plans and Gilbert's unrequited love.

We read. We cooked. We tended our "moon garden," an idea he'd gleaned from a ladies' magazine, turning up a patch of earth beside the back porch and planting it with pale flowers that showed best in moonlight. All through the warm summer nights into the crisp of fall, we sat on the porch steps at day's end, sipping Moxie and watching the river rise and naming our flowers, spring tulips to fall sedums, after angels and apostles: Gabriel, James, Michael, John—even Judas got a flower, one of the shabby ones. We were nothing if not forgiving.

Why did the people not love us? "Here comes Father Mike and his little girl," he crooned, carrying me across an icy road, lifting one hand from my back, but not too far, to wave to a parishioner happening out of Stanley's Meats or Hinton Variety. Their faces, even the smiley ones, held a reserve of disappointment, a disquiet that showed in their faulty features.

"He makes arrangements," Father Mike said of God, meaning me, his treasure. God had taken Elizabeth and Bill Finneran before their time, and I was the thing He had given their brother in return.

THREE

To say I was unconscious for forty-three hours is not entirely accurate. I had no desire to speak. Or to squeeze anyone's fingers. Or to do any other thing they asked me—begged me, I should say—to do. *Open your eyes, Lizzy. Lizzy, open your eyes. Open your eyes, Lizzy. Lizzy.*

I did not open my eyes. I liked where I was.

Afterward, I called it "my accident," as if it were something I owned.

The part you could see if you cared to watch—the nuts and bolts of recovery—that's the part that feels now like a dream. Turning points, epiphanies, miracles aplenty, all those incremental steps toward wholeness. I could tell the story of my stupendous recovery. My convalescence was shorter than anyone expected, especially the humorless neurosurgeon who drained my head. The orthopedist was more hopeful from the outset, but even she had her doubts. I could tell you that story; it is not an uninteresting story, though too heavy with pluck and gumption. The body seeks to remake itself. It is no great surprise that my thirty-year-old body healed. It's true that I count myself now among those tiresome people who can feel rain coming, but other than that my recovery was total. I was amazing. I mended. I am thirty-five now, and to see me walk you might never know.

What I remember with such high-pitched clarity is not so much the bandages and casts coming off one by one, or the pea-green walls of the P.T. room, or the physical therapists palpating the tender spots and apologizing in soft voices, or my record-breaking graduation from walker to crutches to cane to my old shoes, which no longer fit. No. The memories that stuck — crystalline in detail, though temporally obscure — happened in the between-time, in that magical space between the big Before and After, in those softly falling forty-three hours. My head seemed like a room I lived inside.

At the hospital I did nothing but listen. *This one's not going to make it.* That's how they referred to me: *This one.* Maybe they said it out loud, though I cannot imagine such a thing. One of them was plain tired. Another had just discovered a lump in his little girl's neck. Another was ready to quit her residency and didn't care whether I lived or died.

I didn't mind. I understood. These things I heard in my between-time did not feel burdensome, they merely existed. People's desires have a way of curling into a room like smoke, and there I was, breathing in.

They scanned my head. They removed my spleen. They rummaged amongst the bones in my back. I had no idea how many bones made up a back. They put a plate in my knee, screws and pins and a powder made of other people's bones. They stitched a thigh muscle that had split down the middle. They did not do these things all at once, on the same day. But they might as well have. Time felt long, and short.

They picked sequins of asphalt out of my face with

tweezers, and later with lasers. Tick, tick, tick went the sound, like stones being tapped underwater, like time being lost.

They buckled me into a rig that turned like a barbecue spit. Someone came in and rotated me every couple of hours. Or minutes. Time did not seat right. Light and dark did not match day and night.

Later, in the recovery room, or in the room where they clamped me into the spit, I discovered how much Mariette depended on me. I had never known this about my friend, how critical to her was my existing; how, if it looked as though I were going to die first, she would offer to trade places — despite her husband, her little son — if only to escape another loss. These thoughts flew like frightened birds from the friend I thought I knew, and I was surprised.

I heard Drew, too, imagining himself over the long haul failing the test of devotion. That he had already failed the test of devotion in the short haul weighed hard upon him. There was a woman somewhere; he was sorry. I have seen the northern lights twice, and one time I heard them as well, and that's what my husband's thoughts sounded like. Like the northern lights. Sad and unreachable.

❧ ❦

I had been "out" — unconscious but not gone. I had arrowed through the mist and landed on the road. I'd been moved by a stranger, a bystander, my witness. My witness fled, gunned his engine, and raced back to the corporeal world, leaving me stranded. But I did not feel alone. A gate had opened, and my head filled beautifully with memory.

Then, in the cool, humming, middle-of-the-night hospital quiet, came an alteration in the air. A slow warming. My uncle — Father Mike, twenty-one years gone — stepped through that open gate.

After a long struggle, hours or minutes, I opened my eyes. An angel's wing. Threads of silver and gold. The frayed black cuff of my uncle's jacket. A crescent-shaped hole where he'd lost a button. An amber flash of his tiger's-eye ring. His voice sounded like poured cream, exactly as I once knew it.

I was so happy to see him, so unutterably happy. *Finally,* I thought again, and fell asleep, moving mercifully back in time.

Hours later, or minutes, I told Mariette, *Father Mike was here.* In her face I saw relief and tears. *Drew,* Mariette cried, *Drew, get over here, she's awake.*

Hallucination. Morphine. Trauma.

No, I insisted.

You're awake now. Look around.

I woke preoccupied by a life I had not lived since I was nine years old. My explanation — that my long-dead uncle had spoken to me from the great beyond — was not something the people around me were willing to countenance.

So, I was awake. Awake, but still gone. And I would not come back without him.

LAUDS

FOUR

I returned home after rehab in mid-August, having missed most of two seasons. My garden, a tangle of daylilies and crabgrass and clumps of unwatered coreopsis, appeared to have fallen over dead in a fit of despair. I could hardly believe how the physical world had changed in my absence.

What the garden lacked, the florist had made up for. On my porch was gathered a robust delivery of tagged bouquets — from Mariette, from the across-the-street neighbors, from my colleagues in the Hinton-Stanton Regional High School Teachers' Association. I hobbled up the steps and flipped open the cards. Everett Whittier, the school principal, had sent a centerpiece with candles; next to that bloomed a perky spray of daisies from the cafeteria ladies, and a funereal raft of gladioli from the student council. I plucked a single bloom from the rest and held it, admiring its bend and curl, shutting out the world. This is how I was in the aftermath — I'd lost my sense of time as a current, and instead moved stop-motion from one discrete moment to the next. This new acquaintance with the present tense was partly a function of my injuries. I had to think so much about each motion simply as a way to avoid physical pain. But it was more than that. My skin felt thinner and vaguely scorched, as if the barrier between it and the pressing-in of the daily world—its stench and heat and racket—had vanished.

Drew was watching me, gauging my face. We had talked little since the accident, though he had driven to the Portland rehab center every day, fifty-eight miles one way. "Come on, Lizzy," he said. "Let's get you inside."

"Wait." I made a slow circuit along the porch, leaning intermittently on my cane, looking down at my dead garden.

"I meant to keep it up," Drew said. He rattled the door-knob, trying to coax me inside.

"I'm not blaming you."

"I know you're not."

"I'm just looking at everything," I told him. "Looking at how everything changes."

"Probation," Drew said. "Spoiled little brat half kills a person and what does she get? Three months, suspended. We could sue her ass, Lizzy."

I shook my head. "I don't want to be the type of person who sues."

"I want somebody to suffer."

What he meant was that he wanted somebody to suffer more than us. Instead of us.

"They should've strung her up by her pink toenails," he said. His jaw pulsed, and I could see that he was using his entire body not to cry. As part of her sentence, my joyrider had composed a handwritten apology—a yarn-ball of mangled syntax, all the *i*'s dotted with empty circles.

"Drew," I said. "You've been a champ. Don't beat yourself up."

His brow creased. "Why would I beat myself up? I'm not the one who stole a car and tried to kill somebody with it."

The conversation we had been not having all summer was still going on. It was the same conversation we had been not having the night of my accident, when I tore out of the house in anger, in the rain, in the dark.

"That's not what's bothering you," I said.

He shook his head. "You can't hear my thoughts, Lizzy." We stared at each other over the ripple of flowers left by people who wanted my homecoming to look festive. That moment is so clear to me still, the way he burned with rage for the kid behind the wheel, a stranger who had created the circumstance under which Drew Mitchell bumped into the limits of his willingness. I knew this much about my husband of five years: wherever he had been before the accident, he had worked his way back to me since; but he would prefer to have made the journey of his own volition. There was no way now to prove to himself that he would not have left his wife if an Act of God hadn't forced him to be faithful.

We said nothing for a long while, the fact of his emotional infidelity floating between us. Drew looked diminished, worn out, less like the boy I'd known in college and more like the man our marriage had turned him into.

I plucked a flower from one of the bunches and handed it to him.

"It was your own thoughts you heard," he said patiently. "All those drugs made them seem like somebody else's." He rattled the door again, probably thinking that if only he could get me inside our house and reacquaint me with our cluttered rooms, then we could forget the ways in which we had both been altered.

The accident had changed my face. A grayish crescent, like a man's five o'clock shadow, cupped one side of my jaw, and a notched scar folded across my eyebrow like a permanent expression of doubt. I'd been told the scar would whiten and the shadow fade, but at the time these alterations seemed emergent and necessary, as if some long-hidden part of me were struggling to reappear. The way Drew stared made me wonder if I looked freshly harmed in the world outside the hospital, unloosed from the consolation of other patients and their mangled pieces.

"Lizzy. Honey." He urged me toward the door. "Come in."

I wanted to be home, and I was home. But I was remembering a place I hadn't lived in for over twenty years. It was still there, just across town, now inhabited by a priest who had retooled the sign and had the driveway graded. All summer long I'd been on the verge of panic, all through the circus act I'd been practicing like a dutiful child, wearing knee braces and back girdles and ugly shoes, doing squats and wall slides and press-ups and step-downs, all the literal and figurative hoops I jumped through because I believed that jumping through them would deliver me from panic and lead me home. If only my body could remember how to do this and this and this, I would be home. That's what I kept saying, adrift in that feeling: Once I can bend my leg, I'll be home. Once I can lift my arm, I'll be home. Once I can turn my head without a bolt of pain, I'll be home.

Well, now I was home. And it wasn't home.

Before Harry Griggs had a name, when he was still the unidentified voice at the other end of a 9-1-1 call reporting a body in the road, Drew and Mariette referred to him as the "bad Samaritan." A guy who met the barest minimum requirement of human decency before taking off—to a party? to a meeting that couldn't wait?

We were sitting on our porch, Drew and I, a humid Friday evening two weeks after my homecoming. Mariette was there, too, adding to our quiet. Paulie, her son, was toddling after a neighbor cat crossing the lawn.

"I wonder what it looked like," I said.

Drew raised his head, alerted. It had always been my habit to think out loud, but now my husband took my habit as "faulty thinking" or "lack of concentration," symptoms of post-traumatic stress.

"Death," I said. "What exactly did the bad Samaritan see? What does death look like, I wonder."

Mariette eyed me carefully. "Pretty gruesome, I'm guessing, which is why the guy decided to slink off like a scared dog. Paulie! Leave that poor creature alone!"

"No white light," Drew said. "No heavenly hosts singing about the river Jordan." Which, as he knew, was exactly what I was wondering, and he wasn't going to discuss it. Over the summer we'd built a house of cards that we'd learned to live in without breathing, and this kind of gentle, preemptive strike had become our normal mode of communication.

Mariette said, "I hold him just as responsible as that ponytailed sociopath who hit you in the first place. Paulie! Quit that!"

"Besides," Drew said. "You weren't dead. Sitting around wondering what death looked like is pretty much beside the point."

Drew and Mariette exchanged a look. They were sitting together on the porch swing, a united front. Clearly, they had made a pact to stop humoring me, no longer pretending to believe that my accident had opened a misty portal through which stepped my long-dead uncle. Since my return home they'd been treating me like a mental patient on furlough, and now I was inching toward the one subject deemed "unproductive" by the harried in-house rehab counselor with sixty-five other patients. According to him, the circumstances of my accident — gross physical injury, plus the emotional toll of two separate parties leaving me on the road like a squashed frog — had compelled me to substitute an earlier, insufficiently "processed" trauma in order to dodge the one at hand. Hence, my dead, beloved uncle speaking to me from the celestial reach. The sorrow you know being preferable to the sorrow you don't.

How Jungian of you, I said to this guy when he floated his theory, and that was pretty much the end of our rapport. I far preferred conversing with the night janitor, a three-hundred-pound Samoan with a complicated love life and seven dogs.

"Daddy's here!" Paulie said, pitching himself toward Charlie, who was just getting out of his car. Big and bearish, Mariette's throwback husband emitted an aura of durability that his customers found reassuring. He owned a McDonald's franchise in Stanton, and in his starched shirt and razor-creased pants looked like a man who loved his work. We liked to tease him for his obliging ways, his antique manners—but in truth he reassured us, too. "Who wants beer?" he said, swinging a six-pack out of the backseat and tucking Paulie under his free arm.

Mariette raised her hand. "I'll take one."

He set Paulie down and began to pass the bottles around, but when my turn came his ease deserted him. He held the bottle to his meaty chest as if protecting me from harm.

"It wasn't that kind of rehab, Charlie," I said. "A beer won't kill me."

He blushed, averting his eyes. "I'll get you a glass," he said, ducking into the house.

"He's a little nervous," Mariette said kindly. "People don't know what to do."

"You make this sound like a wake," I said. "You're the one insisting that I didn't die."

They swiveled their heads toward me.

Mariette said, "We miss you."

Looking at her made me lonely. My accident had occasioned a paradox of loneliness: I felt most bereft around those who loved me best.

"Just for the record," I said, "the bad Samaritan didn't *slink* off. I heard his shoes."

Charlie reappeared in time to catch the whiff of tension. He offered me the glass, then decamped to the other end of the porch, where he settled into a metal rocker, unwilling to take sides.

"You still set on going back, Lizzy?" Mariette asked. I would be heading back to school on Monday to resume my duties as guidance counselor to the student body of Hinton-Stanton Regional High School. Mariette, whose science classroom was just down the hall from the guidance office, considered me unprepared for active duty.

Drew, of course, agreed. "She could wait another month and nobody would fault her," he said.

Over the summer they'd become accustomed to speaking of me in the third person. The two of them were watching me intensely but trying to disguise their focus, looking all around me as if I just happened to emit an aura they found mildly interesting. Off in the distance I could hear the intermittent traffic on Random Road, a steady whine of cars on their way to someplace else.

"Why should I wait?" I said.

Too much crying, went the unspoken argument. Too many moments of "lack of concentration." Too much appearing to be in a place other than the place my body happened to occupy.

"I hardly even need my cane," I said. "I'm a medical miracle."

"Rick screwed up all the sophomore schedules over the summer," Mariette said. "You'll have nothing but a mess to clean up." She moved to the porch railing now, the better to gauge my reaction. "You could stay out till Thanksgiving," she said. "Even the minor snags will be sorted out by then."

"I miss the kids."

"They miss you too, kiddo. They'll live."

I got up, hobbled off the porch, and began a round of step-ups, using the ground and the bottom step, up and back, over and over, barefoot and without my cane. My knee throbbed, but it felt good to feel something.

"As your husband," Drew said, "I forbid you to go back."

He was joking, of course, but nobody laughed. There was a tinge of alarm in his voice that reminded me of the days early in our marriage when our every interaction burned with significance. You can't live that way indefinitely, though; eventually we had to relax and become the same kind of married as everybody else. I climbed back up the steps, leading with my good leg. I sat on the top step, my back to them. Paulie scrambled up to join me, digging his hard shoes against my shins.

"Give Auntie Lizzy a kiss, Paulie," Charlie said. "Auntie Lizzy needs a big fat kiss." A gentleman like his father, Paulie obliged, squashing his pink, drooly lips against mine. Then he left me, swooning into Mariette's lap.

In the ensuing silence we listened to the sounds of a summer already tainted with the specter of fall: the occasional drop of an acorn, spent lilies rattling with seed pods. I put up my hand. "Listen." We all heard it, a flock of geese barking like sled dogs, high above our heads and hidden in a great smudge of dusk.

"What, Auntie?" Paulie asked.

"Geese." I closed my eyes and tried to conjure the muscular beat of their wings.

Drew came to sit next to me on the step, taking a long pull on his beer. Everybody scanned the sky.

"On nights like this," Drew said, "you feel like nothing has ever happened. It's just *now*, breathing in and breathing out."

I turned to him. "That's exactly how I feel," I said. He smiled at me, and I put my hand on his. Such moments were fleeting and often ambiguous, sufficing over the long haul only for people who didn't need much. But they reminded us that we'd been in love once, could be again.

The neighbor cat returned, eyeing Paulie, who was falling asleep against Mariette's chest.

"Remember the cats, Mariette?" I said.

"The bachelors," she said listlessly. All summer long it had been remember this and remember that. I'd worn her out.

"We never had cats," Charlie said. "My mother always said they were too sneaky."

"The truth is," I said to one and all, "I had a visitation."

"The truth is," Drew said quietly, "you live here with us, on Earth."

"We should get going," Mariette said, hoisting her son, who had collapsed against her, blissfully unconscious. Paulie couldn't be woken, and I envied him that.

"What am I supposed to do?" Drew asked our friends. "Tell me what I'm supposed to do."

"Just wait," Charlie said. "Wait it out."

"I feel like a ghost myself," I said. "Nobody can see me."

I'm so lonely, I wanted to tell them. *I woke up so monstrously lonely.* I slipped into the house, bringing the cat with me. The air inside was warmer, what Father Mike used to call "close." In the living room, among Drew's large-format photographs of house fires and bridge collapses and construction sites, hung a framed snapshot of Father Mike. He is looking off to the side — at me, in fact — his face soft in the magical light of afternoon; but there is another light present, too.

Mariette's mother took this picture in the foyer of her farmhouse, catching him near an oversized window that let in an abundance of light. He had come to fetch me for supper, so he looks hungry, a little. I had spent the afternoon in the Blanchards' parlor, sewing shoes — moccasins, to be precise — my first skill. One or two afternoons a week Mrs. Blanchard put some rockabilly on the stereo and set us to work: Mariette and me, and sometimes Mariette's little brothers, Buddy and Bernard.

He looks hungry, but also bemused, like someone about to open a present. We had just taught him how to sew a shoe. I hadn't wanted to leave the Blanchards' house, so Mariette, stalling, said, "Show him, *Maman*."

He laughed, red hair falling over his forehead as he inspected the heaps of shoe parts. "I wouldn't know up from down," he said, grinning. "Our girls are the experts. Right, Vivienne?"

"Yes, Father," she agreed. "They're the experts, our little chickens."

Experts. I pronounced this my favorite word, ever, right on the spot. And so we were. Our ritual was to gather in Mrs. Blanchard's parlor, choosing a fat, glinting needle and a strand of rawhide from her neatly coiled skeins. Each of us claimed a leather glove — fingerless, shaped to our right hand, darkened with sweat. Next, we lugged a pair of buckets from the foyer, the aroma of freshly soaked leather radiating skyward. After stiffening the rawhide by running it back and forth against a block of wax, we pulled an upper from one bucket, a lower from the other, and lined up their matching holes. Our task called for concentration, strong hands, and sometimes silence. Over and over, we threaded the rawhide through the holes in a piecrust stitch, evenly fluted along the toe end of the shoe. The heel end — a shapeless flap — would be someone else's job back at the factory.

Thirty-six shoes to a case. Crimp, thread, pull. Crimp, thread, pull. Crimp, thread, pull. Mrs. Blanchard dispatched the final tying off in a stupendous *thwip thwip,* fingers flying. Mariette and I were slow by contrast, the little boys nearly useless, but this was piecework, time really was money, and though Mrs. Blanchard sewed five shoes to our one, we often made the difference between meeting quota and not.

They could arrest her for that, Mrs. Hanson said more than once, but left it at that because Mrs. Blanchard was a pretty woman who had married a drinker. Mrs. Hanson was right, of course. The work was highly illegal, a kind of magnanimous sweatshop, really. But who could mind if Father Mike didn't? We sewed sometimes for entire afternoons, the music boosting production, peanut-butter sandwiches stacked on a platter, all of us drunk on Mrs. Blanchard's company and the music and the heady smell of leather and oil.

Why did Mariette and I never recall these times? We were nine years old on the summer afternoon of this photograph; by fall I would be taken from there; by winter would come news of Father Mike's death. How had we allowed the most lighted days of our childhood to fade behind us, unremarked?

He crouched before me that day, picked up my hands and kissed them, admiring the calluses. "This," he said, "is the working girl's stigmata." He was proud of my hands, and I guessed it had something to do with his memories of farm life on Prince Edward Island, where children learned how to do, to make, to fix, to solve. I rested my hands in his, palms up, showing him one more proof of how lucky he was to have me.

"Hey," said Buddy. "I'm an expert, too."

"You too, young man."

"And me."

"And you too, Bernard."

"Show him, *Maman,*" Mariette said.

"It's easy! It's easy! *Maman,* make Father Mike sew a shoe!"

"Make him, *Maman!*"

"Oh, brother," he said, releasing my hands, which meant yes, and there was a pleasant rippling of voices as he sat down and allowed Mrs. Blanchard to guide his fingers through a glove. His small hands looked bigger when he tried to take a stitch. The little boys leaned close, expecting magic, but the hands that could turn wine to blood had no aptitude for piecework. Mariette and I giggled till we had to cross our legs to hold our pee. Finally he sprang up, and to our blank astonishment, began to sing. *You ain't nothin' but a hound dog,* he sang with Elvis, making moony eyes at Major, the Blanchards' earnest basset hound. Father Mike's cassock swung back and forth from his hips, and we all got up to dance, the shabby parlor quivering with movement and raised voices.

I remember this. All this sweetness.

Back then Mrs. Blanchard had a burbling, contagious laugh, and as she danced with her children, side-stepping the for-bearing dog, I was visited by the most unexpected wish for a mother. Father Mike had tried to keep my mother alive for me, but it was like hearing about Rapunzel or Snow White, a seamless beauty who lived in the realm of imagination. I'd never thought to envision her as someone who might cough or sigh or open a breadbox or sew a shoe. But I did at that moment, watching Father Mike move across a parlor rug littered with shoe parts and dog hair, because of how his face looked in the warm bath of a woman's laughter.

Wait, Mrs. Blanchard called, running to get a camera, then caught him just as he danced his way into the foyer and turned to look at me.

On the day Aunt Celie came to take me, nobody thought to stow the Lucy Maud Montgomery books into my tartan carpetbag, or the scapular medal that dangled from my bedpost, or the angel doll that stood atop my dresser. My aunt dutifully packed my dresses and underwear, my socks and schoolbooks, but it was Mrs. Blanchard who appeared like a fairy out of the forest that morning to give me the photograph, thrusting it into my hands like an exposed secret.

FIVE

Not long before Father Mike was sent away, Mariette's own father disappeared. This forever-conjoined loss, I believe, is what bound us through years of separation when most childhood friendships, even one that burned like ours, would have guttered out.

Ray Blanchard's previous desertions had passed unregretted. It was generally believed that when he missed a boat boarding—and two weeks' pay—he either stayed near the docks, prowling the bars, or hastened back to New Brunswick, his original home, to drink and suffer for a mysterious and necessary period of time before joining up again with his true life. The house unwound whenever Mr. Blanchard went away, no *arrête, arrête* from Mariette's mother as he raged around the kitchen knocking pots off the stove. Then, any random midnight, back he'd come, unwashed and unrepentant, blatting in French. Fish talk, Mrs. Blanchard always called it, you save that talk for your fish. I covered Mariette with my body as we snuggled in her attic bed, listening to the commotion, the loud complaints and Mrs. Blanchard's famished pleading, *non, non, les petits. Les p'tits, les p'tits,* is how she said it, meaning us, cowering in the attic, and the baby brothers on the second floor hiding in the closet with the dog.

Tais-toi! The children will hear!

Then, sometimes — not often — a sound that could have been shoe parts slapped into their buckets, but wasn't — followed by a death-white silence.

After a couple of weeks, off he went again, making the long drive along the river to the sea, leaving a wake of relief. Mrs. Blanchard brisked about her kitchen as if God himself had appeared in the night and scrubbed another layer of weight from her bird-bones body.

I kept these things to myself, afraid I'd be forbidden to go back there.

I liked Mr. Blanchard sober. Loosed-limbed and good-looking, he acted out the parts in stories he loved to tell in his zesty New Brunswick accent, mostly about hauntings in his childhood home back in Shediac. Violence hummed just beneath the surface of these tales, which pinned us, thrilled and pie-eyed, against the backs of our chairs with our mouths agape.

"Stop it, Ray," Mrs. Blanchard admonished him, "you give them the nightmares."

"That's how we tell stories up home," he snapped. "You want them to stay babies?" Mrs. Blanchard's people were from Sherbrooke, Quebec, a different strain altogether. Her sisters, with their urgent *sit-sit-sit* accents, tended toward stories of predictable temptations followed by the joy of redemption.

Pauline, the oldest sister, was there on this day I'm thinking of, not long before Mr. Blanchard vanished for good. A warm night, first night of my ninth summer; Mr. Blanchard had his shirtsleeves rolled above his knotted forearms. He called all his wife's sisters "my girl," even Pauline. Mariette and I liked her best. Unmarried, she felt it necessary to advertise, accompanying her tight jeans and pullovers with high heels and lipstick even in daytime. The other sisters were too busy chasing babies to interest us much.

"That's quite the caboose you carrying 'round, my girl," Mr. Blanchard said to Pauline.

"Go catch some fish, Ray," she retorted, swinging the caboose in question down on one of Mrs. Blanchard's kitchen chairs. She had sheathed herself in white shorts and an electric blue tank top with black piping; her brunette hair had turned platinum overnight, cut straight at the jawline like the singers in ABBA. "Make yourself useful for a change."

He laughed then — a clammy, slow-moving chortle that always made me feel funny. Mariette went silent, then laughed along with him. Then I did.

"I can make myself useful, my girl," he said. "Say when."

"You watch yourself, Raymond," Pauline said, her rouged lips slicked into a grim line. Her skinny heels dug into the linoleum. "The Levesque girls don't take shit from the like of you."

Then he made that laugh again, and Mrs. Blanchard told him to stop it or else. "Is that a threat?" Mr. Blanchard asked, still laughing, squeezing Mrs. Blanchard's tiny face between his big thumb and fingers. "Is that a threat from the Levesque girls?" This he said in French. Then he gave his wife a long, embarrassing kiss, and clomped upstairs to take a nap before heading out to sea come night.

I did not know — had no way of knowing, since I lived with a celibate man whose idea of a party was to invite other celibate men once per season to eat hamburgers and smoke cigars and play poker or pinochle half the night — what that kiss meant. It looked like a weapon, but couldn't be.

"Are you scared of him?" I asked Mariette afterward. We were sitting on the front steps of the rectory, surveying our world: church, church hall, the long gravel driveway that ended at the main road, and also, through the wide, tamped-down lane through the trees, the back windows of Mariette's house. "I mean in the daytime," I added. It went without saying that on those hollery nights Mr. Blanchard could be terrifying.

She turned abruptly, her hair whipping against my face. "No. He's my papa." Then she grabbed her tipped-over bike and tore through the shortcut, where I had to pedal furiously to catch her. Her lie felt like a bruise inside my body.

That evening, I asked Father Mike about the kiss. He was spooning fudge batter into a pan. Mrs. Hanson's cake— white cake with white frosting—sat untouched on the counter. I had been instructed to bring it to Mariette's for our sleepover, an unusual gesture on Mrs. Hanson's part, but her pity for Mrs. Blanchard took more than one form.

"He kissed her right in front of everybody," I informed my uncle. "Like this." I demonstrated on the back of the spoon, then licked the chocolate off.

"Stop that," Father Mike said, tapping the pan on the table to even out the batter.

"It looked kind of yucky," I said.

"It probably was."

"How come priests can't get married?" I'd broached this subject before, which he usually took to mean that I wanted a mother. Sometimes he said, "Because we're married to the Church," and sometimes he went all rubbery and confessed that he'd all but stolen me from Aunt Celie, after which I declared my relief and gratitude that I'd landed here, in this house, with our cats and our Lucy Maud Montgomery novels, and not in Aunt Celie's catless, bookless, faraway house full of boys. Then he'd puddle up for my mother and father while I sniffled a bit, trying to feel the way he was feeling.

But that night Father Mike took neither tack. Instead, he said, "Because you don't get everything you want in life." He was cutting the fudge already, his forearms working, shaping messy squares from which a fragrant warmth rose. Fudge was our specialty, though we never cared to follow the last of the directions, the part that said wait. He applied himself to his task, and I felt, as other children must have felt with their parents, a sudden, unwanted realization that his life was a mystery. "Don't burn your tongue," he said as I dropped a gob of fudge into my gullet, baby-bird style. He wiped my mouth with a napkin, then said, "Chapter eight tonight." We were reading *Anne of Green Gables,* our favorite book. I reminded him that I was headed to Mariette's.

"Is he home?" He always referred to Mr. Blanchard as "he."

"He's going fishing." As if to prove my point, Mr. Blanchard's croupy pickup coughed to life next door. Mrs. Blanchard maintained, not without humor, that her husband refused to fix the exhaust system because he enjoyed swearing at it too much.

I scooped a hoggish piece of fudge out of the pan to bring to Mariette — a secret present with which we planned to taunt Buddy and Bernard. "Mr. Blanchard says one of these days he's going out to sea and never coming back."

"Let's hope he's a man of his word," Father Mike said.

"Mariette hates when he talks like that."

"Mariette isn't lucky like we are," he said. "But she's got a good mother. And a good friend, too, hasn't she? Isn't God looking after her in His own way?" He ran the knife under the tap water and covered the fudge. "Ray hasn't been scaring you, has he?"

"Nope," I said, knowing better than to repeat Mr. Blanchard's stories of bloody hauntings. It was true my nightmares had returned, but they weren't about Mr. Blanchard. They were about the cats running away, or the rectory burning down, or Father Mike vanishing in a blizzard. It takes children a long time to understand what they have lost.

"He'd better not," my uncle said, taking my chunk of fudge and wrapping it in wax paper, then wrapping, pointedly, two more pieces for the boys. "Come on. I'll walk you over there."

First he made me brush my teeth and hair. Mrs. Blanchard had her hands full with Buddy and Bernard, and Father Mike was a stickler for good hygiene.

We took the shortcut, the suggestive scent of early summer emanating from the thickety woods. Father Mike still wore his cassock from the evening Mass — Saturdays tended to be breathless affairs, with nursing-home rounds all afternoon and Mass at five and six-thirty, followed by supper and fudge. Father Mike was holding the cake; I kept my hand on his forearm as we steadied through the approaching dusk and its accompanying rustles, expecting to arrive at the Blanchards' back door and find their dog, who knew us, ready to let us in.

But that evening the dog did not let us in; he nosed at the screen door, which had been locked from the inside — an unheard-of custom in Hinton back then, almost an insult to your fellow man. Poor, slow-witted Major butted his head against the door and then gave up, looking mournfully up at us. "Hello?" Father Mike called, peering through the screen.

Mrs. Blanchard appeared then, emerging from the depths of the house into the ill-lighted foyer, holding a package of frozen peas over one eye. Mariette trailed her, crying, Buddy and Bernard draggling behind, Buddy's pee-heavy shorts grazing his knees.

Mrs. Blanchard unlatched the door.

"What happened?" Father Mike demanded, setting down the cake and prying her fingers from her face. She looked like a child being inspected after a fall off a bike.

"It was Papa!" Mariette blubbered. Major raised his tragic muzzle, then scuttled into the next room to search out some quiet.

"*Les p'tits,*" was all Mrs. Blanchard could choke out. "Father, they saw everything." She was one of those rare women who look beautiful crying, and despite the peas hunked against her eye, she reminded me of the Weeping Mary statues the nuns at St. Catherine's gave out for very special rewards.

"That son of a bitch," Father Mike whispered, and did not take it back. Then, remembering the children, added, "Don't be afraid, Vivienne. It's just us now. Don't cry." I was struck by the word *us* as he ministered to this family. He gave the boys a square of fudge and the promise of cake; he calmed Mariette by asking innocuous questions that required only a "yes," "yes," "yes"; he eased Mrs. Blanchard into one of the kitchen chairs. *Us.* He seemed to have entered a place that had heretofore been barred from him.

He did not look like a priest just then, despite his cassock and collar. Neither did he look like my uncle, the one who wore flip-flops and a porkpie hat and embarrassing plaid swim trunks to the beach. Since the age of two I had accompanied him to hospitals and nursing homes, to farmhouses with badly hung doors, to sickrooms ablaze with votives. I had witnessed his kindness, his inclining ways, his bone-deep sweetness. I had seen spits of anger, moments of grief, worshipful bursts of laughter. He was my uncle. He was a priest. This was, I believed, the full repertoire of his responsibility and endeavor.

Until now. Tenderly, he traced the bruised socket of Mrs. Blanchard's eye, and she stared straight at him, emitting a raw, womanly rip of pain. His neck reddened from the Roman collar upwards. All at once, he looked — there is no other way to say this — like a man.

The boys twined themselves mutely around his legs; Mariette squashed her soaked, gummy face against the immaculate folds of his cassock; and I sat down, hard, clobbered by the weight of my jealousy, trying, like a good Catholic child, to wrestle the feeling away. *He's mine,* I breathed to myself, in and out, a premonition of loss eclipsing every need in that room. I was nine years old and he was all I had.

Moments later, Pauline stomped over in a high-heeled rage, *I knew it, I knew it, how many times did we warn you, we knew it, we knew it,* guarding us as Father Mike took Mrs. Blanchard to get her eye dressed. Off they went in his big blue car. Seeing her planted there, her narrow, translucent, finely veined hand still packed over her eye, I surrendered to a form of vertigo, a rolling dislocation that made me look at this crumpled, crying woman, this woman I adored, and think, *That's my seat you're in. Get up.*

After that night, Father Mike forbade me to cross the Blanchard threshold whenever Ray came home. Not that it made much difference, for Mr. Blanchard spent more time at sea than on land that summer, then vanished for good in the fall. Soon thereafter, Father Mike was made to leave. Then me.

SIX

It always began the same way: a startled waking in the terrifying dark. Moonless. Starless. The stairs poured downward, long and endless; my heart seemed to beat outside my body. Perhaps I dreamt of monsters, or bad men who had taken my parents away. Once I reached the landing it was a clear shot to his tiny bedroom off the parlor. His door was open. He listened for me. I flung myself into his bed, scattering cats.

"What is it?" he asked. "What, Lizzy?"

It was the smell of him—the drugstore shaving-lotion smell that to this day brings a wave of longing—that unloosed me. I began to wail, probably for my lost parents, and I wanted nothing but to be held all night by this poor, saddled man who had to get up at five for the early Mass. He petted my hair, told me my parents were watching over us, and Jesus, too, and our guardian angels, and that nothing else bad would happen. He promised.

"It's a nightmare," he said. "Nightmares are make-believe."

"Can I sleep here, Father?"

"You can stay here till you feel better, and then I'll take you back upstairs."

"But I want to sleep here. Pleasepleaseplease."

"I'll carry you up. You just think about your guardian angel, that nice, big angel that's going to sit by your bed all night long, and you'll feel all better by the time we get you tucked in, I promise."

"Why can't I sleep here?"

"Because girls aren't supposed to sleep in boys' beds."

"But you're not a boy."

"Actually, Lizzy, I am." That's just how he said it, too: *Actually, Lizzy, I am.*

"You're *not*. Please, Father. Pleasepleaseplease."

Most people's memories do not go back this far. I was so small on this night I'm thinking of that I did not know girl from boy. So small that he could not refuse me.

He tucked me into his bed. He put me on top of his blankets, then covered me with a quilt. He then slipped back beneath the covers and kept his arm around me. This was not exactly the arrangement I wanted — I wanted to sleep under there, where he was — but it did the trick. I woke in my own room in daylight.

Waking in terror every few weeks, I fled down those stairs again and again, beelining for Father Mike's bed. He picked me up, carried me back upstairs, talked me back to sleep, but after two or three more trips he'd relent and let me burrow into his bed. Who would blame him? Who would imitate the unique loneliness of the parish priest, no live-in brothers to buoy him, no wife to comfort him, no friend to stand with him on equal ground? He let a child into his bed, always arranging the blankets in that fussy chasteness, and let her take her comfort. What was he thinking, waiting for my breathing to slow, my quivering body folded against his? Was he thanking God for me? Was he wishing to be a normal man, a father who had to get up not to say Mass but to make first shift at the shoe shop or the mill?

I always woke in my own bed, no longer afraid. I believe he might have been trying to teach me something about solitude, though in a month's time I would again barrel down the stairs and into his bed to fracture his sleep.

He let me do this at two years old. At three, and five, and eight.

And once at nine.

April first, the rectory buttoned up, our small town cloaked with the quiet of a late spring snowfall. At one point the plow made its lumbering rounds through our parking lot. The muffled night had been filled with shadows, and because I had come to him in a state of terror, not once but many times, he lay sound asleep, exhausted, when Mrs. Hanson opened the unlocked kitchen door. Normally, Father Mike would be up, coffee made, the paper open on the table; I would be drowsing down from my bed, waiting for Mrs. Hanson's mushy pancakes or soupy eggs.

But she was early that day, and Father Mike was late. His bedroom door was open, as it always was. He had not moved me in the night.

In my memory the doorway fills with her face, mouth turned down like a hound's, cheeks enflamed, eyes watery and shocked under her magnified glasses. I sat up, mortified, certain that her coiled face was a reaction to my childishness, a nine-year-old having come crying downstairs in the night. Nine years old! A big girl like that!

How ashamed I must have looked. How caught.

The rest she filled in herself.

Very slowly, with the patience of an uncoiling snake, an ugly story began to take shape in our town. Spring to summer to fall, it wound its way in near silence through the parish, an unseen presence that finally struck — with no warning and no mercy — at the end of November. Father Mike guided me into his office after supper, looking glum and vacant. I took one of the stiff visitor chairs and gazed across at him. Of course I was in love, the way all nine-year-old girls love their fathers. In his cassock and collar, with his swatch of red, untidy hair, he was handsome-man, perfect-man, daddy-man, mine-mine-mine. Women brought him apples and brownies; men fell out of their way to greet him on the street. Middle-aged millwrights came to him for spiritual advice, young parents asked him to bless their babies, the Daughters of Isabella cajoled him into singing "Mrs. Murphy's Chowder" at the church bazaar.

Up until that fraught season, that is, when the rectory's front door stuck in its frame, logy from disuse. There was an undercurrent in the parish, an emotional imbalance that I had no way of understanding.

"I couldn't love you any more if you were my own child," he told me that evening, sitting at his desk. His back straightened, and his fingers — nails bitten to tatters — rested lightly on the desk. Normally his declarations reached me like an umbrella opening inside my chest, but not on this night. He kept brushing back his lovely hair as if the very fact of it wounded him.

"I love you too, Father," I said. And though I had said these words numberless times, I detected a change in my own voice, a foreknowledge that frightened me.

"I have to go the Chancery tomorrow, Lizzy. I might be gone all day."

"I can't come?"

"Not this time. You can stay with Mrs. Blanchard."

"But it's Buddy's birthday. You said we could make a coconut cake."

"I have to go, though. It's a very important meeting."

"With who?"

"Father Jack, you remember him."

I nodded. When Father Jack visited I lay awake well into the night, in thrall to their loud stories and rips of laughter and clinking glasses.

"And Monsignor Frank, and maybe Bishop Byrnes."

"What's the meeting about?"

"Just Church business. Nothing to worry about."

"All right," I said, worrying already.

He got out of his chair and onto his knees. "Pray with me, Lizzy?" he asked, and my first memory came back to me then, my uncle melting in his chair after unspeakable news, asking was it all right to cry. I scrambled to my knees, overcome by maternal fervor. He had a rosary in his hand; from my pocket I took my own rosary, which he himself had blessed on the occasion of my First Holy Communion. I laid my hand on his shoulder and let it warm there. We weren't halfway through the second decade when my uncle began to weep. I clung to him, afraid he might fall. He got up, crushed me to his beating chest, and for a moment I thought we were about to dance, the way we did sometimes at parish weddings, my legs dangling free. But no, he simply squeezed the breath from me and put me down.

Early the next morning, before leaving for Portland, he gave me a real guardian angel, one he'd been saving for Christmas: a winged doll in sequined robes, sixteen inches high. It would be up to her to keep nightmares away, and in her glittering glory she appeared to be up to the task. After breakfast, Father Jack arrived, inexplicably, accompanied by a priest I knew just a little, and a pink-cheeked, nunlike woman who asked me a series of bewildering questions. The woman stayed with me that night, and when Father Mike finally returned, a day later, he was in the company of a monsignor whom I didn't know at all. *I have to go away, Lizzy. For a little while.* His coursing tears silenced me. Within minutes, it seemed, he was gone.

The angel reposed on my dresser for the brief remainder of my time at St. Bart's, a dark-haired doll with a porcelain face and large, dolorous eyes and wings fashioned out of real feathers. Her lips parted faintly, as if she'd been created in the midst of confiding a secret. I thought he must have retrieved her from heaven itself. Whenever I woke in those last blunted days, there she would be, this benevolent specter to whom I whispered each night before falling into feverish sleep. I could scarcely breathe under the weight of ending. Father Mike gone, the house so quiet you could hear the padding of cats, the light snoring of a kindly woman sent to supervise my last days there.

Your uncle went to a nice place called a retreat center. They're going to help him there.

Help him what?

You'll see. Everything will be fine, she said to me, and it was the sad-eyed angel whom I beseeched, night to night, *When?* A week later, when I finally left there myself—that awful, high-cold day—my angel got left behind, and no amount of pleading could persuade Aunt Celie, herself reeling from the concussion of change, to drive back to Maine to reclaim her.

I believed I would never see her again, my shining, gold-threaded angel, but twenty-one years later, in my fog of recovery, she returned to me—her dark hair, her voluminous gown, her snowy feathers. She seemed to hover, warming the air, then stepped aside in a hush of wings to let him speak.

The Little Hours

TERCE

SEVEN

From *The Liturgy of the Hours:*
The spirit of the Lord God is upon me, because the Lord has anointed me; He has sent me to bring glad tidings to the lowly, to heal the brokenhearted . . .

His life is a pleasure for which he thanks God seven times daily, guided by his Breviary, a set of four prayer books bound in soft leather, one for each liturgical season. The Breviary contains the complete Liturgy of the Hours, a flawless scheme of psalms and canticles, inspirational readings, intercessions, scripture, hymns. Sometimes he sings aloud, sometimes he hums, often he whispers. Since his ordination he has woken each day to murmur the Invitatory: *Lord, open my lips.* Before breakfast comes Lauds, then The Little Hours: Terce at midmorning, Sext at noon, None at midafternoon. Vespers is said as evening falls, Compline in the dreaming moments before sleep. Sometimes he adds Matins, a prayer for the middle of the night, which has become obsolete for all but the occasional insomniac. Like any careful design, this one offers more than one application: balm for the wounded, calm for the fearful, solace for the griefstricken, celebration for the blessed, inspiration for the ambitious. For him, in these radiant days of a dual fatherhood, the Breviary gives form to a free flow of gratitude.

Seven times a day: *Thank you, thank you, thank you, thank you, thank you, thank you, thank you.* He seeks holiness in the poorest moment, a fulfillment of his calling. Seven times a day, he consecrates time.

As Vivienne Blanchard knocks at the door for their weekly session, he recognizes that in some ways he is no different from the men in his parish who do shift work at the shoe shop or the mills. He never expected his life to resemble a layman's, but like them, he has a child to raise, a job with routines. In all other respects his days resemble no one's but another priest's. Custodian of secrets, shepherd and steward, God's stand-in, he opens the door to his neighbor and friend with the heady certainty of the chosen.

I have a problem of faith, Father, says Vivienne, her small face pinkening. *I require advice.*

He has always found the odd formalities in her English enchanting. The way she speaks makes him feel necessary.

She requires him.

He takes her hands, which are thin and hard, bony, but in a pleasing way. He squeezes her fingers, meaning to reassure, to appear older than his years. *Faith is not the problem,* he says, and she smiles, answering, *Faith is the solution.*

Most Wednesday afternoons, just before supper when the girls like to play together after Mariette's nap (Lizzy flat-out refuses to nap, ever), Vivienne presents to him a problem of faith, and they talk. Her questions interest him because, unlike the questions of his other parishioners, they strike him as a plea for a more meaningful life but not necessarily an easier one.

If God is always with us, as He claims, then why do we so often feel alone?

Do you often feel alone?

Doesn't everyone, Father? Clearly God wants us to feel alone at times. There must be a reason.

What do you mean by alone?

Surely you know, Father. You of all people. Tell me where God goes when He leaves me.

He goes to me, he tells her, smiling. *He says, Remind Vivienne Blanchard that I can exist in two places at once.*

At these times, her problems of faith appear to be nothing more than an excuse to talk to somebody who is neither a child of four, nor her sisters who don't know everything about her, nor her husband who doesn't listen. This, to his private satisfaction, is something he gleans between the lines.

Not that she tells him much.

He is thirty-three years old, flatters himself that he looks forty: permanently windburned from all those seasons on the Island, his skin exudes an illusion of experience. Despite his toughened complexion and the auburn stubble he has to shave twice a day, during his first years here the parishioners treated him like a little boy. He came to St. Bart's as a freshly minted curate, straight-shouldered and long of limb, consigned to the tutelage of Father George Devlin, the mulish, much-loved pastor whose sole concession to Vatican II was to say Mass in an English so grudgingly unintelligible that a good third of the congregation didn't notice the switch from Latin. Night after night, Father Devlin installed himself at the dinner table, masticating one of Mrs. Hanson's overcooked pepper steaks, wondering loudly what in heaven's name the Church was coming to. After one of the teenagers in the parish youth group asked to do an interpretive dance for the Offertory, Father Devlin abruptly retired, leaving his understudy in the thankless position of reviving the headliner's beloved and long-running role.

Because he was young — the youngest pastor in the diocese, a point of pride for the congregation — they treated him as a mascot, a class pet, the freckle-faced boy who had followed his beneficent older sister into the bosom of the Hinton Valley. Among the first seminarians to be ordained in a hometown parish, he had made his vows in this very church, prostrating himself before the Almighty and the bishop and this same congregation, light-headed from incense and suffused with the most exquisite joy and submission. At the reception they pressed upon him like so many uncles and aunties, balancing tea cakes and punch as they pinched his hands and patted his back, wishing him well on his first assignment as a prison chaplain and hoping aloud to get him back as their own pastor. That wish came true — it was his wish, too — but he'd become a man in the meantime, to no one's notice. Even when officiating at a wedding, or following a slow-moving casket out of the church into a bright cold day, he felt their sticky indulgence: *Don't worry, Mikey, you're doing great. And people do improve.*

That was then. With a child in the house he can no longer be their child, thank the Lord. They look at him differently now. Askance. He senses their discomfort — at a parish-council meeting, say, or during a homily in which he invokes one of Lizzy's childhood milestones. He's good at reading faces: They doubt his commitment.

They think: That kid takes too much time.

They think: How does he give her a bath?

They think: At least there's a woman in the house.

But Mrs. Hanson keeps so busy. She is pleasant enough, attentive toward Lizzy but not especially affectionate, closer to General MacArthur than the Mary Poppins he might have wished for. Surely Lizzy must find comfort in her cushiony figure, her graying hair, her female presence in these bachelor rooms. Mrs. Hanson drubs Lizzy's hands every afternoon before she leaves, scuffing under the nails as if sending him a message. Lizzy seems not to mind being tended like livestock, and he cannot help but believe Mrs. Hanson knows something he doesn't. Everyone else seems to.

Lizzy and Mariette have lined up all of his shoes on the coffee table. The girls are four years old, it's a snow-gray afternoon, and they've transformed his parlor into a make-believe shoe store. Mariette plays the salesman, Lizzy the customer. She follows Mariette's instructions, tying the laces over and over — a triumph he mentioned just last Sunday as a metaphor for perfecting the act of prayer. His oratory is a vanity he fights to control. He registers with glee the upturned faces, the unswerving eyes, none of the rustling or coughing that accompanies Joe Poulin's tone-deaf bromides or Stan Leary's syntactical rotaries and cul-de-sacs. St. Catherine's, across the river, is a two-man parish with a school and convent and a spired church made of fieldstone and blue glass, yet he has spotted some crossovers slipping into his pews on Sunday. No matter the few (unimportant, he hopes) misgivings about his loyalties, when he preaches people sit enthralled. He brings God to them in his own best way — through his vanity, truth be told — and they cannot resist. He would gladly have become an actor, had God asked.

But God asked no such thing. A scent wafts into the house through an ill-fitting window, a weak premonition of spring whose origins he can't guess; it brings back his boyhood in a sudden rush: the high Masses, the silent adults, the quilted fields and golden haystacks, the surging, suggestive seasons. He knew nothing of men and women. He witnessed the workhorses, the dogs in the lane, a pair of doves on the weathervane, and wondered about the world of the body, that strangest manifestation of God's glory. He discovered his body in secret, marveling at its shudders and heat, peeking sidelong at the girls in the schoolhouse, throat afire.

Of course he did. He was a boy. But he found something more powerful than the body's wonders, something more marvelous and astounding.

God called him.

It happened in the north field, just after planting, the red furrows with their promise of potatoes, his uncle's tractor at the far end, parked beside the lilacs. The sky, starched flat and white as a pillowcase, thrilled him. He looked into it and found the face of God bearing down. Like St. Paul being knocked off his horse, he fell to his knees, crying out, his body vibrating with news. He rushed to the house, past the stone cap of the well, over the flattened front steps and into his mother's kitchen. The fragrance of molasses filled the drafty room. *I've been called,* he told his stunned mother, who was months from dying, her vine of cancer almost fully bloomed, the bad luck of this family a whisper down the long, long lane. But he did not yet know this. His sister, Elizabeth, who did know, wiped her reddened hands on a dish towel. *Tell us.*

Light carpeted through the dusty windows. His mother had been spooning cookie batter onto tin sheets, and now her hand stilled, the spoon suspended and full. The stove glowed. For the moment, the family's impending grief waited politely outside the door. Tears pearled on his mother's cheeks, for she knew, as everyone did, that the mother of a priest goes directly to heaven. He often imagines her there, basking in the grace of her son's vocation.

Look what our smart girls have done, Vivienne says, casting a bemused eye over the pretend merchandise: the black Keds he wears in the garden, the shiny wingtips he saves for high holidays, the flip-flops he takes to the beach. She raises one winged eyebrow, sliding him a look, parent to parent. This thrills him.

But he wonders: Should Lizzy always play the customer? Shouldn't he be teaching her to be less accommodating? *Children need rules, Father,* is Mrs. Hanson's stock answer to questions he's given up posing. *My Rosie always had rules.* He longs to ask Vivienne, whose every maternal motion he examines like a map of heaven. Sometimes she is brusque with the children, all business. At other times her face loosens, her hair swinging like a girl's as she turns to answer one of their endless questions.

Her ladies' magazines gather on his desk. Clipping recipes and columns, he commits to memory the tips on child-rearing, window-dressing, fruit-arranging, bathroom-disinfecting. With Mrs. Hanson on board he finds little room to implement his ideas, unable to get past a certain awkwardness with this housekeeper who used to put supper in front of him only after Father Devlin had been pointedly, deferentially, served. With Father Devlin now gone, she guards her history, an impulse he understands. Her former tenure in this house lives on: those humdrum, codified years. No longer live-in, having been relieved of supper duty (sent home now at three), Mrs. Hanson nonetheless keeps the laundry a secret, the cooking a mystery. The disposal of trash resembles a multistage exercise worthy of a world war. She keeps the pantry in stern order, a barracks of soup cans and cereal boxes. Phone messages are recorded on coded index cards placed — *this way, Father, not that way* — into a converted recipe box. Her absence on Tuesdays and Saturdays turns him giddy and slightly panicked, as if he were a soldier absent without leave.

Buy some shoes, Maman! Mariette calls, installed officiously behind the coffee table. Lizzy grins, picking up his black Keds and thrusting them into Vivienne's arms. She plays the salesman convincingly, he notes with relief.

That's enough, he chides gently, embarrassed by his shoes. Not one of them resembles the glossy, clean-smelling moccasins that materialize from Vivienne's hands every week. *Maman is here on a spiritual matter.*

Vivienne frowns. *Surely I have time to buy one shoe.* She

produces two quarters—from where? his smelly shoes? how does she manage always to produce exactly what they need?—and drops them into the girls' pink palms. Vivienne puts the shoes back, pretending to eye the remaining merchandise, then examines things that are not for sale: his sister's glass bookcase, the uncomfortable rocking chair, the plain white curtains, the three cats. *Not for sale! Not for sale!* the girls holler, pushy and self-important, which makes him laugh.

I was looking to buy a badger, he says, joining in. *Do you sell badgers?*

No, Father Mike! We sell shoes!

Earmuffs, then?

No-ho-ho-ho!

How about a nice little tub of snails?

Besotted by this game, Lizzy collapses on the sofa, so wilted by laughter that Vivienne bends to check her, bends slowly, since she is hugely pregnant. Lizzy is fine, eyes alert and focused, looking very much like her mother. In a brief time he has learned some things about children, but not nearly enough. Certainly a child requires a schedule, some discipline. In this arena he has not done well. *Spoiled,* he's heard Mrs. Hanson tsk into the telephone. *Spoiled rotten.* He wants Vivienne's opinion before cutting Mrs. Hanson's hours any further than he already has. But he is unwilling to sound as befuddled as he feels.

The gloomy evening renders the parlor especially close, its leafy wallpaper encasing the four of them briefly as the girls settle down again, adding items to their store, recruiting Fatty, the only willing cat, to serve as an extra customer. *Play nice,* Vivienne warns them. *Be nice to the kitty.*

He invites Vivienne into his little office, leaving the door ajar. She sits down gingerly and hugs her blooming belly. He is hoping to pick up their discussion about the presence of God. After their talk of loneliness they concluded that God is most accessible to us in extremes—when we are in great need or in great bounty—and almost invisible in our daily endeavors, when we feel neither completely empty nor completely full. How can God seem most absent when we are doing exactly what He wants? They talked a long time about this, and now he would like to know how she has sorted out the paradox.

Instead, she has something else on her mind.

Must a good Catholic follow all the laws, Father, even the stupid ones?

Nothing she says insults him. She speaks without irony when she speaks of Church law. She wishes to be a good Catholic, to live a Christian life, to raise Catholic children and die anointed. In this way she is unlike most of his parishioners except the very old; most of them come to him wanting loopholes and shortcuts and permission to remarry. They want from him the minimum required to please their grandmothers. They expect their wedding rite to include a high Mass that will become their last memory of receiving the Eucharist. In two years they will bring a baby to be baptized in a Red Sox outfit and running shoes.

The stupidest laws, in Vivienne's view, are the ones governing birth control and the strict obligations of certain sacraments. He thinks she means the sacrament of Holy Matrimony but can't be sure. What comes to him is a vision of Ray Blanchard hogging all the space in the marital bed, all the space in his wife's body, Ray of the muscular forearms, Ray of the well-upholstered chest, Ray of the blue eyes his own sister once said reminded her of Paul Newman's. When Vivienne wants to discuss the Church's stupid laws, it is always just after Ray has left for the sea.

That's not a problem of faith, Vivienne.

No, she agrees, smiling. *Faith has nothing to do with the Church.*

I wouldn't go that far.

No. You wouldn't.

They have their customary debate about the Pope's unyielding reign. At the end he leans across the desk as her co-conspirator: *I agree with you, Vivienne. Don't tell.*

I was testing you, Father. From time to time I must remind you what you really believe.

He blushes, which he does too easily, and her eyes crease merrily at the corners. He minds, very much, that he amuses her sometimes, but he doesn't know how to make things different. Vivienne knew Lizzy's father back in grade school; for this alone he needs her. For this, and their mutual memories of Elizabeth and Bill in this house for Sunday-night cook-outs, the two baby girls gabbling in the twilight. Sometimes Ray wandered over to join them, toting his own six-pack and sitting on the steps, wrapping his big hands around a can and popping a top, that distinctive summer sound. The babies crawled over the grass with the mothers standing watch; Bill helped grill the steaks. Ray mostly kept his own company—not unfriendly, exactly, but perhaps cowed a little by the presence of the priest.

They had been family and neighbors, assembled on a pretty stretch of yard beside a river. Such happy times, these bouts of normalcy, these glimmers of God's ordinary gifts. He and his sister reminisced about the Island, but never for long. There was too much here-and-now: the tiny girls, the rising moon, bloody steaks spitting on the grill. *How did we land here, Mikey?* Elizabeth would say, astonished. *Why such beautiful luck?*

Elizabeth is gone, but Vivienne remembers. For this alone he loves her.

When they emerge once again from his office, Lizzy waylays him: *Here's your badger,* she cackles, handing him a shoe. *Ha! Ha! Ha! Ha!* Her little teeth make him feel bitten.

Is this what people mean when they claim to have fallen in love?

I don't want this particular badger, he informs her, *I don't care for the sunglasses he's wearing.* He waits for her face, the entire apple-shaped miracle of it, to crinkle hilariously.

Is it normal, this feeling of bursting, this sustained longing? She pitches herself toward him, her stick arms branching around him, the smell of soap or snow or dirt or strawberry ice cream rising from her coppery hair. Is it normal, this monstrous, engulfing anguish that feels like no other thing? Like no other single thing?

He nearly ate her once. She was so small, so newly arrived in his life, he'd just lifted her out of the bath, warm water dripping from her ringlets and the lobes of her flushed ears, one pink leg dangling from the towel he'd wrapped her in. *Arrgh-arrgh-arrgh,* he growled, hoping to make her laugh, kissing at her toes, pretending to be a monster—a nice monster, the one they'd invented and named Biggy. *Arrgh-arrgh-arrgh,* and then he was nipping her, *arrgh-arrgh-arrgh,* one pink, beloved toe at a time. Then—this is what troubles him—he took in her entire foot as if he meant literally to devour her, to swallow her whole, to eat her up. Expecting laughter, he found her gaping at him instead, her eyes big and blue and startled. He spit her out, ashamed.

Is this normal? To feel so ravenous, so heartsplit? He's heard prayer described this way, but has found the opposite to be true. Prayer is his journey toward stillness, a calm, white hollow, a noiseless comfort, the opposite, in fact, of the mysterious, disquieting *forwardness* of parental love.

He does not want his love to be desperate, the result of having lost his family. He does not want his love to weigh too much.

Vivienne steps into his kitchen now, to copy a recipe onto a pad he keeps hidden from Mrs. Hanson. Lizzy is trying to sell them another badger and also a kangaroo. Sometimes he fails to distinguish between his love for her and his fear of losing her. *Too,* he adds in his head. *Losing her, too.*

It is he who requires advice.

He admires the quick strokes of Vivienne's handwriting, her confident presence in another person's kitchen.

Of course, she will say. *Of course it's normal.* But he does not ask.

EIGHT

On my first day back, the school seemed like a place remembered from a dream. From far down the hall came the staccato notes of a new term, the slam-bang of teachers flinging open cabinets, filling trash cans, stapling lists to bulletin boards, dragging desks into optimistic configurations. The students weren't due back for a week, but already the place ballooned with the sound of industry, destruction, hope, effort—the main ingredients of any school year.

I stepped out of my office and into the guidance lobby—a misnamed cranny containing the reception desk, a cranky copy machine, and a walk-in vault that sheltered a few decades' worth of student records. Another door opened into a shabby conference room that we shared with the school nurse. Our school district had more hope than money, and the discrepancy showed especially in the high school, which had been converted, unconvincingly, from a defunct shoe factory. Oxblood dye still showed in the floor planks outside the cafeteria.

Jane Rodgers, an old-fashioned secretary who'd been trained in the fifties, was installed behind her desk, talking on the phone and stapling orientation booklets. *Stay put,* she mouthed, and I did, pouring myself a cup of coffee. I had been home for three weeks, had slept in my own bed—my sheets, my pillow, my husband—but only now did my former life begin to seem familiar.

"You all right?" Jane asked, hanging up. She gave me a worried squint from above the tortoisey rims of her half-glasses. "You look paler than when you first got in."

"I'm fine," I said. In truth I felt a little sad, wanting to call Drew. Breakfast had been a tense affair even though the word "forbid" didn't formally enter our conversation.

"That was the Harmon girl," Jane said. "None too happy with her course schedule, big surprise."

Andrea Harmon was none too happy with anything. "Jane?" I set my coffee down. "Why isn't this place hopping?" I was the sole guidance counselor for a population of three hundred and fifty kids; on a normal pre-opening day, the place would be a-clamor with complaint.

She set her mouth, her pink lipstick puckering. Jane remembered me as a child and retained her right to mother me. Usually I didn't mind. "I thought you'd want to wait until Rick got the schedules unsnagged," she said. "He balled them up, Lizzy, he can vet them himself."

"Excuse me," I said carefully, "but isn't this my job?"

She lifted her eyes without moving a single muscle in her face. "You look as if you just escaped from a labor camp."

"This is the labor camp. I escaped from Limbo."

"Mariette says—"

"Mariette doesn't have a medical degree. *Actual* doctors have cleared me for takeoff." I looked down at my blank appointment book. "Apparently I have openings." Then I limped across the hall to reclaim the schedules from the main office. From there I detoured to Mariette's classroom, moving as nimbly as I could without my cane just to prove a point, but as a result the plates in my leg seemed to be heating up.

Mariette looked surprised to see me. "I thought you were staying home today."

"The only people who thought that were you and Drew."

She was in the back of the lab, uncrating boxes of rats. "I love these guys," she said. "I hate like hell to feed them crap." She picked one up and kissed its pointy, polka-dotted, disobliging face.

The rats, which would be named for famous scientists, were the stars of her single-quarter, one-credit elective course called "Our Magnificent World," a garage sale of her favorite topics, ranging from the properties of light to the effects of junk food on unsuspecting rodents. Every year she managed to accidentally kill one of them — Madame Curie drowned in the janitor's water bucket, Copernicus expired in a heating vent — occasioning her annual, suspiciously canned, sermon on accountability.

"You could sound a little more sorry," I said. I glanced around her classroom, an underfunded lab that brimmed with life. Literally. A village of gerbils, two tanks of fish, and a bashful chinchilla had joined their rat brethren in the aid of scientific inquiry. "I don't know how you keep this up."

She put up one finger, obviously rehearsing. "It is the ever-marching quest for knowledge that separates man from beast."

I set my schedules on the lab table. "Mariette, is it my imagination, or are people looking at me funny?"

"Who?"

"Jane," I said. "And both janitors. And the new guy in English, who dropped off a syllabus and acted as if I had rabies. Tell me the truth. Do I look that pitiful?"

"No." She carried the rats to a six-foot cage outfitted with rat-sized chutes and ladders and let them go, *plop, plop, plop,* into a heap of wood shavings, like a platoon being released on a beach. "People hear things, that's all."

"What things?"

"Some people around here still think of you as the town orphan. And now this," she said, grazing her eyes over my creaky body. "Maybe the thing with Father Mike came up again in certain quarters."

I closed my eyes. During my first year back in Hinton, I ran into parishioners, former friends of the family, certain shopkeepers in whose memory I had continued to exist as the damaged child. I endured their tiptoeing conversation, their undisguised amazement that I had not wound up on the street conversing with phone poles. "What did you hear?"

"I didn't, my mother did." Mariette closed the cage lid. "She told the offending party to shut her fat face, if that makes you feel any better."

I laughed. "It does, actually. It's nice to know she's still got some of the old spit and polish."

"Sometimes it comes back," Mariette said. The intervening years had thwarted her mother's natural effervescence, aging her in ways we could not have predicted. Fire to ice. Mariette blamed her father.

She opened a cabinet and began to unload glassware — petri dishes, beakers, test tubes — and arrange them on a slate table that lined one wall. With no small effort I hoisted myself onto the table and watched her rattle test tubes into a rack.

"Remember our first year here, Mariette?" I said. "That girl Everett sent over? Amy Frye, her name was, skinny little freshman. She'd been hauled back home by the cops after a two-week runaway. They figured she's afraid to start high school, she's got the wrong friends, she's a spoiled brat, get her insolent little butt back in school where it belongs, and pronto. So Everett shuttles her across the hall to the new counselor to work out a course schedule, but I can see she's a mess, I'm not an idiot, for God's sake, I graduated *first*."

Mariette cocked her head. "You're amazing. I don't know why you still talk to me."

I blinked, caught short, for Mariette had not spoken to me in this, her old way, since my accident. A reprieve is what it felt like, because we were standing not in a hospital corridor or even on my front porch but in this classroom, this starting-over place, at the glossy beginning of a new year. "So," I continued, "I'm with this kid, this kid I've never met, and it's my first month into my first job, sure, but I'm not so green I can't recognize a few things, including that crushed look in the eye before the truth comes tumbling out. So I wait. She's sitting there, the schedule's done, and I'm waiting, because I know she wants me to wait, it's going to take her a while to say it. Which it does."

"I remember that girl," Mariette said. "It was the mother's boyfriend, right?"

"He ended up in jail, but it took two years. So I call the mother, alert the police, get the DHS referrals lined up, set the kid up at her grandma's house for the meantime, and at the end of the day Everett saunters back into my office to congratulate me on a job well done. 'You really had her pegged,' he says, like it's this big compliment, only he says it with this morose, drippy smile that means, 'Of course you had her pegged, it takes one to know one.' "

"Everett's an idiot," Mariette said.

"It's not just him. I don't want people thinking I'm good with kids because I've *suffered*."

"People don't think that," Mariette said quietly.

"I'm good because I studied my ass off. Because I'm *suited* to the job. Is it too much to ask for full credit?"

"In real life?" she said. "Yeah."

"What am I supposed to do, go around telling everybody, 'Hey, speaking of fall schedules, nothing hideous happened to me in childhood.' " I slid off the table and faced her. "How guilty sounding is that?"

"Nobody thinks you're guilty of anything."

"They think *he* is," I said. One of the rats had paused at the cage door and appeared to be listening to me, though probably it was merely enchanted by the rattling test tubes. I stuck my finger through the wire and petted its head, which felt like much-washed cotton. "It took me so long to figure out why they sent him on that so-called retreat," I murmured. "Can you imagine a kid nowadays being so dense?"

"I was just as bad," Mariette said. "I had to ask my mother what 'molested' meant."

Father Mike had been sent to someplace called Baltimore to think about his sins — that's how Celie explained it, refusing to elaborate. When she broke the news of his death a few weeks later, her voice went mild and squashy, but her face did not. She believed in sin and punishment. Father Mike died of a premature heart attack like his father and uncle before him, she said, implying that God Himself had set into motion this genetic calamity to ensure an instant penance should one ever be required. Penance for what, I had no idea, until four miserable years later when my boarding-school roommates passed around a copy of *Lolita* and I thought, Oh my God, that's what they think *we* did. The questions that nun-woman asked me, they were about *this*. Until then, I had believed the Church exiled him because he let me eat chocolate pie for breakfast, because he danced at weddings, because he let me act like a baby, because he said son of a bitch. Now, in my own exile at Sacred Heart School for Girls in Bryce Crossing, Minnesota — where Celie had sent me after a short, edgy stretch in her care — I could see that my uncle's heart had buckled under the weight of false accusation.

I stared out the windows of my dorm room, taking in Sacred Heart's maidenly lawns, with their prim, sculpted trees, feebly seeking a target for my uncontainable rage. Who could I punish? Mrs. Hanson, now in South Carolina with the daughter she'd brought up on rules? Celie, who so robustly believed the worst? The titanic institution of the Catholic Church? My true home — my house and room, my ribbon of river, my friend next door — lay fifteen hundred miles from this stone windowsill on which I flailed my fists till they drew blood, scaring my room-mates into silence.

At dawn, sick from weeping, it came to me. FORGIVE THINE ENEMIES, exhorted the sign over the chapel doors. Well, I would. Oh, yes. I would forgive everybody but God. God was omnipresent, and so, too, would be my punishing silence. God would be forever denied my company. Collapsing into my bed as the bells sounded morning prayer, I plunged my face into my pillow and refused the call. For the first moment since my arrival there I felt a sweet, muscular spasm of control.

"Listen," Mariette said, racking another row of test tubes. "You're back. Just do your job, and screw all the gumflappers in this place."

I had to blink hard, feeling another crying jag coming on and determined not to falter here, in this place of shiny starts. "What if he tried to reach me" — here I avoided her eyes, but it had to be said — "because he wants me to clear his name?"

Mariette regarded me stoically. "Clear his name?" Her voice softened. "Lizzy, it's been over twenty years. It's just a story now." She cupped my face. "Nobody cares how a rumor turns out. After enough time passes, the truth doesn't change a thing." Then she hugged me, smelling of rats and rubbing alcohol, which wasn't an awful smell on her. "Heaven is awfully far away," she whispered. "Maybe he was asking you to let him rest."

There was a period at Sacred Heart, as the copy of *Lolita* was being passed from room to room, when I spent most of my time writing letters to people from the parish, hoping for a reasonable explanation to my dawning suspicion. *Why did they send him away?* The few responses I received — out of pity, I suppose — were brief and noncommittal. Father Mike had been transferred to "nonpastoral" duties. They made it sound like a promotion, but even through the mail I sensed their averted eyes. The transfer had been cloaked in a telltale secrecy; it was not commonly known that Baltimore was his destination, nor even that he had died. It took months to pry the truth out of Celie, longer still to get Mrs. Blanchard to admit, yes, there were accusations; from Mrs. Hanson, yes; that's why the Church took him away. Mrs. Blanchard persuaded me to stop writing letters. *The more you say no, dear girl, the more they will think yes. This is how people are.*

Mariette was moving through the room now, wiping down her lab tables.

"Mariette?"

She looked up.

"Did you ever — ?"

"Not for one second. I never believed it for one second."

After a moment, I asked, "Do you ever wonder if your father might come back?"

She resumed wiping. "No."

I'd been wanting to tell her that since the accident her father, too, had been on my mind. "You don't think he might be out there someplace?"

"He hasn't spoken to me from the dead, if that's what you're asking."

"That's not what I'm asking."

"Lizzy," she said. "I'm tired of talking about fathers."

I lowered my eyes. "I know I've been kind of hard to be around."

She finished her chore, then picked up an armful of schedules. "Come on. Let me help you with these."

We walked to my office together, out of words, our tandem footfalls echoing in the empty hall.

That afternoon, after the schoolwide in-service — a tedious primer on our new attendance policy — I found Jane on the phone and a lurid bouquet of roses on her desk. She banged down the receiver. "Jerk," she muttered.

"A parent?"

"A *bully* who wants to talk to you this very instant and won't leave his name." Jane always got tense when school started, though her patience at other times flirted with legend. She had trouble with beginnings, is all. I had trouble with endings. "I told him we had a school year getting underway and he'd have to wait in line like everybody else."

I looked around at the empty office. "And yet I see no line, thanks to you and your accomplice."

She slid the roses toward me. "For you," she said. They had fully opened, petals flung back wantonly.

"Who brought them?" I asked.

"The flower man. No card."

I took the flowers into my office, where I found Andrea Harmon pinching my plants. "Hey, Mrs. Mitchell," she said, as if no time had passed since my accident. No time, no loss, no change.

One thing I admire about teenagers is their ability to remake themselves over the course of a summer. Some of the transformation is beyond their control, a six-inch growth spurt or a mouth whose baby curves have flattened out. The rest they assiduously tend — a new vocabulary, a pair of boots that hitches their natural gait, a copy of *On the Road* poking artfully out of a torn-back pocket. *I'm not that kid from last year,* these props warn all who witness, *Don't even think I'm that kid from last year.* Andrea, however, looked the same. Same clotted eyelashes, same masky makeup, same gossamer hair dyed the color of a cheap merlot.

"You got a boyfriend?" she asked, eyeing the roses.

"I'm married, Andrea."

"That doesn't stop some people."

I set the roses on the sill. "How'd you get past Mrs. Rodgers?"

Andrea gave me a methodical once-over, then dropped some plant parts into my wastebasket. "Mrs. Rodgers doesn't have eyes in the back of her head," she said.

I had to laugh, for this was Jane Rodgers's perennial claim, and the other ninety-nine-point-nine-nine percent of the student body appeared to believe it. Even the biggest, most galootish boys cowered in the lobby waiting for Jane's say-so before making a dash for my office.

I closed the door, a metal rectangle with a peephole placed far above eye level. Despite the plants, the window, the plaid rug, the photo of Paulie in an electric-blue frame, my little chamber could not shirk its original identity as a stall for dyeing shoes.

I gestured toward a seat. Andrea would sit eventually, but she liked to meet even the smallest requests on her own timetable. It drove her teachers crazy. She would someday become the kind of adult other adults admired, if one of them didn't kill her first.

"I got my schedule," she said, fishing it out of the same handbag she'd toted all the previous year, a scabrous vinyl pouch that matched her jacket.

"That's not final," I informed her. "The prelims got mailed out by mistake."

She slapped the printout on my desk. "I got the Rattlesnake for English."

"I can't imagine who you mean."

Andrea tsked significantly. "Mrs. Ratclef."

"Oh, Mrs. *Ratclef.* That would be the same Mrs. Ratclef who, as a member of our faculty, is entitled to our respect whether she is standing in the room with us or not?"

Andrea stared me down for a few moments, her eyes etched in thick swipes of black, deceptively ferocious-looking. "That's the one," she conceded at last.

"Shall we start again?" I said, sitting down. "How was your summer?"

She allowed me a small smile — I'd never seen her laugh. "Better than yours," she said. Finally she sat, draping herself over the chair as if she were made of seaweed.

My desk faced the wall. My chair was turned out to face whoever landed in the student chair, as a kind of invitation. Across the hall Rick used his desk like a barrier, which I could understand. As vice-principal he likened himself to a prison warden who couldn't afford to start feeling sorry for the inmates.

"How's your mother?" I asked.

Andrea thrust out her wrist and consulted her watch. "Drunk," she said.

I waited.

"My dad finally bailed on us," she said, stroking the eyebrow ring that had more than likely been applied to commemorate the event. "He moved in with Miss Teenage America on August twelfth. Which he totally and completely forgot was my birthday."

I nodded. The saga of her father and the girl from the hardware store had been a recurring theme the previous year.

"You want to talk about it?"

"Nope," Andrea said, her vinyl jacket, spotted from the day's rain, creaking around her as she sat up. "What I want is to switch to English 2 2 0. This class you put me in is for morons." Her eyes flickered over my face. "Or whoever put me in. Obviously it wasn't you."

"No," I said. "I was kind of busy."

Until that moment I had never seen that girl choke up. Not over her feckless father, her pickled mother, over the shack she called home, an unpainted heap of planks with a dirt yard, fourteen miles from a cup of coffee or a tank of gas. She lifted her hands as if to touch me, her black nail polish looking like gangrenous wounds. Instead, she peered at my face, squinting closely at the scar along my eyebrow.

"I thought you weren't coming back," she said. Her hands returned to her lap.

"The pay's irresistible."

Andrea didn't smile. "I felt really bad," she said.

"Me too." My eyes stung unexpectedly as I took her schedule. "Let's see how we can fix this."

My buzzer sounded. "Line one, Lizzy," Jane said. "That bully-man."

Andrea sat up with the alacrity of a federal agent. I picked up the phone.

"Did you get the flowers?" came a voice from the ether.

"Who is this?"

The moment hovered, and the voice said, "I'm the guy that saved you."

NINE

He'd been waiting for me, hands knuckled hard into the pockets of a used London Fog with shiny spots and a broken belt loop. His head lifted edgily as I parked the car. He was scrawny and raw-skinned, with the white, wet-combed hair of a man in deep middle age trying hard not to look like a former drunk. I checked his boots, recalling the *tink-tink-tink* they made on the wet night road.

"Hello?" he said, heading toward me. I felt ridiculously glad to be recognized, though of course my cane is what gave me away. I couldn't have looked much like the heap of bones he'd found on the road. "Harry Griggs," he said, putting out his hand. He closed the space between us, taking my hand—clasping it. *Complicity* is the word that came to me. I put him at sixty: slack, heartbroken mouth, corded neck, wiry eyebrows. Old enough to be my father, though my actual father—the sunny Bill Finneran—would have been older still, more filled out, bonny and robust and easeful. Harry Griggs's face, veiny and scrupulously shaved, sheened with regret. I wondered if he had always looked this way.

"You came all by yourself?" he asked. We were in the parking lot of Portland's back cove, where sprightly people jogged in place, getting ready to run the perimeter.

"My husband thinks I'm at a soccer game," I said.

He shrugged nervously under his Goodwill coat. "I didn't know but what you might bring him with you."

"He wouldn't be interested in seeing you, to be honest."

He shifted on his feet, thinking. "He knows I'm the guy that called the 9-1-1?"

I looked into his eyes, a chipped, not-unappealing kaleidoscope of blue and green. "He thinks you should've stayed with me till the ambulance came. I was sort of wondering myself why you didn't."

Harry Griggs took a couple of darting looks around, as if searching for a protocol he was ill-equipped to deliver. "I thought you were dead," he said. "I was moving a body. But I saved you anyway. Next car around the bend coulda run you clean over." His accent was a surprise: inland Maine, thick and reminiscent, the same dropped *r*'s and draggy *o*'s of the old ladies from St. Bart's.

"I figured you called me to apologize," I said.

On the phone he'd been confusing and inarticulate, but he was the only witness to my death, or whatever it was, and I was in no position to be picky.

"I wondered how you made out, is all," he said. "Things haven't gone too goddamn fabulous lately, and saving you was the one decent thing I could think of that's happened in a goddamn ice age, pardon my French." He looked at my hands as if I ought to be bearing gifts.

"It was a very decent thing," I said. "It's just that most people would've stayed."

"You ever see those TV shows where the rescuer gets to meet the one they rescued and everybody's so goddamn glad to be alive, pardon my French, and they thank God and all the saints in Heaven and sit down to a meal?"

"That's what you thought was going to happen?" I asked. "Six months later?"

"I know," he said, "six months later, Jesus Christ, it's about goddamn time, but I've kinda been out of the loop for the duration." His eyes slid sideways. "To tell you the truth, it wasn't till recently I looked it up in the newspaper. The library's got all that stuff, and I spend my free time in there. They did a thing that told you were gonna make it. They said a motorist called the 9-1-1. A passing motorist."

"I know."

"That was me. The passing motorist."

"I know that."

"Well, I was pretty goddamn glad to find out you lived." He shook his head. "The girl got probation, I saw."

"She was only fourteen."

"She call you?"

"I got a letter. It was part of her sentence."

"Can I buy you a cup of coffee?" he asked. "I would've asked you to my place, but it's a shithole."

"I wouldn't have come to your place. You're a stranger."

He looked mildly offended. "You want a sandwich? How about a tuna sandwich? My treat." He pointed toward a shopping center across the busy boulevard, one nicked-up hand darting from a too-short sleeve.

"No thanks," I said, realizing that sending roses must have pretty much broken the bank. "I'd rather just walk a bit, if you don't mind."

"Mind? Christ, no, why should I mind? Anything you want, that's great, sure. We'll walk. After you." He swept his arm toward the water and I stepped ahead of him, my leg hitching badly even with the help of my cane. "I'm doing better than this, really," I said. "It's just when I first get out of a car."

"Oh, Jesus Christ," he said, gritting his teeth. "What a goddamn shame." His eyes followed my body — head to shoulders to arms to legs to feet, then back up again, resting on my face. I could almost feel the trail of his gaze, a kind of shimmy over the places that still hurt.

There we stood, face to face, the water at high tide and lashing softly just below us. Strangers passed. "Let's just walk," I said.

"Sure, you bet, anything you want." As we set out he hovered at my side, not quite touching me, but cupping the air around my shoulders.

The sky appeared dark and held back, the air moist, soft as cloth. We walked in silence for a minute or so — he was even slower than I was. Finally he had to stop, holding his wheezy chest. We'd gotten only as far as the end of the lot where the footpath began. "Cigarettes," he said. "I keep swearing to quit." We sat on a guardrail and gawked at the cove. A gull shrieked overhead, then spiraled down to perch on the banking.

I turned to face him. "I heard you, you know."

"Say what?"

"When you carried me off the road. You said something like 'Jesus on a stick.'"

He let out a long sigh and patted his pockets, a smoker's impulse. "I don't see how you could've heard that. You weren't even breathing."

"I did, though."

He patted his pockets again.

"You can smoke if you want," I said.

He glanced at me, then worked a cigarette pack out of his coat. "It's a powerful yearning," he said, his lips mushing together. He lit up and drew in a breath.

"You said 'sorry,' before you ran off. 'Sorry sorry sorry.' I heard you."

He breathed out a trail of smoke. "Okay, so you weren't dead. I'm a shit, first and last, a genuine class-A shit, and I swear to God what I did to you is the worst thing I ever did to anybody, I swear to God, leaving you there all alone in your dying hour." He shook his head. "I didn't want to get caught with a suspended license, and that's the truth of it. I didn't need one more goddamn problem, so I ditched and ran."

His chipped eyes flickered over my scraped face. How had I looked, lying there in the road?

September was barely a week old, but already fall seemed imminent. In the trees that lined the cove, stray leaves flamed prematurely in colors that intensified in the dampening air. "It's going to rain," I said.

He checked the sky. "Yeah." Then we caught each other's eyes for a second, and I found myself glad of the impending rain. It was just weather — I understood that rain was just weather — but maybe it recalled something for us that it did not recall for other people. *You saw it,* I thought. *You saw exactly what happened to me.*

"Was I on the yellow line?" I asked him. "When you found me?"

"Matter of fact, yeah. Lined right up."

"You moved me from there."

"Yeah."

"To the side of the road."

"Yeah, I remember thinking, What're you doing, Shit-for-Brains, you don't move somebody in this condition, she could get paralyzed. But it was either that or you get run over twice."

"You were sort of crying. That's how it sounded."

"I was sober, in case you wondered," he said, smoking hard. "I was on my way to see my daughter up to Dixfield. I swear on her head I was sober."

"You don't have to swear on her head," I said. "I believe you."

"I wouldn't believe me if I was sitting where you are. I wouldn't believe a word I said. But I'm telling the truth anyway. I was sober as a judge." He trembled the cigarette to his mouth.

"You've had some convictions, I take it?"

"Good guess," he said, grimacing. "I'd just got myself cleaned up again, got my sorry backside over to A A for a couple of months. I was waiting to get my license back from the friggin' State of Maine Department of Motor Vehicles. I'd even wangled my old job back." He glanced at me. "I'm an electrician by trade." He cupped the cigarette in his pink-raw palm and looked at it. "And I really wanted to see my daughter. She had a brand-new baby and said she'd see me. I hadn't set eyes on her in years."

"How many?"

"Eight, nine. Seven, I don't know. I was a shitcan of a father. But I don't know, the new baby softened her up some, I guess. Her candy-ass husband said forget it, but she's a good kid, that Elaine, she figured to give me one last shot no matter what he said." He sucked on the last of the cigarette and threw it to the ground where it landed with a hiss. "I never paid a cent in child support. I treated her mother like dirt." He looked at me. "That's who I am, and still, she said she'd see me, give me one more chance. She's a good kid, that Elaine. I'm one lucky god-damn bastard."

He didn't look lucky, though; he did not resemble a lucky man.

"The thing is," he said, lighting up again, "and I'm just telling you this so you know I didn't leave you there and go on my goddamn merry way, I never got to Elaine's that night. I mean, I left the goddamn *scene,* so to speak, because I didn't want to fuck up — *screw* up, sorry — I didn't want to *screw* up the big reunion. The first time in ten, twelve years she says she'll see me, but I don't want to get there all shook up and she says what's wrong and I say nothing and she says I know there's something wrong and I say well I just left some poor kid dying on the side of the road in the pouring rain. So I didn't go. Too ashamed." He shifted uncomfortably. "Instead I drove back home and drank myself blind for a coupla months. Then I checked myself in for the old get-better, same goddamn twenty-eight days. Went for the VA counseling, the AA, the whole goddamn alphabet, except I didn't get my job back this time. I'm down at Barber Foods, which is rock goddamn bottom on the ladder of gainful employment in this town, let me tell you, me and a buncha Cambodians deboning chickens, nobody to talk to and nothing to look at but a conveyor belt splattered with chicken guts." He took a drag and exhaled loudly. "And I got to thinking how goddamn great it might be if somebody I saved said thank you."

"Oh," I said.

He was waiting.

"Thank you," I said.

"You're welcome."

I looked him over, his decaying boots, his secondhand coat too warm for the day. "Lucky you had a cell phone," I said.

"I stole it off a job," he admitted. "It was sitting there in this lady's open purse, right out there on the kitchen counter. I was running wire in this gigantic goddamn kitchen, all slate this and copper that and a monster Jenn-Air and the whole jeezly shebang, and me with no phone at the time because the last time they cut me off it cost upwards of three hundred bucks to get the phone put back in, and I really wanted to call my daughter because of the new baby, which I found out about through her aunt who also never talks to me but ran into me in a 7-Eleven and spilled the beans. I figured there's no time like the present, so I took the phone out of the lady's purse and called, then stuck around for the rest of the day while she asked this one and that one where was her phone, did she leave it at Nancy's, maybe it was in the car, did Jeff forget to lock the car again. When I finished the wiring I waved good-bye and struck out for Dixfield, phone in the glove box, and it even rings once or twice but of course I don't answer it, knowing it's them calling themselves, thinking to trap a bonehead like me with their superior wits and ingenuity, but I figure I'll use it just for the meanwhile, Elaine's kind of squirrelly about saying yes, she wants me to call back at this time and that time, so I figure if I'm calling her from my goddamn no-heater dinged-windshield leaking-radiator shitpile of a car that's on its way up to goddamn Dixfield maybe she'll cave, and she does, it takes forever but she finally says all right as long as you're halfway here, you can stay an hour, but that's it, an hour, just to see the baby and no drinking whatsoever, which I wasn't doing anyway, I swear." He looked at me. "So, yeah. I had a phone. Their loss, your gain. That's how things work, usually."

The clouds began to move along in gray tatters, allowing weak breaks of light into the sky. "So you're a guidance counselor," he said after a while. "How do you like it?"

"A lot," I said. "I like teenagers."

He lit another cigarette off the end of the one he'd just smoked. "Nobody likes teenagers," he said.

I smiled a little. "I do."

"My guidance counselor was an asshole."

"A lot of people say that. They have to blame somebody."

He inhaled deeply. "I thought you were a teenager yourself, you know," he said. "When I looked up the articles I didn't expect you'd be a grown woman with a good job like that."

"I'm back at work," I told him. "I went back even though everybody said wait." What came to me then was an odd little fillip of pride. I wanted him to think well of me.

"How old are you?" he asked.

"Thirty."

"That's how old Elaine is. Somewhere around there. Thirty-five, maybe, now that I think about it. Time flies." The water slapped against the rocks, and the gull lifted off again, circling out toward the bay. "Elaine's a teacher, too. Little kids. It's a good job, good benefits, time off to take care of the baby. She did great, that Elaine. Dental insurance and that. The works." He set his elbows on his knees and looked at me sideways. "Why did you come down here?"

"The girl who hit me never even slowed down. You're the only one who actually saw me."

He shook out another cigarette, and I waited while he smoked it. It had begun to mist, but he seemed in no hurry to move. "I was in the United States Army for four years in the sixties, but I never saw a dead body."

"Vietnam?"

"It was early on. Before the shit hit. I did my whole tour stateside, fixing radios."

"What I want to know, what I wanted to ask you —" I swallowed, and it hurt, like ingesting a thistle. "I wanted to ask you what it looked like."

He paused. "What do you mean?"

"I mean, did you see anything. Something that you might not want to admit to the average person. To, you know, to the average person who wasn't there when it happened."

"Did I *see* anything?"

I nodded.

"Like what?"

"A spirit?" I said, embarrassed. "An angel? Something along those lines?"

His eyes rested on me in a way that showed not surprise, but something like what I felt — inevitability. "I — Christ, no, I didn't see angels, nothing like that."

"It's just that I felt a certain — like I was waiting for something."

"Waiting. Sure, okay."

I looked at the ground. "If someone was there — an ambassador from Heaven, something like that — I'd kind of like to know for sure."

"I wouldn't know an ambassador from Heaven if he spit in my face."

"What about light? You always hear talk about the big white light."

He regarded me intently, for some moments. "I wasn't going to say anything."

I hiccupped, or gulped. "You saw something?"

"Now that you mention it." He stamped out his cigarette, frowning. "I did see a buncha light. I can tell you that. Buckets of light, just like you said, all around you."

"What kind? What color?"

Harry Griggs jittered his hands through his film of hair. "White, I guess. Whatever color light is. That's all I can tell you. Nothing more specific than that. But light, yeah, loads of it, like you said, all around."

Looking at him, I saw a man in pieces, a heap of parts that had never quite converged, and I suppose I began to shape something necessary out of the broken bits. Maybe I was already making believe this was my father, or a version of a father, in any case a man who had left me and was now making up for his mistake. "Something *happened* to me, Harry Griggs," I said. "You're my only witness."

"Hey," he said, taking a step toward me. "Hey, now." My teeth were chattering so hard I feared I might break them. I put up my hands and composed myself. He did not touch me. He was close enough, though, that his voice contained the properties of touch.

"Come on, deah," he whispered—*de-ah,* he said, like the elders of my childhood—cupping my elbow, urging me back toward the car, my cane squeaking against the dampening pavement. "Let's get you in out of the rain."

⁓⁓ ⁓⁓

His apartment, one half of a third floor on Hanover Street with chattering windows, contained few possessions. The neighborhood, an ethnic mishmash crammed between City Hall and the cove, felt both thriving and luckless, possessed of dented cars and gabled apartment buildings and municipal facilities and beautiful trees. I saw men and women carrying soft, thin briefcases, Somali immigrants with their brightly swaddled children, teenagers thickened onto street corners, and a few men like Harry Griggs, loosely stitched, looking only one way before crossing.

I liked it there. I felt gloriously invisible, a feeling intensified by the sheer quantity of air space in Harry Griggs's apartment. It took me a while to make the stairs, but once inside he guided me into his one chair, a stuffed armchair, bone white. Next to it stood a floor lamp with a mustard-colored glass shade.

"A guy was loading a truck up on Cumberland," he said, "and took off in too much of a hurry. I carried this home brand spanking new." He peered down at me. "Feeling better?"

I nodded. "I'm not usually this emotional."

"You're entitled," he said. "Cry all you want."

I wasn't crying, though; I was taking inventory. In one corner resided a seedy-looking guitar, a stack of CDs, and a stereo that sat directly on the floor. There were curtains, sheer ones, that looked clean. Through an open door I could see part of a bed—neatly made up—and a small TV tray with a lamp sitting on it. The whole place emanated the futility of misplaced effort.

He offered me a Gatorade. "It's all I drink when I'm not drinking," he said. "It's supposed to load you up with electrolytes."

He went into the kitchen — clean and empty — and got one out of the fridge. He took down two glasses and divided the liquid.

"Cheers," he said.

It was awful, but I drank it anyway, thinking a few extra electrolytes couldn't hurt. I could see the water from where I sat, over a cascade of rooftops and a flat swatch of concrete where the city parked snowplows and dump trucks.

"What do I call you?" he asked.

I wiped my eyes. "Lizzy. You?"

"Harry's fine. My friends called me Hank back when I had friends."

Now that we were inside he looked caged, his feet moving in little forward-and-backs even while he was seated. "You having some kinda delayed reaction?" he asked. "The va's full of those."

I shook my head. "I'm fine. You can't imagine the relief. I was starting to think I was going a little crazy."

It is not an exaggeration to say that I loved Harry Griggs in that moment, the way disaster victims are said to love their fellow survivors. I wanted to tell him the whole story now, to live through it again and again the way those same survivors are wont to do.

"I was out there running in black clothes," I said to Harry. "Did you find that strange?"

"It's a free country," he said. "You can wear anything you want."

"My husband was thinking about leaving me, and I didn't want him to say it out loud." I hesitated, surprised. "I was running from that." What I wanted from Harry Griggs was beginning to form — a kind of witnessing, a confirmation, an accounting. What he wanted, besides gratitude, I couldn't say, but if we were at cross-purposes our desire contained at least one mutual ingredient: confession.

"I got hitched four times total," Harry said. "Technically I'm still married to the last one, Loreen. She's a good egg, that Loreen. We fought like raccoons from day one. You hear of happy couples, happy trails. What a load of crapola."

I nodded, glancing around his starved apartment. "He's stuck with me now, my husband," I said. "He thinks I'm not altogether — healed. So he's stuck with me because it turns out he's not the type to get out while the getting's good."

"Then he's a stand-up guy," Harry said. "He didn't cut and run."

Nothing I said appeared to surprise him. It was a feeling like drifting back down to earth after having been temporarily relieved of the force of gravity. I marveled at the unfilled space, how little there was here to touch. You could move very fast from one room to another here if you wanted to.

Eventually Harry got up and went into his vacant kitchen, returning with more Gatorade. He refreshed my glass, then set the bottle on the floor and sat himself next to it, his back to the windows.

"How long have you been here?" I asked.

"Fourteen years, off and on," he said. "I tend to hole up here between marriages. Me and the landlord are tight, ex-Army. I saved his sorry backside once or twice with our so-called superiors, so he keeps returning the favor."

The water appeared nearly black from this far off and had begun to recede. The rain was beginning to look serious. Waiting there — and I did think of it as waiting — in the bare rooms of a stranger, a man of dubious scruples, a man who had done me an ill turn and waited six months to make good, I did not feel in the least afraid. I felt, if anything, safer than usual. Despite his raw skin, his flattened clothes, his insinuated past, there was something undeniably fatherly about him. He made me think of the men in gabardine shirts who came in for the early Mass on Sundays at

St. Bart's all those years ago, the guys from the shoe shop working Sunday double time and clearing a bit of room in their day for God.

"So," I said. "Harry."

"Yeah."

"Did I say anything?"

"On the road, you mean?"

"On the road. In my white light."

"Nope. Nothing."

"Were my eyes open?"

"No."

"Are you sure? I keep remembering things, like how the rain looked from where I was lying."

"Well, it was dark. Maybe they opened for a second. They could've opened for maybe a second."

"I was on the yellow line."

"Yeah. Lined up like you planned it."

Each word reached me as a discrete, critical bit of information. Vital information, without which my connected parts could not function normally. It was like rehab all over again. Put your foot here. Contract that muscle. Step down.

"You moved me."

"Course I moved you," he said, suddenly defensive. "You were in the middle of the goddamn road."

"And you moved me to the side."

"Yeah."

"To the shoulder. It was kind of muddy there."

"There wasn't really anyplace else to put you."

"Oh, I know," I said. "I'm not complaining. Did you say 'Jesus on a stick'?"

He shrugged. "Sounds like me."

"Out loud? Or were you just thinking it?"

"Considering the circumstances, I'm gonna say it was out loud. Pretty goddamn loud."

"I thought I could hear people's thoughts," I said. Again, he didn't look surprised. "That's why I'm asking," I added.

The sky finally opened, and out poured a relief of rain. The windows shuddered, not hard. It was coming on dusk.

"My husband will be wondering where I am," I said. "He had a wedding today. A big one up in Sidney. He's a photographer." I glanced out at the cove again, the tide fading into the distance.

"You can call from here," he said. There was a phone sitting on the floor, a black rotary phone, no desk or stand, just the phone. "Cost me two-fifty this time to get reconnected. Can't get a job without a phone."

"What happened to the cell phone?" I asked.

"Well, you know," he said. "They had it turned off."

"Wouldn't they have traced the calls back to you?"

"Not these people. I had them pegged." He smiled sheepishly. "Not that I'm in the habit of stealing, I'm really not. It was a crime of opportunity."

I sat there for a long while, too tired to move. The phone was in my lap, and therefore I thought I had called Drew; I was sure of it. I went over the brief conversation in my head. *I'm delayed, don't wait dinner.* The conversations I conducted in my head were more or less permanently merging with the ones I had with actual people.

Harry got up at one point and made me a cup of instant coffee. I sipped at it as the evening encroached, a grainy darkness shaping itself around the lighter squares of window, the rain tap-tapping against the panes. I could no longer see his face clearly, but his shadow remained an attentive presence. The ice in his glass moved; he was on his third or fourth tumbler of Gatorade. He was still wearing his coat.

"So," I said. "Here we are." A veil dropped then, the faintest suggestion of secret.

His boots moved on the bare floor, but he didn't speak.

"Can I tell you something?" I asked.

"Anything, sure, anything you want."

"I had a visitation." I blinked into the dark. "When I was in the hospital."

"A visitation? From who?"

"From my uncle, who died when I was nine. And I have to tell you that 'uncle' is a small word for what he was to me. I was really, really glad to see him."

"You saw your dead uncle?"

"I heard his voice, too, clear as yours."

I had said this very thing to the doctors, to an orderly, to a nurse and chaplain, to my husband and my friend and my friend's husband and my friend's mother, all of whom initially responded in various patient and compassionate and ultimately cold therapeutic ways, but nobody, not one person, thought to ask what Harry Griggs now asked: "What did he say?"

I blinked hard. "He said, 'my child.'"

"My child. Okay, sure. My child. That makes sense."

"He was in the company of an angel."

"An angel? Well, sure, if he's dead, why not?" He nodded, agreeing with me. "It was just the one visit?"

"Yes," I said, "although I've been wondering if he was also there with us, on the road. I was hearing so many things, everything felt so strange, so out of order. So *rearranged*. Maybe that was him. Or Heaven itself."

"Oh. Whoa." Harry's shadow had angled somewhat, a full attending.

"But what struck me most," I said, "what strikes me still, is how his voice seemed so present, so *in* the present, I mean. It was so, I don't know how to explain it, so *in* the world." Outside the lights along the cove appeared as apparitions out of the dark. "I saw his sleeve, the cuff of his sleeve, and it looked exactly,

exactly like his cuff, just the way I remembered it, a missing button and a little hole. It was so real."

"Stuff like that happens. My old granny saw ghosts all the time."

"Exactly," I said. "There are certain things we can't explain but it doesn't mean they didn't happen."

"Goddamn right."

I was trembling again, wholly unbuckled. Harry materialized at my side, removing his coat to wrap it around me, revealing a wrinkled white shirt. I let my face drop against that whiteness, allowed his arms to encircle me. "Hey, hey," he said. "Steady now."

We sat together in the dimming light for some time, not talking, as I felt myself being transported back, into the velvety between-place I'd inhabited just after my accident, that cushiony here-nor-there where my senses both blurred and sharpened.

"The weirdest thing," he said quietly, "when I got out of the car to look, I thought you were Elaine. I thought it was my own daughter somebody'd run over." He reached into the coat I was now wearing and fished out another cigarette, the feeble glow of the tip making the rest of the room seem darker. I snapped on the lamp to look at him, and we both flinched, blinking hard.

"Why on Earth did you think that?" I asked.

"You look like her, if you want to know," he said. "She has red hair like yours. Skinny like you. It kind of kills me to look at you, if you want the truth." He got up, looking for an ashtray, grabbed one off one of the deep windowsills and stayed there, looking out the window. "Course I knew right off, I mean after that first impression, you know, that it wasn't her, couldn't be her. But it was somebody. If it wasn't my daughter that was all bunged up, then it was somebody's daughter."

"Except that I'm not," I said.

"Pardon?"

"I'm not somebody's daughter."

He stubbed out the cigarette in the loaded ashtray. "Now there's another goddamn shame."

During my months of rehabilitation I came to accept the pitiful pace of range-of-motion, the futility of desire and the reality of anatomy. I took the incremental mercies visited upon my body — a receding pain, a small rotation — with an accumulating, grudging gratitude. Healed and whole and a stranger to my loved ones, I had another rehabilitation ahead of me, and right now Harry Griggs felt like step one in a range of motion that I was a long way from getting back.

"Do you have pictures?" I asked. "Of your daughter?"

"Sure, yeah," he said, whisking into the bedroom and returning with a creased snapshot in a frame. Despite her red hair she looked nothing like me except for a certain blunted look, as if she'd been caught in the moment between being hit hard and realizing she was going down.

"Any pictures of the baby?"

"I haven't seen it yet."

"Boy or girl?"

"I don't know. She told me, but I forgot."

"You never went back? You didn't try again?"

"Nope."

"Didn't she wonder what happened?"

He shook his head. "Probably figured car trouble. I'm kinda famous for that."

"You got your phone reconnected. You could call. Or write her a letter."

He put the photo on the windowsill. "Coulda woulda shoulda. Listen, you want something to eat? All I've got is canned."

"No," I said. "I should go." But I didn't. Instead, I watched him for a moment, and — either because he had compared me to his daughter, or because at the advanced age of thirty I was still looking for a father—I found something familiar in the set of his shoulders, the farm boy's surrender that my uncle had also carried.

"Can I tell you about him?" I asked.

"Go ahead, deah," said this shiny-coat heartwreck of a man with one chair. "I got nothing but goddamn time."

TEN

From *The Liturgy of the Hours:*
We all have secret fears to face,
Our minds and motives to attend . . .

Of all his pastoral duties, marrying brings him the most pleasure. He loves engaged couples, especially the young ones who come to him ruddy and thrilled. For some, marriage occasions their return to a faith they have lost, or misplaced. When he utters the word "sacrament," the engaged couple lift their faces as one face. The word is a poetic intrusion, crisp with consonants, the very sound of it both precise and evocative. He introduces the word with gravity, a hint of melodrama. Even the ones who come reluctantly, at the behest of Catholic parents footing the bill, or out of plain nostalgia for the rituals of their childhood, even they perk up at this unexpected word for what they are about to do and promise.

One of the first changes he made after succeeding Father Devlin was to institute new guidelines for marriage at

St. Bartholomew's Catholic Church. In brief: No more cakewalks. To earn the privilege of entering into the sacrament of Holy Matrimony, engaged couples would meet three times with the pastor and register for a daylong engagement retreat, offered six times per year. Some balked. A few accused him of grandstanding. Others said: *Who does he think he is?*

He reminds them that his own sacrament, so similar in magnitude and permanence, required a college education and then a formal training of four years. What is a few meetings with the priest, what is a day of study and reflection in the face of a lifetime promise? If you begrudge yourselves this feeble requirement, then kindly find yourself another priest.

He says it more politely than that. But he's not fooling around and they know it.

Hear, hear, say some. *Dictator,* say others. Vivienne says: *I wish I'd done the engagement program. What a wonderful idea.*

He uses an outline sent from the Chancery and redlines it like a movie director, adding a role-play here, a wish list there. *List two goals for the next two years. Five goals for the next five. Ten for the next ten.* Brides discover grooms who don't want babies. Grooms discover brides who long to flee their hometown. They discuss these things in the cloistered privacy of the pastor's office. Then, at the retreat, they undertake similar tasks in a friendly group, and listen to speakers brought in expressly for them: pediatric nurses, financial advisors, real-estate agents. Some couples decide not to marry after all, despite two hundred embossed invitations sitting in a box on an enraged mother's dining-room table, a four-hundred-dollar deposit already cashed by the resort hotel, eight disgusted bridesmaids stuck with nonreturnable salmon-pink dresses.

They think he's a stickler, or a killjoy; but really he's a romantic, sending God's lovers down the marital path with all due preparation, metaphorical rose petals floating in their wake.

His custom is to have the engaged couple to dinner a few days before the wedding. His ostensible mission is to review the details of the ceremony, but really he wishes to have a happy couple at his table for the edification of Lizzy, who cannot remember her parents. See what happiness marriage brings? He serves lasagna and garlic bread and a single toast of champagne (Lizzy is allowed a taste, diluted with ginger ale) served in the crystal flutes that were his wedding gift to Bill and Elizabeth. Removing them from Elizabeth's breakfront is Lizzy's favorite task — she loves to turn the slim brass key in the old-fashioned keyhole — and he beams at her as she opens the glass doors.

"Mrs. Hanson says I shouldn't drink champagne," Lizzy informs him. Claire Gagnon and Will Cleary wait in the dining room, dressed for the occasion, Claire in a lightweight yellow dress, Will in a starched shirt and pants that are not jeans. With few exceptions (Sandra Leighton, who was forty-four years old with two kids and an annulment, arrived in a tube top and shorts) the couples he marries rise to this particular occasion, dinner with Father, feeling proud and (he believes) grateful to have prepared for their sacrament with such focus and alacrity. Some, like Sandra Leighton, are just humoring him. But that's all right. He does his job, putting as much Holy into Matrimony as the couple can bear, and mostly the fruit of this labor ripens just in time.

"Tell Mrs. Hanson that I said it's okay," he says.

"I told her," Lizzy says. "She did that thing with her mouth, you know the way she does."

"I know the way she does," he assures her, petting her head. She is seven years old, an intelligent child with hair the color of old pennies. A few drops of champagne to honor this couple's joy before God won't do her a bit of harm. She loves toasting — *All joy, all love, all good wishes to you, in God's good name* — and they both believe that ginger ale alone doesn't count.

They bring the flutes into the seldom-used dining room, where the table is set in a precise imitation of an article from *Good Housekeeping* entitled "Spice Up a Special Occasion."

"What are all these tags for, Father?" asks Claire. Such a pretty, solid girl, whom Will Cleary, God bless him, cannot stop gazing at. She has glossy black hair and dimples.

"I'm learning French," Lizzy explains, lifting a tag from the curtain that reads *le rideau.*

"Say 'good evening' to Claire," he tells Lizzy.

"Bonsoir, Mademoiselle," Lizzy says. He can't help but smile; she sounds exactly like Vivienne.

"Wow," says Claire.

He has a good feeling about this couple. Their children will be smart and rosy and profoundly loved. Claire is a student nurse; Will's applying to law school. They want two children, but not for five years. Their plans are perhaps too exact, but he believes they will weather surprise or disappointment gracefully. They each placed "friendship" at the top of their priority list. They will not be back in his office nineteen months hence looking for a way out.

"She can read all these?" Claire asks, moving lightly around the room, picking up tags at random: *le mur* taped to the wall; *le tableau* stuck to the framed print of a babbling brook that Vivienne gave Lizzy last Christmas; *la fenêtre* lying loose on the windowsill. The tags make the room look festive, fluttering like confetti.

"She's picked up a lot from the neighbors," he explains. "We're working mainly on her accent."

It's the one thing that annoys Vivienne: *You're a snob, Father, and God knows it,* she tells him, only halfway joking. True enough, but in one of his many daydreams of Lizzy as a grown woman, she is captivating a roomful of Parisians with her formal, melodious French. In another she sits in a brocade armchair with a view of the Seine, singing *"Fais Dodo"* to her newborn baby as a smitten husband looks in from their grand, tiled kitchen.

"Aren't you, like, seven?" Will asks, exchanging a quick look with Claire: *Jeez, I hope we end up with a kid like this.*

"She was reading at four," he tells them, which is a tiny stretch. "Now she's the top second-grader in the county," which is either true or should be. Lizzy grins, either believing him or delighting in his slippery facts.

Lizzy has her mother's face, pliant and rubbery, her grin reaching all the way up to her eyes. He doesn't spend enough time with her. She comes to the weddings but not the funerals. She accompanies him to the Saturday five o'clock Mass and the Sunday ten-thirty, but not the Saturday six-thirty or the Sunday nine. She seems to enjoy her duties — passing out the church bulletin, collecting the hymnals after Mass, arranging donuts on paper plates — and would happily attend four Masses per week-end, but how much time must a normal child be expected to spend in church? She likes Mrs. Hanson well enough, loves Vivienne, spends every spare moment with Mariette. He's never left her alone. Is this enough? Can the thing he provides be called a happy childhood?

Vivienne taps at the back door and slips into the kitchen, surprised to find a crowd in the dining room.

"Sorry!" she calls lightly, draping Lizzy's red sweater over a chair back. "Lizzy, you left this." She makes to leave but he stops her. Claire and Will come out to say hello — Vivienne knows Claire's mother.

"We're just about to toast the engaged couple," he tells her, offering her his glass. "Join us."

"A toast," Vivienne says, delighted. "I don't remember the last time I lifted the glass."

He rushes to get another flute, fizzing champagne into it without spilling a drop, then gathers with the others, who wind up thronged between the narrow archway that separates the dining room from the kitchen. One side of the wall reads *la cuisine,* the other reads *la salle à manger.*

"Lizzy?" he says. "Would you do the honors?"

Lizzy holds her glass high above her head. "All joy," she quavers, "all love. . ." Her face knots with effort.

He prompts her: "All good wishes. . ."

"All good wishes to you in God's good name!"

"Beautifully done."

"Santé," Vivienne adds, the glass resting in the nest of her fingers as if placed there expressly to be admired.

Good cheer wakens the room. The glasses flare beneath the kitchen light. Moments like this are reputed to perfect the vocation, to bring into play the full intention of the priest's own vows. He is husband to his parish, father and brother and friend. In this brimming moment, however, there arrives a notion so fleeting it comes and goes like a burglar with surprise as his sole weapon. What if—what if he misheard God all those years ago? His head buzzes briefly with the possibility of missed connection, then the notion is gone before he can catch it, gone before he can detect how it got in and what it took on its way out.

He blames the champagne rushing down his gullet, and the cat's cradle Vivienne makes of her fingers around that filled, flashing glass of celebration.

ELEVEN

Drew and I couldn't go back, like Mariette and Charlie, and point out some fall-dappled tree under which we first locked eyes. In college Drew was just a guy cutting through the cafeteria line, another student bounding out of the art building with a roll of sketch paper tucked under his arm, one face among many in a history class or at a football game. We never really spoke. The first time I noticed his voice — that soft, anxious monotone — was in one of those impromptu gatherings that pop up just before graduation, where everybody feels a little sick with nostalgia for good times they never had. By then it was too late to make friends.

When we re-met, three years later at a homecoming weekend we had each separately decided to attend out of a desperate loneliness, he was in Boston, a twenty-four-year-old freelance photographer living in a monkish apartment on Hemenway near Northeastern. I was back in Hinton, doling out advice to sixteen-year-olds whose social life contained layers of intrigue entirely lacking in my own — which consisted mainly of helping newlyweds Mariette and Charlie pick out wallpaper for their kitchen.

Roiling inwardly, I arrived at the alumni reception pretending to be the type of person who liked crowds. Drew was the first soul I encountered, pretending the same. In that sense, it could be said that we re-met under false pretenses.

The one who will save me, he thought.

And I was thinking the same thing.

During the first weeks of our re-acquaintance, I drove to Boston after school every Friday afternoon, then tunneled home through the dark on Monday morning, barely making the early bell. I'd enter the school building in a kind of trance, my body humming with the memory of him. Our courtship took us from September to December, fall to winter, but in my memory it is a single season, the trees aflame with autumn reds as we walk the city, aimless and untrammeled.

We often wound up in the North End, stopping here for ice cream, there for flowers, loving time, Earth, traffic, strangers, each other. Evenings we chose some noisy Italian joint catty-cornered into an intersection, then caught the T to Newbury Street to find an art opening or simply to ogle the window displays. We saw a couple of Celtics games before Boston Garden sold its soul and took up the parquet tile by tile.

I can still see us there. Drew and Lizzy, holding hands, a game ticket or show schedule jammed into their pockets. They spend all their money, stay up too late, walk the city as if running a search pattern. They talk till dawn, choose this single season to behave entirely out of character. They have been alone, separately and for different reasons, for a long time. They enjoy the reassembled selves they become in each other's presence. For the moment they are the fully formed people they always intended to be, counting on the moment to forecast the rest of their lives. They slip into this new skin and hope it holds. Maybe that's all love is.

At Christmastime, I told him. In the version he already knew, the same one I'd been telling for years, I'd granted Father Mike his heart attack at our local hospital, no extenuating circumstances. I'd been wanting to tell Drew the real story since the homecoming weekend at our alma mater, but it was a hard story to tell.

We had reversed our pattern come holiday time, so it was Drew now who made the trek from Boston every weekend, often to help me with unshirkable duties: the H–S Regional Key Club food drive, the H–S Regional holiday concert, the H–S Regional Snowflake Dance. I'd agreed to be club advisor, ticket taker, and chaperone, respectively. Already I was turning back into myself.

"We should put up a tree in here," Drew said. My apartment was spartan in the sense that I hadn't much furniture. Most of my mother's things had been left unclaimed at the rectory, though Mariette's mother had rescued the dishes and saved them for me. I didn't have much in the way of wall decor, either, except the photograph of Father Mike, the one of my parents in the silver frame, and a portrait from Mariette and Charlie's wedding. I had no curtains, two rugs. The landlord forbade pets. But my place was not empty. I'd kept things from as far back as Sacred Heart: old mittens and programs from school plays and macramé god's-eyes and cotton pouches containing cheap jewelry and beach stones. I still had all the clothes I'd taken with me from St. Bart's, my good shoes from then, my child-sized winter boots. I had souvenirs from college—mugs and sweatshirts and bath towels and emblazoned bric-a-brac of all kinds—and from grad school I still had the papers I'd written and a dozen tapes of practice counseling sessions and all my evaluations. I had a glass bell I'd bought on a trip to Quebec City with Mariette and Charlie. These things were in boxes, mostly; but they did exist.

Since meeting Drew I'd begun laying everything out — flowers long dead and badly dried, a new umbrella, some books we'd read together, a stuffed elephant he won for me at a carnival — displaying them on a low table like objects about to be either sold or enshrined. As the bounty grew, between September and December, I began to feel full.

"I wouldn't mind a tree," I said. "I don't remember the last time I had my own tree." Though I did.

"They're selling them over at the Catholic church."

I'd been back in Hinton for six months, but had yet to approach St. Bart's. Not for Mass, not for the spring bazaar, not for the Christmas pageant, not even to look at my old house and mourn. "Whatever you say," I told him, standing up, suddenly glutted with hope. St. Bart's was a beautiful place. I had been happy there. Besides, Drew was looking at me as if I were the gold he'd just turned up in a streambed, and I felt lucky.

I had told the true story only twice before, once to a girl in my dorm at Sacred Heart on the last day of school, and again to the first boy I slept with, in college. At the time, the news was full of lurid stories about recovered-memory syndrome, adult women remembering all manner of mayhem years after the fact. This new climate of suspicion made it hard to tell the truth — *nothing happened; the accuser lied* — without sounding like a liar myself, or a memory-repressor, a textbook case. I thought I had chosen carefully the people in whom I would confide the truth, but in both listeners, first the girl and then the boy, two years apart, I saw the same quick light of alarm, an ambiguous eyeblink, as if I'd flicked a ribbon at their faces. The girl in my dorm said, "Ick," and turned over in her bed; the boy I slept with didn't call back.

Drew pulled over just short of the St. Bart's turnoff, next to the newly painted sign. He listened to the story all the way to the end without speaking. When I finished, he said, "Why would your housekeeper say such a thing?"

I shook my head. "She never liked him, really. I think she wanted him out, and she wasn't the only one, I guess. Anyway, she got her wish."

" 'Nonpastoral,' they said?"

"People drew their own conclusions."

"And then he died?"

"He was thirty-eight. Bad hearts ran in the family, and you can imagine the strain he was under."

"That woman's going to burn in hell," Drew said.

"It's not something I dwell on," I told him. Which at the time, I believe, was true. "But I did want you to know."

He looked up and down the road. "Is this common knowledge around here?"

"Once in a while I'll get a look — pity, I guess. But the town's changed a lot now that the shoe shop's gone. More strangers, which suits me fine. Not as many churchgoers, either."

Drew went quiet for a while. "I wonder how things would have turned out," he said finally. "If he'd lived, I mean." This was exactly the right thing to say, the thing I remember about that evening with perfect clarity. During my exile at Sacred Heart I had imagined, over and over, my alternative life: Father Mike, alive, back from retreat, the two of us recommencing our jeweled existence.

"They reassigned priests all the time back then," I said, "even after the most lurid allegations. They'd whisk them off for some therapy, pronounce them cured, then place them somewhere else. Everything stays in the family that way."

"Until somebody blows the whistle years later, and it ends up in the papers."

I nodded. "The old system would have been a godsend, though, in my case. It's a terrible thing to say, but it's true. After submitting to the so-called retreat, he would have collected me from Celie and brought me to our new parish, no questions asked."

"Your aunt would have unhanded you, just like that?"

"She didn't want me. She packed me off to boarding school and took me back for three grudging weeks every summer. Besides, she would never have crossed the Church." I looked at him. "In other words, things would have turned out fine. I would have gotten my old life back. I'd be an entirely different person."

"I like the person you are." He kissed my cheek. "Come on. Let's get our tree." He started the car—one hand on the wheel, one hand on me. We were off.

The place had changed little. The same ring of trees, taller now, a little thicker. The same river appearing between the arthritic tangle of branches, the same sealed-off quality where the driveway angled toward the house. A light from the Blanchards' old farmhouse showed dimly through the shortcut, which had grown over from a dearth of footfalls. No more neighbors ferrying back and forth, no stampeding children ramming sleds or bikes down and back, down and back, down and back. No picnics on the boulder, no raspberry-gathering, no stomping dead leaves just to hear them crack. The rectory had been painted—the black trim changed to green—but otherwise looked the same, a bright porch light casting down on the shiny, bluish snow.

I got out of the car, not bereft, as I might have expected, but wistful; perhaps I even felt a touch of awe. *Come in,* the place insisted, even now. *How we've missed you.*

The Christmas trees had been set up beside the church hall. People milled and moved, cheerfully dragging trees by their chopped trunks back to idling cars. Some people had moved their cars into the official lot, anticipating the Saturday-evening Mass. Making the transactions with the aid of a much-used money pouch was a young priest I'd never seen, wearing a lumberjack-plaid coat and earmuffs that didn't quite cover his flappy ears. His boots looked comically out of fashion, the same buckle boots

Father Mike used to wear, and it occurred to me that they might be the same boots, a pair that had stayed in the closet to be passed down from priest to priest.

Drew's arm came around me. The light in my old room burned yellow; something, a vase or figurine, showed through the window, in silhouette. I had no great yearning to go inside, to see new things in an old place; it was enough to know that the lights still worked, that if a child wanted to send signals through the trees to the house next door, she needed only to wave the curtain back and forth. It struck me that I'd been furious at God for so long it felt like my own form of religion, but something moved inside me right then, and it was the church itself I was drawn to. This was my first experience of nostalgia; maybe that's what grief becomes over time.

We bought a tree from the young priest, and he thanked us. "Are those your boots?" I asked him.

"Pardon?" He was smiling, merry as all get-out. Christmas was a convivial time in the parish; the church filled up, the coffers swelled, the priest felt more useful at this time of year.

"Your boots," I said.

He laughed, a dry ripple that reminded me of falling acorns. "My sister's idea of a joke." He lifted his foot. "We wore these when we were kids." We smiled with him, wished him a merry Christmas, and carried our small tree back to the car, where Drew tied it to the roof. We looked like a family in the type of Christmas movie where some lost soul who needs a miracle gets one.

The ride home was quiet. Not until we'd muscled the tree up the stairs and into my living room did we realize we had no tree stand and not a single decoration.

"Maybe we could put it in a bucket of water and kind of lean it against the wall," I suggested.

"Not too festive," Drew said, but he found a bucket under my kitchen sink and did the honors. The tree looked like a post-holiday castoff left out for the trash man.

"I'll go out and get a stand right now," Drew said, but he didn't. Instead, we left the tree as it was, plain and leaning, and laid ourselves down beneath it. In the morning we were still there, the tree looking green and well watered.

"Hey," Drew said when I opened my eyes.

"Hey." I sat up. "What?"

His voice was soft and sleep-graveled. "Why did you come back here, of all places?"

I rolled onto my back, not knowing how to answer. When I first came back there must have been people who asked the same question. Why Hinton? Of all places? They had no way of imagining the wing-lift of relief the sugar maples gave me, the comfort of remembered streets, the blessed nearness of Mariette and her mother, who had known me as a safe and cared-for child. When I finally finished at Sacred Heart I joined Mariette at the University of Maine, following her like a homeless dog for four solid years and two grad-school years beyond. She came back here, so I did. Why *not* here?

"I wouldn't have," Drew said, "if it had been me. I wouldn't want to be reminded of everything I lost."

"It's home," I said simply. "I had no other place to come back to."

Later that morning, after we'd rustled up some red crepe paper to put on the tree, he said to me, "Lizzy, you're the most rooted person I know."

This is what he thought he learned about me in our season of re-meeting. That I was fiercely rooted. For Drew, who had grown up on shifting ground, following his sergeant father and mouselike mother from base to base, this one fact—my rootedness—struck him, hard, as his one missing piece. You could almost hear a click as he pressed it into place. For this he married me, after a ten-week courtship, in front of a Justice of the Peace in the Hinton-Stanton town hall. Mariette brought balloons, which we released into the air as we descended the courthouse steps, thrilled and oblivious. Boston was calling him, but he chose me.

❧ ❧

After leaving Harry Griggs's apartment, I hit heavy rain. The storm barreled down the turnpike at such a pitch I had to keep pulling over, cowed by the racket. Water broke in waves against the windshield. It took me two and a half hours to drive fifty-eight miles. By the time I got home the driveway was sheeted with roiling water, and behind the blur of rain my house looked like a pretend house, like the ones I remembered from Six Gun City, a corny theme park in New Hampshire where Father Mike took me for my fourth birthday. "Main Street" had been tricked out with sepia-toned facades, including a pair of swinging saloon doors with nothing behind them but a mashed and shocking stretch of grass. I planted myself on the fake road, howling with outrage, refusing to surrender to Father Mike's blandishments. This is how unused I was to having expectation open into nothing.

I loped from car to house, dragging my leg through a stinging, horizontal rain. "Where the hell have you been?" Drew demanded, jerking open the door. It was all there—our clutter and books, every corner spoken for. He picked up the phone before I could answer. "She's okay, Mariette," he said, "she just walked in."

He put down the phone and looked at me. "Is this a test?" he asked. "Because if it is, I flunked." His voice shook with anger, or possibly relief. I was having a harder and harder time reading people.

"It's not a test," I said. I looked at my watch, twice, unable to believe it had somehow gotten to be eleven-thirty. "Is this right?" I asked. I'd been thinking, nine o'clock. Nine-thirty, tops.

And of course I hadn't called. I was sure I'd called, but judging from Drew's expression, I couldn't have. This I kept to myself, this evidence of the dreaded "faulty thinking."

I checked my watch again. Apparently I had spent hours in Harry Griggs's company, taking chips of my childhood and holding them up to the light. He was a good listener, resting on the floor of his barren place, his back against the rattling windows, head tilted just so.

"I thought it was earlier," I said lamely.

Drew closed his eyes, probably counting to a hundred. At last he said, "You can't just take off in weather like this and not tell anybody where you're going." He looked tired—the kind of weddings he photographed often tired him: the grubby function hall, the cottony sound from the band's terrible speakers, the drunken cousins, the blue garter slipping down the bride's dimpled thigh. In truth, Drew was not good with people. Word of mouth followed him only in the bad ways; he was not the jokey type, not given to coaxing laughter from a jumpy bride. I imagined that he worked in almost complete silence. Perhaps his bedecked subjects sensed his true yearnings—to be photographing murder victims or apartment fires in Southie, capturing the human spirit in its moments of disbelief. Instead, he was in Hinton, Maine, taking pictures of three-tier sponge-cakes and tipsy groomsmen. Amongst the obligatory shots of bouquets being tossed and rings being swapped, he always managed to unearth something interesting to him, but not nec-essarily to the people paying him. Look at this, he'd tell me, coming out of the darkroom, a still-damp replica of the single aunt's averted eyes, a close-up of the mother-in-law's bared teeth. He liked these moments of accidental honesty, and I did too, but these mementos also troubled me, as if they proved that even the luckiest, happiest times contained unrealized potential for violence.

"Where were you?"

The water dropping from my hair to the carpet sounded unnervingly like tapping fingers. "Portland."

"All night?"

"Yes."

"In *this?*" he said, flinging his arm at the rain.

"It wasn't raining there. Not like this."

My answer sounded almost stagey, as if I were trying too hard to pretend I lived in this house we had bought and filled together. Drew looked so wretched that I wanted only to take him upstairs and lay him down and erase our long months of silence. We had made love only once since I'd come home, a clumsy, grasping dance: Not there, not there, no, that hurts, too. Everything hurt.

"Did you eat?" he asked.

"Yes." Canned spaghetti. A lemon Gatorade. A slice of spongy bread with margarine. A paper towel laid across my lap.

"Where?"

"Some restaurant," I said. "I forget where."

"You don't know where you ate?"

I wrung out my shirttail, kicked off my wet shoes. "I didn't notice. I wasn't looking."

He peered at me. "Have you been drinking?"

"No," I said, but there was a certain inebriated swirl, a swampy imprecision, to my words and gestures.

He stared at me the way he stared at fresh photographs, as if determining how closely the facsimile matched up with his recollection. I figured he was wondering how to leave me, when to leave me, without looking like a heel. I didn't blame him for thinking that.

He fumbled toward me and I rested against him for a moment, but my hair was wet, and my clothes; our joining felt clammy and strange and unwanted. We disengaged and I sat down.

"Come back," he said, very softly. "Please."

I rested in the chair, exhausted. It was a wonderful chair, made for two, a more sumptuous version of the one Harry Griggs had rescued from the street. I'd bought it just before my accident, imagining that the two of us, Drew and I, might find our way to repose there, reading, legs entwined. Somehow we hadn't managed to broach the chair's vicinity at the same moment. I felt sorry for him all of a sudden, living an itinerant childhood only to land in my arms and believe he had hit solid ground. He still had the power to move me this way; I hung onto that.

"You could have left a note," he said evenly. "You could have found a phone. Would that have been so much trouble? We called everybody we could think of in this stupid, washed-up, goddamned *town*." He shook my arm, hard. "Lizzy. Come *back*."

"I'm already here," I whispered. "This is me. I don't know how else to say it."

I remembered an evening early in our marriage when we drove back to Boston for an awards ceremony at the Marriott Long Wharf. Enchanted, we sat through witty speeches from columnists we'd heard of, then the presentation of three dozen awards, some to the big guns, some to small-town papers with a staff of two. Drew won for a photograph that had appeared in the *Globe,* a soul-crushing image of an exhausted, middle-aged man whose burning house appeared as a reflection in his eyeglasses. As his new wife, I pulsed with pride, but when he sprinted back to our table with the plaque seized into both hands I caught something in his face, a confusion of purpose that fleeted across his brow. That moment was the beginning of a protracted and ambiguous struggle between us, but at the time I merely blinked it away.

Gradually, reluctantly, we defined the terms of the struggle and named it Boston. He wanted to move back and I didn't. He was sick of selling tickets at school dances and I wasn't. On the night of my accident, I came home from a baseball game and found him bent over his light table, inspecting a contact sheet.

"We won," I said. "Eleven innings on soggy grass."

"Go, Bobcats," he said, not looking up. At his elbow lay a stack of duplicates from a sixtieth class reunion, eight apple-faced senior citizens arranged around a yearbook.

"Some of us went out for a beer after," I said.

He kept sorting. "I would've joined you guys."

"But you wouldn't have," I said, and in an eyeblink we found ourselves *en garde* in full armor, the word "Boston" standing in as the problem and the solution and the slow fuse and the tripwire. We didn't yell, we were not yellers; we used quiet, controlled, reasonable voices, which was worse. Just before Drew opened his mouth to release the thing I refused to know, I stomped upstairs, pulled on all that black, then tore out of the house, heading straight for the soaked road. As I rounded the first corner I tossed back a look at what I could not yet know would become my old life, and there was Drew watching me from our house, his face scorched with sorrow.

The one who will save me, he had once thought.

And I had once thought the same thing.

Now here I was in the that same house—my home—looking, apparently, like a wet drunk, unable to explain what I had been doing in Portland for the past seven hours.

"So," he said, still studying me. "You went to Portland, a city where you don't know anybody, in a *monsoon,* to eat alone in a restaurant."

He sat down in the chair with me—it was a bit small for two people after all. "Can I tell you something, Lizzy?" he said. "Sincerely, now." He stroked my wet hair, and his face—the high-angled face with a yearning expression that never failed to move me—inclined toward mine. "You counsel kids for a living, Lizzy, you know the drill. There's no shame in asking for a little help."

I looked at him. "I know that."

"Call someone. Talk to somebody."

"I found someone, Drew, I did," I said, the lie taking shape almost before I saw the full range of its possibilities.

"You found someone?"

"In Portland."

"Oh." He exhaled. "For crying out loud, Lizzy, why didn't you just tell me that in the first place?" He was still doing calculations in his head. "What time was your appointment?"

"Five," I said. It was so easy.

"All right, five, and it was what, an hour?"

"About that."

"Who—"

"Griggs. Doctor Griggs."

"On a Saturday?"

I shrugged. "Those are his hours."

"All right, so we're at six o'clock by now, and you ate someplace, so that's, what, another hour?"

"It was pretty busy."

"Hour and a half, then. So now it's, what, seven-thirty, eight, tops?"

"Where are you going with this, Drew?" My head was starting to ache.

"It's eleven-thirty, Lizzy, and you're not yourself, is where I'm going with this."

I closed my eyes. "God, Drew, I'm so tired."

"I'm doing the best I can here," he said.

I nodded, listening to the rain batter the roof we'd replaced, all those shingles we'd spent a week picking out on the first anniversary of our marriage.

"Remember the tree we put in the bucket?" I said.

I felt him smile. We stayed there awhile, in the double chair. Our breathing sounded deceptively peaceful.

"Drew?"

A pause. "Yeah?"

"Is she anybody I know?"

Then, perhaps because the rain outside slashed and fell, a persistent lashing against our jointly bought shingles, he relented. "Was," he said quietly. "She *was* nobody you know."

We were staring ahead, not looking at each other. What I saw was our house, our merged clutter, the hopefulness implied in the mess we kept. Shelves sagging with paperbacks missing final pages, a box of socks with no mates, a kitchen burgeoning with mismatched cutlery and topless pots. *Fear not,* our earthly possessions seemed to say, *the rest of this stuff'll turn up someday.*

"I met her at a wedding," he said.

"When?"

"Last February. The Lauzier wedding in Lisbon. Maid of honor's roommate."

I turned toward him. "Did you — ?" I asked.

"We talked on the phone a few times, Lizzy, that's all." Now he looked at me. "It ended before it started."

I nodded. "That's kind of what I figured."

His mouth, which tended downward even when he was content, seemed to slide off its mooring. "I didn't see any point in telling you," he said. "It's irrelevant now."

"But I knew anyway."

"Right," he sighed. "I forgot about your supernatural powers."

"Don't."

He didn't say anything more. We remained there another while, but the double chair really was too small and we both stirred eventually; I'd all but wrecked it anyway with my dripping clothes.

"I should get out of these wet things," I said.

He stood up, folding his arms such that he appeared to be hugging himself, a gesture that always masked unease, a gesture he made many times in a day, for Drew Mitchell did not feel easy anywhere. For now, he looked like a guy at a bad party in search of a graceful exit. "I was working," he said, gesturing vaguely toward his office.

"Go ahead. I'll be up for a while." I peeled off my coat. "I'm sorry I worried you."

"Mariette jumps the gun," he said. "It gets contagious."

"Tell her I'm doing better than she thinks."

He nodded. "Will do." He started to leave, then turned to me. "A kid called for you earlier."

"Who?"

"I don't know. A girl."

"Trouble?"

He tried to smile. "What else?"

Sometimes, not often, I got a call from a heartbroken freshman at the liquor-store phone booth, or a cheerleader whose boyfriend had popped her in the jaw, or a friendless outcast with nobody, absolutely nobody else, to talk to. It was still early in the year for night calls; but I was in the book, easy to find.

"I'll be out back if you want me," Drew said. His sober gray eyes took my measure, then he left the room.

A minute later, the phone rang. It was Andrea Harmon.

"Where are you?" I asked her.

"ShopRite."

"Are you crying?"

"No," she said irritably. "I'm wet. I feel like a gerbil on Noah's ark."

"Well, it's raining, Andrea." I peered out the window. The storm had let up, having swept through quickly and left a gentle, autumny-cold rain in its wake.

"Look, I'm kind of stuck here, Mrs. Mitchell, and I had nobody else to call, all right? You've probably got like a house full of people, but like I said I'm totally stuck. I mean, if there was anybody else on the face of this friggin' planet, I would've called them."

Her flattery notwithstanding, I said, "Are you asking me for a ride home?"

"Look, I know you're probably like in the middle of a dinner party or whatever, but I've got no shoes on and I'm about four hundred miles from my house."

I had no shoes on either.

"Are you *laughing* at me?" Andrea said.

"Of course not. Your mother can't pick you up?"

"The state yanked her license."

"All right," I said. "Stay put."

I stopped to wash my face, get some dry socks, put on a raincoat. Drew was at the back of the house, where he kept a separate set of rooms. A tiny front office, which used to be a sun porch, had an entry that opened into the side driveway. Unlike the rest of our house, the office was spare: a desk and computer, a light table, two chairs for clients. On the walls hung prints of brides, graduates, toddlers in birthday hats, old ladies blowing out candles, families posed in front of fake trees, plus a few human-interest shots from his part-time work for our local weekly— city councilors in pressed suits, a new teacher holding a beaker, a crowd gathered around a burst water main. Next to that, in the previous owner's spare bedroom, Drew kept screens and backdrops and other portrait gear. The darkroom resided in a former bathroom, just out of sight.

His own phone, his own entrance, a separate existence in our home. Not long before the accident I had stood in this very spot trying to retrieve the exact moment when we began our drifting, but it was like trying to pinpoint twilight, or midtide, or peak foliage. He was squinting into his computer screen, in an uncomfortable quiet.

"I'm picking up Andrea Harmon at the ShopRite," I told him. "Some jerk left her there in the rain."

He looked up wearily. I felt in an unwanted flash the toll I had taken on him since the accident. "You're in no shape to go chasing after kids, Lizzy."

"She's desperate," I said. "I won't be an hour."

"Let me drive."

"I'm fine. It's letting up." In truth I didn't think we could bear being in the car together just then; the silence had begun to hurt.

He started to say something but lost his zeal. "Do what you want," he said quietly.

I knelt next to him, and he placed his hands on my shoulders. In only a small way I wanted our beginning back, that torn-flesh feeling of our Monday-morning partings. Hello or goodbye, he used to trace the shape of my face, one finger down each temple and cheek, ending at the point of my chin. Hello, Lizzy. Good-bye, Lizzy. More than that, I wanted the stage that was supposed to come later, the thing Mariette and Charlie seemed to have. Friendship, I guess, is one word for it.

"Touch my face?" I said.

He did. Not like before. "Hello, Lizzy," he murmured. "I miss you."

How strange that he would miss me. Maybe he meant an earlier version of me — the girl who went with him to get the Christmas tree.

"Me too, sometimes," I said.

There was a moment that could have gone either way, our whole house a held breath: the thrumming rain, the MITCHELL PHOTOGRAPHY sign swinging outside on its hinges, the refrigerator starting up in the kitchen. Then it was gone.

"Bring a blanket," he said as I got up. "She's probably cold."

I left my house, shouldering once again into the wet night, thinking, Things end. They just do.

I edged into the parking lot at the ShopRite near a bank of phones. Andrea tottered out of the mist like some undead creature in a horror film, a threadbare shadow in sock feet lurching toward the car. She sloshed into the front seat and slammed the door. "I owe you so big, Mrs. Mitchell, anything you want, you got it."

Sometimes Andrea just plain broke my heart. What did this sopping slice of girl think I could possibly want from her?

"Take this," I said, offering her the blanket. She slung it over her shoulders. "Your mother know you're out here?" I asked.

She looked me over. "Maybe. Maybe not. Either way she'll figure out a way to blame this on me."

"Who else should she blame it on?"

Andrea leaned sideways, making sure I could catch the theatrical roll of her inked eyes. "Are you winding up for one of your little treasure hunts?"

"There's no such thing as a free ride, Andrea. Buckle up."

Andrea paused, thinking it over. Then, apparently deciding that beggars couldn't be choosers, she buckled up, loosening the belt just enough to fall halfway between the letter and the spirit of the law.

I pulled onto Random Road and headed south along the river, the noise of the wipers making the car seem quieter by contrast.

"You're soaking wet," Andrea said. "I can't stand the smell of rained-on clothes." She herself smelled of discount wine, though she appeared to be sober. She pulled her own wet shirt away from her skin, then flinched as it slopped back into place.

"Would you care to wait by the road until a more appealing driver happens along?"

"Not really," she said sullenly.

"Where are your shoes?"

She ignored me, picking at her nail polish, humming something just under her breath.

"Did somebody hurt you, Andrea?" I asked, measuring my volume.

"I had a fight with my boyfriend, all right?"

"And he took your shoes?"

"They were already off."

"Your jacket, too?"

She nodded. I was beginning to get the picture.

"Do I know him?" I ventured.

After a moment, she said, "Seavey."

"Glen Seavey? Seriously?"

Her chin jutted out preemptively. "He can't stand you, either."

"Imagine that," I said. Glen Seavey was a nineteen-year-old senior who had not once condescended to *sit* in my office. He elected, always, to stand, all six feet of him, one hammy fist anchored on my desk, the other jammed provocatively into the pocket of his too-tight jeans. It did not surprise me one bit that Andrea Harmon had scraped up a boyfriend from the dry-rotted bottom of the barrel.

"How long have you been seeing Glen?" I asked.

"Six days."

"Why did you get out of the car?"

"He called me a bitch."

"Why?"

"Because I wouldn't suck his you-know-what."

I slid my eyes sideways. She was testing me, but also telling the truth.

"Then I'm glad you called me, Andrea."

She let go a conciliatory sigh. "I'm sorry if you were right in the middle of a dinner party or something." I realized then how important it was for her to imagine me presiding over a long table, a ring of faces flashing in candlelight, a burble of congenial wordplay. My guess is that she wanted to be anchored, however tenuously, to the kind of person who gave dinner parties.

"We were just wrapping up anyway," I said.

"Was it fun?" she asked.

I nodded. "You have to spend time with decent people, Andrea."

"I don't know any decent people."

I found Andrea's driveway, a rutted gravel lane with a prefab house of discolored planks sagging at its bitter end. Her mother had parked a rusting Escort so close to the door that the car's front bumper appeared to be resting on the steps. She'd left a lamp on in one window, a cold yellow square crossed by a flickering bluish light from a TV. From inside came the yapping of the jittery, unhinged terrier that Andrea adored.

"Look, Andrea," I said. "I'm assuming you've got enough sense to be using birth control."

She gave her eyes a long, exaggerated roll. "Haven't we had this conversation, like, six hundred times?"

"Yes," I said pointedly.

"I'm not a moron. You think I can't learn from my sister's mistakes?" She stroked her neck absently, darkening a hickey I'd just noticed at the top of her collarbone. "There hasn't been one single solitary minute of silence in that nuthouse since the second her kids were born. They're always howling and yowling, either they fell down, or they dropped a cookie, or somebody had the nerve to say 'no' when they tried to put the dog in the hamper." She looked at me. "I guess your nerves kind of short-circuit after a while, because she doesn't even hear it anymore. Or maybe she's just gone deaf—as a whaddyacallit, defense mechanism."

"Which is the long way of saying you *do* use birth control?"

Andrea pursed her used-looking lips. "Usually. It's kind of a pain." She swiveled her head toward her house.

"I'll walk you in," I said.

"Don't," she said.

"Andrea, I've been in your house before."

She hesitated, then got out; we had to step over the bumper of her mother's car to get to the steps, keeping one hand on the hood. The rain had stopped altogether, leaving a greasy film over everything in the yard.

Mrs. Harmon grunted when Andrea crowded through the too-small kitchen door. She was making a potholder at the kitchen table, on which rested a year's worth of newspapers and a portable TV broadcasting a middle-of-the-night infomercial for a hair-removal system. She looked up and saw me. "What're you doing here?"

"I brought your daughter home, Mrs. Harmon," I said. I had to shout a little over the TV and a lot over the dog, who was yapping psychotically, jouncing side to side. Cat-sized, with a dirty muzzle and hardly any tail, he jounced and yapped: *Ark ark ark ark ark ark ark!*

"I suppose this is my fault?" Mrs. Harmon yelled. *Ark ark ark ark ark ark ark!* "This is all my fault, right? My daughter trots her backside all over two counties and you figure out a way it's my fault, right?" Her swimmy eyes bulged; she pointed a crochet hook with an alcoholic's self-righteous bravado. On my previous occasions here she'd been sober and edgy, quoting accurately from the state's toothless truancy code. I decided I preferred her drunk.

"Ma!" Andrea hollered. "Ma, shut up!"

Ark ark ark ark ark ark ark!

Mrs. Harmon teetered in my direction, her boxy figure taking all the space between the refrigerator and the stove. There were so many pots and pans — clean ones, incongruously shiny — stored on the stove top that you couldn't see any of the burners. The place smelled faintly of propane. "You people keep your nose stuck out of my business, why don't you," Mrs. Harmon said. She'd been drinking long enough that her voice could rise only so far, for which I was grateful. The dog was springing up and down, but not toward me, more like a jack-in-the-box, stuck in a witless boomerang. "If you people had kids of your own," she added, "you wouldn't be so stick-your-nose about mine."

The dog kept at it, a persistent pitch that lodged just behind my eyes and grew nails. "Your daughter is a tenth-grader, Mrs. Harmon," I said irritably. "It's twelve-thirty in the morning."

"Aren't you one to talk," she said. "Aren't you a fine and dandy one to talk." She grabbed two pans from the stove and banged them at the dog, who turned tail for about a fifth of a second, then resumed barking. Andrea scooped him up, and he finally stopped. For a moment we all stood there, blinking in the silence.

"Ma, will you just shut up?" Andrea lumbered to her room, a long groan trailing her as she picked her way through hillocks of laundry, the dog tucked mutely under her arm. Her door slammed with a cardboard-sounding clunk.

"At some point," I stammered, "at a more appropriate time, Mrs. Harmon — " As a rule, I didn't like to confront parents; they either blew up or shriveled before your eyes and neither scenario made for sunny times. Mrs. Harmon didn't say anything, so I added, quietly, "Andrea's a bright girl, Mrs. Harmon, but she's barely — "

"Who do you think you are, telling me how to raise my kid?" she snarled. "You think I don't know you got tried out by a priest?"

I was so stunned that my ears rang. I started to speak, but the saliva caught in my windpipe and I began to cough, first lightly, *hic-hic-hic,* then hard, helpless. Mrs. Harmon waded through a cymbal-crash of fallen cookware, yelling, "Andrea get out here your teacher's about to croak," and there was Andrea appearing out of nowhere, hammering on my back with her bony fist, rejuvenating my healed wounds and releasing spirals of pain as the TV show droned in the background and the dog resumed its electroshock barking and a glass of water was thrust into my hands and I stopped coughing and the room righted itself and I found myself outside again, climbing back over the bumper of the Harmons' low-hipped car as the barking came to a stunning, merciful stop.

"She wasn't this bad before my father left," Andrea said. She stood in the open doorway, her silhouette wiry, tough, rigid, mitigated by the frizzy outline of the dog hanging purselike over her arm. "It's my father's fault I'm turning out like this."

"Get some sleep," I told her. "We'll talk on Monday."

"Okey-dokey," she chirped. "We'll talk on Monday."

"Andrea," I said, turning into the dark. "You mean something to me."

The house blazed behind her, but her face consisted only of shadow. I believe I saw her eyes move. "Oh," she said, then slipped inside, the door catching so quietly that a moment passed before I understood she was gone.

By the time I got home I had bitten my lips nearly numb. Drew came out of his studio and studied me.

"I had a dustup with Gwen Harmon," I told him.

He was pulling off my coat. "I told you not to go."

"I wish I hadn't. She said something really hateful."

"You want a bath? I'll run you a bath."

"I don't want a bath. I want a gun."

We looked at each other, time stretched briefly, and we laughed a little, another one of those connecting moments.

"I want you to go back to that counselor," he said.

"I will. I know." I kicked off my shoes and sloshed into the living room, Drew trailing me.

"It's nothing to be ashamed of," he said. "Anyone would be a little at sea."

He was trying to help me. I let him hold me for a while as if I were any ordinary wife. Then, after a long silence in which I felt his body adjust and readjust against mine, his voice re-emerged from the muted dark. "People have things, Lizzy," he said. "Things that kill them a little. They find ways to keep going."

I nodded, my face resting on his chest. "Were you going to leave me?" I asked him. I tried to imagine a woman Drew might leave me for, but came up empty, just a dim, see-through figure, weightless and floating, nothing real.

"I don't know," he said. His shirt smelled like us. "I was thinking about it."

"Are you thinking about it now?"

"What kind of man would leave you now?" His breath warmed my temple. "What kind of man would I be?"

As dislocating as it was to stand in my house with this man who wanted to leave but wouldn't, I didn't push him any further. I did not want to be the kind of woman who got left.

"You coming up?"

"In a minute," I said. "Give me a minute."

We extricated ourselves—awkwardly, it seemed. I followed him only so far; he paused on the stair, but maybe he saw in my face that now was not the moment if he cared to seize one.

I was on my way upstairs, I believe I was on my way upstairs, but instead I fitted myself into the double chair and wrapped myself in the throw Mrs. Blanchard had given us for our wedding. It shimmered with white flowers.

I turned off the lights and sat in the dark, trying to conjure the feeling of angels' wings near my hospital bed, the flash of ring. The weightless woman Drew might have left me for vanished utterly, replaced by the more tangible specter of a black sleeve, a freckled hand marked with downy red hairs, a hand that looked as if it might actually weigh something, a ring so real it took the color of earth itself.

The Little Hours

SEXT

TWELVE

From *The Liturgy of the Hours:*
My soul yearns for you in the night;
yes, my spirit within me keeps vigil for you . . .

The women in the parish dress up for him. He finds it touching, their lipstick and good shoes, these signs of respect and distance. How endearing, the businesslike way they straighten their skirts across their knees in advance of the inevitable tears, the admission of weakness or guilt, the confession that will make slush of their voices. Their ladylike attire — tiny earrings, small purses swinging on long straps — serves as a kind of disguise, a loophole in case they renege on promises made while wearing these very clothes. Later, stripped of their armor, they can tell themselves, *That wasn't me in there,* making their betrayals and inconsistencies easier to bear.

From the beginning, from his first, mercifully brief assignment as a prison chaplain, he set out to make leaders of the led, shepherds of the sheep. His mission, in the words of the more progressive teachers at Grand Séminaire, was to help his parishioners "find their own priesthood." He undertook the parable of the loaves and fishes — the first self-help article in recorded history — as the central metaphor of his calling. Now, entrusted with four hundred families in a town he loves, he strives to show his people how to become their own prophets of God's word, their own keepers of the sacraments. He jokes that he wants to work himself out of a job, to bring them a bit of bread and a gutted trout and watch them multiply the bounty. Cultivate faithful marriages; maintain forthright friendships; pray with your children. Find your own priesthood.

He tries to make it easy, doling out advice the way he doles out penance after Confession, discrete tasks (on the order of six Hail Marys and four Our Fathers) that appear easy but (in the ideal, at least) nudge the penitent toward reflection and forgiveness:

Give a sincere compliment to the child who harries you most.
List three reasons why you married him in the first place.
When God says no, try to rephrase the question.

He hopes and believes that his people — the men, too, when they come — leave his office feeling fortified, not judged; renewed, not encumbered; opened, not diminished. Though ill-prepared for the confounding miscellany of human endeavor, he has learned to meet his congregation's often muted cries with a certain amount of grace and, increasingly, experience.

He believes he has made a good job of it, discovering on his own that spiritual guidance is often a matter of reassurance. *Father, would you bless me?* they ask him. His fingers rest on their sheening foreheads. Their faces slacken; it has the effect of a magic spell. How glad he is to have been called to service now, with condemnation out of vogue and compassion in!

Unlike the other women, Vivienne comes to her appointments simply dressed, in her softened shirts and much-washed jeans, her hair corralled by a brown barrette. How else, in this house they've come to jokingly call the "north wing" of her own, might she dress? Even so, when she comes to him for guidance she enters by the front door and steps into the narrow hall like any other parishioner. Her formality both dismays and disarms him. Is she taking care to appear unexceptional because she believes she is an exception, or because she believes she is not?

He does not yet understand that he has fallen hard in love.

Wednesday evening. He can hear the girls outside, tending the moon garden in the dusk, nipping spent blossoms with the excellent German-made clippers he gave Lizzy months ago, on her seventh birthday. (*Too young!* said Mrs. Hanson. *C'est beau, ah?* said Vivienne.) The baby boys — Buddy just ten months old, a dimpled troll whom Lizzy and Mariette carry around endlessly, their favorite doll — are next door with Pauline. Ray's gone fishing. Vivienne arrives, cool outside air filling the tiny hallway through which normally enter so many forms of demand: *Father, the parking lot needs paving. Father, my mother took a turn for the worse. Father, my son is taking drugs.* Vivienne brings something else altogether. Her presence, despite its physical lightness, seems so urgent, so blessedly necessary.

Drawing her into his office, he opens the whispering door. He runs his hand over the light switch, but it does not take. *I'll have to replace that,* he says. Here is a man with no wood shop, no riding lawn mower, no bowling night or shift work, but he has a lightbulb to replace and wants her to know it.

He crosses to his desk, where he snaps on the lamp Elizabeth bought for him in celebration of his pastorship. The lamp shade shows hummingbirds and lilies floating in thick glass. It casts a quiet, pinkish light. Over the years, so gradually it feels almost like a secret, he has attuned himself to his friend and neighbor with ever-increasing precision. He can recognize her footfall on the porch, the rabbit-quick flick of the knob when she turns it. He knows when she's been in his garden, certain careful partings amongst the thickets of flowers. When the Blanchards' car starts up in their driveway a hundred yards away, he senses whether it is she or Ray at the wheel. He can pick out her voice anywhere: her scratched-glass alto in the recessional hymn, her waterfall laughter at a school play; a single word in a grocery line. She is, quite simply, present. All the time.

And he—who possesses no frame of reference, who depends on God to keep his mission clear, who accepts sexual desire as a path to prayer and psychological strength, whose sister was his only woman friend, whose passion for his child both anchors and terrifies him, who wants no life but the one he's been given—he names her presence only as a form of relief.

The certainty in her face, those strong, high bones: relief.

Her composed elegance, in her customary pew, hymnal opened on her lap: relief.

The marigolds bordering the moon garden, her recipe for preventing pests: relief.

Her presumptuous reach into the spice cupboard, a fistful of oregano added to his kettle of pallid spaghetti sauce: relief.

He endures thoughts of Vivienne as a passed test, a measure of his focus as a man of God and his willingness to renew his vows on a daily basis. He respects his vocation more, not less, because of her. He is proud of his friendship with her and what it asks of him as a mature man with a calling. He believes he has come to embrace its complications.

Father, she begins.

We've been friends for years, Vivienne. Do you think you could call me Mike?

I call you Michael in my head, she says. At least, that's what he thinks she says. He does not ask her to repeat it for fear he heard it wrong. His own head rings. When she speaks again, she calls him Father.

Tonight, as it happens, is also his own counseling night—once every six weeks he drives up to Bangor to visit with Jack Derocher, his confessor, an older man good at parish work. He talks to Jack about parish demands, his impatience at meetings, his annoyance with the housekeeper. He does not, as he suspects some of his brethren must, discuss doubts about God's plan or presence. Who can doubt God's plan or presence with Lizzy in the house? In the face of another unendurable loss, God waltzed Lizzy into this rectory, hung her red coat on the newel post, and let her stay.

No, he thinks, I've got no quarrel with God.

It's an arrogant notion, Jack Derocher would say, to believe God selected you for special favors. But he does believe it, and because he does, he cancels his standing appointment. He would rather see Vivienne Blanchard tonight than Jack Derocher. He would rather talk about children, act like a family man, push up his sleeves, work the collar off his chafed neck, talk to a mother. So he switches on the lamp, admiring the pinkish light on Vivienne's face.

I let her stay up till eleven last night making a leprechaun trap, he says. *Her eyes were nearly swollen shut this morning when Mrs. Hanson came in.*

Did you catch one?

Not yet. Maybe tonight.

Vivienne smiles. *Children love to stay up late,* she tells him.

I can't seem to put my foot down, Vivienne.

Oh, so! she scoffs. *She has all her life for people who put their foot down. You go ahead. You keep your foot right where it is.*

This is what she says to him, all the time: *You go ahead.*

He is not without friends. But Vivienne is the only person he knows who appears to believe he is really a parent. He shows her the trap, a shoe box decorated with crepe paper and green glitter. Her head bobs a little, her hair shivers in the light.

Vivienne inspects the leprechaun trap, then puts it down, turning suddenly formal, distant. *I wish to talk about Ray*, she says. *I have nowhere else to turn. I require advice.*

Something curdles within him. He waits. He does not yet know that he will come to her house one night and find her eye blackened, but the foreknowledge resides in his head already, for he expects her to say something about violence.

Instead, she comes up with the words "marital intimacy." The term fills him with dread, though Vivienne is not the first woman to confide in him this way. He has talked about this with his brother priests. How do we advise wives and husbands? We, with the experience of eunuchs! *We're choirboys!* Poulin booms over a card game, throwing back his head and showing his fillings. *Choirboys masquerading as grown-ups!* He laughs, slapping the table, four aces, no doubt, quivering in the opposite hand; he laughs when winning.

We know plenty about commitment, Leary likes to retort, defensive and (few people know) thinking about "jumping the league," Jack Derocher's words for leaving the priesthood.

Who understands commitment better than we do?

We're more than qualified.

You do fine, Poulin concedes, letting them down easy, a bitty little token before he fans his winning hand and collects their quarters.

And he *has* done fine. Indeed he has. He is a fine priest! But this?

Vivienne hugs her stomach. *Having Buddy was not easy, Father. I'm not yet myself again.* Her voice, even in its wavering, contains the clarity of a spoon tapped against a fine glass.

His tongue swells. He offers her silence.

I fall tired so often, Father, she tells him. *I find some obligations of marriage difficult to fulfill.*

What he wants to say: *A kick in the nuts should do the trick.*

What he does say, without inflection: *Marital obligations apply to both husband and wife.*

This is more or less the party line, a point he addresses perfunctorily when preparing young couples for their sacrament. Tonight he sounds not only embarrassed but cloddish and unprepared.

Is he drinking? he asks, clumsily. He can't even say Ray's name, and it occurs to him in a knife-slash of shame that he is afraid of Ray Blanchard. He finds Ray at early Mass on occasion — Ray considers it lucky to pray before going to sea — and when he places the host into Ray's sea-scarred hands his concentration breaks. *The body of Christ,* he says to his neighbor, and his neighbor responds *Amen* with a throaty, early-morning rumble that borders on — what? Is it disrespect, the way he snatches Christ and chews him? Is it presumption? The ritual changes then, feels rote and hollow. Because of Ray and his manly bluster. Ray and his ice-blue eyes. Ray and his idling truck weighted down with metal hooks and coils of bristly rope and mysterious clanking tools. Only two days ago, as the farmhouse filled with Vivienne's sisters for Bernard's birthday, he heard Ray, smoking on the porch with one of the brothers-in-law: *Father likes to stay inside with the women.* Said in that same throaty rumble, without a jot of rivalry, or envy, or suspicion; said, instead, with a throwaway humor, the way one would speak of, or dismiss, a boy.

Vivienne's head picks up. *I can certainly refuse him when he's drinking, Father.* Not a question, this: an instruction. She frequently instructs him.

What he should say: *Is he hurting you? Do you need help? Does he?*

What he does say: Nothing.

He offers nothing, sitting like a potted plant, a root-bound ornament, behind the prissy shield of his desk. Heart flapping, he offers not a word of counsel. He will not pick up the edge of the rug she has dragged in here. He will not peer at the dirt and then be obligated to start sweeping.

Vivienne sees this before he does, to his great chagrin. *It was only a little question,* she says, backtracking, shepherding both of them back to safer ground. *Just something I wondered about. My sister, same thing. Wives get tired. Men, they don't know.*

In the ideal, he says, *obligation is something the husband and wife work out for themselves. It should, in the ideal, be part of the communication in a good Catholic marriage.*

Yes, yes, she says, dismissing him. His irrelevance stays his throat. *I work toward a good Catholic marriage,* she adds, unsmiling.

He has helped other husbands. Prayed with them. Listened to them with patience and compassion. Neutralized their anger and frustration. Sent them to programs. Shamed them, even, into becoming better husbands, more devoted fathers. He could name five men, right this second, who changed. But they did not have Ray's sunburned swagger, Ray's whiff of the street. They did not make him feel pale and cloistered by contrast. Like a nun.

Ray believes in God. Ray could be helped.

Why does his will fail him? A surreptitious inventory of Vivienne's exposed skin shows not the slightest bruise, merely a creamy, uninterrupted sweep, save for her calloused hands.

Anyway. In this sudden, hooded silence, Vivienne decides not to tell.

He knows this. She knows this.

They sit uncomfortably in this weird intimacy. It will be another two years before he rattles the latch on her kitchen door and finds her holding a bag of peas to her punched eye. There he will be, thoroughly unmanned, carrying a cake.

It will be two years, but he knows already.

At the back of his head, far enough back that he can barely ascertain it, a thought flitters, a faint pumping: If Ray Blanchard became a good husband, then—?

I do not want another baby with him, Vivienne says suddenly, her voice a twinge in the charged air. It is a voice he has never heard from her: heartless.

With him are the words that reverberate. Everything she says seems to take on double meaning. *If not with him — ?* goes the second faraway thought.

Pardon? he asks, blinking.

Nothing, Father, she says. *Forgive me. I act like the new mother and I should know better after three times, yes? It was just a silly question.*

She gets up, smoothing her stomach. He lets her go. She will come back next week at their regular time. Ray's name will not come up.

I am helpless.

I am helpless before you.

I require advice.

❧ ❧

Because Vivienne Blanchard is so slight of frame, the girls, at nine years old, flank her at nearly her own height and weight. Lizzy has shot up over the summer, all leg, while Mariette carries her height in the torso, a strong-looking girl with her mother's wavy dark hair. He sees the three of them gliding down the flattened lane between the pines and bramble and laden maples, three lovely creatures in fluid motion. This always happens when Ray goes away. Vivienne's spine appears to loosen, all her flinching caution drains away. Mercifully, Ray is gone more often than not of late, and Vivienne's body looks reclaimed, fully returned to loveliness, an ease of motion that the girls replicate to near perfection.

He watches them approach, and sees that Lizzy, too, will be a woman someday. With the precision of a hornet's sting comes the recognition that he has not prepared her.

Mariette calls out first, waving her bathing suit over her head. They are going for a swim. Now they are all calling—these three feminine specters—calling to him in varying, equally pleasing pitches. The little boys, comical afterthoughts thumping after their mother like a pair of boots tied to the tailpipe of a Mercedes, suddenly shoot ahead, hollering across the lawn to the short trail leading to the river's bend. The water there is cold but tolerable, not too deep, far enough upriver from the mills that it runs clear. A massive, flattened boulder where they all like to sit is close enough to the house that he can hear the phone when it rings. Lizzy tears off to her room to change clothes, Mariette following; he hears Mrs. Hanson shouting directions from the laundry room—*Not those towels, take the ones in the basket*—as he follows Vivienne down the trail after the boys.

They sit quietly, watching Buddy and Bernard, who have been told to stay close to the bank but can't be trusted. Their eternally skinned knees recall his own tumbling boyhood. Ray plays too rough with them, he believes. Secretly, he hopes that Vivienne brings them over here to show them a different way to be a man.

Only recently has it fully dawned on him that he and Vivienne are raising their children together. And as Lizzy gets older, he needs Vivienne more. A week ago, in civvies and blistering with shame, he bought a copy of *Our Bodies, Ourselves* at a Bangor bookstore. The title alone mortifies him, but how else is he to introduce even the most rudimentary topics of a female's physical development? Surely he requires more information than he can glean from this embarrassing book (whose graphic illustrations of fully developed women torture him in all the tiresome, predictable ways) and a stash of articles on the sexual development of girls that he has hidden—*hidden,* for God's sweet sake—beneath his socks and handkerchiefs. For months now he's been lifting copies of *Seventeen* from waiting rooms, looking exactly like the kind of reprobate he must now find a way to warn Lizzy away from.

Vivienne, he begins. Fortunately she's got her eyes on the boys, and so, with a sigh, he confesses the subject that worries him through sleepless nights. He tells her about the book.

I don't know where to start, he tells his friend.

Vivienne keeps watch on the children, and her mouth does not move, but he can see how she is struggling not to laugh. He feels, maddeningly, like a child himself. Since his refusal to brook the topic of Ray two years past, there has evolved a subtle shift in their relationship, a reversal that completed itself on the first night of this very summer, when he arrived at her kitchen door with a cake in his hands and found the children crying, the dog cowering, Vivienne emerging from the shadows with a bag of peas pressed against her eye. Though he saw to her, after a fashion, bundling her into the car and whisking her off to a doctor who stitched her eye, he was the one who felt seen to, for she allowed him to minister to her without once mentioning Ray's name. And Ray made himself easy to forget, grabbing every fishing trip that came up, giving wide berth to his family. Her eye healed as the desire to forget spread across the two households. Now, with her cheek restored to its former smoothness, she comports her-self just as before — except for a slight, oddly appealing defiance that makes ordinary speech seem rehearsed and ordinary tasks appear choreographed. A bystander would scarcely notice, but there it is: The parishioner has found her own priesthood. He has achieved what he so often publicly wished for — obsolescence. That was the night she ceased to call him Father.

And yet she courts his company, and in her company he feels renewed.

I feel foolish asking, Vivienne. But she's nine years old and knows nothing about — about certain things.

Now she looks at him. Blood rushes straight up his neck and deep into the roots of his hair. He envisions Ray's hands on her breasts, his mouth at her neck, then flings the thought away.

I'm afraid I've kept her too innocent, he says. *When she was four I told her babies came from God.*

Don't they? she says. Her bright, dark eyes strike him mute. Finally she laughs out loud. *Lizzy knows where babies come from, Michael,* she says. *Don't worry! You think those girls never talk to me?*

Lizzy and Mariette are working their way down the bank, tiptoeing over the dirt and rocks, bare-limbed and summer-tanned and wearing bright swimsuits on bodies that are short of puberty but nonetheless seem to have transformed—this very summer—from young girl to young lady. Young lady. How in God's sweet name does he plan to raise a young lady?

Besides, says Vivienne—as the girls explode into the water, spraying a geyser of river foam onto the howling boys— *there is no such thing as being too innocent.*

But, he says, *certain matters are unavoidable. She'll be maturing. Certain matters will have to be addressed.*

Vivienne smiles generously. *On her next birthday I'll bring over a package of sanitary napkins,* she says. *She can keep them in her bathroom. Then, when the time comes, you can have a calm and peaceful day.*

I won't have a calm and peaceful day, Vivienne, he says, his blushing now so intense it causes physical dismay. *How can I ever have a calm and peaceful day? I have to prepare her to live in the world as a mature woman. What do I know about living in this world as a mature woman?*

You don't have to know, she says. *I know. Besides,* she adds, patting his hand: *We have plenty of time.* Then, as an afterthought that washes him white with relief, she adds, *It's not just you, Michael. Men are no good at the talking.*

The phone rings from the house, and he scrambles to his feet, sighing inwardly. Somebody else needs him; someone he knows (or doesn't) is in mourning, or in labor, or in trouble.

Mrs. Hanson hands him the phone. She's been washing clothes, so the receiver is wet and smells of bleach. She is brusque, and he guesses the reason: At the Sunday ten-thirty he called everyone with a July birthday to the communion rail and led a chorus of "Happy Birthday." The children were delighted, and others, too. But it's the very kind of thing some in his parish detest.

Some people don't get birthdays at home, he tells her.

She counters pleasantly, *We're God's children, Father, not God's spoiled brats.*

He brisks away, to take the call in his office.

It's Frank Flannagan — Monsignor, now — from the Chancery, a functionary who was a pastor in Aroostook County before his rise through the ranks. Flannagan's made no small hints that he doesn't approve of the circumstances at St. Bart's — nor does the present bishop, whose predecessor, a soft-hearted, grandfatherly soul who held Lizzy on his own lap after approving the unorthodox arrangements for her guardianship; nor do other church officials, who go unnamed. Flannagan's call feeds a generalized paranoia that has begun to dog him: the feeling that his brotherhood has shrunk since he became a father, small "*f.*"

By how much, or in which quarters, he has no way of knowing.

Reflexively, he counts his friends. There's Matt at St. Dom's, Bob at St. Stan's; there's the bunch he plays cards with once per season. Loyalists all. And he relies on Jack Derocher at St. Pete's in Bangor. Once a year he has dinner with Luc Bellefleur, who jumped the league two years in and now meets God in a fifth-grade classroom in Peekskill, New York. He finds time for these people, and others, too, parishioners and colleagues who open their homes and their hearts, they really do. He has cleared an impressive amount of room in a life designed for one.

But in fact, Vivienne Blanchard is his only true friend.

We've had a complaint, Flannagan says on the phone. The complaints are always anonymous and strike the same sour notes. Father Murphy is not present enough to this congregation. He appears distracted by his other duties. He cut the number of weekend Masses. He missed three council meetings in a row. He posted office hours — posted hours! like a dentist! or a hairdresser!

Other pastors, one-man bands like himself, have resorted to the same tactics simply to find time for reflection, for stillness — for *God,* dammit. Do their personnel files also bulge with complaint?

Too much father and not enough priest, says Flannagan. *A little more focus, Mike. This isn't coming only from one quarter.*

Yes indeed. Thank you, Monsignor.

Do you need anything, Mike? We have a regional retreat coming up. I could send somebody up there to fill in.

My spirit is in fine shape, Monsignor. God and I are getting along famously.

And this, he thinks with a quiet whoosh of joy, is the plain truth. He is close to his God and sure of his mission, despite coming to service in the rancorous aftermath of Vatican II. Scores of his brethren have since abandoned their posts, but he harbors no such desire. In seminary he learned the Mass in Latin with his back to the faithful, but when the time came for him to take up service he found himself face-out, speaking English to a room bejeweled with the gleaming eyes of a waiting assembly who, he believed, wished him well.

He believes he has done right by his congregation. Spend some time every day in the silent company of God, he exhorts them. Is this so difficult? Is the presence of God so terrifying that you can spare no time?

But not everyone wishes to become his own prophet of God's word, as it turns out. Not everyone wishes to find his own priesthood. And, frankly, Vivienne reminds him, sometimes he can be a nag.

In this one way, he is old-fashioned. People think he came from another place and time.

Which he did.

Others think him an upstart. In his weekly homily he flaunts his taste for the theatrical, not above crooning a few bars of "Lean on Me" as the springboard for a meditation on friendship under pressure.

Who's your confessor? Flannagan asks.

Jack Derocher at St. Pete's.

You want someone else?

Why would I want someone else?

Well, nobody wants an unhappy parish. Maybe you're not getting the best advice.

There are some unhappy people here, Monsignor. It's not an unhappy parish.

He wants to add: *I've inherited eight families from that windbag across the river because I know the difference between preaching and anesthesia.* But considering the hot flash he experienced in Vivienne's company just now, he decides not to add the sin of pride.

He hopes God can laugh with him about this later.

THIRTEEN

Three buses pulled into the flag circle and dispatched Monday morning's load. Only a third of our students lived in town. The rest came in from Stanton, or from one of the townships flung like dropped beads along the haphazard outer edges of the county. To look at them you might not see the differences — Hinton kids acted like teenagers everywhere, influenced by TV — but differences did exist, often acutely felt. Some got dressed in the dark, wrestling their brothers for first dibs at a bathroom sink that ran out of hot water after twelve minutes. Some sipped pressed orange juice with their not-divorced parents in the oaken alcove of a restored farmhouse. Some slogged down a rutted gravel lane to wait for the bus in the cold. They knew who they were even when we didn't, surging en masse into an entrance hall once used for punching timecards that, depending on the color, marked you as a line-worker or line-leader heading into the pigeonhole of your eight-hour shift.

I stood by the entrance doors, one hand on the wall for balance, as the kids surged through. "Andrea, third period, please," I called as she whisked by, disappearing into a hole in the crowd.

"Did you hear me, Andrea Harmon?"

"I heard you," came her voice out of the din. Glen Seavey was avoiding me, too, I noticed, but I'd left a note with his study-hall teacher to send him up during fifth period.

"Trouble with the Harmon girl?" It was Rick, who had also posted himself at the doors.

"Just the usual."

Rick wasn't hunting up anybody in particular — he reserved the power of the intercom for summoning his charges — but he'd taken to joining me for the morning bell. I softened his linebacker image, so he claimed, but in truth the kids didn't seem to mind his end-zone baritone, his chunk-of-granite silhouette. It hadn't yet occurred to me that he was there not to inspect the morning maraud, but to inspect me.

We'd reached the fourth full week of school — a mild time, my duties mostly confined to perfecting schedule adjustments, inaugurating study groups, separating teacher-student combos that bore early signs of calamity. The second bell sounded and I scurried to my office, where I found six kids waiting, one of them in tears. *Honeymoon's over,* Jane telegraphed to me with her eyebrows. She sent the crier in first — Cassie Driscoll, who'd gained thirty-five pounds over the summer; our triage system, which we'd worked out over our six years together, was on go. The morning vanished; not until Glen Seavey swaggered in at the beginning of fifth period did I realize that Andrea hadn't shown up for third.

"Sit down, Glen," I said mildly.

"I'll stand, thanks."

I stood, too, though I still had to look up to eye him. I folded my arms to give my shoulders a better square. "She's a little young for you, don't you think?"

His long-lashed, pewter-blue eyes narrowed. "I thought this was about my history class."

"Nope. It's about tossing a young lady out of your truck and not having the good manners to throw her clothes out after her."

He looked surprised, but only momentarily. "That's none of your business." Out of my jurisdiction, he meant. Not a school matter.

"She's a minor," I said. "I'm speaking to you as a citizen."

He scowled at me. "She's sixteen."

"Fifteen," I corrected him. "She skipped fourth grade. The girl you ditched in a downpour is the youngest student in the sophomore class."

He leaned on my desk in a way that enraged me, his face close to mine. "What can I say? I like the smart ones."

"I wish I could say the same for her."

For a few electrical moments, we stared each other down. My leg throbbed, but I preferred the possibility of collapse to the aid of my cane at that moment. I was cataloguing the run-ins we'd had during his endless tenure at H–S Regional. This was year five; he'd missed the equivalent of a year and a half in various programs: drug rehab, behavior mod, two luckless stretches in private school, plus an expensive, sixteen-week evaluation program that failed to reward his parents with an explanatory syndrome other than Rotten Person. No doubt he was doing some cataloguing of his own, beginning with his first freshman year when I reported him to Rick for fighting. His parents—father a tax attorney, mother an ophthalmologist—had threatened the school with assault charges on the grounds that I'd ripped the cuff of Glen's new shirt while detaching his fists from the ribcage of a freshman who played clarinet in the jazz combo. The suit never went anywhere, but the senior Seavey retaliated by running for school board and siding every time with the Cheapskate Bloc.

"You're nineteen years old, Glen," I said evenly. "An adult, legally speaking. A charge of statutory rape isn't out of the question. And I might add that consent is entirely beside the point in the eyes of the law." I set my face carefully, as if I had his best interests at heart. "I'd hate to see you go to jail just for being stupid."

"What did she say to you?" he snarled, all pretense gone now, the well-sculpted knot of his jaw seizing up. His lips were perpetually flushed and pliable, an Elvis sneer that certain girls predictably found enthralling. He had a pseudo gang he ran with, five or six head cases with hip-hop pretensions and tricked-out cars — except for Glen, who drove a Blazer. He wore army fatigues, a gaudy gold disk around his neck, and his left forearm was permanently marred by a tattooed snake entwined around the words BORN NAKED. The thought of Andrea Harmon in that Blazer with him made me sick.

"She didn't have to say anything, Glen. I found her where you left her."

His eyes picked me over. "There are two sides to that story."

"I'm sure there are," I said, flipping through his student file, my sole weapon of intimidation. "However, in a Maine court, your side won't hold much with a judge."

"Really," he said. He looked amused, which launched a fresh shot of adrenalin through my percolating bloodstream. "Who presses charges, Andrea's dog?"

Not the dog, no, and not Andrea's mother, and sure as hell not Andrea. "*I* do," I said. "*I* press charges. *In loco parentis.* Look it up."

He blinked first. "You're supposed to be the student advocate. I'm a student. You're supposed to — advocate."

"You're special, though. You're the exception that proves the rule."

"Fuck you," he muttered.

I stalked past him and flung open the door. "Don't mess with me, Glen," I said. "That's your only warning."

He slipped out, in a waft of nicotine and marijuana, leaving me seething. Jane peered around the doorframe. "You all right?"

"Just ducky," I said. "I adore that kid."

Jane studied me for a minute, hands on hips. "You've got two waiting," she said. "I'll shoo them off."

I shook my head. "Bring 'em on."

They kept coming—with the notable exception of Andrea, who avoided me all day—and before long Jane was packing up in that secretarial-school way of hers that drenched the end of each day in an unmistakable, if misleading, sense of order. First she covered her computer with a plastic sleeve, tugging the sides all the way down; then she watered her plant; then she swiped her desk with a damp cloth and straightened the ink blotter. She put on her sweater, gathered up her purse in exactly the same way she did every afternoon. It pleased me to watch her, though she was eyeing me in that new way. "Good luck tonight," I told her. Mondays she bowled with her husband in a league in Lewiston.

"Thanks." She hovered in the doorway.

"What are you waiting for?"

"I'm not waiting," she said. "You need anything?"

"Jane. Get."

"Remember when Alice Fernald came back too soon after her hysterectomy and then ended up being out for the whole semester?" She gave her gloves a crisp pull at the wrists. "There's no law that says you have to stay just because you came back, Lizzy."

"There isn't? Are you sure?"

"All right," she said, slipping her purse strap over the crook of her arm. "See you tomorrow."

Then it was just me in there, and the sounds from the building—the far-off squeak of sneakers in a practice, the buses huffing out of the circle, a door slamming here, a chair moving there. My phone rang. "Lizzy?" Rick said. "Got a minute?"

I crossed the hall to his office, where the walls fairly clanged with plaques, for Rick had coached seven different sports in his twenty-five years at H–S Regional, including a one-time shot at a rugby team with six kids.

"Statutory rape?" he said, raising an eyebrow. "*In loco parentis?* What the hell's gotten into you?"

I sat down in one of his famously coming-apart chairs. "I take it Glen Seavey made a complaint?"

"Glen *senior,*" Rick grumbled. "Glen H. Seavey, *Esquire.* I'm surprised the phone didn't catch fire."

"I meant to let you know. I'm sorry. One of those days."

"It was one of those days on this side of the hall, too." Rick wore short-sleeved shirts year-round, and the sleeves strained against his biceps as he lifted both hands to the top of his head, showing two robustly sweat-stained armpits. "And where were you," he said, "where were you when Mr. School Board shows up? On the other side of the building engineering some kind of goddamn group hug."

I relaxed a little, realizing he wasn't angry. "Study Circle," I corrected him. "We don't hug unless we're studying American diplomacy."

"Well, a fat lot of good it did *me* today."

I shifted to avoid pinching my legs on the cracked vinyl. "I'm sorry, Rick. Really."

"So," he said. "Andrea Harmon, in the surprise of the century, decides to act like a delinquent and gets caught with her panties down."

I gave him a look but didn't say anything.

"Then the big, scary guidance counselor, singlehandedly and with zero legal standing, informs Glen Seavey, the son of a son-of-a-bitch *tax attorney,* that she's going to get his ass hauled down to the crowbar hotel." He spread his arms the way he sometimes did with the kids. "Is that it? Do I have that straight?"

"More or less. Yeah."

Rick sighed. "Do me a favor, Lizzy. Next time you hatch a plan like this, run it by me first."

I scanned the appalling clutter of his desk and realized I'd just added to the mess.

"Look," he said, "I don't give a shit about Glen Seavey. I don't care if that meachy bastard ditches every course he's taking, come June I'm going to gift wrap a diploma, stick it up his ass, and boot him out the door." He rocked back in his chair, which made a cheap cracking noise. "But you can't tell a kid you're going to sic the law on him, Lizzy. Especially on something that happened out of school, reported secondhand by a notorious liar. You were way out of line on this. You know that. Right?"

"Right. I know that."

"And you know that your gal is sitting in detention right now because she was lounging in Glen Seavey's lap at lunchtime and Irene Ratclef had the nerve to ask her to move?"

I didn't say anything.

"So, I'll handle the Seaveys. I don't know what the hell you were thinking."

I leaned forward. "I was thinking that he stands in my office with his hand stuck in his pocket, and I don't like it one bit. I was thinking that he makes his women teachers' skin crawl. I was thinking that Andrea got out of that obnoxious, over-priced, overbuilt *vehicle* of his about four seconds from a rape." I gripped the wobbly arms of the chair. "I was thinking of a little payback for every miserable kid he's victimized since he was old enough to throw a punch."

Rick rubbed his hand over his thinning hair. "I know this kid, Lizzy. I've seen a dozen just like him over the years — no more than a dozen, though, and believe me I'm grateful for small mercies. If he were haunting the girls' bathrooms then yeah, we could do something. But what am I supposed to tell his father? That the loosest cannon in the sophomore class did a song and dance for her guidance counselor about needing a lift?"

"It wasn't a song and dance."

"You had no business picking her up in the first place." He looked at me. "This is rookie bullshit, Lizzy, and I have to tell you I'm standing over here on my side of the hall scratching my head."

I didn't say anything for a while — I certainly didn't say anything about visiting Andrea's mother in the middle of the night. Instead, I sat there, fiddling with a tuft of stuffing that I'd picked out of the chair's split seam. "My fuse is shorter now, Rick. I can't seem to let anything stand."

"I get that," he said, "I do. But forget the Seaveys. I've been fending off the Seaveys since the day their precious little criminal set foot in my school. This is just one blip on a screen that's full of blips, all right? My real concerns lie elsewhere."

"What?" I looked up. "You mean me?"

He came around the desk to my side, and sat on a sheaf of papers. "Can you see why I might be getting the feeling that you're not all the way up to it?" he said gently. "You want sick leave, you got it. I'll go over to the super's office right now and sign the damn form myself."

"I don't want sick leave. Who told you I needed sick leave?"

He crossed his arms.

"Mariette?" I asked.

"Mariette says you're fine."

Good old Mariette. "Jane, then. She can't stop mother-henning me."

"You're crying in there, Lizzy," Rick said. "In the middle of the day."

"Not for long," I said, mortified. "And not often. Jane told you that?"

"Not just Jane."

"Then who?"

"You hear things," he said. "From the kids."

"The kids?" I sat up, stunned. "What things?"

"Nothing bad," he hastened to say. "More like, oh, like an unusual abundance of empathy, even for you."

"Is this about Josh Wilkes? His *mother* died, for crying out loud. *You* try adjusting a schedule while this poor motherless kid is sitting there right in front of you pretending his entire universe isn't in the process of being sucked into a black hole."

"It's not just him."

"This place is full of awful stories. Get worried when I *stop* crying." I spun toward the door, feeling suddenly light-headed.

"Lizzy," he said, coming after me. "Listen, wait." He squared me gently by the shoulders. "I'm starting to think maybe we dropped the ball over the summer, all of us. We should've organized a visiting schedule or something, shown our faces a little more than we did, eased you back in."

"Nobody dropped the ball. I didn't need easing."

"We're glad we didn't lose you, Lizzy, is what I'm trying to say."

I nodded. "Okay. Thanks. I'm sorry about the Seaveys."

He gave my shoulders a squeeze. "A heads-up next time, that's all."

His sympathy trailed me back across the hall. I sat at my desk, gazing out the window. All the stragglers — the kids held for detention or tutoring or theater rehearsal or basketball practice — stood in a loosely bound throng, waiting for the late bus. Andrea Harmon, freshly sprung from detention hall, sat on the weathered grass a deliberate distance from the group, her back propped against the listing chain-link fence that surrounded a practice field, smoking what I hoped was a cigarette. Her hair shone a muddy maroon color in the afternoon light and her eyes from a distance looked like cigarette burns, but there was something beautiful there, too, in her long legs bared to the cold, delicately turned wrists poking out from the cracked cuffs of her jacket. I had looked just the opposite at her age, in my school uniform and tied-back hair, though I'd cultivated a similar solitude, acute and palpable. I was glad to see she'd recovered her jacket; there were so few things she loved.

For all the drama of the day, I felt curiously serene; you could even say I was happy. My recent hours with Harry Griggs reverberated still, an afterglow of reliving my childhood days with such pleasure and relief. Perhaps because he was a stranger, Harry had elicited my most sympathetic readings. My stories unfurled without the stain of loss. My years at Sacred Heart had been marked by bitterness, an ugly, fanged thing that left me friendless and unreachable until I rejoined Mariette at college and started living again. I did not recognize this revival as temporary until the accident shook loose that old bitterness from its hiding place inside my own body. Released, it began once again to dog me, until this — this *telling* — began to dull its bite. *Let him rest,* whispered Mariette's voice in my head; and it came to me that at long last I was doing just that. What did it matter now that my uncle died accused? He lived innocent in memory, *my* memory, and it struck me now that the words "My child" held no imperative, no veiled directive; they were merely a declaration of presence. I am here. I exist.

Maybe that's all he was asking, the same thing we all ask: to be remembered.

FOURTEEN

The last time anybody could swear to seeing Mariette's father, he was headed up Random Road, northward, in the dark middle hours of a night in early September. Chummy Foster saw the truck—its flame-orange running boards left over from the previous owner—hugging the black curve, the tailpipe whacking the roadside weeds as the truck wended ditchside and back, over and again. Drunk, Chummy figured. Ray Blanchard, drunk again.

This information did not turn up until mid-November, more than two months after Mr. Blanchard missed the boarding of Gus Fournier's boat. By then it appeared that Ray Blanchard had taken off this time for good, and an unaccustomed watchfulness had overtaken Mrs. Blanchard, who exhorted us to play near her, as if afraid to lose us, too. Flattered, we cleaved to her, resorting to board games despite the cold and tempting sunshine outside.

We were playing Sorry at the kitchen table. Mariette chose a yellow marker, not her usual green. "I'm a new girl now," she explained, meaning a girl with no father. She spoke in a complicated timbre, as if acknowledging that she both missed him and didn't, or missed the idea of him more than the fact of him.

This is what I say now. At the time she might have been wrecked by grief. I can say only that she did not appear to be, which I suppose people must have said of me when I arrived at Sacred Heart to begin my long sleepwalk through the remains of my childhood.

A knock at the back door. Major drooled across the floor to let in the florid, bald-headed Chummy, no stranger himself to the bottle. "I saw Ray," he announced to one and all, avoiding Mrs. Blanchard's gaze, which had fallen upon him with the ferociousness of some animal I had no name for. "I'm sorry to be just getting to it, Vivienne, I've been off on the boats myself." He kept hiking up his green work pants, a nervous gesture of sympathy, I realized even then, but the effect on Mrs. Blanchard was that she kept retreating, *merci,* ok, *merci,* her arms violently folded across her middle, taking little mouse steps, back, back, back, until she'd pasted herself against the stove.

"Ok, *merci,*" she repeated, her lips closing tightly.

"He was headed north, up the Random Road, two-three in the morning," Chummy said. He made a half-gesture toward the newly fatherless children and said, "This was back in September, but I thought you'd want to know in case you need to track him down. I could stop by the police station for you, tell Ted and them, get them looking around in case he turns up."

"Ok, *merci,*" said Mrs. Blanchard, who had run out of room, her backside pressed against the knobs of the stove. For a moment I feared she might burst into flames.

Chummy hiked up his pants again. "A family man shouldn't take off like that." He gave Mariette's little brothers a single pat each, on the top of their fusty heads, with one of his big, knobbed hands. They gaped. Mariette and I, sharing a kitchen chair, watched him lumber off in embarrassment at this family's trouble, nearly steamrolling Pauline on the porch.

Pauline clicked into the kitchen and cast a glance at her

sister. "Mr. Foster saw Papa," Mariette said. "The police are going to make him come back."

"The police?" Pauline took off one of her high heels, shook out a pebble onto the linoleum, then picked up the pebble and plinked it into the sink. She turned to her sister. Their heads tended together, and they murmured in that way they had when discussing even the simplest matter.

"You think the police care one little bit where Ray went?" Pauline said.

"They might," Mrs. Blanchard said. "They think men should always come back." She went to the sink and scraped out a frying pan. It was almost lunchtime.

Pauline said, "You girls get the boys' hands washed. *Vite!*"

We each took a boy—I liked Buddy best because at two and a half he was still very small and loved to be carried—but we didn't leave the kitchen. Why would we? Pauline and Mrs. Blanchard were launching an irresistibly adult conversation, Pauline still holding her pointy red shoe.

"Ray disappears all the time,Vivi."

"Not this long."

"Oh, so!" Pauline said, tossing her hair. "Every time he goes he says he won't come back. He tells everybody he's leaving this town and never coming back."

Mrs. Blanchard hung on to the edge of the sink for a moment, then plunged her hands into the dishwater. "This time is different." She whirled around, soap flicking off the tips of her fingers. She looked frailer than usual, more papery and brittle, the skin beneath her eyes still soft and punched-looking, though she'd had all summer to heal since the night she answered the door with the bag of peas held to her eye.

"Papa's gone," Bernard whimpered. "He left us."

As if summoned by our voices, Father Mike appeared.

Major nudged the door open and in he came. Everything in the room returned to balance, as if a seesaw had just stopped, flattened at midair. Here was Father Mike, trim and well-kept, his fingers smooth as a woman's, his face scraped clean of stubble, his clothing predictable, pressed, black and white. He seemed, every time he entered this house, to have come a long way, without sweating, for the sole purpose of refining a place unused to finishing touches.

"Mrs. Hanson's looking for you, Lizzy," he said. "Lunchtime."

"Can I stay here?" I said, shifting Buddy to my other hip. He was heavy, but I liked the work of him.

Father Mike looked around. He looked at Pauline's shoe, at the lacy ribbon of soap dripping down Mrs. Blanchard's dress. "Did something happen?" he asked.

"Chummy Foster saw Ray's truck," Pauline said.

Mrs. Blanchard made a little cry, turning to face away from us.

"Oh, the children," Pauline said.

Was Mrs. Blanchard crying, I wondered, because the Ray who hollered at night might come back, or because the other Ray — the one who step-danced and told stories and made money — might not?

Father Mike began putting the boys' coats on. "Tell Mrs. Hanson I said to feed the lot of you," he said.

"But Father," I whined, "Father."

"No buts," he said. "Now." Because he never made commands, we obeyed, all of us, glancing over our shoulders as we scampered down the shortcut to the rectory, the crisp November air strafing our faces.

Mrs. Hanson was hardly thrilled to see us — four kids to feed instead of one. "He said what?" she asked, scuffing her hands on her apron lest her consternation be not plain enough.

"He's helping *Maman*," Mariette said. "He doesn't want us to see her cry." I gawked at Mariette, her weight distributed evenly, defiantly, on both feet.

"Fine, then," Mrs. Hanson sighed. With each passing year her lips paled another shade, as if keeping pace with the rest of her diminishing reserves. I had never thought her unkind, merely underpowered for the job. "Make yourself useful, Lizzy, and put out some plates."

We ate tomato soup and buttered bread in relative silence. Father Mike and I had made the bread the night before, way past my bedtime, listening to *The Barber of Seville* on the radio. The boys were miraculously quiet, anesthetized by the unfamiliar table, new food. The bachelors had wisely hidden themselves away.

Mrs. Hanson was glaring at me. "Take that off," she ordered.

I looked up. The shirt was my best, a hot-pink shell with a wave of sequins glimmering across the front. Crissy Miller had one exactly like it. Father Mike had thought it too loud, had done his best to talk me into something else, but in the end he relented, as he always did. "It's my favorite," I protested.

"You look like a tramp," she said. "It's beyond me why he puts up with your shenanigans."

At nine I did not understand innuendo. "Tramp" meant a hobo, a drifter, homeless and unwanted. "Shenanigans" was her word for finding me in Father Mike's bed back in the spring. The humiliation still burned—in both of us, it seemed, for she had changed utterly toward me since then. Her impatience, which had never struck me as personal, had turned to a pointed disgust. Clearly she was remembering anew, her face resolving into that same expression of shock and insult, her prodigious wrinkles converging into the open O of her mouth. Such a baby, I imagined her thinking. Such a tramp, wandering the house at night. The little princess, running downstairs after a nightmare. What shenanigans.

"I'm not changing unless Father says," I informed her, emboldened by Mariette's stolid presence and the audience of little boys.

My defiance stunned us both. Her eyes shuttered open. "You think I'm not on to you?" she said. "You think I don't know what you've been up to?" She ripped off her apron. "I won't stay in this place a minute longer. You tell that uncle of yours, that so-called *priest,* that I will no longer abide." She snatched her coat from the rack in the hall as we gawked at her, goggle-eyed. Her own eyes, amazingly, spilled a thin, tearful trail. "I once had a perfectly satisfactory life," she said, then turned and left for good.

Just like that, we four found ourselves baffled and abandoned, inexplicably insulted. Mariette cried first, then her little brothers startled into tears, then I did. By the time Father Mike returned, we'd worked ourselves into a state and ran to him in a kinetic, sticky throng, wrapping ourselves around his narrow middle, seeking the comfort of his body and lamenting the sudden caprice of our world.

It was Harry Griggs I told this story to, two months after our first meeting. I'd made a visit per week, sometimes two, during that window of time, in secret. I suppose it could be said that I was "seeing" him, but that admission would point in the wrong direction entirely. Nevertheless, I left school at the earliest possible moment like a woman aflame, scooting past Jane's desk without a word, my coat halfway on as I fumbled for my car keys.

When he opened the door to me on this particular evening, I discovered a second chair placed near the white one, a TV tray between, and two matching coffee cups, with matching saucers, arranged on the tray with a tower of Fig Newtons on a new plate. Each time I returned I found something else placed there just for me.

It was four-thirty and he seemed a little breathless, having rushed home from his shift gutting chickens to make coffee for two, as he had from the start. I would stay an hour (believing, perhaps, that adhering to the length of an actual therapy session mitigated my lie) and leave rested.

Outside Harry's windows the vanishing daylight glowed; doomed leaves rattled on their branches. "I love Fig Newtons," I said, picking one off the plate. "I used to eat them all the time when I was a kid."

"I know," he said. "You told me."

We smiled at each other. During the term of our acquaintance he'd become more and more regretful, his eyes sagging over me. He claimed that if he could do it over he'd remain at my side on the muddy shoulder to listen for signs of life and hold my hand. I didn't honestly believe him, but so what? The bad Samaritan was making up for his half-good deed by remaining at my side now, listening now, holding my hand — figuratively speaking — now.

"It's starting to look really nice in here," I said.

"I got the car fixed. Busted head gasket cost me a shitload, but now that I've got wheels I figured I might's well fix the place up a little. So I drove out to Ames last night to get the chair." He patted the back of the new chair, a high-backed rocker with tweed upholstery. The TV tray was fashioned out of a wood laminate stamped with green acorns.

"The cups I had left over from Loreen," he said. "She kept every other friggin' thing we owned." He examined one of them, as if looking for spots.

"Maybe you should ask her for another chance."

"You wouldn't say that if you knew how many chances she already gave me." He handed me a cup — bright green china with a border of pink tea roses. "You'd think it was the drinking, wouldn't you, but Loreen's a funny one, it's not the on-and-off wagon ride that got to her in the end. She says she's gonna find a man who listens to her next time around." He shook his head. "I'm a piss-poor listener, that's Loreen's theme song. My daughter always said the same thing."

"Actually," I said, "you're a very good listener."

His face brimmed; it had probably been a long time since he'd felt complimented. "Huh. Well, it feels like one more goddamn second chance — you being here." He stared at me over the rim of his cup. "Isn't your husband kinda wondering what you're up to?"

I felt caught, ashamed. "I told him you're a shrink."

"Hah! My VA counselor would get a kick out of that." He looked at his watch — a cheap Timex with a battered strap. "I charge by the hour, lady, so you better start talking. What have you got for me today?"

Stories. That's all I had. I'd intended to proceed chrono- logically, to recapture as many of those lost days as I could, but the story broke down almost instantly, as stories will. On this day, as before, I told things out of order, feeling little hinge-clicks as the hour wore on, one memory begetting another from two years earlier or two years later, the narrative resembling not the straight line I might have been hoping for but a circle that hid its beginning and end. Despite this disorder, I felt landed, tranquil, the way some people describe the act of prayer.

For his part, Harry seemed to like being confided in. He kept at attention, his head cocked, as if he were not so much listening — though he was — as rehearsing for a role he was just beginning to believe himself capable of.

"She's a piece of work, that housekeeper," Harry said.

This is how he referred to the characters in my story. The priest. The friend. The friend's mother. The housekeeper. Something about the way I told it. I sipped my drink, recalling Mrs. Hanson's face, which in my memory appeared perpetually wronged, wearied by the changing world. "I thought she quit us because I defied her," I said. "Kids are always making the wrong connections."

"Adults, too," Harry said. "Adults do it even worse. Take Elaine, she makes everything I do into an angle. Everything's an *angle* with you, that's the tune she's been playing since she was eighteen years old. I make the slightest goddamn attempt to make up for my mistakes and she thinks I'm hitting her up for cash. So what happens is, I ask her to visit me sometime, and she's thinking, okay, he wants cash, he wants cash, he wants cash, and I'll be goddamned if it doesn't pop into my head to ask for cash out of spite, and so I do, and there's her jackass jumped conclusion all tied up in a bow and handed to her on a velvet cushion."

"I thought you hadn't seen her in years."

"Yeah, well. Time doesn't move too fast when it comes to Elaine."

She seemed to be with us that day. Harry had gotten into the habit of moving his few sticks of furniture around, and on this afternoon, he'd placed her picture, the snapshot in the frame, on one of the windowsills. As I talked and her father listened, she stared out at us, eyes alight.

Just then a motion sensor from the facing building snapped on; a wide swath of light teetered in through the big windows — the apartment's one beauty — reminding me of an afternoon in some season where the sun made that same sudden appearance, slanting down on an oval of bread dough that rested on the kitchen table. It was a memory I loved because of its light and air, its aroma of molasses, its vision of flour clouding up from the dough as I patted it with both hands. Vivid and immediate, the memory nonetheless came disembodied. I couldn't say how old I was, or what time of day we were in, or what I was wearing, or any other thing I did on that day or on the days leading up to or away from that single moment. I *could* say exactly how my hand looked making those clouds: Band-Aid on my pinky finger, fingernails newly clipped. I could say that despite its lack of context, this vision recalled what childhood felt like—homey, fragrant, containing just enough surprise.

It wasn't all one way. Harry told stories, too—war stories, mostly, from his stateside stint in the early years of the Vietnam War. He preferred high-concept tales heavy on hijinks and starring officious superiors shanghaied by their own arrogance. He often told the same one twice, with different endings.

"They did that on *M*A*S*H* once," I said after a tale of a private mistaken for a major by a visiting colonel.

"Yeah, well. The army's so goddamn boring, sometimes you have to borrow your stories."

"You've told me plenty of good ones," I assured him.

"I took my first drink when I was fourteen and a half years old," he said. "That's pretty much the only story I've got." He checked his watch. "It's five-thirty," he said. "You don't want your people sending out for the Mounties."

Each time I left there—passing over from such stillness into the teeming reality outside—I felt submerged, at an exquisite distance from the actual world. Telling felt like resting. I was resting. Just like Father Mike.

FIFTEEN

From *The Liturgy of the Hours:*
Now my soul is troubled,
yet what am I to say:
"Father, save me from this hour"?
But it was for this very reason that I came to this hour.

September intoxicates him. Some lost memory of the Island drifts in on the bitten air: the rattle of leaves, the taste of apples. September! The natural world in full crackle, a rapturous harvest surfacing at roadside stands. The altar abounds with pushy, pie-faced sunflowers.

Though Lizzy's return to school grieves him a little — fourth grade! can it really be fourth grade? — it also brings a thrill of newness. Mornings, she runs down the path to collect Mariette and wait on the road for the bus to St. Catherine's, and he watches her go, colossally happy. Like Lizzy, he loved school. The four-room schoolhouse on the Island where every spring an exhausted blackbird winged through the open window and flapped against the blackboard. The public high school in Maine where he had his own desk, all the paper he wanted, books he could take home and not give back till the term ended. Notre Dame, where he missed home so badly he hid in the field house and wept beneath the bleachers. He sought refuge in books, his big love — his own books, he owned them, a wonder in itself, all that Latin and philosophy and theology and mathematics, each guiding him toward a different possibility for his God-made mind.

At Notre Dame he abstained from alcohol, unwilling to enfeeble his percolating intellect, though he did go to parties. He was not an odd boy, just a committed one. His classmates liked him. He moved among them as a peacemaker, a storyteller, a pillar of dependability, already practicing for his intended life. His vocation revealed itself in his outer aura, obvious as the color of his hair.

Girls adored him, for he was green and guileless and kept his hands to himself. He liked them, too, their feminine company, and there were occasions, one or two, when he wondered whether he could make the big sacrifice when the time came.

At seminary he found more books, oceans of thought as yet unnavigated. He found learned men who did not fear irony. And some, of course, who did. He disappeared for hours, even days at a time, into the oiled mahogany carrels of the central study room — reading as meditation. He studied religion in general and Catholicism in specific, loving theory and practice in equal parts, reveling in the nuances of doctrine in transition.

Outside of the books and lectures, he discovered prayer. Real prayer, not the romantic notions of his fervid boyhood — God is my father, God is my friend, God is my protector.

No. God is not this, God is not that. God *is*.

In his solitary hours at chapel, he came to understand that the opposite of God is not Satan. The opposite of God is not evil. The opposite of God is absence.

Perpetually present, he was; fully alive in body and spirit. A stupefied seminarian, throbbing with purpose, speaking French and Latin, afire with erudition and scholarship. Willing not only to make the big sacrifice (no wife no child no mortgage no garage no tools no physical refuge), but also the myriad little ones, the finely calibrated interpersonal adjustments required to maintain warm but reasonable relationships with both men and women. It didn't seem so difficult a projection; he would have his sister and brother-in-law, after all, and his fellow priests. He believed these people would shore him up in the hours of spiritual darkness he did not quite believe would befall him but nonetheless felt required to anticipate, if only to maintain a modicum of humility.

On this first day of September, watching Lizzy run off to school with her hem flapping against each headlong step, he hopes she will also enjoy a life of the mind. Already she shows the capacity to encounter God every time something new reveals itself: long division, the order of planets. Lizzy will think her way to the soul, as he did, and discover it with her eyes open. She will not be called to a vocation — she's awful at rules (his fault, he fears) and would make a terrible nun. Vivienne harbors a futile wish for Mariette to be called, but that's only a mother's impulse, the contemplative life the one sure path to prevent Mariette from finding a man like her father.

Lizzy will be no nun, he thinks, fondly. This summer, noticing her kindness toward the bratty baby brothers Mariette suddenly can't abide, he has come to understand that Lizzy is the sort of person who will require an earthly mate. Already he imagines the man, intelligent and good-natured, a teacher or housebuilder. Already he envies him, the man who will guard Lizzy's dreams.

He feels his vocation most keenly in September, too, everything starting anew as the ground begins to die. The church hall humming with industry. The Daughters of Isabella planning the fall bazaar. The parish council prepping for a new election. The choir regathers, their rehearsal notes fluting into his open windows at suppertime. All this amidst the flowers' last bloom before death and resurrection. He loves paradox, the best thing God made.

Looking across the moon garden — a final glory of physostegia, phlox, and white sedum — he imagines Lizzy and Mariette terrorizing some unsuspecting community of nuns, Mariette too bossy and headstrong, Lizzy unable to countenance supper at five, the two of them pulling up the community herb garden in order to plant something useless and beautiful. He chuckles, liking the sound of his laughter in the snappish, open morning. Intensely happy, he stands at his back door with a mug of coffee fisted into one hand, behind him the clacking of Mrs. Hanson doing up the breakfast dishes, across from him, at the other end of the path, the sound of the Blanchards' door banging shut and the girls calling good-bye.

This is how that last season begins: a happy man with a calling, holding a mug of coffee and seeing a child off to school.

Later in the week, on Wednesday, the air gone brittle and the first leaves curling, he sets out for Bangor to see Jack Derocher. He'd prefer not to go, but has missed his last two visits. He likes Jack, but the thing that occupies his mind right now — nothing too pressing, just something he thinks ought to be mentioned — is not, he realizes while gassing up the car, something he especially wants to say to his confessor.

Along Random Road, the first wash of autumn gleams in the leaning trees. Halfway to Bangor, he gets stuck behind a line of cars. Construction, backup, men shouting to be heard over backhoes and cranes. The radio sputters irritatingly — he's in one of Maine's many dead spots, where hill and valley conspire for poor reception—so he turns it off. He ticks his fingers on the wheel—like Lizzy he is bad at waiting. His parlor beckons, his chair and lamp, his stack of books and fleece slippers.

U-turn, and the smallest click at the back of his mind: *You're afraid of confession.*

He heads for home.

Since the house will be empty, he stops to eat at a family restaurant stranded along an ill-traveled stretch. A teenaged waitress serves him a platter of clams. He returns the polite nods of strangers, accepts the owner's offer to cover the check. *Let me rip that right up, Father.* He feels full to bursting, foolish and punch-drunk, headed home, away from confession and toward Vivienne.

There. There it is, the notion forming into words. Words in the head, but still, there will be no taking them back. He wants to see Vivienne.

"I want to see her," he says aloud, pulling out of the restaurant's gravel lot. He takes in his breath—it sounds wet and unfamiliar—and now he does not know what is happening. Talking to himself (to a passerby he'll appear to be praying), he begins a conversation with the safely absent Jack Derocher:

Tell me again, Jack, why that particular sacrifice.

Sacrifice? Sure. Call it a sacrifice. Our gift to God. But isn't it also our gift from God? A means to reject the corporeal and embrace the spiritual? A channel for maintaining the great, ongoing conversation? Not that I don't complain at times. I do.

What does God say then?

Celibacy's not for sissies.

Hah.

Jesus chose it, Mike. St. Paul chose it. You could do worse for role models.

You're right about that.

We keep our vows, they keep theirs—fidelity in marriage, constancy in friendship. We show them how to keep tough promises.

And anyway, if we fully belong to someone else, how do we husband our parishioners?

Now he's annoyed by Jack's logic. He does not say: *She's married, Jack, did I mention that?* Instead, he reminds his confessor: *But I do belong fully to someone else. I have a child. And here's the thing: she's made me more available. Really, she has. I love my parishioners more because of her. I understand what they want for their children.*

Do you understand what they want from you, though? That's the trick, Mike-o. Are you hearing me?

Yeah, I'm hearing you. I hear you.

Then why do I get the impression you've gone stone deaf?

It's a man-made law, for Pete's sake. God didn't make this one up.

But you chose it, Mike. And still you wound up with a kid. Are you grateful?

Yes, of course. Of course I'm grateful.

Then say thank you and move on. God gave you a gift-wrapped present the rest of us can't have, and you're ticked that he left off the bow.

That's Jack for you. Not a man to mince words. The road unwinds, reddish trees lacing above him. He keeps his hand on the Breviary — his talisman, his dialogue.

Once home, he stops in the empty church to kneel in the sacristy, communicating his weakness and also his resolve. Then he waits for that feeling, that white, interior blooming that signals God's forgiving presence. He is almost glad for his feverish urges, to have something messy and pressing to wrestle with; the rest of his life is too easy. His arrogance returns, for he has won another struggle, which he offers to God as a trophy.

He goes into the house. The bachelors twine through his legs. He strokes Boo's silky fur, admiring the ingenious design of this animal, the grace and muscle, the gloss and striping, the mysterious internal mechanisms that produce a trippingly lovely sound at the merest touch. It's coming on dark but he doesn't flick the kitchen switch. Instead, he feeds the cats in the soothing dimness and goes straight to his bedroom to get ready for bed. He'll read from his Breviary, watch the news, sleep the sleep of the righteous, dream the dreams of the chosen.

On the bathroom hook hangs a robe he got from Lizzy and Mariette last Christmas — an embarrassing sea-green bathrobe with cat appliqués on the pockets that he wears every night anyway. He completes his ablutions, snaps on his reading light, picks up his Breviary, and settles in, Fatty and Mittens squashed companionably into his lap, Boo staring from atop the dresser. Next door, Vivienne would be moving through her house, getting the boys to bed or doing up a few dishes. He imagines Lizzy and Mariette in the attic with a board game, listening to the lightness of those footfalls.

"Michael?"

The cats scatter. He bolts up, heart flapping like a trapped bat, and cracks open his bedroom door.

Astonishingly, it is Vivienne, standing in the middle of the parlor.

"What happened?" he cries, pulse still jumping, hand gripping the doorknob. He registers her gold earrings, the touch of lipstick.

"They're fine," she says. "Pauline's at the house."

Swept-back hair. White dress dotted with tiny, cherry-red snowflakes. Not even Snow White on her bower, covered with rose petals, glistened so.

"I'm sorry to bother," she says. He feels caught and idiotic in this ridiculous bathrobe. Hairy legs sticking down. Broad, flat, hairy feet.

"I heard you drive in," she says, very quietly.

He tries to hear the insides of her words but nothing arrives except a pulsating silence, a freighted, ringing, something's-happening brand of silence.

"Construction," he says. "I had to turn back."

"I, too, I had to turn back," she says. "But I didn't."

What does he do now? Should he ask her to leave, change clothes, meet her in his office? Instead he steps back, dopey and stuck, like a boy at his first dance, hands dangling off the ends of his arms.

"Michael."

It's his name, *Michael,* spoken in this new way, that tips him over. His Christian name, iridescent as a butterfly, lolloping into the stark little room. Such a beautiful name, spoken this way. A secret, fluttering thing, spoken this way.

At this moment he loves his name more than any other thing in Heaven or on Earth. His name becomes food and water and miles of sky and ten thousand violets. His body fully wakes now, listening for his name.

"Michael." She comes to him. The door swings to, whispers halfway closed behind her.

His arrogance vanishes. As if he has any gift God wants! As if this wretched aching is a gift God gives! What of the gifts God took back? Mother, father, brothers, sister. Rage, shocking and elemental, stuns him; it crashes over the breakwater of prayer and intention and routine and good sense and responsibility that he has constructed so fervently, so dutifully, so *sincerely* over the years. He braces hard, but over the wall it roars: *I have lost so much,* he cries inwardly, seeing her here, her eyes wet, her hair freshly brushed, all his losses converging in a soupy craving that he cannot bear, he truly cannot, it seeks release, it seeks a home, and so he takes in his name and lifts his arms and lets her walk straight into them.

God made her, he breathes to himself as her hands twine his neck and pull his face toward hers. God made her powdery skin, the scent of warm ground floating from her worked hands. This woman, Vivienne, in his arms — a joy unlike any in his repertoire of joy. Unlike the dizzy joy he feels for this season. Unlike the layered sympathy he feels for a congregation at prayer. Unlike the gut-twisting longing he feels for Lizzy. Something else altogether, this: another facet of God's mystery emanating from her face, her apple-clean lips. Caught and helpless, he tries to speak but can manage only a pitiful bleating, he is pitiful, he is nothing but a garden-variety, all-purpose, ordinary sinner. What relief.

For a second, eyes closed, buffeted by his own breath, he sways on his feet and she catches him. *Thank you,* he says, laughing a little, and then she laughs, returning him abruptly to his real life. He is a celibate man wearing a bathrobe with cats on it. The woman he has always desired — there, there it is, he has always desired her — rests against him in a pretty dress she picked out thinking of him.

But he is spoken for. As is she.

He lifts his head, eyes wide open, clasping this small, soft woman. He understands how the world was born, how trees and sky and dogs and lava and dragonflies and water came to be: the whole saturated mess sprang from the swamped insides of God's unutterable loneliness.

She touches his face, a soft pressure on his cheeks. He feels like a freshly released exile returned to the world with his faculties altered. She studies him, her own confusion surfacing as a slender discord in her features, a slackening of her eyebrows, a fidgety lower lip. He gentles his hands to her shoulders — how narrow they are beneath the soft, small cotton sleeves of that dress — and nudges her away, a motion so shreddingly painful he could be tearing off his own skin. *Oh,* he says, *oh, I wish,* and that is all, the rest is just noise, a muddy whimpering, but he has done it, it took all his might but he's dug out this space between them. To bridge that space again, to move so much as a knuckle, will be to practice, with his faculties intact, the forked gift of free will.

Something drops in the parlor. Vivienne's eyes spring open: *Oh mon Dieu, it's Ray.* The door hitches as Vivienne collapses to the bed and grasps the quilt to hide herself in one swift slide, but it is not Ray who pushes the door open but poor, shocked, mute Mrs. Hanson, her eyes shifting toward the bed and the blurred shape clawing to hide itself. He yelps at her, furious and ashamed. Mrs. Hanson holds up a pair of eyeglasses, filling the doorway absolutely, muttering something he can't catch before he slams the door in her face.

Vivienne, Vivi, he whispers, tendering his hand, helping her wriggle out of the quilt in which he will recall her scent only minutes from now. *It's all right, it's no one.* She gets up, squinty as a child after a nightmare, her fingers working at her hair. *I thought it was Ray,* she cries, *I thought it was Ray.*

But he tells her no, it wasn't Ray, Ray's out fishing, it was no one, just Mrs. Hanson, she saw nothing, that's her car leaving just now, don't cry. Thoroughly rattled, he nonetheless thrills to be comforting her, a balance returning, his lately up-ended world righting itself. He becomes the leader again, not the led; once again he retakes full charge of this ambiguous dance.

It must be a sign ——, she says. *If anyone did see . . . You would be required to leave. What would become of me if they required you to leave?* But he tells her nothing will happen, no one saw, and he begins to believe it. He has not been caught; Mrs. Hanson was merely embarrassed to find him in his bathrobe; she thinks the motion in his bed was cats, the cats she complains about endlessly, how they're always chasing each other over the furniture, knocking things over, causing a ruckus.

This was another test and he passed.

Forgive me, Michael, she says, *I'm so foolish. So ashamed.*

Don't worry, he says. *Nothing happened,* he says, *we won't speak of this again,* holding her, calming her, urging her toward the door and out of his scraped, wounded life, offering up his misery and grateful for his name.

SIXTEEN

This is how marriages end, I thought, parking my car on the slope of Hanover Street. It had begun to occur to me that I was having the equivalent of an affair, but here I was anyway, back on Harry Griggs's doorstep. Same three flights, same dark hallway, same badly fitted door, same hollow sound when I knocked.

Harry opened the door, cheerier than usual. "Hey," he said. "Hey, hey!" Boomy and expansive — energized, I thought, by his weeks of restitution. He ushered me inside and offered me a Gatorade. "It's been a hell of a day," he said. "You picked a hell of a day."

"What happened?"

"I deboned my last goddamn chicken. It was one of those take-this-job-and-shove-it kinda moments." He laughed, loud and wide-mouthed. A back tooth was missing, I noticed, and the other teeth looked flattened by old fillings.

"What are you going to do for money?"

"Man, it felt good," he said, missing my question entirely. "No more Cambodians clackety-clacking at me all day. I got a bellyful of them in the war."

"You were stateside," I reminded him, accepting my drink.

He pointed at me. "You listen too close. Bad habit." He stretched out in the tweed chair. "Free at last, free at last, free at last."

"Well," I said. "Congratulations, I guess."

"You said it!" He laughed again—a new laugh, not the pleasant, rueful chuckle I was used to. This was a big, loud, horsey, vaguely libidinous chortle. His face got very red. Drinking, I figured—but not much, I hoped.

"I missed you last week," he said, pulling his chair close to mine. "This place was a goddamn tomb."

"How was your Thanksgiving?"

"I sat here and ate a chicken that was still half froze. You?"

"We ate at Mariette and Charlie's. Mrs. Blanchard made mince pies," I said, extracting a package from my bag. "Here. I saved you a piece."

It disappeared in two bites. "She's good," he said.

"The boys were both home, too, Buddy and Bernard? We played cards for about six hours." I took a languid sip of my drink. "It's kind of amazing how easy it is to pretend to be living a normal life."

"You said it!" Sipping from Loreen's prissy cups, Harry resembled a bear at a tea party. "What've you got for me today?"

I had few stories left, and we both seemed to know it.

He lifted the cup to me. "You must have something. Give me the ending."

"A house full of strangers," I said. Or near-strangers. Father Mike was gone and in his place appeared some men I knew a little—Father Jack and Monsignor Frank—and a woman with a big, frightening smile. She asked me questions I didn't get and showed me dolls with no clothes on and urged me to tell the truth, which, when spoken aloud, sounded like the exact opposite of the truth. In the end I fled to the back of the house and hid in our coat closet, cowering in the muffling dark, listening to them look for me and hoping to hear his voice lancing through the noise. I stood under the hangers and pulled the arms of his jacket around me because it was the closest I had to the real thing. Clutching the empty arms, I picked and picked at the cuff, working at a hole that had started with a swipe of Boo's claws, then worrying the nub where a button had come off as the strangers in my house called my name. He was already gone. He was not coming back.

I shut my eyes. I was back there. I'd been waiting in that closet, comforting myself with my uncle's empty coatsleeves, for long enough.

"What's wrong?" Harry asked.

I sighed. "I'm out of stories."

"Yeah, well," he said. "I've kinda been waiting for this. Somebody's dead as Moses, all the stories in the world won't bring them back."

On that point, he was wrong. My uncle had been returning to me little by little since Harry Griggs first brought me out of the rain and into this apartment. In his own ham-handed, accidental way, Harry Griggs had restored my life to me twice. I rested my head against the back of Harry's chair, allowing a sweet, accepting melancholy to overtake me. My bones felt pleasantly soft. I wondered if I'd made a precipitous lurch into adulthood, as my students so often did, seemingly overnight. At the age of thirty, I felt, suddenly, no longer a child. I'd come to Harry Griggs with my stories not to search out a beginning, but to make peace with an ending. This was an adult's job, one I had been bucking all my life, preferring the child's task of eternally wishing things otherwise.

"He died," I said. "The end."

"Where'd they put him? Some kinda priest mausoleum?"

"Someplace in Canada." *The Church took care of it,* Celie had said. *Back to the Island, where he came from.* "But I preferred to think of him out in the world somewhere, a traveling spirit who could come and go as he pleased."

"Yeah, well," Harry said. "Whatever it takes."

"You're kind of edgy today."

"I quit my job. So. Go ahead. What else you got?"

"Nothing. He's gone."

"Aw, come on."

"No, really," I said. "The story *ends*."

In a slow-burning hindsight, I understood that the notion had been with me for months—present, but not fully arrived: Grief is not endless. "You've been a good listener, Harry," I said peaceably. "Maybe that's what strangers are for."

"That's not what strangers are for," he said, and I looked up just in time to see the lurching blur of his face. His lips didn't quite meet target, and what he clearly intended as a first move ended up feeling like a good-bye kiss, a harmless little smack just clear of my mouth. His jaw felt clean-shaven and smelled of cologne. And liquor, too—I caught it as I drew back, stunned that he'd kissed me and also that it had not been as awful as I might have guessed.

I covered my mouth. "What are you *doing?*"

"Strangers are for filling up space," he said hazily. "They're for sitting next to in bars so your stories sound brand-new." He lifted the cup to me in an ambiguous toast. "I spiked mine. You want some?"

I got up. "No."

"Jesus on a stick, I think I hurt your feelings," he said, pulling a bottle from beneath his chair. A quart of whiskey, a label I'd never heard of, probably the kind that ended up in storm drains all over America the beautiful. He knocked back the rest of the faux Gatorade and filled his cup exactly halfway, measuring scrupulously in a skewed show of decorum. Then he set the bottle down with a clunk of relief. "Now, come on," he said. "Don't look at me like that."

"I—" Standing there, I felt small and needy and ridiculous. "That was—inappropriate." I cringed at the word, one of the words of my profession.

He waved me off. "I just figured what the hell." He himself drew back now, wrapping his hands around the flimsy cup.

"It never occurred to me—" I searched for words that wouldn't shame me, and failed. "I thought—you seemed to—think of me as a daughter." But not an actual daughter, of course. A pretend daughter, a vapor daughter, something to be reshaped on an as-needed basis. Surely I had done the same to him. It was so much easier to consort with vapors; unlike actual people, they didn't demand much.

"The last thing I need is another goddamn daughter," he said. "But you're the only company I've had in two solid years and beggars can't be choosers." He controlled his cup with slow, practiced trips to his mouth, nodding after each one, as if trying to prove to me he could drink like anybody else, in moderation. "Your husband thinks you're in a goddamn shrink's office. What was I supposed to think?" He took a messy swig, all pretension gone now. I could see that he was embarrassed. I'd embarrassed him by being young and insulted.

"You're more like my daughter than I thought," he said suddenly.

"What's that supposed to mean?"

"I mean she's always wanting to go back. Go back, go back, go back. Me, I like to stay where I am."

"That system's served you very well, I can see."

He gave me a crooked look. "Why don't you just say good-bye to the priest and get it over with? I got three other kids out there who flipped me off for good a long time ago and they're doing just fine. Elaine, she's the only one, she never figured out how to do it." His eyes took on a watery vagueness as he drank again from the cup, a good, long pull.

"I *am* going to say good-bye, for your information," I

said, deciding on the spot. "I'm going to pay a visit and lay some flowers on the headstone."

He seemed to be enjoying himself again. "First you gotta find out where they put him." He saluted, knocking his eye in the process. "You gotta face down the boys in black."

"So I do," I said, buckling inwardly. After twenty-one years, it would be back to church for me.

"What the hell," he said. "Here you are, you caught me, so have a drink."

I crossed my arms. "Were you drunk when you found me?"

"As a skunk." He lifted his cup. "Bottoms up."

"I don't suppose you saw any white light."

His demeanor shifted again. "I might've," he said quietly. "Once you mentioned it, I thought I might've. I'm not that much of a liar."

"I'm leaving, Harry."

"Aw, come on," he said. "Stay. Talk some more. I like your voice." When I picked up my coat, he added, "Hey. I saved your life. You owe me." He splashed some whiskey into my cup. I perched on the edge of the chair arm, halfway between sitting and standing, not committing myself.

"Stay here," he said. "I thought we were friends."

"We're strangers, Harry. Perfect strangers, and you know it."

"Fine, sure. But if you've got so many goddamn friends, how come you're not home talking to them?"

"I have plenty of friends," I said. I took one burning sip out of my cup. "There are times when a stranger can come as a great relief."

"Touché to that."

We remained like that for a few more minutes, pretending not to be drinking alone.

"My husband calls you the bad Samaritan," I said after a while.

"I've been called worse by ladies' husbands. Not in years, though, sorry to say." He looked up. "I didn't do the whole job. I know it, all right? I never do the whole job. I owe something to everybody I've ever known. But I was kinda hoping that me and you, we'd come out even." He shook his head slowly, looking dwarfed and tired in a freshly bought chair that wouldn't last three years.

"You listened to me all the way to the end, Harry. We're even."

I did not want to be owed. I wanted to be seen.

"Even up?" he said. "No loose strings?"

"No strings."

His mouth relaxed into an approximation of a smile. "So. You coming back here, or not?"

I rested my gaze on the bottle. "Seems like you're going to be kind of busy for a while."

"It's the damnedest thing," he said, then settled back in his new tweed chair with the resignation of a man so used to losing things they no longer registered as losses.

I leaned down and put a hand on his shoulder. "I wouldn't operate any heavy machinery for the next couple of hours if I were you."

"Hah. Good one."

I buttoned my coat. He struggled out of the chair—no small effort—to shake my hand.

"All right, then," he said.

I took his hand and kissed it, half expecting him to vanish like a genie. "Even up," I said, and left.

I got home well before Drew, who had gone to Boston for a Celtics game. "Did you guys have fun?" I asked as he tiptoed into our bedroom, hoping not to wake me.

"Charlie bailed," he said. "Two of his line workers didn't show up for their shift, so he had to cover for them." He was moving carefully through our bedroom, taking off his clothes. "I went by myself."

I snapped on my bedside lamp. "Did they win?"

"Yeah," he said. "Pierce had a triple double."

This is how people managed to drift along in a marriage — being polite and going to bed at different times.

"Did you call anybody? You could have given away Charlie's ticket."

"It was last-minute," he said. "I didn't mind going alone."

Unlike Charlie — hat-tipper, baby-kisser, favorite brother in a family of brothers — Drew was a loner by nature. The thought of him sitting by himself in a cheering crowd made me sad. We had friends, but not many; we were alike that way. People still came up from Boston for the weekend sometimes; we went to faculty get-togethers; occasionally someone we knew in college would find us in the phone book. But except for Mariette and Charlie there was nobody we spent much time with except each other.

I glanced around our bedroom, at the shelves and baskets and closets and dressers landfilled with broken watches and un-opened packages of underwear and broken-backed novels and too-short belts and too-long shoelaces and owner's manuals for obsolete appliances and clothes we would never wear again and canisters of ruined film and plastic knick-knacks and porcelain gewgaws and moth-eaten pennants and greeting cards with no envelopes and entire, undiscovered layers of things we were psychologically and probably pathologically unable to part with simply because we had once touched them and because they were — though useless, though ugly, though out of style, though crumbling at the core — ours.

"Do you think it gets harder to make friends as you get older?" I asked him.

"It's starting to look like everything gets harder as you get older." He was standing beside the bed, taking off his socks, wearing nothing else but a pair of grayish underpants whose listless waistband barely held at his hips. This, more than anything else right then, made me feel married.

"Maybe we should have had more friends," I said.

He got into bed with me, lying still, staring at the ceiling. "Maybe."

"You meet someone new, you get to talking, and the person really seems to be listening, and you feel so, I don't know, *revealed*."

His voice tightened, though he didn't move. "Is this about whoever you've been seeing?" I felt his eyes slide over. "Your therapist with the really strange hours?"

I steeled myself as he sat up to face me. "It's not an affair," I said, which wasn't quite true.

His face filled with resignation. "No? Then what?"

"A friendship, I guess you'd call it." I let a moment pass. "I've been seeing the bad Samaritan."

His face wrinkled in confusion for a second—then he got it. "You can't be serious."

"He phoned me at school."

Drew snapped his mouth shut. Stared.

"I was just curious at first," I said, trying not to look at him. "I figured I owed him a thank-you and he owed me an apology, but then I noticed that when I was with him this feeling, this awful feeling I've had ever since the accident, it just went away." Out came the truth, a ribbon of relief. "He lives in Portland."

Drew swung his legs over the edge of the bed, his feet thunking to the floor. "Name?"

"It's over now anyway."

"What's his *name?* It's a simple question."

"Harry Griggs."

"And he's not a shrink, I take it."

"A vet — ex-Army. He's an electrician now. Well, not at the moment. There's a slight drinking problem."

Drew stood up in his ill-fitting underpants, his skin mottled where he was cold and fish-white where he wasn't. "This, Lizzy, this, I have to tell you — I don't know what to say. I thought, okay, she's seeing somebody, but at least — at least the guy's *alive,* some guy from rehab, probably, but at least it's something we can fight about, something real. I thought seeing ghosts was the problem. But this pretty much takes the cake. What can I say except — well, there's nothing. I have nothing to say."

"He saved my life."

"He moved a body off the road."

"*My* body, Drew."

"And we, what, give him a medal for that?"

"It's not what you think," I said quietly. "He's, like, sixty years old."

Drew began to move around our bedroom, picking up the clothes he'd just shed and returning them to his body as if trying to put time in reverse.

"He listens," I said. "He believes everything I say."

"I don't see why he wouldn't. A drunk with nothing to lose."

"That's why I didn't tell you, Drew. I knew you'd figure him for some lost soul with nothing better to do than listen to me talk."

"I didn't say that. You did." He returned to our bed, fully dressed again. "Was he drunk when he found you? Is that why he ran off?"

I looked away.

"This fucker left you in the mud without even checking for a pulse. In the meantime, I've been *right here,* running out

of ways to put you back together." He squeezed my shoulders—
out of frustration, protection, left-over love—looking eerily
like the pictures I'd seen of his father, the military man who
never had enough stripes, who expected the worst and mostly
got it, whose grip on his son was such that the son could not
speak of the father.

"There's something else, Drew."

He looked at me.

"It's about Father Mike." I wanted to say, I've *moved on*.
I've *snapped out of it. Time has healed all wounds.* I wanted to say,
Forgive me.

"You know what's ironic?" he said. "After the accident,
my big fear was that you'd lose your memory."

"Drew—"

"Tell it to your boyfriend," he said, swiping his keys off
the dresser. "I'm going to see Charlie. Don't wait up." I couldn't
imagine anything more lonely-looking than Drew knocking on
the door of Charlie's McDonald's after hours, the crew gone
home, the grill cleaned, the yellow sign darkened for the night,
Charlie fumbling with the lock to let Drew in. Two grown men
in their own Hopper painting, sipping coffee at a booth in the
window, talking about whatever men talk about. My name
would not come up, because Drew did not speak of the things
that most pressed him.

Before leaving, he paused at our bedroom door. "Lizzy,"
he said. "You expect too much of me."

The words landed hard. We flinched, each of us, at the
bare, bald truth of our marriage: *You expect too much of me.* Two
empty vessels hoping to be filled.

The Little Hours

NONE

SEVENTEEN

From *The Liturgy of the Hours:*
This guilt of yours shall be
like a descending rift
Bulging out in a high wall
whose crash comes suddenly, in an instant . . .

He is watering a lawn in Conlin, Ohio. A flat landscape. Flat and uninspiring in the weak light of early morning. Over the pickets of his fence — yes, a picket fence, and a twelve-year-old boy getting into the family car parked on the stiff sheet of driveway that smells of fresh resurfacing — he can see ten, no, fifteen houses, vinyl-sided and shallow-pitched, like his. This neighborhood, so like the watercolor neighborhoods from the educational primers of his youth, rarely fails to please him. At fifty-nine years old, he can hardly believe he landed himself here. In this evenness. This place of straight lines.

His wife, a husky, sandy-haired woman named Frannie, moves past him over the black, sealed driveway, her heels clicking smartly. She has a boy to drop off, a hundred errands, then work. He envies her. Urgency is one of the things he misses about the life he once led.

They have been married five years now — five solid, blessed, uneventful years. Frannie likes having a husband; after nursing Alfred through his cancer, she seems glad to feel like a wife again. Frannie brooks no hesitation when it comes to second chances. She does not love him, he feels; but she likes him. They are friends. Every time he comes home at the end of an endless day, he feels rescued anew.

She gets into the car to drive her son to school. The boy is an easy boy who still misses his dead father. Before Frannie starts the car she unwinds the window, blows a big, cheery kiss. Her smile will sustain him over the next few hours. This is how he measures time.

He is due at work himself in two hours, though today will be a dark one. A nervous condition that comes and goes. Frannie understands. She knows that he used to be a shepherd of men, that turning into a sheep takes its toll.

His work, a cobweb of a challenge compared to what he once had, unfolds at the Good Deeds shelter in East Cleveland, a place for men who have fallen upon hard times: fallen down, fallen off, fallen away, fallen sick. He's good at listening, and unlike the others who work there he does not tire of their tales of woe. Their putrid breath does not sicken him; their encrusted clothes make no impression. He doesn't roll his eyes behind their backs. Without complaint he swabs toilets and traps rats and strips beds and boils rice, working like a man at Heaven's gate. Sometimes he prays with the men, if they ask.

The phone rings from within the house. He shuts off the hose, wrapping it quickly. He leaves nothing unwrapped, uncoiled, unboxed, unhung. By the time he clamps the hose to its hook outside the garage, the phone has fallen silent and the machine does not engage.

His wife's son calls him Mr. Clean. With affection, he hopes. He tries so hard to shelter them, to keep the gutters clear, the driveway shoveled, the roof sealed, the grass clipped. The fridge never wants for milk; the breadbox stays full.

The boy also calls him Dad. It's not that he doesn't care for the boy. It's just that it is very hard to fall for a child, knowing how suddenly they can be lost. How suddenly abandoned.

The phone rings again. Bounding up the steps, he feels better. Movement always helps. For years he did nothing but drive, across the country and back. Twenty times, stopping here two months, there eight months, working just long enough to keep moving. On the twentieth return trip he stopped in Ohio, exhausted.

As he crosses the foyer he notices a curl in the wallpaper that will have to be re-stuck. He envisions exactly where in the basement he left the bucket of sizing and the tub of glue. The kitchen looks nearly beatified at this time of day: sunlight raging through the bay window, his plants a wondrous, living green. For a moment he misses the smell of an empty church. That feeling of just him and the Eucharist, that private, shared space.

He picks up the phone. Listens a moment. His shuttered past throws itself open. Smack in his face.

~⁓~

When Frannie comes back for her briefcase she finds him packing.

—A niece? she asks, befuddled. You have a niece?

—She's had an accident.

—You never told me you had a niece. Who called?

—A friend. An old friend from there.

—I'll go with you, then.

—No.

—No? What do you mean, no? Of course we'll go. David and I will both go. You'll need us.

—No, no, he says, I can't explain right now. He puts his keys in his pocket.

—You're driving? To Maine?

—I can't get a flight till tomorrow.

He stops what he's doing, ticking off a litany of preventable catastrophes.

—Don't forget to lock the patio door. Don't let David leave his bike outside. I just had your oil changed, so you should be all set, carwise. Aaron's covering for me, they put me on for the weekend so we won't lose anything in my check.

—I lived without you for fifty-one years, Mike.

He stashes some shirts into a suitcase. The shirts are white, mostly; one of them is a pale blue. This wardrobe has been a source of merriment in the household, for he has never learned to dress as a layman. When Frannie withdraws from their bedroom—*clack, clack clack,* go her hurt feelings down the stairs—he steals into the closet and reaches into the back, unzips the garment bag wherein hang his blacks, two complete sets. Black jacket. Rabat. Shirt, slightly yellowed. Black pants. Cassock and collar. They still smell like home. On the floor, next to the black shoes, a small leather case containing the essentials for a sacrament he cannot bear to consider.

He must hurry. She needs a priest.

For a long time after he left Maine, he tried to make God forsake him. Alone and despairing, he determined himself unheard. Landscapes blinded him, sunrises mocked him, Earth's abundance salted his wounds. Seven times a day he spit into the abyss, reading his Breviary with moving lips, repeating words that vanished into the ether. Driving endlessly, a long escape, endless and to no end. He found himself in large, anonymous cities, ducking into churches to hide and finding God there. Trysts, he thought of these impulses: illicit moments of undeserved relief.

—Who's the friend who called? Frannie asks as he puts the one valise (a flight bag, they used to call these small black bags) in the trunk. She eyes the garment bag but says nothing.

—Her name's Vivienne, he says. She was my neighbor back then.

—Back when?

—Frannie. I have to go.

She studies him, confused.

—All right, she says. Call me.

—All right. I love you.

—Me too. She kisses him briskly, her eyes wet.

He wants to explain, but where would he begin?

—I'll pray for her, she says.

In his rearview he catches the worried folding of Frannie's arms as she stands at the end of their straight, swept, blacktopped driveway in neat, safe, featureless Conlin, Ohio. He stops, backs up, rolls down the window, suddenly frightened.

—The roof is not going to collapse, Mike, she says wearily. The boiler isn't going to blow. Now, go.

But the boiler *could* blow. A tree branch could smash through a window. The boy could come down with pneumonia, and he will be nowhere in sight. He starts out again, his rearview filling this time with the well-appointed house that, for lack of anything sturdier, will have to pass for shelter.

❧   ❧

Fourteen hours and Maine appears, much changed after so much time. Clearing the tollbooth at the border, he finds more sky than he expected. More sky and fewer trees. Fewer trees, wider roadways, construction everywhere, the innocent land looking hacked and abused. He sucks in his breath, escaping at the first exit in search of a less violated route. In and in he goes, his Maine, his old life, his younger self appearing before him as the road unrolls like a spool of remembered cloth. *God, my God,* he prays: *Is it here you have waited?*

He is quaking now, feeling the old white light of divine connection, hands knuckled ferociously around the steering wheel. *God, my God, is it here you have waited?*

He rolls down the window, inhaling: pine, hay, a small, agonizing thwack of ocean. He can barely drive for the din of blood in his head.

No one called a priest. It is up to the husband. The husband said: My wife isn't Catholic.

❧ ❧

On a neatly made bed in a chain motel at the turnpike exit, he lays out his former clothes. The motion—the careful smoothing, the softness and gloss of the fabrics—reminds him so much of laying out the altar that tears come to his eyes. He wipes the black shoes with the bedspread until they shine. In the inside pocket of the jacket he finds the pyx, a now-tarnished silver case in which twenty unconsecrated hosts have crumbled with age. Kneeling at the bed, he consecrates them in Latin and swallows them all.

The clothes have aged at the back of the closet, the material soft and starchless. The outfit looks shabby, dulled by time or moths or disuse, an extravagant symbol for the moment he is inhabiting. He sits, exhausted, in the ugly motel chair, staring at the laid-out clothes as if they might get up and walk off without him.

The husband said: My wife isn't Catholic.

Soon he gets up, strips, and dresses himself, applying the clothing to his body like bandages on a burn. From his flight bag he extracts the leather case, surprised to find everything there but the prayers—he wonders if the boy has taken them, if the boy has considered a vocation. The stole is there, and the oil; in his head he retains the prayers for the dying. They are not long.

I baptized this child. Let me now anoint her.

Once every spring, he took Lizzy to Portland for a trip to Porteous, where they looked at all the pretty dresses and chose one for Easter. They would shop awhile, drop in at St. Dom's to see Matt Flynn and his goofball dogs, then drive down to the waterfront for fried clams at Boone's. Back then Portland was just a big town with city pretensions; in his absence it turned itself into the real thing: more people, more cars, more buildings, more signs, more loitering souls wearing two coats. He drives through the West End, heart-crushed to find the doors to Saint Dom's closed. It is no longer a church. He wonders what happened to Matt, who used to win at pinochle and gloat like the devil himself. Matt was one of the priests named by the Diocese in the recent full disclosure, the great purging that exposed some men as privately accused child molesters from decades back — men he knew and respected, men whose skills he admired, whose siblings he'd met, whose parents he'd helped bury. He himself would be on that list. How many of them are innocent? he wonders. How many are not? He finds himself hoping Matt's dogs are still alive, especially that wire-haired, smiley one, though they couldn't be.

The hospital, where he made monthly pilgrimages to visit his ailing, homesick parishioners, has grown wings. It looks taller, too. All at once he relaxes; he won't be recognized in this new, changed place.

He, too, looks much changed.

The parking lot used to be free but now charges by the half hour. He works his way through the bright hospital lobby, looking for a phone. He calls Frannie, leaves a message, assures her all is well, he'll be home tomorrow. He says it again — *all is well, I'll be home tomorrow* — aware of the machine in his house recording these words as a prayer that must now be answered.

He takes the rooms floor by floor. Occasionally a patient in paper slippers accosts him in the hall, asking to be blessed. But mostly he is ignored. No one mentions the doll tucked under his arm.

Entering a waxed corridor from the fourth-floor stairwell, he spots Mariette, whom he recognizes even from the back. The sight of her feels like an avalanche of feathers. She is a woman now, and when she turns to speak to the man standing next to her, he sees that she turned out handsome and sturdy-looking, more like her father than her wrenlike mother. The man she speaks to reminds him of the Pelletiers—the incarnation of Leonard Pelletier, though too young. Charlie, then. He takes a few steps into the hall before withdrawing into the shadow of a doorway, feeling like a thief, listening for the voice of Vivienne. Instead, he hears a man. The husband, Drew. A gut-twist of envy visits him from some place he can't begin to name.

It strikes him that in this disguise he could get in anywhere. He ducks into the stairwell and skirts through the other floors, biding time, moving, moving. No one bothers him. He is asked not a single question, stopped by not a single aide or doctor as he slides from floor to floor in the lengthening night, staircase to elevator, returning to the fourth floor every twenty minutes to see if they have gone. He could be a murderer, a terrorist, an imposter with bad intentions. He could be the thing they said he was.

Around one o'clock, everything quiets. Night takes over, muffling the corridors and stairwells. Returning, he finds the hallway deserted for the moment, the family gone home to wait, or to the first floor for a soda or a bottle of water, possibly to the chapel for a desperate prayer.

Intensive Care, immediate family only. The alcove near her room is quiet, the nurses' station, shiny and partitioned, occupied by a woman who frowns into a manila folder. He waits until she disappears behind a screen. He hears a busy rustling of paper and takes a chance.

It is the hair he knows first, that distinctive shade of red, her mother's hair, golden at the ends. Her face spasms from what has been done to it. It is hard to tell whether she turned out beautiful. He gazes upon her, unable to speak. Her hair fanned against the pillow, her body embalmed in a rig with a steel framework that resembles gritted teeth. Just after he baptized her, thirty years past, he stepped around the baptismal font, flanked by Elizabeth and Bill, and lifted the baby to the congregation as if introducing the Christ Child to a delivered world. Everybody smiled; he can still hear the wave of applause.

How can she be thirty years old? On her bed he places the angel, having unearthed her from the pocket of the garment bag where she has resided all these years. *You have a package,* the orderly had told him as he sat in his tenth-floor room in the Baltimore "facility." He'd been looking out the window, trying to locate his car in the lot. He had an extra set of keys and they'd been too polite to search him on arrival. They had let him drive to Baltimore himself, everyone pretending he was making an act of free will, that he would seek voluntary care and counsel and then return, renewed and whole, to a life stripped of children, of tenderness, of responsibility, of meaning. He'd left everything behind: his books and cigars, his sister's breakfront, his dishes and curtains, his cats, his only child. Jack Derocher, in a show of sympathy, had sent along some things he didn't even want: his shaving gear, his other shoes, his winter coat, a set of blacks—his backup set, with a button missing at the jacket cuff. This new package looked the same, another useless item, but it wasn't. Inside he found the angel, a note pinned to her silvery garments: *I am sorry.*

He drapes the stole over his neck, his anguish becoming a thing with wings, flapping in his throat. How can he explain himself now? To her, to anyone?

Muh, he says, trying to form the words, hacking out syllables that demand release. *Muh.* Her body appears frail and powerless, swaddled and still. *My,* he manages, finally: *My child.* He thanks God that she looks loved.

He wets his thumb with holy oil and anoints her forehead, whispering in rapid Latin. *In nomini Patri, et Filio . . .* If she dies tonight she will die in God's arms.

Briefly, her eyes flutter open.

He flinches as she takes his measure.

Then, once again, he vanishes.

EIGHTEEN

The bishop wouldn't see me. Instead, I was ushered into the high-ceilinged office of the co-chancellor, a sprightly man, fiftyish and young for his station. He still had all his hair, an impressive pompadour of faded gold. Twenty years back he'd probably been the type of curate who inspired a full choir top-heavy with sopranos.

This co-chancellor, Monsignor Fleury, greeted me from behind an imposing desk—in "civvies," as Father Mike used to say. I sat down, recalling our summer excursions to the beach, the way Father Mike kept his collar in the glove box, tacking it onto his madras shirt about a mile short of the tollbooth. *Go ahead, Father,* the toll collectors enthused. *Go right on through.* Nowadays they'd make the priest pay twice.

"I didn't know Father Murphy," the chancellor told me. "I was still a curate up in Van Buren around the time he left St. Bart's."

"He didn't leave," I said. "He was removed."

He slid his glasses down. "You're the little girl."

"I *was* the little girl."

He met my eyes, for which I gave him credit. "The Church is making every effort of late, Mrs. Mitchell, to right the wrongs of the past."

"So I've read."

His eyes flicked sideways and back; he'd misunderstood my intentions completely. To him I was part of the recent posse of victims gunning for justice — and a settlement — after the fact. Probably he thought I'd been talking to either a lawyer or a reporter. "I don't believe it was fully appreciated back then how damaging — " He waved his hand around as if I were smoke. "The scars — "

I leaned in, close enough to catch a syrupy whiff of aftershave. "Nothing was done to me, Monsignor Fleury. I'm *good* news for you. I was not damaged. I am not scarred."

He looked confused, for of course I *was* scarred.

"I'm glad to know that," he said. "What can I do for you?"

"You can tell me where my uncle is."

Another furrowed look. "Are we talking about Heaven and hell?"

I placed both hands on his desk, which was not the pristine expanse I might have expected, but a landfill of papers and manila folders. "We're talking about Earth," I said. "Canada, specifically. I'd like to visit his grave."

"The Church wouldn't have had anything to do with his burial, I'm afraid. That was handled by the family."

"But — " I took a moment to re-orient myself. "He died in your care. In your so-called facility. Where you sent him for no good reason."

He didn't answer right away. The day's gloom lifted; a wide blade of sunlight cut the room in half, separating us. I squinted into the glare. He lolled out of his chair, looking suddenly older, and adjusted the blinds. "If you know he was sent to Baltimore, then you must be aware that he was the subject of an investigation."

"I'm aware, yes."

"There was an accusation, on your behalf, from a parishioner."

"Not on my behalf."

"Well, you were just a child."

"Believe me, it was not on my behalf."

"You're aware of the nature of the accusation?"

"You're aware that I just told you nothing was done to me?"

He cleared his throat. "The state sent a caseworker to speak to you."

"The state?" A small click, like a distant lock-and-load heard through a thicket of trees, sounded very far back in my head. I had not come here to be surprised. "I thought she was a nun," I said.

"The accusation against Father Murphy differed significantly from other — incidents — of that era. It came from the Department of Human Services. The Chancery had little control over its course." He observed me warily. "You recall the investigation?"

"A little," I said. "I was nine. A very young nine, Monsignor. Innocent. Sheltered. Uninformed. I was scared to death and didn't understand the questions."

He sat down again. "We send our clergy to the Baltimore facility for a variety of reasons. Some have drinking problems that surface now and again. Some suffer crises of faith or vocation. And as the whole world now knows, some have abused their office. Others go for less obvious reasons. We used to call them nervous breakdowns."

"He had a nervous breakdown? Father Mike had a nervous breakdown?"

"That's certainly how it appeared." He paused. "You understand, the breakdown happened after he arrived in Baltimore. He wasn't sent there initially—"

"I know why he was sent there initially."

"I wasn't privy to any inside knowledge then. I'm just going by the records."

"The records?" I was beginning to sound like a talking bird.

His fingers moved almost imperceptibly toward a manila folder lying atop a crush of other folders. I had a pretty good idea whose it was, though he made no indication that it was anything more than part of the mess on his desk. "I was told there were no records," I said. Our eyes met, an electrical charge. "The woman on the phone—Sister Helen Dunley?—she told me there were no records."

"You didn't identify yourself very precisely."

"Would it have made a difference if I had?"

He pushed his seat back a little, holding the lip of the desk with both hands; he had most likely been explaining processes like this to victims—real victims, that is—for weeks, sitting in this very office, staring into the unmarked faces of the genuinely damaged.

"My uncle had a weak heart," I said. The clicking in my head sped up; I could see that everything I said surprised him. "I don't believe there was any breakdown, Monsignor, and I find it ironic beyond words that he died while receiving all this so-called help from the Church."

"Except," he said, "to be perfectly accurate—not that I'm minimizing the Church's role in his life, Mrs. Mitchell, I'm not—Father Murphy died after having refused the Church's so-called help."

"No," I said evenly. "He died in Baltimore. He was probably wearing a regulation johnny and robe."

Monsignor Fleury's bearing changed then, taking on the befuzzled cant of the hard of hearing. "Father Murphy left our facility," he said, enunciating, "without being discharged. The Church had arranged for him to join a retreat center in Pennsylvania. He would be trained in keeping archives, fielding requests for marriage annulments and the like. It was not work he looked forward to." He buckled his hands over his stomach. "After leaving Baltimore, Father Murphy sent a letter to the bishop, informing him that he had—well, that he had left us. Left the fold. We received word of his death not long after that."

Now my head was in full throb. "*Received* word? From where?"

One quick spark of the eye toward the folder. "From his sister, I believe. A Mrs. Cecilia Barrett. As next of kin, she was the one notified by the authorities."

The room pitched a little. "She wasn't his next of kin. I was."

"As his sister—"

"She wasn't his sister. She was my father's sister. They weren't related."

"We were given to understand—"

"And it's the Church who sent word to *us*. They sent a priest to my aunt's house. *We're* the ones who received word."

He gazed at me, his eyes very still, the watery, bonny blue of a homesick Irishman. "You were just a child, Mrs. Mitchell. Perhaps you got the story turned around somewhere along the line."

It's true, I'm sorry, but it's true, Celie had insisted in those first lightless days. Stage one, disbelief. *I can't help it, Lizzy. The priest who came here, Lizzy. He told me himself. A priest would never lie.*

"Are you all right?" Monsignor Fleury asked.

"I didn't get my story turned around."

He seemed reluctant to contradict me; his lips pulsed like a guppy's before he spoke again. "My understanding is that the Church got word of his death from the family. His confessor, Father Derocher, made a personal visit — to Rhode Island, I believe it was? — hoping the family might know where he'd disappeared to. We might never have known of his passing otherwise." He regarded me with an unctuous sympathy. "It's Father Derocher you recall coming to the house. We *were* concerned about your uncle, regardless of how it might appear to you."

"You just took her word for it?"

"We had no reason to disbelieve the family."

"Do you have an obituary?"

"As I said, Father Murphy's death occurred after he left the priesthood. Everything was over, so to speak, and as he had no interested relatives here, there would be no need — "

"He had a very interested relative, Monsignor."

"Forgive me. I meant to say no interested *adult* relatives."

I was remembering the funeral of Father Devlin, Father Mike's predecessor at St. Bart's, and my unmitigated awe at the spectacle of thirty men in black worshipping in one voice. I'd wheedled my way in and had been spectacularly rewarded. Until the arid service of Mariette's grandmother, I had thought all funerals vibrated with that same pomp and circumstance. I'd imagined my parents' funeral as a cortege of gowned and chanting friends.

"One of its own priests dies in the prime of life," I said to the chancellor, "and the Church doesn't bother to run an obituary? Wouldn't they want to bear his body home, see to his burial? Don't you do a high Mass, don't you all file in together, don't you fill the pews like an honor guard? Like the police, or the firemen? Isn't that how it's done? So what if he jumped the league, so what? According to you he was having a breakdown. Where is this famous Christian compassion? He was still one of yours."

The chancellor cleared his throat again, dainty as a girl. "Mrs. Mitchell," he said, "your uncle was dead and buried by the time we received word. But even if the Church *had* known in time, we would have been in somewhat of a quandary over funeral rites."

"Why?" My voice was getting higher, tinged with something like hysteria. "Those accusations were *wrong.*"

His mouth took a downward turn. "As I said, Father Murphy appeared to be suffering from intense remorse."

"He was suffering, Monsignor, but not from remorse."

"After his arrival in Baltimore, there was a general impression—a fear that he might take his own life."

"That's ridiculous. I don't believe you."

"Father Derocher made a personal visit expressly to prevent such a catastrophe. When Mrs. Barrett informed him of Father Murphy's death, she was loath to provide details, but the conclusion was a foregone one. And the Church, I'm ashamed to say, was probably relieved that someone else tied up the details in the case of a problem priest. I'm being very open with you here, Mrs. Mitchell." He unlocked his hands and lifted them, his mission complete. "I have no idea where your uncle is buried. You would have to get that information from your aunt. I'm sorry. The details were kept very quiet. Understandably so."

The words "problem priest" scorched me. We might have been talking about a house pet being carted off to the vet. "Do you need some water?" he said—or, I think he said. The room was taking on a muffled quality, his voice coming through a cottony fog. Despite this scrim of confusion, a finely etched image began to form: that little hole in the cuff of my uncle's jacket. That hand at my bedside. That frayed hole, yes, and the missing button. The ring. I had seen them in my consecrated between-time—same cuff, same hole, same ring. Except, not quite. The hole was bigger. The ring was scratched. The hand was older. As if they'd been worked over by time. As if the cloth were real cloth, the ring a real ring. The hand a real hand and not the memory of a hand.

For a moment I could not unstick a single word from my throat. I was running back through those initial weeks in Aunt Celie's too-small house, all those frightening, big-footed boys, the one dresser drawer set aside for me. My dresses, my socks, my few photographs shoehorned into a space the size of a child's coffin. I slept on a cot in Celie's room, somewhere in the helter-skelter state of Rhode Island, an eternity away from my quiet pink bedroom. She kept my hair braided, my clothes washed, she slapped her youngest son for hitting me, but I could tell from the start there would be no room for me. *Where is he?* I wailed. *Where is he where is he where is he where is he where is he?* At wits' end, Aunt Celie applied cold washcloths to my pulpy eyes. *Please, Lizzy, please. People will think I've been beating you! For God's sake, can you pull yourself together?* But I didn't pull myself together, I wouldn't, *where is he,* I wanted him back, *where is he where is he where is he where is he where is he?* until finally she spurted the words: *He's dead!* And he was. Suddenly, unbelievably dead. *It happened in Baltimore, I don't know, they buried him somewhere in Canada. Back to the Island, where he came from.*

Not until I faced Monsignor Fleury across the mess of his desk did I recognize in retrospect the lie in her voice, the desperation. She was so sick of listening to me, and frightened, too, of my uncle and me and the thing she thought we had done. A by-the-book Catholic, she had suffered the bruising humiliation of divorce, and now this. My soaked and blotchy face and its myriad suggestions — the shame of me — must have been more than she could bear. *He's dead!* she cried, two irreversible words dangling at the frayed end of her rope. The front door opened, some time later, a week or a day or two days or three. A priest stood on the stoop and I thought, for a single sanctified second, that it was Father Mike, back from the flexible land of the dead.

I lifted my eyes to the face that was a face I knew—but not his, not his face, an insult so eviscerating I fled to my private space behind the parlor drapes and held my stomach in fear of a literal spilling of guts. *We've received word,* is what I heard, but the words must have come from Celie, not the priest, whose name, Father Jack, I shouted after he left. *They come to give the news officially,* she told me quietly, *like in the military,* and I wondered for some time afterward whether Father Mike's heart had given out in the midst of battle.

I dropped my head and rested my forehead against a stack of papers on the chancellor's desk, feeling, for the first time in many years, like making my confession—but I could not think what I had to confess, unless it was a sin to hold this long to grief. "My uncle isn't dead, Monsignor," I muttered into the ink-smelling papers. "My aunt lied." I tempered each breath, in and out, in and out. The chancellor said nothing. "None of this would have happened if you'd had a little faith in him to begin with. Such an ugly story about a man who loved a child, and you believed so easily." I lifted my head.

"There was an investigation," he said quietly. "We believed what we were told."

"So did I," I snapped. "My excuse is that I was nine years old." I looked him directly in the eyes. "It must have seemed too good to be true, the problem priest resigning just before his problem death. And a civilian only too willing to tidy up the details. It must have seemed like a miracle."

He looked old. Exhausted. Sorry. "Father Murphy was accused of molesting a child," he said, "after which he resisted treatment, fled without a word, left the priesthood, and suddenly died. What else would you have us believe?"

"The truth."

The chancellor slipped his fingers beneath his eyeglasses and rubbed his eyes, then drew his hands down along his cheeks.

Fury thundered within me, but it was God I was fighting, not this mild-eyed monsignor posing as God's unlucky stand-in.

"Elizabeth," he said, very gently. "Elizabeth. You were not going to see your uncle again in any case. Not until you turned twenty-one years old. There was an agreement."

I folded my arms involuntarily, as if my body knew something I didn't and was getting ready to fend off the news. "What agreement?"

"Between the Diocese and the state. You would be remanded to the care of your aunt. Father Murphy would be sent to Baltimore for counseling and treatment, and after that to a non-pastoral assignment, in return for which the state would drop the inquiry. Nobody wanted this to advance to the stage of official charges, and Father Murphy agreed to the terms."

"Are you telling me he *admitted*—"

"I'm telling you that he did not deny it with the vigor we might have been hoping for." The chancellor looked unfathomably sad. "And neither, my dear woman, did you."

All my injuries, even the healed ones, stung fleetingly. The room felt tipped over, I couldn't quite get a breath, and then came a clean, white-light image of Father Mike spreading honey on toast. I'd tasted some at the Fryeburg fair on my fifth birthday, blueberry honey, and we'd been eating it ever since. Mrs. Hanson didn't hold with honey; honey was out of the ordinary. Honey was not unsalted butter. I yearned to sit at that table, in the warm light of the kitchen window, and spread honey on toast.

If I could have done that, just for a second, I believe I might have left the chancellor's office and returned to my former self.

"I'll take that water now," I said, swallowing and swallowing. "Can you get me some water?"

He was up in a flash, relieved to have something to do. Alone, I breathed ten times, measuring out my fury and confusion, bent on keeping my feet in contact with the floor. Drew had offered to accompany me here, expecting that I'd be handed a map to a gravesite on Prince Edward Island. He'd be the shoulder to cry on. We'd made up, after a fashion, and I vowed to put Father Mike to rest, to get on with my life—our life—and pronounce my rehabilitation complete. But I'd insisted on coming alone and now I knew what I'd come for. As if guided by the hand of God I filched the folder, jammed it into my purse, and left.

The chancellor was just outside in the carpeted ante-room, filling a glass of water from a pitcher.

"My uncle is alive, Monsignor," I said. "I saw him last March. He visited me in the hospital."

He closed his eyes—praying, probably—and made a disconcerting noise that sounded like humming. Finally he sighed. "I'm very sorry for your trouble, Elizabeth."

"Thank you," I said, preposterously.

He nodded once. Then he set the glass of water down, intending to shake my hand, I suppose, though for a moment I thought he meant to bless me. His hand lifted. "Don't," I said—not gently, I think—and left there, unblessed.

NINETEEN

He thinks he knows grief in its every shade. As a dread of nightfall. A glue that has to be walked through. A ticking clock in an empty room, each *tock* like something taking bites inside his body. He thinks he knows how grief works: It sucks taste from apples, it drains color from trees, it makes absence into a presence.

He thinks he's ready.

But grief does not prepare the bereaved for future grief. Grief is not something you get good at. Practice does not perfect anything.

Driving back to Conlin, Ohio, unable to loosen the vision of his grown, broken child from the locked cage of his own head, he cannot remember a worse sorrow than the one that weights him now: this stinging knowledge of time lost. Lost and irrecoverable. For two decades he deluded himself, shaping the past into something immutable and fully formed. A museum that might be visited. But the past, that slippery traitor, evolved without his permission. It refused to stay put. Waiting in the unbearable quiet of a hospital room at night, gazing down at a grown woman, a stranger, he felt the past lurch violently and then collapse like so many bricks, and he lost her once and for all.

Outside Allentown he stops at a Citgo, not because he needs gas but because the road has begun to change shape before his eyes and he hasn't eaten in two and a half days. Nothing but a few sips from the drinking fountain in the hospital lobby, a glass of water pulled from the bathroom tap in the motel. He buys a hot dog from a boy at the counter, gets back into the car. When he stops again, this time for gas, he realizes the hot dog is gone and can only assume that he is the one who ate it.

Then, a stretch of land in northern Pennsylvania that reminds him of Prince Edward Island.

No strangers to grief, people once said of his family.

But he was, as it turns out. He was a complete stranger to grief.

A few miles past the Ohio border, at the crest of a long, ambling hill, sits a country church: copper cross, white clapboards, medium-sized parking lot, tidy house with an add-on office. It is so open to the sky and fields that he already believes in the benevolence of the man who lives there, but not until he pulls in does he recognize this church — St. Anne's — as the place he stopped the last time he took this very journey. He'd found his car in the Baltimore parking lot, feeling poised and calm and guided. They had given him medication — what, he didn't know. He stashed his few belongings in the trunk, and headed north. He arrived in Maine seven hours later, mailed a letter to the Chancery, shut his bank accounts and transferred everything to the modest trust left to Lizzy after the death of her parents. He kept two hundred dollars for himself, then turned around and drove south again, over the same highways. In Pennsylvania he switched to the side roads — more hills back then, more untouched land, but the same journey, the same instinct for open land propelling him. He had been a man with nothing left but his own name. He had shed everything: his family, his home, his vocation. But he found himself unable to resist that simple church, its doors opened to the broad, sunny day, and after a time a priest strode in — a young pastor like himself, engulfed by duties that had taken him by surprise. The pastor raised his eyebrows in a question, which he answered by saying: *My name is Father Mike Murphy.* A priest once, a priest always. A permanent vow. They shook hands, the other priest saying nothing about his colleague's demolished eyes, his growth of beard, his gnawed fingertips. *Hungry?* he asked. After supper, this kind priest offered to hear his confession.

I abandoned a child, he whispered, risking forgiveness at last. *But this is not all of my sin.*

On his last day there, he asked to use the phone.

Stop calling here.

Let me speak to her, Celie. Please. Five minutes.

They said you quit. Nobody knows where you went.

To purgatory, Celie.

A priest came here looking for you. Concerned, not that you deserve it. A nice man looking for souls to redeem.

Just let me speak to her.

Not for another twelve years. As you very well know.

Just so I can reassure her that I'm still —

This was my responsibility in the first place, but I didn't take it, and look what happened. They told me everything, so don't try to soft-pedal this to me. I should have taken the responsibility, I realize that, but I didn't, and now here I am with this damaged —

Surely you don't believe —

God is punishing me but good, and I won't lay one more stick on my conscience.

I'm just asking for five minutes, Celie. Five minutes. She needs reassuring.

I told her you died. She thinks you're dead because of your horrible heart.

You told her——?

I told the priest the same thing. You want to resurrect yourself, be my guest, but it won't make a lick of difference for twelve years.

One minute. You can time me. Give me one minute.

You're not to speak to this child until she's twenty-one. That's the agreement, that's the legal agreement, you agreed. If you call again, if you show up here, if you so much as write a letter, I'll report you to every authority in the United States of America and you can tell your side to a judge.

Panicked and speechless, he held the disconnected phone. In his head he shouted her name as surely she would be shouting his. Her name bled in his throat as he weighed his narrowing options. For a child like his—a stubborn, meddling, wonderful girl who brooked no compromise, for whom there would be no predicting how twelve years of severed ties might disintegrate her soul—would not his death be more bearable than years of separation? In his fever of grief and shame, he decided to grant her the mercy of a gradual forgetting.

And so he died. And took to the road, to endless driving and temporary jobs and years of misery that would bring him eventually to Frannie and her son and their oblivious consortium with a dead man. A walking tomb.

This very church, on this very hill. The moon is up, the trees silhouetting grandly against the empty, almost dark sky. He pulls in. Again. He knocks on the rectory door, finds an old priest, not a twenty-years-older version of the young one who opened the door back then, but a truly old man in his eighties who could be retired right now had so many of his brethren not jumped the league.

Father Mike Murphy, he says.

Or thinks he says. The world is tipping and pitching.

St. Bartholomew's, Hinton, Maine. That balm again, allowing him to engage properties of time that he had forgotten all about. It stands still. It moves backwards and forwards. It deposits a dozen layers upon a single moment. Standing on this tilting porch that needs paint and a new number for the door post, he can believe that nothing has happened yet. This feeling used to visit him during prayer.

If I could sit in your church for a while, he says to the old man. *If I could compose myself.*

The old priest leads his visitor to the church, which is well lighted and decorated with lilacs bubbling out of glass jars that look like the ones Vivienne used to bring into St. Bart's when she was in charge of the altar.

Thanks, Father, he tells the old man, who looks him over and asks, *Do you need to say a Mass?*

He nods, and the old man, who knows a priest in distress when he sees one, leads his visitor to the sacristy, opens the door, shows him a drawer containing a tiny key that opens the tabernacle.

Everything's laid out, he says. *I'd stay, but I'm waiting for a pair of souls I'm trying to talk out of a divorce.*

Not for years and years has he stood on this side of the altar, but the composing moment returns untrammeled, that instant calm, the silent white expanse of laid-out linen filling his vision, his mind, and what comes to him first is the Latin of his seminary days, and the memory of one of his first Masses, at a prison in Thomaston, and the inmate who grabbed his sleeve afterward, saying: *Father, I watched your face when you were foolin' with the host, and I said to myself, Christ, this guy buys the whole works.*

He's become used to sitting in the pews, as a husband and stepfather, a parishioner like any other, and he believes in the liturgy still. But this is different, standing here, bent over the altar with his hands on the chalice. He remembers anew, believes anew, believes in a way no one can know except another priest who lifts the brittle white disk — *Do this in memory of Me* — the bread no longer bread, the wine no longer wine.

As a boy of twelve he believed wholly. A called boy, he believed. Time shifts and flitters, loops and flattens. He is fourteen, in spring, riding in his sister's bottom-heavy Dodge Dart station wagon, hanging his head hard out the window, eager as a dog. Oh. His first whiff of Maine.

His sister calls to him, his big sister, Elizabeth, his beloved: *Get your face inside, Mikey, I don't plan to lose you too.*

Their mother, their father, their uncle, their baby brother, gone. He counts, too, the cats and dogs that vanished over the years, and Johnny-Boy, the crippled crow that patrolled his mother's flower patch, yelling "Hi, Johnny! Hi, Johnny!" all day long. All of them gone, dust to dust beneath the furrowed earth.

They drive and drive. Maine is not beautiful in the way of Prince Edward Island. It is beautiful in a way he has not thought to imagine. He takes in the flooded sky, the changeable, spooling land.

Look how much life is left, he wants to say. Not in those words. He is young, tongue-tied, alight with possibility. He invents a sort of poetry for this place, naming everything he sees as a way of receiving it. His sister's loaded car wends south along the shimmering coast, then inland, away from the water. *I'm sick of ocean,* his sister tells him, following a river in and in. They encounter furred ridges and tree-lined roads, purple valleys split by rivers. He glimpses the arrogant stacks of mills and factories shouldered into the landscape, senses a dropping away of farmland, ocean, the calm and rolling countryside they have left forever.

His sister slows down, creeping down a main street in a town upon a river, a shoe factory just across the bridge. *How about this?* she asks.

He spots a rock in the river, an emergent, gray-backed boulder. Upon this rock, he thinks, then blushes at his audacity. He is no St. Peter, but he will try.

He loves God. He is in love with God. There is nothing but God, and the state of Maine, and his sister.

Now I'll have to find us a man, his sister says, laughing.

So he prays and prays. At last they find him: Bill Finneran, a setup man at the shoe shop, his commodious Irish laugh the most enthralling of all his enthrallments. He doesn't mind that the woman he wants comes packaged with a little brother. And why would he mind? She's strong and redheaded, quick to kiss, looking for a place to land.

You learn to meet God everywhere, is what he was taught as a child in church, so he meets God here, in Maine, in this town on a river, the ocean many miles away but close enough to smell if the wind blows right. He meets God in the parish church that he will, years hence, be called to and then banished from. He meets God in Bill Finneran, who will become his brother-in-law and send him to college on the strength of a bank account stashed with overtime and moonlighting, who will welcome him back home eight years later and smile through the ordination rite in his ugly brown suit and applaud with hands stained orange with shoe dye. In time a baby will arrive, a new beginning named for her mother. They'll call her Lizzy.

Okay then, his sister says, halting the car. Factory, river, town. *What do you think, Mikey?*

Meet God everywhere, is what he thinks, flush with certainty. Here at the beginning, on this clear spring day in the State of Maine, United States of America, meeting God seems easy. It is Elizabeth, after all—Elizabeth, his favorite—whom God spared.

Time is layering again, moving back and ahead simultaneously, expanding and contracting. Dressed in sweat-crushed clothes and a borrowed surplice he lifts the chalice, the consecrated host: *Do this in memory of Me.* God, my father, my savior, my every breath, I meet you. You who punish and forgive, You who weep and rejoice, You who have given and taken all I have, You who refuse to abandon me, You son of a bitch, my only friend.

He lifts his head as if to find his lost parishioners, Vivienne in front with the girls at each side, the little boys squirming on the lap of one aunt or another. Row upon row of fine faces, hymnals opened to the same white page, mouths opened to the same word of the same prayer. He can almost smell the wet coats and incense, hear the thudding of children's shoes against the kneelers, Vivienne's awkward vibrato, Lizzy's effortful alto, the swaggering off-key stylings of the parish-council treasurer, the flutelike notes emanating from the kissed throat of Vivienne's sister Pauline, who stands in the low balcony with the twelve-voice choir. In time's layered way, his parents seem to be sitting out there, too, and the churchgoing farmers of his boyhood, and the complicated seminarians with whom he prayed and fasted in a city that spoke an effervescent French and loved dessert.

Outside, the stars begin to blink on. He thanks the old priest and resumes his journey, the road dark now, and winding. So little traffic here, off the highway. The road pleases him; the smallest sensation of pleasure, or remembered pleasure, reaches him through the air lock of his grief. He took this road on instinct. The codger's route, Frannie calls roads like this. He can drive as slow as he likes, praying for his anointed child. It will take a long time to get home.

TWENTY

I opened the file in nearby Payson Park, where Father Mike used to take me after our twice-a-year shopping trip, or as my reward for waiting in a room with no books as he conducted church business in the Chancery. We liked to stroll the winding lanes, often all the way down to the cove to feed the ducks that snapped up the Cheerios we brought in wrinkled bread bags. The park had changed since then—cobblestones thrown over for asphalt drive-throughs, ball fields chain-linked into territories.

The file contained Father Mike's resignation, a perfunctory note that nonetheless began, *With bottomless sorrow.* There were also a couple of letters between the Chancery and the Department of Human Services, and three transcribed interviews, each headed "Unofficial." The transcripts—signed by a nun in the front office, everything prepared within the family—began with a set of names, each of which opened a flower of memory.

Monsignor Frank Flannagan, co-chancellor, Diocese of Portland. Snowy beard and glittery blue eyes, Santa Claus in disguise.

Father John Derocher, pastor, St. Peter's, Bangor. High summer, hot weather, Father Jack arriving with a bottle of wine and photos from his trip to Italy.

Mrs. Ida Hanson, reporting party. Shoes unlaced on sore feet, support hose rolled to the ankles.

Ms. Shelley Costigan, Licensed Clinical Social Worker. Bloomy cheeks and a nunlike mouth, hair cut high across her brow. Her face came to me with unbidden clarity. Of course she was young and out of her depth, in a difficult job impossible to prepare for.

MS. COSTIGAN: To be absolutely clear, Mrs. Hanson. You witnessed Father Murphy engaging in improper sexual activity with the child?

MRS. HANSON: I just told you they were in his bed. It was April first, I remember, because we had a snow overnight and I said the snow must be an April Fool's joke.

MS. COSTIGAN: Okay, so you're saying that he was molesting her in his bed?

MRS. HANSON: You tell me.

FR. DEROCHER: What kind of an answer is that?

MSGR. FLANNAGAN: Let her talk, Jack.

FR. DEROCHER: These aren't answers. You never stayed with them, Frank. The child adores him, it's as plain as the nose on your face.

MS. COSTIGAN: May I?

FR. DEROCHER: If Father Murphy is going to be accused of something this foul, I for one think the accuser should be more specific.

MRS. HANSON: I've been a member of this parish for sixty years, Father Derocher. I was here when Father Devlin was a curate. Even if I wasn't a Catholic, I think I know that a grown man isn't supposed to share a bed with a nine-year-old girl. He keeps books in his dresser, about girls and their private parts.

MSGR. FLANNAGAN: This is informal, right?

MS. COSTIGAN: You're the one recording, Monsignor.

MSGR. FLANNAGAN: I'm just confirming. For the record.

FR. DEROCHER: This goes nowhere, right? You're calling this informal.

MS. COSTIGAN: Preliminary, Father. We'll see what turns up.

FR. DEROCHER: Nothing is going to turn up.

MRS. HANSON: It's always the ones you don't suspect. There was that young day-care worker in Delaware, sweet as pie. Abusing babies with forks.

MSGR. FLANNAGAN: Mrs. Hanson, you were about to explain what you saw.

MRS. HANSON: My sister-in-law belongs to St. Bonaventure, and there's all these stories about what's going on up there and nobody's doing one thing to stop it.

MSGR. FLANNAGAN: Whatever the troubles at St. Bonaventure, they have nothing to do with this interview, Mrs. Hanson.

MRS. HANSON: People talk, is all. And it's not impossible for a priest to commit a mortal sin.

MS. COSTIGAN: Can we get back on track?

MRS. HANSON: The Church had no business putting a child in a situation like this in the first place. What would a priest know about raising a child? A girl especially. She wasn't even toilet trained. They should have known full well the effect this would have on the parish.

MS. COSTIGAN: Can we please get back on track please?

MRS. HANSON: No limits, anything she wants. You would not believe what he allows that child to eat. I might as well have been invisible, nobody so much as gives me a how-do-you-do. And it wasn't just this household affected, I can tell you, it was the whole parish. The child wants guitar music, presto, everybody has to suffer a hoedown before the Offertory without so much as a do-you-please to the parish council.

MS. COSTIGAN: You said you saw Father Murphy molesting her.

MRS. HANSON: Well, that first time I didn't actually see it happening. This is April first I'm talking about. Father Murphy overslept. That was highly unusual all by itself, I can tell you. He's always up early because he doesn't like my coffee. He mixes eggshells in with the grounds, some notion of his from who knows where.

They do things different where he comes from. Eggshells. I got there at six to start breakfast, as usual. The bedroom he uses is downstairs, just off the parlor. The door was wide open, and there they were. A nine-year-old girl and a thirty-eight-year-old man. I'll never forget the way she looked at me. Guilty as sin, I can tell you that.

MS. COSTIGAN: Did Father Murphy say anything?

MRS. HANSON: Nothing. He got up, looked at the clock. Not one word of explanation. He might have said something about snow in April being unusual, I'm not sure. By the time I had breakfast ready they were both dressed, acting like everything was normal. Normal as pie.

MS. COSTIGAN: And the second occasion?

MRS. HANSON: A couple of months ago. First of September or thereabouts. It was right around when our neighbor's husband ran off. The Blanchard children were moping around. Their mother was keeping to herself. It was a bad time as it was, so I decided to keep shut.

FR. DEROCHER: It's my understanding that you in fact did not keep shut, Mrs. Hanson. In fact, it's my understanding that the rumors in this parish have been flying around like a plague of locusts.

MRS. HANSON: I'm not the child molester here, Monsignor. He gives her liquor.

                                   ❧ — ❧

MRS. HANSON: Father Murphy cut my hours, like I said, around the time she turned four. He wanted to cook suppers himself, and that's fine, he has every right. I cooked all the meals when Father Devlin was here. I was live-in, you know, before Father Murphy came as a curate. Father Devlin didn't honestly need a curate. God rest his soul. He was a peach. And he knew the meaning of thank you. Believe you me.

MS. COSTIGAN: Can we?

MRS. HANSON: Oh. Well, you said every detail. All right. We're talking about the second occasion now? Around the first of September? I worked until three that day, as usual, but after I got home I realized I'd left my glasses in the parlor. I had a letter from my daughter in Florida, which naturally I wanted to read, so after supper I went back for the glasses. I thought Father Murphy had gone up to Bangor like he said he was going to, to visit you, Father Derocher. After school Lizzy was to go straight to the Blanchards'. In my opinion, Monsignor, that's where you should have placed her from the start-up, with somebody like Vivienne Blanchard. God knows the woman could have used the help.

MS. COSTIGAN: So you went back for your glasses.

MRS. HANSON: St. Bart's isn't but a mile from me, so I thought, why not, it'll take a few minutes and then I'll be able to read Rose's letter. It wasn't exactly dark, but you'd need a light on inside, so I figured no one was home since there were no lights on that I could see. I thought Father Murphy was still in Bangor. He parks in the carport next to the parish hall, so I never noticed the car. The house wasn't locked, but I figured he forgot. He forgot things all the time, absent-minded, his mind every-where else but where it belonged. So I let myself in, thinking I was alone. I wanted my glasses. That's all I was doing.

MS. COSTIGAN: And you saw what?

MRS. HANSON: Heard, at first. Certain noises.

MS. COSTIGAN: What kind of noises?

MRS. HANSON: The driveway is a long one, you know. The only house within eyeshot is the Blanchards', and even at that you'd have to really be looking. All those trees. And in fall everything gets kind of filled in, with the goldenrod and whatnot. It's a handy little spot if you're put in mind to do things you don't want seen.

FR. DEROCHER: I'd like to know where this is going.

MRS. HANSON: Well, I found my glasses in the parlor, and like I said, his bedroom is right there, and I heard these — I heard noises. Of a certain type. It was, they were certain noises of a certain type of intimate nature. I was so shocked I dropped my pocketbook right there on the parlor floor.

MS. COSTIGAN: What happened then?

MRS. HANSON: Well, there was some noise behind the door. It was open just a little ways. I heard her voice — well, it was like a cry. But not sad crying. The other kind. This is embarrassing.

MS. COSTIGAN: You're doing fine.

MRS. HANSON: I couldn't make out any words, but she sounded ashamed, and who wouldn't be? I went over to the door, I don't know why, and then the door flies open and there he is.

MS. COSTIGAN: Did he say anything to you?

MRS. HANSON: He asked what on Earth I was doing in the house. All snappy, too, I might add. He's in this bathrobe, which is on every which-way, and his hair, too, all sticking up, it was disgusting. I was disgusted right down to the last rattle of my bones.

MS. COSTIGAN: Then what?

MRS. HANSON: I caught her turning over in the bed, covering herself up, but I could see the shape of her there, and the tail of her nightgown plain as day, this white one she wore all the time with red dots on it. She was hiding. Protecting him. You should have seen his expression. He slammed the door in my face and I wanted to throw up.

FR. DEROCHER: He keeps cats. Could you have seen cats moving in the bed?

MRS. HANSON: I think I can tell the difference between one of those filthy cats and a girl in a nightgown.

MSGR. FLANNAGAN: You came back the next day?

MRS. HANSON: Same as usual. Six o'clock. He didn't say a word about it.

MS. COSTIGAN: The first time was on the first of April, the second time in early September. We're almost into December. Why come forward now?

FR. DEROCHER: That's what I'd like to know.

MRS. HANSON: Her shirt, is what it was. One of those shirts, tanks I think they call them, hot pink, sparkles on the front, very suggestive. Just disgraceful. Like some kind of showgirl. I hadn't seen the thing for a while, but there it was again. Like a streetwalker would wear. That was it, the last straw. I said to myself, that's it, you can't hold still another instant. My niece's daughter works for the State. I called her that very afternoon. She's the one who got everything rolling. Well, I suppose you know that.

FR. DEROCHER: You suspected that an innocent child was being abused on the premises since last April, and yet you stayed on as the housekeeper, going into that house every day.

MRS. HANSON: I needed the money, God help me. And besides, I just told you: She isn't an innocent child.

TWENTY-ONE

Monsignor Frank Flannagan, co-chancellor,
Diocese of Portland.
Father John Derocher, pastor, St. Peter's, Bangor.
Ms. Shelley Costigan, Licensed Clinical Social Worker.
Elizabeth Finneran, age nine.

MSGR. FLANNAGAN: Just a couple of little questions, Lizzy.

ELIZABETH FINNERAN: Where is he?

FR. DEROCHER: He went down to Portland to visit Bishop Byrnes, remember? It turns out he's going to spend the night. You can stay with Mrs. Blanchard for a couple of days.

MS. COSTIGAN: That's not quite true, as I understand it, Father.

ELIZABETH FINNERAN: Did something happen?

FR. DEROCHER: Nothing happened. All you have to do is answer this nice lady's questions, Lizzy. Nothing happened.

ELIZABETH FINNERAN: Then why did Father Mike go to Portland for overnight without telling me? Did I do something wrong?

MS. COSTIGAN: Of course not, sweetie. You did nothing wrong. You have to remember, no matter what, you did nothing wrong. Now. I want to tell you something. Lots of girls just like you, exactly your age, they're afraid to tell if somebody did something wrong to them. They think maybe they're the ones who did something wrong, or that if they tell on the person who did something wrong to them, everyone will be mad.

ELIZABETH FINNERAN: What do you mean? Is somebody mad at me?

MS. COSTIGAN: No, not at all. That's the whole point. You didn't do anything wrong, and nobody is going to be mad at you for anything you say here, no matter what it is. In fact, everybody will be extremely proud of you for telling the truth.

ELIZABETH FINNERAN: I do tell the truth.

MS. COSTIGAN: Of course you do. You're a good girl, that's why. So, when I ask you questions, you'll tell me the truth, right?

ELIZABETH FINNERAN: Right.

MS. COSTIGAN: Even if the questions are kind of embarrassing or make you feel ashamed.

ELIZABETH FINNERAN: [no response]

MS. COSTIGAN: So, I'm going to ask you some more questions now, Elizabeth. Okay?

ELIZABETH FINNERAN: Okay.

MS. COSTIGAN: I'm going to ask you about where you sleep at night, things like that.

ELIZABETH FINNERAN: [no response]

MS. COSTIGAN: I was wondering if you always sleep in your own bed. You can answer yes or no, sweetie, there's no need to be nervous. You always tell the truth, right?

ELIZABETH FINNERAN: I sleep in my bed. That's where I sleep.

MS. COSTIGAN: Can you speak up a little, Elizabeth? So. Every single night, you sleep in your own bed?

ELIZABETH FINNERAN: Yes.

MS. COSTIGAN: Good. That's wonderful, Elizabeth. You're just telling the truth, right?

ELIZABETH FINNERAN: Yes.

MS. COSTIGAN: Isn't this easy? See? Everybody's really proud of you for being so grown up and just answering the questions.

ELIZABETH FINNERAN: Thanks.

MS. COSTIGAN: Oh, you're welcome, Elizabeth. Now, you sleep in Father Mike's bed sometimes, too, don't you? Did you forget to tell about that part?

ELIZABETH FINNERAN: [no response]

MS. COSTIGAN: Just tell the truth, Elizabeth, just like you've been doing. We are so, so proud of you.

FR. DEROCHER: She just told you, she sleeps in her own bed.

MS. COSTIGAN: And you sleep in Father Mike's bed, too, sometimes, right?

ELIZABETH FINNERAN: [no response]

MS. COSTIGAN: Answer the question, sweetie. Yes or no, okay? Do you sometimes sleep in Father Mike's bed? Yes or no, sweetie. You're doing really great.

ELIZABETH FINNERAN: I get nightmares.

MS. COSTIGAN: Can you speak up, Elizabeth? What happens when you get nightmares?

FR. DEROCHER: She goes by Lizzy.

MS. COSTIGAN: Is it all right if I call you Lizzy?

ELIZABETH FINNERAN: Uh-huh.

MS. COSTIGAN: All right then, Lizzy. What happens when you get nightmares?

ELIZABETH FINNERAN: I go downstairs and get Father Mike. Just sometimes. When I really, really have to.

MS. COSTIGAN: You have to speak up, sweetie. Just a little bit, okay? Now. Do you sleep in Father Mike's bed all night when you really, really have to?

ELIZABETH FINNERAN: He carries me back upstairs after I fall asleep. So I wake up in my own bed.

MS. COSTIGAN: But Mrs. Hanson says she saw you in Father Mike's bed in the morning. And once in the evening.

ELIZABETH FINNERAN: What?

MS. COSTIGAN: Mrs. Hanson said she saw you in Father Mike's bed with him. Right?

ELIZABETH FINNERAN: [no response]

MS. COSTIGAN: Just tell the truth, sweetie. We're really proud of you right now. You sleep in Father Mike's bed all night sometimes, right?

ELIZABETH FINNERAN: She thinks I'm a baby. But I can't help it. I get nightmares.

MS. COSTIGAN: Are they scary nightmares?

ELIZABETH FINNERAN: I'm nine. You don't have to talk to me like that.

MS. COSTIGAN: I'm sorry, sweetie. I know you're really grown up. You're telling the truth, which is really a grown-up thing to do. What happens when you have a nightmare and go in Father Mike's bed?

ELIZABETH FINNERAN: What?

MS. COSTIGAN: Does he ask you to do things? Is that what happens?

ELIZABETH FINNERAN: He says to think about my guardian angel.

MS. COSTIGAN: Can you speak up, sweetie?

ELIZABETH FINNERAN: I know Mrs. Hanson saw me. Is that why you came here? Because I'm spoiled?

MSGR. FLANNAGAN: You're just upsetting her, Miss Costigan.

ELIZABETH FINNERAN: Is it because my parents died? Am I too babyish to stay with Father Mike?

FR. DEROCHER: This is ridiculous, Frank. Why are we allowing this? She's scared to death. She doesn't understand the questions.

MSGR. FLANNAGAN: It has to be done, Jack. We're due back by noon. Father Murphy's interview is at one.

FR. DEROCHER: All this cloak and dagger. We should be ashamed of ourselves.

MSGR. FLANNAGAN: Go ahead, Ms. Costigan.

MS. COSTIGAN: Just a few more little questions, sweetie.

ELIZABETH FINNERAN: Is this because I'm an orphan? Crissy Miller says I'm an orphan, but I'm not.

MS. COSTIGAN: Who is Crissy Miller?

ELIZABETH FINNERAN: A girl in the fifth grade. I'm not an orphan.

FR. DEROCHER: Fifth-grade girls don't know up from down, Lizzy. Don't pay any attention to a word she says.

MS. COSTIGAN: Can we continue, please?

MSGR. FLANNAGAN: Go ahead.

MS. COSTIGAN: Elizabeth, Lizzy, remember how you said you always tell the truth?

ELIZABETH FINNERAN: Yes. I'm not an orphan, though. I have someone.

MS. COSTIGAN: So you have to tell the truth here, with me, even if it's the truth about another person who did something really, really wrong.

ELIZABETH FINNERAN: What person? Did I do something wrong?

MS. COSTIGAN: You did nothing wrong, Elizabeth. Lizzy. It's Father Mike who did something wrong.

ELIZABETH FINNERAN: What? What did he do wrong?

MS. COSTIGAN: He put you in his bed, Lizzy, when he wasn't supposed to. Right? Didn't he do that?

ELIZABETH FINNERAN: [no response]

MS. COSTIGAN: Elizabeth, you want to help Father Mike, right?

ELIZABETH FINNERAN: Yes.

MS. COSTIGAN: A little louder please, sweetie. I can't hear you. Do you know how you can help Father Mike the best?

ELIZABETH FINNERAN: How?

MS. COSTIGAN: By telling the truth. He'll be really proud of you when he finds out you told the truth. By saying yes or no to my questions. That will make Father Mike really proud of you. Can you do that?

ELIZABETH FINNERAN: Yes.

MS. COSTIGAN: Okay. Remember now, you're making Father Mike really proud of you.

ELIZABETH FINNERAN: It's not his fault I'm spoiled.

MS. COSTIGAN: You're not spoiled, Lizzy. You're a perfectly nice girl.

ELIZABETH FINNERAN: He gives me everything I want.

MS. COSTIGAN: Well, that's simply not true, Lizzy. You're a nice girl. Now, listen, I'm going to ask you the rest of my questions now, and we're going to use these dolls to help us out. Okay?

ELIZABETH FINNERAN: I guess so. I don't really play with dolls that much.

MS. COSTIGAN: See this doll, Lizzy? Can you do something for me? Can you pretend this doll is you?

ELIZABETH FINNERAN: But she doesn't have any clothes on.

MS. COSTIGAN: We're going to pretend this doll is you, and we'll pretend this cushion right here is Father Mike's bed. All right?

ELIZABETH FINNERAN: Doesn't she have any clothes?

MS. COSTIGAN: And can you pretend this other doll is Father Mike?

ELIZABETH FINNERAN: I don't — Can you put some pajamas on that doll? He looks very ugly like that.

MS. COSTIGAN: Speak up, sweetie. What do you mean?

ELIZABETH FINNERAN: His, you know, his weenie is, you know. He looks like Buddy. Buddy takes his clothes off sometimes. He's just a little kid, though.

MS. COSTIGAN: Can we play with the dolls like this for a minute anyway, even if they look ugly?

ELIZABETH FINNERAN: [no response]

MS. COSTIGAN: Let's pretend this pillow is Father Mike's bed, all right? So here's Father Mike, putting you in his bed.

ELIZABETH FINNERAN: I guess so.

MS. COSTIGAN: And he gives you special things to drink, too, right?

ELIZABETH FINNERAN: Like what?

MS. COSTIGAN: Like champagne, right?

ELIZABETH FINNERAN: That's for celebration.

MS. COSTIGAN: For celebration, right. What are you celebrating when he gives you champagne?

ELIZABETH FINNERAN: Love.

MS. COSTIGAN: Love. Okay. Well, Lizzy, sometimes what one person says is love is actually very, very wrong. I'm going to play with the dolls for a little while here, and we'll pretend this doll is Father Mike, and this other doll is you, and Father Mike is showing you love. Okay?

ELIZABETH FINNERAN: You should put some clothes on those dolls, though.

MS. COSTIGAN: Just for now, we'll keep them like this, all right?

ELIZABETH FINNERAN: [no response]

MS. COSTIGAN: Okay. Elizabeth. Lizzy. I'm going to show the dolls doing some things, and you tell me if Father Mike ever did the same thing to you. Even once, okay? All you have to do is say yes or no.

ELIZABETH FINNERAN: Yes or no?

MS. COSTIGAN: Even once. Just tell the truth, remember?

ELIZABETH FINNERAN: Uh-huh.

MS. COSTIGAN: Did Father Mike ever put his hand on your forehead, like this?

ELIZABETH FINNERAN: Yes. Is it because I'm too much of a baby? Is that why you're mad at him?

MS. COSTIGAN: Nobody's mad at anybody, sweetie. You're a great girl. Very, very grown up. You're doing great. See how easy it is to just say yes or no? Now, did he ever touch your back, like this? Look at the dolls, sweetie. You have to answer. Yes or no, sweetie.

ELIZABETH FINNERAN: Yes.

MS. COSTIGAN: Good. Just tell the truth. Did he ever touch you here? Even one time?

ELIZABETH FINNERAN: Yes.

MS. COSTIGAN: Here?

ELIZABETH FINNERAN: Yes.

MS. COSTIGAN: And here?

FR. DEROCHER: Oh, for the love of God.

MSGR. FLANNAGAN: Is this absolutely necessary?

MS. COSTIGAN: Lizzy? Can you look at me for a minute? Okay. Can you look at the dolls now? Thank you. No, look at the dolls, sweetie.

ELIZABETH FINNERAN: [no response]

MS. COSTIGAN: Listen, you're doing really well, Lizzy, you're really helping.

FR. DEROCHER: Lizzy, come on back.

MS. COSTIGAN: Lizzy, come back, sweetie.

FR. DEROCHER: Wonderful.

MS. COSTIGAN: This is what happens. This is what we're seeing now. This is classic.

TWENTY-TWO

His Excellency Patrick L. Byrnes, Bishop of Portland.
Monsignor Frank Flannagan, co-chancellor,
    Diocese of Portland.
Father John Derocher, pastor, St. Peter's, Bangor.
Father Michael Murphy, pastor,
    St. Bartholomew's, Hinton.
Mr. Douglas Dearborn, Case Supervisor,
    Department of Human Services.

MSGR. FLANNAGAN: I don't see the point in going over this again. I'm sure we can come to some arrangement.

BISHOP BYRNES: I would like to have it recorded that we have held a proceeding with all due opportunity for discovering the truth. This proceeding is private, as discussed. Sealed, as discussed.

MR. DEARBORN: Just to clarify, though: You don't deny that you gave your niece alcohol.

FR. MURPHY: I told you this twice already. A sip. Diluted.

MR. DEARBORN: Right. On several occasions.

FR. MURPHY: Occasions of celebration. I told you.

MR. DEARBORN: To celebrate love.

FR. MURPHY: I don't like your tone, Mr. Dearborn.

FR. DEROCHER: Mike, you're not helping anything.

MR. DEARBORN: And you don't deny that your niece often slept in your bed with you.

FR. MURPHY: I didn't say "often." I said "occasionally." How many times are you going to ask me this question? She has nightmares. There is no comforting her. Anyone with a child knows this. I arranged—I always arrange the blankets in a proper way, Mr. Dearborn. I've already told you this.

MR. DEARBORN: What is a proper way to arrange blankets?

FR. MURPHY: I really don't like your tone.

FR. DEROCHER: Can we just finish this?

MR. DEARBORN: To clarify, then, your housekeeper said—

FR. MURPHY: I know what she said. I don't need to hear it again.

MR. DEARBORN: Her word against yours, then.

FR. MURPHY: I'm afraid so.

MR. DEARBORN: Well, we interviewed your niece this morning.

FR. MURPHY: What? You did what?

FR. DEROCHER: Take it easy, Mike.

FR. MURPHY: You said you'd leave her out of this. If I came down and answered these asinine questions, you'd leave her out of this.

MSGR. FLANNAGAN: We're not the only ones making decisions right now, Father Murphy. This is taking on a life of its own.

FR. MURPHY: What's wrong with you? She's nine years old. Was Mrs. Blanchard with her? My neighbor, Mrs. Blanchard, was staying with her today.

MR. DEARBORN: We sent a female caseworker, Father Murphy. She's very gentle when interviewing children, I assure you.

FR. MURPHY: I don't believe this. I don't believe this.

MR. DEARBORN: Your niece told our caseworker that you gave her alcohol, took her into your bed, and touched her inappropriately.

FR. MURPHY: What? What?

MR. DEARBORN: This is someone used to interviewing children, and her professional opinion is that abuse did occur. If you have an explanation, Father, now is the time.

FR. MURPHY: She's a little girl. What in God's name is wrong with you, asking her questions about — questions like that? Monsignor, you gave me your word.

MSGR. FLANNAGAN: Are you saying the child lied about being touched improperly?

FR. MURPHY: Lizzy doesn't lie. I can't imagine what you're talking about. You had no right. I'm her legal guardian. You had no right to put things in her head. You had no right to harm her like that. Why are you doing this?

FR. DEROCHER: Take it easy, Mike. It wasn't like it sounds.

FR. MURPHY: You were there, Jack? You let this happen?

FR. DEROCHER: I asked to go. I figured a familiar face might make her feel better.

FR. MURPHY: What did they ask her? What did they put in her head?

FR. DEROCHER: Mike, it was nothing, honestly. Totally preliminary. It took ten minutes. Calm down.

MR. DEARBORN: Well, she'll be re-interviewed in a day or so.

FR. MURPHY: What? Over my dead body. Over my dead body.

MR. DEARBORN: Sit down, Father. Please.

FR. DEROCHER: Mike, take it easy.

FR. MURPHY: Help me out here, Jack. Help me.

FR. DEROCHER: Mike, for the love of God. What are we supposed to think? You can't tell us what exactly Mrs. Hanson saw or heard. You can't tell us why Lizzy hid herself. You can't tell us why you slammed the door in Mrs. Hanson's face. You can't tell us why you put in for a transfer. What are we supposed to think?

MSGR. FLANNAGAN: Father Murphy, you've put the Church in a difficult position.

FR. DEROCHER: Please, Mike. You've got something to say, haven't you?

FR. MURPHY: I'm afraid not.

FR. DEROCHER: Maybe your housekeeper made the whole thing up? Maybe you did something to make her angry and she's using this to get you back?

FR. MURPHY: I never called her a liar. I said she was mistaken.

MR. DEARBORN: The child indicated otherwise.

FR. MURPHY: You will not ask her another question. You will leave your caseworker and your questions out of my child's life. Not a single question, do you understand me? Are you listening to me, Mr. Dearborn? The one thing I gave her was an innocent childhood.

MR. DEARBORN: With all due respect, Father, you don't make the rules here.

FR. MURPHY: Let's wrap this up, then. I won't have her questioned.

FR. DEROCHER: Mike. Wait. Can you see what's happening here?

FR. MURPHY: I'm afraid so.

FR. DEROCHER: So help us out.

FR. MURPHY: I'm afraid I can't. I'm finished here. Whatever you want, I'll agree. Anything you want, I'll sign. But this ends here. Now.

FR. DEROCHER: Mike. I'm begging you. Think what this means.

BISHOP BYRNES: Mr. Dearborn, perhaps we can talk about terms.

TWENTY-THREE

In graduate school, as counselors-in-training, we practiced on strangers, recruiting the secretaries and janitors who worked in the building, the occasional landlord or cab driver or store clerk, students from a neighboring high school, a dragnet of the walking wounded who populated an average day. Under the pitiless supervision of Professor Alice Talbot, we taped our sessions and submitted a written summary, after which she would have our tapes transcribed and force us to mark discrepancies between the wishful recollections in our summaries and the transcripts' cold, unbending truth.

Talbot, imperious and near retirement, refused to trifle with the layered suggestions of body language, considering such investigations the first refuge of amateurs. "Words first," she warned us. She believed, controversially, that our intuition as practitioners would be thwarted at every turn by a slovenly reliance on body language for cues. Body language served mainly to distract us from what she called "direct hits," bald truths that are harder to discern in some people than others.

She began with voice, the first language of the body. Some voices sounded more naturally mournful than others.

Mumblers sounded less truthful than articulators, men sounded more convinced than women. "Voices mislead," she told us. "And your client can do nothing about it. Not just voices, either." Her lacquered hairdo tacked around as she eyed us each in turn. "A comely, heart-shaped face appears less desperate, does it not, than a face shaped more like a water bucket? Crossed arms might signify defensiveness, or it might be that your boiler's on the fritz." She lifted one powerful finger — her own body language tended relentlessly toward clarity. "Discipline yourselves," she warned, "to hear the actual *words.* Difficult, yes, which is why most of us would rather throw our energy into guessing why our client's picking lint off his collar. Until you learn to *listen* — and judging from these slaphappy summaries you've got a ways to travel — the transcript is your best shot at the truth, and your client's best shot at being heard."

We understood that our training would be inadequate; that experience would be a slow and ruthless teacher; that we would fail a few souls, maybe even ruin them, before training turned into skill. "Fuzzyboy" was Talbot's name for those of us so eager to help that we defined problems in advance and heard only what we needed to fill in the right blanks.

As I sat in my car, turning the pages, my teeth gritting and ungritting, it occurred to me that Ms. Costigan might have attended my same graduate program. One of Talbot's Fuzzyboys, Ms. Costigan was off to the rescue, a nine-year-old girl lashed to the tracks. A child who has never seen a naked man answers "yes" to a question that fuels the train, thinking of the cold she had when she was eight, the Vicks VapoRub her uncle massaged into her chest, the baths he gave her when she was three and four years old. She has been instructed to tell the truth, yes or no. This child raised on the Ten Commandments follows the directions exactly. Listen to the kid, Talbot would say. She wants to know where her uncle is. She is afraid of you.

As I turned the last page, however, I felt all of my training drain away in the bright wash of afternoon. A transcript was nothing but words on a page. I wanted to *see*. To *hear*. I could easily picture Mrs. Hanson's expression as she told her first story, for I had seen firsthand the shocked collapse of her chin when she found me, innocently abed, on that April morning after a nightmare. But the second tale, of a wanton girl in a white-and-red nightgown, provocative noises behind a closed door—this is the story I wished I could see on her face, this preposterous lie. Were her thin lips sweating with shame?

Most of all, I wanted to see and hear my uncle, to find in him the thing that held him back. Did his glasses fog slightly, as they did when he felt angry or greatly moved? Did his hands drum anxiously on his thighs as if looking for the comfort of his cats? Did he for an instant believe I'd said those things to the caseworker? Why did he not rise up and knock over the tables, like Jesus in the temple?

Words first. Read the words.

I'm afraid so.

I'm afraid not.

I'm afraid I can't.

Black and white. He's afraid.

Worn out and near tears, I started the car. The park was empty, nothing but a few prospecting crows silhouetted against the waning afternoon light. My teeth chattered; I'd been sitting too long in the chill. December was a day away, but only now did winter seem possible. Where the park road drained onto the boulevard, I flicked the left-turn signal—I was heading home, of course home, where else but home?—but as I waited for a break in traffic, the sun dropped behind the cove, which glittered with water and birds. I turned right instead of left, drawn cityward, recalling the radiance of my childhood river. Father Mike seemed close indeed, such that any water became that water, any man became that man.

Harry's lights were on. I ascended the knotted stairs, desperate to lay eyes on someone who recognized me. Before I could knock, the door swung open, revealing a woman clutching two lumpy paper bags.

"Elaine," I said, astonished, recognizing the daughter from the photograph. In person she looked a little older, though less fierce. Soft, in fact. Born tired.

"Do I know you?" she asked.

"Your picture's on the wall."

She looked me over for several unnerving seconds, then stepped outside the hallway. "He shows everybody my picture." She had a key ring looped around one finger and was trying to lock up with part of one free hand. "What do you want?" she asked, unable to aim the key with her arms encumbered. Finally she sighed, dumping the bags on the floor. They made a puff of noise: clothes.

"I was looking for your father."

"Then you're out of luck." She gave the deadbolt a few tries, then jammed the key into the doorknob. "I don't know why he locks up," she says. "He owns squat."

"Where is he?" I asked.

"Drying out." The lock caught. "You Loreen's daughter?"

I shook my head.

Her gaze, fretful and discomfiting, washed hotly over me. "Natalie's, then?"

"No," I said.

"Serena's?"

I shook my head again, distressed to find him gone, shocked at my disappointment.

"Then I'm out of guesses," Elaine said. "If you want to see him you'll have to wait another twenty-six days. They don't allow visitors in the booze barn." She scooped up the bags again. "These get dropped off at the front desk."

I stood in the grimy hallway, digesting this. Though she was holding the bags and the keys and had her coat on, I didn't get the impression she was in a hurry. "Did you reconcile?" I asked.

"Reconcile?"

"With your father. I was told you hadn't spoken in years."

"He loves that story." Her eyes lingered over my creased eyebrow, and the remaining speckles of road rash that still marred one cheek. "Oh my God, you're the one from the accident."

I didn't say anything.

"According to him, you died and came back."

"I'm fine now."

"All's well that ends well, huh? Have you really been coming here to visit him?"

I nodded, reassessing my impression of her as a creampuff.

"I'll be damned," she said. "He was telling the truth for once in his life." She chuckled softly, a staccato muttering. "He leaves you for dead and now you're bosom buddies. I don't know what it is about the guy. Women are so desperate."

"I'm not desperate," I said, though I suppose I was.

"Sorry," she said, "long day. Look, you want to sit for a second? You don't look so good."

I waited as she fumbled again with the keys and opened the door. I followed her in. The place looked ransacked: empty liquor bottles lining the sticky windowsills, the new tweed rocker grotesquely stained on the seat, broken glass scattered like spilled ice cubes, the funk of unwashed body and softening fruit emanating from the pores of the place.

"I thought this only happened in movies," I said. Even Ray Blanchard had never left this kind of trail.

"The movie of my life," she said. "You want water? I might be able to find a glass that doesn't have fur growing on it."

"I'm fine. Really." I glanced around. "Looks like he really tied one on." I had a flash of sympathy for Andrea Harmon; it was a wonder she ever made it to school at all.

"In the old days I would've cleaned up," Elaine said. "I'm down to the bare minimum now. It's like my own personal twelve-step program. Two more steps, maybe, and I can stop picking up the phone."

There was nowhere clean to sit. "So, what'd he do," she said, "give you the old sorry-deah?"

I didn't know what to say. "How's your baby?" I asked her, hoping to change the subject quickly and then get the hell out of there.

"Beautiful," she said. "Thank you for asking."

"When did he, when did he tell you about me?"

"Let's see . . . July, I guess. He was fresh out of rehab after the mother of all benders, not counting this one. The booze barn usually fills him with the fear of God after twenty-eight days of trust-in-a-higher-power bullshit. He goes all soft and religious. But this time, instead of true confessions, which I definitely do *not* want to hear, he's got a doozy of a story about snatching some poor girl from the jaws of death and asking nothing in return."

"It's not a story," I said.

She blinked at me a few times. "You're saying what? That he actually saved your life?"

"You could look at it that way."

Her eyes widened, and remained flung open. *"You* could, maybe. My father's managed to keep his pathetic life cobbled together by the misguided graces of people who think like you."

I said nothing, feeling small and silly, resenting her for being so much better versed in the methods of certain men.

"I can't believe he just left you there," she said, her voice softer now. "Correction. I *can* believe he just left you there. That's what he does. I bet he swore he wasn't drinking." When I didn't answer, she added, "Well, you're entitled to believe what you want. Obviously you're new at this."

"He did call an ambulance," I said, feeling defensive — on my own behalf or Harry's, I wasn't sure. "He moved me off the road."

"Oh, yes, I know, the passing motorist," she said. "That's my father, all right. The passing motorist."

"He didn't have to stop," I said. "The kid who hit me certainly didn't."

"Let me tell you something about my father." She touched me briefly on the arm. "If he'd been the one who hit you? He wouldn't have stopped."

"That's a terrible thing to say about a person."

"The voice of experience, believe me." She rested her eyes on me and I felt judged. "My father doesn't give a dime about anyone. He can't remember my daughter's name for more than a couple of days at a time."

For a few minutes we breathed the fetid air of Harry's apartment.

"What *is* your daughter's name?" I asked her.

Her face changed utterly. "Anna Kate. Isn't that gorgeous?"

"It is," I agreed. "He was on his way to see you that night. You knew that, right?"

She nodded. "I figured he was drinking, or else his car broke down. Or both. When he finally called again, the body in the road sounded like another one of his ridiculous excuses. But I checked the papers. Lo and behold. Of course, in his version he drove you to the hospital."

"You don't seem much like him," I said, though in fact they possessed the same jittery energy.

She coughed up an unhappy splat of laughter. "Thank you very, very, very much. I'm like my mother, thank God, who was pretty much perfect if you don't count her one obvious mistake. If she'd lived long enough to marry again, I wouldn't have to be here at all." She snapped her eyes away. "Look," she said, "I've got to go. I left my baby with a sitter."

"Is your husband—" I began, hoping to find him downstairs in a parked car. I wanted to lay eyes on the sort of man this sort of woman had finally settled upon.

"Hubby flew the coop," she said. "I don't do so great with men, big surprise." She rattled the keys and led me out the door. "I bet I'm the only woman on Earth who doesn't enjoy falling in love. The feeling doesn't suit me." She paused. "Except with my daughter. I'm mad about her."

"I don't understand what you're doing here."

She yanked on the doorknob and turned the key. "He checked himself in, but no clothes. They give you one phone call, like in jail."

"I meant *why* are you here? If you hate him so much, if he can't even remember your baby's name, what are you doing here?" I really wanted to know.

"I never said I hated him." Her face changed again, her large eyes welling. "Every single time, I swear to myself, This is it. The end. But it never is."

I walked her downstairs. She let me help her put the bags in the trunk, a deflated plaid shirtsleeve dangling out of one, a folded pair of pants topping the other. "Good luck," I said.

She was harder to read now, for the light was vanishing in that quick way of late fall. "He told me you're looking for your father," she said.

"It's a long story."

"Save yourself the heartache." She got into the car. "You know why my father's so keen on you? You're the only woman he ever touched who ended up better off." She looked at me for another moment, then pulled her seatbelt across her chest.

I suppose I should have been angry at Harry Griggs for seducing my sympathies with his accent, his shabby coat, his Fig Newtons and Gatorade, his fatherly pantomime. But watching his daughter drive off with a sackful of clothes, I could only wonder at the human animal's insistence on stitching one life to another's with the flimsiest of thread. My uncle had been torn from me once, and now it seemed a repair was possible. Stitching had been my first skill, and I believed I could do it again. Crimp, thread, pull.

TWENTY-FOUR

Father Mike once lost Boo for a single frantic week in which we scoured the house, the cellar, the yard and the river, calling and calling, bereft and hopeless, thinking *drowned, shot, grabbed by coyotes.* Finally the choir director discovered Boo, alive, trapped in the church-hall basement. *He was there the whole time,* Father Mike muttered for days, inconsolable. *He was there the whole time,* which I took to mean that finding Boo swiftly dead of natural causes would have brought Father Mike less pain.

Now he himself was by all indications alive somewhere; not eight months ago I had opened my eyes and beheld him. *He was there the whole time.* But it was my aunt, not my uncle, on whom I dropped the tonnage of my accreting anger. Celie Barrett had looked into a child's face and told her a heartwrecking lie. *He was there the whole time.* Toward Father Mike himself I could muster nothing but fresh grief. As I drove home, I kept one hand on the file next to me, and the ride became a rite of sorts—the humming car, the unfolding road, the two of us together again.

Drew met me at the door. "Well?" he asked. "Did you get to see the bishop?"

"Chancellor. He's alive."

"The chancellor?" Drew said, bewildered.

Mariette and Charlie materialized behind him, Paulie jumping in place and hollering "Surprise! Surprise! Surprise! Surprise!" But it was only noise; I rifled through my address book, located the number, and seized the living-room phone. She picked up on the sixth ring.

"Where is he?" I demanded.

"What?" my aunt said thickly. I'd woken her from a nap. Once a year I called her on her birthday, which fell in February, a day after mine. A few awkward minutes, pause, thank you, good-bye. She'd managed a single visit after my accident, but I'd scared her with my ghost story.

"It's me, Celie. Where is he?"

I heard a rustling. Probably she was putting in her teeth. "What time is it?"

"High time. That's what time it is."

"Surprise!" Paulie was shouting. "Surprise! Surprise! Surprise!" Mariette was shushing him, trying to listen.

"We never went to a funeral," I said to my aunt. "His death was something *told* to me. It was nothing but *words.*"

"Is this about all that foolishness at the hospital? Are you still on that?"

"I'm still on that. The nerve of me."

"Why on Earth would I take you to that man's funeral?"

"Are you listening to me, Celie?" I said, louder now. "I've just seen the church records. I have them in my hand." I expected capitulation, confession, maybe even apology, and got nothing but silence.

"Where is he, Celie?"

Where is he where is he where is he where is he where is he? Nothing.

I imagined her sitting on the side of her bed, pitiful and

curled-in and old, and I would have been happy to smite her on the spot if such a thing were possible.

Her voice returned, disarmingly gentle. "You think it was easy to take in a child who'd been — disgraced — the way you were? I could have done better by you. But I had five boys, Lizzy. They were *boys.* Boys, they get ideas. And you pining over that man morning noon and night. Listen to me. For once, please, just listen. You grew up saying white was black and black was white. You're well out of it now. He's gone. Let him *be.*"

"Where did he *go,* Celie?"

"How should I know? I haven't the faintest idea."

My anger fully ignited then, a crimson, blistering rage. "If you don't tell me, Celie, I'll come down there and *make* you."

Charlie and Mariette were murmuring to each other, a worried hum.

"Come on," Drew was saying, "Lizzy. Hey."

Celie tried to wait me out, but I was better at waiting.

"They made a *law,*" she said finally. "People like that aren't allowed near children. They're coming out of the woodwork these days, every day another one in the paper. All these children misused by sick, sick men. If I ever had a shred of doubt, which I *didn't,* then I certainly don't have one now."

"Where is he?"

"Dead, I hope!" she shouted back, giving as good as she got. "Dead of shame! And if he's alive, you ask yourself, you *ask* yourself, young lady, if he had nothing to hide, if he was so innocent, why didn't he ever come back?"

From time to time since the accident I got a painful jolt that I attributed to a minuscule shift in hardware, a screw rubbing lightly against tissue, a minor discomposure in the way I'd been put back together. At this moment, violently and without warning, all the hardware in my body seemed to convulse. "Shut up!" I shrieked at her, clobbered by physical pain. "Shut up! Shut up! Shut up!"

"Lizzy, stop," Drew said, "that's enough." But I didn't stop. I kept shouting until Drew finally wrested the phone from my hands. Paulie had run to his mother and tunneled into her midsection. Charlie spirited him to the kitchen where I could hear him howling, afraid. Of me.

I leaned against the wall, panting. Drew took the phone and talked to my aunt. Charlie reemerged with Paulie, who was smashing the remains of an Oreo into his red bow mouth.

It was then I saw it, sidling out from behind the couch. A cat. I had to look twice, a cartoon double-take. A cat in my house, beelining toward me as full of purpose as if we were wounded soldiers who had followed separate, perilous paths to the same destination. The rest of the room appeared to me then in surreal stages, a picture developing in the chemical bath of my own head. Chair. Window. Husband on phone. Friends mute and staring. Cat trotting toward me.

Stacked on the floor were feline accoutrements better suited to a cheetah than a housecat: a drum of cat litter, a stuffed mouse the size of a breadbox, a bushel or two of dry cat food and several towers of canned.

"What is this?" I asked, stupidly.

"Drew got him at the shelter," Mariette said. "Lizzy, is this really—? He's alive?"

"Surprise! Surprise! Surprise!" Paulie shouted, tiny teeth bared in ecstasy, both feet smashing hard on the carpet. "Surprise, Auntie!"

It was not a very pretty cat, a faded, patchwork creature reminiscent of a much-washed dishtowel that had been left too long in the spin cycle. Paulie was now beside himself, cheeks aflame. "Hahahahaha!" he shouted, lobbing himself into my legs and haha-ing wetly into my knees. Then he pitched back into the room, kidnapped the stuffed mouse, and tossed it over his head. The cat just sat there.

Drew hung up the phone, his expression cemented into the grim square that since the accident had more or less become the permanent shape of his face. "God," he said, crossing the room toward us. He cupped my face, drawing his fingers over the tender side, then folded me into a hug.

"It's true?" Mariette asked him.

"Yeah," Drew said. "Celie made it up."

Charlie's eyes welled. "She told a kid with no parents that her uncle died of a heart attack? Why?"

"To shut me up," I said. "Grief gets so annoying."

Mariette regarded me with something close to awe. She, too, had mourned my uncle, at a time when her father had gone missing and she was mourning him, too. Now, a resurrection. All at once I felt as if I'd just entered familiar territory after a sojourn in a faraway land where nobody knew me. The cat, lulled by the drop in our voices, squinted approvingly. "He's beautiful, Drew," I said. "You picked a good one." I scooped it up. The thing weighed nothing, apparently one of the boneless variety that suffered endless lugging around by children and old ladies and shaped to whatever vessel it happened to land in.

"It's a present," Drew said. "I figured you were in for a long day."

Paulie was back, clutching the stuffed mouse, eyes snapping with light, face aquiver. "What's the kitty's name?" he asked, trying to match his voice to ours and coming up with a hammy stage whisper.

"Here's the thing, my man," Drew said. "We've got ourselves a little problem."

"Uh-oh."

"Exactly. Some little granny-type named him Peachy. I would've taken the one named Boris. This one's ten years old with no prospects. I figured he could use a guidance counselor."

"Did she die?" I asked.

"Who?"

"The granny-type."

"Oh. Jeez, I guess she must've."

Mariette petted the cat's narrow face. "He looks something like Mittens," she said.

Celie couldn't take the bachelors. Instead they'd been separated into parish homes by Mrs. Blanchard, who also couldn't take them, on account of Major's terror of felines. Before my enrollment at Sacred Heart, I spent weeks languishing in Celie's boy-smelling house, speaking to no one, praying that whoever took the cats had thought to ask what they liked to eat, each of them spleeny and spoiled rotten in separate ways. I spent the rest of my ninth year and most of my tenth worrying myself sick over the cats, unable to bear the thought of them sitting in separate windows, befuddled by new names.

"So," Charlie said slowly, like one of Mariette's worst students trying to memorize an impenetrable formula, "he could—be out there? Now? Alive someplace?"

"Could be," Drew said. "Probably is."

"They didn't direct you to the gravesite?" Charlie asked. The question didn't surprise me. Working with teenagers had taught me to expect people to accommodate shocking news in something other than chronological order.

"There's no gravesite," I said. "There was no death." Four words. We fell silent at the sound of them.

There was no death.

"Is she all right?" asked Charlie, whose version of the world, though expansive in its way—he expected his line workers to look back on their McDonald's experience as the birth of ambition—did not easily take in a sudden reversal of the received truth.

I had foundered into the double chair and curled up with the cat, vowing to make this animal glad his old mistress had died. Paulie came over to inspect me, and attached a humid kiss to my forearm.

"Thanks, my little man."

"She's all right," Drew said. "You're all right, aren't you, Lizzy?"

"Auntie? Auntie?" Paulie crooned. "All right now?"

"Yeah," I assured him. "Happy tears." The cat smelled of medicine and animal shelter but would soon smell like us. It relaxed into the destination of my arms, its purring as fulsome as an acceptance speech. I guessed its age to be closer to twenty than ten. Maybe Drew misheard them. Maybe they lied. It loved me already.

Paulie grinned his rubber-man grin. "He's *loud.*"

"We'll have to do something about the name," Drew said. "I mean, he's a *guy.*"

I tipped the cat's face to see it better. It stared at me benignly. "We could call him Mr. Peachy, maybe."

Paulie hurled himself to the floor and cycled his legs into the air, this is how hilarious he thought we were.

"I'm switching him to decaf," Mariette said.

"Hahahahahahaha!"

I looked up. "Thank you, Drew."

Drew smiled, appearing suddenly older, radiating crinkles showing around his eyes. When had that happened? Charlie, too, already possessed the earnest frown lines of a franchise owner. Paulie, on the other hand, had the complexion of a snowfall, nothing in his face but unblemished jollity and applause.

Mariette kissed the top of my head. "We've got to get him home before he implodes. I don't know what to say, Lizzy. Can I tell my mother? She'll want to know."

"Go ahead. It's not a secret."

"My God," Mariette marveled, "she'll die when she hears this."

Charlie scooped up Paulie—upside down, so that by the time Paulie was done laughing he'd be strapped into his car seat, thoroughly outwitted. Their sounds left me in stages, and then there I was, left alone with my husband and this restful purring.

"Alive," I whispered. "Drew, imagine."

His jaw was working fervently, as it did when he was trying to solve a problem. "Celie said he was barred from contact. Why would he agree to something like that?"

"To shield me, I think. A child-protective investigation is no pretty thing." A decision worthy of Solomon, I realized; Solomon would have restored me on the spot to the parent who refused to chop me in half. "You can read the transcripts for yourself," I said. "I stole them on my way out of the chancellor's office."

He got up, put his hands in his pockets, and stared down at me. When had he lost weight? Had I done this to him? "You stole them," he said evenly. "Okay. Where are they?"

I got up, laying the cat gently on the chair, and retrieved the file. Drew leafed through it, frowning. He led me into the kitchen, where we turned on lights and cleared the table and I made us something to eat as Drew set to reading. The cat hopped onto one of the kitchen chairs, apparently pleased with his new digs. Every once in a while Drew would read a sentence or two aloud—*I never called her a liar; I said she was mistaken*—to signal how far he had read and what struck him as especially significant. I felt curiously content, considering the circumstances, for this is exactly how we used to be in our beginning, hanging around his apartment on a Sunday morning with the *Globe* spread out in sections, reading snippets to each other and building unlikely intersections out of our thoughts. Back then, this seemed like the apex of romance.

At last he closed the folder and looked at me. "What the hell was going on here?"

"I thought the woman was some poor stupid thing who had *forgotten* to dress her dolls," I said. "I had no idea what she was getting at. Of course he touched me. I was a baby when I first got there. How do you not touch a baby? He had to tend me when I was sick, or filthy, or hurt. I had bad dreams—where else would I go? What was he supposed to do, throw me out the window?"

"This isn't your fault," Drew said, and my eyes welled up, because of course I'd been thinking exactly the opposite.

"If you'd screamed up and down that he never touched you at all, ever, they would have said you were protecting him, or repressing it. Something."

"That's exactly how I read it, Drew. I had no power over their good intentions."

"Something's off, though," he said. He tapped the folder. "On his end of things."

"Something," I conceded.

"He makes himself sound so guilty." Drew's gray eyes—trimmed with the wet-looking eyelashes I had always loved—narrowed with calculation. "It's like he's measuring the words, you know? Why not just deny it to the hilt?"

"I have no idea," I said. "All I know for sure are two things. He loved me. And he loved being a priest."

"He's hiding something, though. That's why they don't believe him."

"It's not what they think he's hiding. That's the third thing I know for sure."

"Whatever it is, it can't be worse than people thinking he's a child molester."

"Then what is it? I turned twenty-one nine years ago. Where has he been?" I felt the hot-splashing tears of a child. "Did he just—forget?"

At this point, Drew could have said, *I guess we'll never know.* He could have said, *You have to take this file back.* He could have said, *Are you sure your memory isn't playing tricks, Lizzy? Is it possible you've forgotten something?*

Instead, he said, "He didn't forget. He was in your hospital room."

This, as it turned out, was the actual apex of romance. To be absolutely believed.

"Maybe Celie really does know where he is," Drew suggested. "She might have called after the accident, out of pity. Or else he's been watching you somehow, this whole time. Nearer than you think." With his long, tender fingers he wiped my wet cheeks. "I'm sorry I didn't believe you."

I fell weak with love and was stunned to feel it, awash with the sudden animation in my own body. It struck me then— *struck* is the right word, too—that a certain richness might be returning with the knowledge, however mystifying, that Father Mike lived in the world somewhere. Everything around me took on a solidity that I associated with childhood, those nine and a half years in which every object seemed permanently earthbound, three-dimensional, as fixed and lasting and unassailable as museum objects displayed under glass. Thirty spice jars reposing fat and aromatic on the kitchen shelves. The fire of Father Mike's tiger's-eye ring as he nails a page with his finger, marking our place in a book that smells of must from my mother's breakfront. All these moments and objects, and days and years, dense with substance.

Everything after that felt almost airy in its inconsequence. Twenty-one years—that long pause—had accumulated so little weight.

"Lizzy," Drew whispered. "Come upstairs."

A good healer, my doctors called me. Amazing. Resilient. Plucky as hell.

I held my husband, who was no expert at healing. Tamping his body with the pads of my fingers, I craved imperfection, yearning to feel every snag and fissure straight through the feeble sheath of his skin. By contrast, I felt anointed—because, of course, I had been. Father Mike had found me in my needful hour and anointed me.

The cat trailed us and hopped onto the bed, treading the coverlet in a tight circle, claiming a space at the foot. Drew and I took up the rest.

We moved languidly beneath the covers. At one point he rested his hand on my forehead as if I were a child with fever, and it struck me that any one form of love borrowed from all the others. Love comprised thirst and quench, pain and repose, mystery and recognition, lust and purity, the ingredients shifting, more slightly than we might think, depending on the object of our affection. In this bed, with this man, at this moment, the formula found its ideal: equal amounts of everything, generously flowing.

"Is this all right?" Drew murmured, petting me gently.

I felt the way I had back in Boston in our early days, a slow fire burning up through my limbs into my center, where nothing existed but sensation and release and a shameless, idiotic joy.

I expected to enter a bloomy stupor that would last beyond the morning's first alarm, but instead thudded awake around five-thirty, coiled and scared. It was Friday, and in two hours I was due at school. Mr. Peachy arrived at my elbow and began to knead on my arm. His former mistress had had him declawed, I was dismayed to discover. "Poor thing," I whispered. He tucked into the crook of my arm and collapsed asleep; Drew stirred but did not wake.

I wanted that long pause back. Twenty-one weightless years. Two hundred and fifty-two months, went my furious calculations. More than seven thousand days. Almost two hundred thousand hours. More than ten million minutes. Two-thirds of my life, hovering in the blue distance like a let-go balloon. I lay back in the dark, and when I woke again the covers had been tucked under my chin and Drew was gone. I found him downstairs in the kitchen. He shot me a tentative look, a half smile, the morning-after glance of a man who'd been taken home by a stranger and wasn't sure now where he stood.

My first feelings for him had arrived much as they did now, as a kind of homesickness. Isn't that what the first blush of love is, a thirst for your true home, the ancestral place you've been dithering toward, unbeknownst? *I can't believe I found you!* Desire and enchantment, naive tallies of shared passions *(Me, too, I like Saul Bellow, too! Yes, and folk music! Oh my God, gambrel roofs! Helicopters! Dobermans!)*, that perpetual aha.

"I feel as if I've been someplace else for a really long time," I said from the kitchen doorway. "It's like a waiting room. You kind of float there, waiting for your name to be called."

Drew was seated, unmoving, his face still morning-squinched and blinky. "*I* called your name, Lizzy," he said.

Our kitchen that morning radiated a comforting heat. "Can I tell you a secret?" I asked him. I, too, felt shy.

"I hope so."

"When we got married I thought of myself as your helpmate. Something old-fashioned and worthy like that. I had this ridiculous idea that you needed me to freshen up your worldview."

His look was warm. "I did need you to freshen up my worldview."

There was a tingling moment of recognition that we were each referring to the same thing—the photos from his Boston days, print after print of smashed storefronts and car wrecks, anguished widows and bawling orphans. He'd shown them to me after our first date. These were his "work." The brides and babies and ninety-year-old birthday girls—these he called his "Kodaks." *I give it eight months,* he was fond of saying, unloading his gear after a hoop-skirt wedding. He scorned his Kodak subjects because, I believe, he envied these beaming families, he who called his mother but once a year. Despite the evidence of human misery tacked all over his walls, he'd been a bringer of flowers, a candy-and-wine guy.

"How'd I do?" I asked. "Freshening up your worldview, I mean."

He shrugged. "Not so great. But I'm thinking maybe we could start over from here."

His voice caught on the words *start over,* as if it pained him to acknowledge that our marriage had ended without our permission and we'd wound up in the position to have to begin afresh.

It was only then I noticed what he had been doing at the table: sorting proofs. The pictures were from the wedding he'd shot a few weeks earlier — often he chose a souvenir from a shoot for his personal gallery, something that resembled his "work" more than his "Kodaks." The bride and groom were teenagers, yet their stormless faces shone with a certainty more common to elderly couples for whom vigilance has become irrelevant to happiness. In the picture Drew had separated out from the rest, the bride and groom, two dimpled Italian kids, faced the camera square on, their hands twined, rings glimmering. What struck me about this choice was its lack of guile, an absence of irony that bespoke more of the photographer than his subject. A straight-on shot of confident, cornball joy.

I was still in the doorway. We seemed to require this physical distance after the intimacy of the night before. "I stopped in on Harry Griggs after I left the Chancery," I said. "I thought you should know."

"Okay. So I know."

"He was out. But whatever those visits were for, Drew, they've run their course."

"It kind of felt like you threw me over. I don't care that he's sixty years old."

"It wasn't what you think."

"I wasn't listening, and he was. That's what I think."

After a moment, I said, "Is that all she was to you? Someone to listen?"

"I'm a man, Lizzy. There's always more."

The silence that followed seemed like a forbearing one, doleful as it was; it did feel like a beginning. I went to the counter to pour some coffee, drawing my hand across my husband's shoulders as I passed his chair. Outside a breeze stirred across the yard, rattling the spent stalks of daylilies I'd first planted with Mariette on the day Drew and I moved in. *Grasping at straws,* I thought when I saw them. I stared out at the drained light that comes between fall and winter; every so often I'd hear Drew pick up his coffee cup, then put it down.

I made a brief inventory of our sideboard: four mismatched crocks holding wooden spoons and spatulas and broken chopsticks, a flower pot spilling over with ancient receipts, a set of candlesticks from Mariette's mother, dishtowels and stamps and two bottles of wine and a set of Tupperware still encased in plastic. I touched each thing in turn, and they in turn touched me with something akin to pity. "Look at this, Drew," I said. I heard his chair scrape back. "Look how we've crammed this place with stuff. Do you think maybe we did this to make it harder to leave?"

"I thought we were just bad housekeepers."

"Look at all this effort, though. How hard we were trying. The whole time we were fighting about Boston and feeling miserable and blaming each other, we were filling up this house as a kind of insurance policy. It would take a really long time and a thousand packing boxes to leave this place."

"Maybe so," he said.

"Drew, I don't know how to begin looking for him." I meant to say that I had lost two essential men, my first love and my last; I didn't have the heart to look for one until I found my way back to the other. "Maybe I don't want to know why he didn't come back. Maybe it was just—easier—for him to stay gone."

"Lizzy," Drew said.

"What?"

"Don't leave me."

I whirled around.

He said, "You think I don't know you've been furious?"

He said, "You forgive the ones who leave, and you blame the ones who stay."

He said, "I stayed."

I lifted my arms. He crossed the room and collapsed against me. It was my turn to hold him up. So I did, rocking him a little: my husband, my sweetheart, my injured one.

TWENTY-FIVE

My uncle now lived in the world someplace, but it was Drew I
moved toward.

I took the day off. Good, excellent, Rick said, take all the
time you need, nothing ever happens on Fridays. Drew canceled
two portraits, and because it was the first day of December —
drought season for weddings — he had no brides to immortalize
over the weekend. We unplugged the phone, feeling like fugitives
holing up for the duration. I felt willing, even glad, to drop out
of the stream of hours for a while, to let my life go on without
me. To pause again, but on purpose. *With* purpose.

By Saturday afternoon we'd lost any sense of routine,
eating at odd hours, sleeping when we felt like it. We watched
some television — sitcoms and game shows and animal docu-
mentaries — and dug into Drew's store of old movies. We ate
meat. We played Scrabble. We made a chocolate-meringue cake,
the blind leading the blind, that required six separated eggs and
a double boiler. We made a stew with beets and potatoes and a
pound of beef. We made love. We made a bubble of time.

"We're on vacation," Drew said.

"How do you like it?" I put the cake in the oven. It was one in the morning, between Saturday and Sunday. We'd done our sleeping in the afternoon.

"I feel stranded," he said. "Like in a mountain cabin after an avalanche."

I licked the spoon. "We've got cake. Stranded people eat tree bark."

"I've never been stranded before," he said. Which, metaphorically speaking, was not true. "How about you, Lizzy? How do you like it?"

"Actually, it feels just like rehab. Except it doesn't hurt."

Drew said, "Maybe he was afraid if he came back you'd hate him for leaving you in the first place."

All weekend it had gone like this, Father Mike popping in and out of our ongoing conversation, seemingly at random. "I wouldn't have hated him," I said. "If he'd shown up, say, at my college graduation, I would have been so happy."

"What about now?"

I'd been happy to see him in the hospital — I could still conjure that feeling of revelation — but then I'd believed he was speaking to me from an unreachable place. "I'm not sure," I said. "Just knowing he's out there is so — jarring — that it's kind of hard to imagine the next step."

"You don't have to start looking right away."

Where is he where is he where is he where is he where is he?

"It's entirely possible," I said, "that he died anyway, that it really was a figment I saw, or a hallucination, and that sometime between back then and now his heart gave out after all. Do I want to know that?"

"If it were me? I'd want to know." He'd been whipping frosting in a bowl, and now set it aside to paw through the Yellow Pages. I peered over his shoulder at two columns of names under the heading "Investigators."

"Wow," I said. "Who is everybody looking for?"

"Makes you wonder," he said. "Do you want to call one of these guys?"

I shook my head, tears welling, bludgeoned by the notion of Father Mike in an actual *place*—not in the chiffony anywhere of Earth, but in the bordered somewhere of Denver. Chicago. Honolulu. Marseilles. For the moment I preferred my uncle in his half-imagined state, the specter who had appeared to me in my hour of need.

We ate our cake on the living room floor and watched another movie, a depressing, handsomely shot indie film in which the six windburned sons of an Italian patriarch sleep with each other's wives and ruin the family winery before expiring one by one in the Second World War.

"The point?" I asked, which is what I used to ask.

"Of life?"

"Of the movie."

"Oh, that," Drew said, lying back on a heap of cushions and easing me down with him. "It's a rotten world."

"That's the point?"

"That's always the point," he said. "Why else do you think people watch these things? To confirm their core beliefs."

We lay there a moment, fingers twined. "It isn't a rotten world," I said.

"Actually," Drew said, "it is. What with war and famine and jerks at intersections." He kissed my temple. "You didn't like the movie?"

"Which part? The pretentious story line or the zombie acting?"

"That long vineyard shot at the end was something. They filmed it in black-and-white, then colorized it afterwards."

"Really? They did?"

"It was subtle, my friend. Not for the casual observer."

He blushed a little then, having inadvertently let slip his desire to become a cinematographer, a secret he'd confided when we first married but hadn't mentioned even obliquely in quite some time. Not to me, at least. Maybe he told the woman at the wedding as she canted her heart-shaped face and pursed her engorged lips and bestowed upon him the grace of being seen.

"That one shot was worth the whole price," he said.

When we were first together and going to a lot of movies and art openings and makeshift theater productions of Beckett and Ionesco — when we were, in other words, courting each other by borrowing from lives whose darkness appeared artful and therefore necessary — Drew always salvaged something that was worth the whole price. A brush-shaped paint stain on the artist's leather skirt. A hummable, apologetic soundtrack behind the final credits. The toupee tilting off Estragon's existential head at curtain call.

I sat up. "My God. Drew Mitchell, you're an optimist."

"Am not. *You* are."

"Ninety minutes of the film equivalent of gall-bladder surgery and you think forty seconds of camera voodoo is worth — what did you pay for this thing? Twenty bucks?"

"*You* work with teenagers," he countered. "On *purpose*."

"There's that," I said, thoroughly trumped. "Touché."

Our house, at that wee-morning hour, felt still and shuttered. There was something reminiscent about the turn our conversation had taken. We used to argue all the time about things like the relative rottenness of the world. Good arguing, I mean; not the kind of arguing that started after a couple of years in Hinton.

"This reminds me of Boston," I said softly.

He smiled. "Boston's a fine town."

I gave Drew a haircut. He painted my toenails. Like two animals from the same pack keeping tabs on each other by smell, we padded around the house, sitting in all the chairs and lying on all the beds and handling each other's things. Sometime before dawn Drew crumpled candy wrappers into balls and tried to teach the cat to fetch, which made me laugh, and then Drew laughed, too, really hard. Clouds parting, water giving way, fences collapsing, such a sound. We looked at each other, startled, a little ashamed. How had we gone so long without laughing like this?

At sunup we unearthed Drew's photographs. His "work," that is. We propped them against books and lamps and windows, arranged them into groupings on the floor, and sat in the double chair, surrounded by all manner of human misery. A drunk tottering out of a wrecked Corvette. A second-grader being loaded into a strobing medi-van. A woman in a bathrobe embracing a two-hundred-year-old chestnut tree as its companion tree falls under a chain saw. Drew had caught these people, every single one, at the exact moment when Before becomes After.

"My worldview definitely needed some freshening up," Drew said, surveying the photos.

I put my legs over his legs. "No," I said. "I was wrong." These bruised people shored me up, and I wanted them near me, not because misery loved company but because the business of human striving felt common to us all. In this was the presence of God.

Well. I had married a religious man. Here was news.

In all, we lost three days. Or, found three days.

We hardly slept, and when we did sleep, one of us would wake every so often, and, in the manner of the woman and her chestnut tree, embrace the other as the last tree standing.

On Sunday, midmorning, I said, "I bet there's still a ten-thirty at St. Bart's."

His eyebrows lifted. "Mass? Seriously?"

"I want to see the church again. The inside, I mean. It wouldn't kill either one of us to say a prayer."

A week earlier he would have talked me out of it. He would have looked at me funny. Now, he shrugged on his coat, saying, "Next stop, the distant past."

It had snowed a little overnight, the first snow of the season, a weak sheen that nevertheless rendered the morning as a white light that had to be blinked back. Already the snow was melting away; we didn't even need a shovel. We had reached the end of a season of benevolent weather that had not yet yielded a deep frost.

Standing on the porch, I squinted into the daylight. "Where have we been?"

"Staying married, I hope," Drew said. Our sequester finally over, we escorted each other to the car, entwined. Our town seemed deserted and coiled in that Sunday way that never changes. Inside the car, I felt protected from the outside quiet and its intimation of something about to spring.

"I wonder if it might have been a relief for him to land in Baltimore," I said. "Maybe it felt a little like this. Everything on hold."

"Maybe," Drew said, easing the car into the street. "People take comfort from the damnedest things."

What had it felt like, wearing a cotton bathrobe and terrycloth slippers, eating three squares a day on a Formica tray, shuffling downstairs for individual therapy in the morning, group in the afternoon, at night sitting around with other damaged clergymen watching reruns of *The Mary Tyler Moore Show*? A nervous breakdown, the bishop called it, but I preferred the notion of suspended animation, found time, a reprieve of the sort you might get in jail or at boarding school or inside a forty-three-hour sleep or during an isolated weekend with your husband of five years, a stop-time in which you cease trying to connect the before and the after, because in fact you are balanced on the point of connection. All weekend I had thought of my uncle this way, precariously balanced, a form of suspension that a growing part of me felt loath to disturb.

Drew steered us through town, driving slowly. "Hey, isn't that whatshername?"

So it was. Andrea Harmon, strolling past Hinton Variety, squashed against Glen Seavey like a sock stuck to a shirt in the drum of a dryer. "Pull over for a sec," I said, rolling down my window.

"Hey, Mrs. Mitchell," Andrea called, waving mightily, which was quite a trick considering the restrictions imposed by the straitjacket of Glen Seavey's forearms. The sight of Andrea, a living reminder that I'd managed to do something with my life besides wait, pleased me. Not that Andrea Harmon was the greatest exemplar of my success, but she proved that at least I'd been trying, and against long odds.

"They're up early," Drew said. "Don't teenagers sleep till noon?"

"Up *late,* is more like it," I said. "To them it's still Saturday night."

Approaching the car, Glen twisted Andrea's unblemished jaw skyward so that he could kiss her, ostentatiously, for my edification — *you can stuff your "in loco parentis," lady* — before allowing her to proceed.

"Long night?" I said. Andrea's lips looked mauled, and Glen's grip gave her the lopsided bearing of a hostage being lugged out of a held-up bank. The fact that Glen was wearing fatigues under a long black coat didn't help.

"We're looking for Glen's truck," Andrea said cheerfully.

"Blazer," Glen corrected her.

"Ty Sprague borrowed it around three-thirty but we forgot where he said to come get it." Andrea looked cold, and as usual didn't have enough clothes on. High thirties under icy sunlight, yet there she was, bare-legged beneath eleven inches of fake-leather skirt, her vinyl jacket flapped open to reveal a scalloped tank top and a tattoo of a bleeding heart lodged between her breasts.

"My burka was in the wash," she said, reading my mind.

"Hell of a party over at the Dusons'," Glen offered, his lip curling in that way I hated. "Music sucked, though. Destiny's Child all night long. Andie likes girlie-bop music."

"I do *not*," Andrea squeaked, banging flirtily on his chest with a lightly closed fist. Glen's medallions rattled like padlocks.

"Girlie-bop, girlie-bop," he chanted. I detected a low growl from Drew, who was watching all this with his hands still on the wheel.

"*Quit* it, Glen!" said Andrea, in a whiny, squealy, girlie-bop way.

"It's Andie's birthday," Glen said. His eyes went tin-colored and mean.

"Happy birthday," I said.

"It's not till January, we're just pretending," she said, giggling — buzzed, obviously — then Glen laughed, now that I had duly noted the pharmaceutical provenance of their expansive spirits. He looked straight at me as his hand roved beneath Andrea's half-zipped jacket. Then he turned his face and licked her ear, his other hand clamped against her backside as if palming a basketball. If they'd been in school I'd have sent them both home.

"*Quit* that," Andrea snarled, pulling away. She looked momentarily irritated, and even had the grace — or the minimum required sobriety — to look embarrassed.

"Well," I said, "much as we'd love to see the whole show, we've gotta scoot."

Andrea looked at me. "Where were you on Friday?"

"Away."

"Are you sick? You kind of look it."

I shrugged. "After thirty you start aging in dog years."

Drew leaned across me and said to Glen, "Offer the girl your coat, for chrissakes."

Astonishingly, Glen shed his coat on command, dropping it onto the frail rack of Andrea's shoulders, then stepped away from her to cross his arms.

To Andrea, Drew said, "You should be ashamed of yourself."

"Drew," I said softly.

So he pulled away. Before I got the window rolled up I heard her laugh again, a falsetto ripple so full of desperation that I had to count the seconds until it vanished in the distance.

"You missed your calling," I said to Drew. "Rick could use you in the office."

"Guys like that make me sick. What is she, twelve?"

"Fifteen. She breaks my heart."

He put his hand on my knee. "Who doesn't?"

I watched Andrea recede in the side-view mirror, looking more and more wretched as her image diminished. She seemed to have been standing there both a very long time and no time at all. Her image was getting smaller but more present, and we seemed to be driving both slow and fast, and the laws of time and space lost their authority, as they had so often since my accident. I was sitting here in the car with my husband and our new beginning, and I was also standing on the sidewalk with Andrea, my arm around her where Glen had taken his pointedly away, and I was also lying in my childhood bed, listening to my uncle and the cats move safely through the house's well-remembered rooms. Like childhood itself, this moment of simultaneous experience lasted and lasted.

The church at St. Bart's had been painted inside, everything an uneven, sickly yellow — walls, ceiling, trim, baseboards — the obvious result of a close-out sale. Probably the Improvement

Committee had hoped to spread sunshine, but the result looked more like jaundice. St. Bartholomew himself, standing at the entrance in life-size plaster, had undergone a political correction, blue eyes dyed brown, fair hair painted over in a more Mediterranean hue. As before, his robe glinted gold and red, and a symbolic flaying knife rested ominously at his feet. The face-lift made him look slightly less smug about having led his brother to Christ and slightly more mindful of his imminent death by skinning. The patron saint of surgeons and tanners looked more like a Hebrew with second thoughts than the vaguely Nordic know-it-all from my childhood.

"Surgeons and tanners?" Drew said. "That's a joke, right?"

"Nope. Some books add taxidermist to the list."

"Didn't your uncle think it was kind of gruesome, booking this guy as the maitre d'?"

"Maybe. Nobody ever mentioned it. I figured St. Bart died like all the other martyrs — a pleasant little burning at the stake. I thought the knife was a bookmark that dropped out of his Bible."

Drew and I slipped into a back pew. The trifling snowfall had prompted the faithful to don their winter goods, so the church bloomed with the wet-wool smell I associated with winter Masses. The priest was not the hale fellow who'd sold us our first Christmas tree but a man in early old age with nothing of the actor about him. He shouldered through the liturgy in an indifferent monotone, his bald head absorbing the fluorescence of the upgraded fixtures in the sacristy. In my former place, far down the aisle in the front pew, sat a family of redheads with two grinny babies. Behind them, the extended family, also ruddy and carrot-topped, politely inclined their heads for a lugubrious homily that I could not quite make out despite the addition of a microphone, an accoutrement that Father Mike's honeyed tenor had not required.

Comparison was unavoidable. The new priest, slope-shouldered and weakly spoken, managed to look smaller than life in his dazzling vestments, like a turtle posing unsuccessfully as a bird. Father Mike had so easily risen to the costume and transformed himself in a dozen intangible ways, understanding that religion was not the same as faith. Religion required a touch of theater even in God's own house. He had an actor's voice, high color, and a theological certainty that doubled as charisma. He created an illusion of eye contact with scores of people at once. My uncle's hands were short and square, but from the altar they appeared long and luminous, lifting the chalice to the soft jangling of bells. There was no explaining the sudden breadth of his shoulders in his immaculate vestments, or the uncommon span of his arms. God's presence transubstantiated more than bread and wine.

At the end of every Mass I raced to the sacristy door but never caught sight of the haloed specter who held up the host. Week after week I flung open the door and found no one but my only uncle shrugging off his vestments or adjusting his watch. I suppose this was both a relief and a disappointment.

Drew and I sat through the Gospel, the sermon, the Offertory—Drew standing, kneeling, and sitting a few beats behind everybody else. I'd forgotten nothing and was glad. At the Sign of Peace, the air eddied as seventy-five people turned to shake a neighbor's hand.

"Peace be with you," I said to my startled husband, holding out my palm.

He glanced around, saw what was happening, and smiled. "You too." He kissed me. "Peace."

TWENTY-SIX

After the initial Monday rush, I ducked into Mariette's room, where she was standing over a granite lab table grading a set of quizzes. Behind her hovered a ten-foot-wide paper mural depicting the universe as seen from, apparently, the Eye of God. Above the speckle of gold that signified Planet Earth was written, in red paint: YOU ARE HERE. LOTSA LUCK.

"Where have you been?" she asked.

"Home."

"Home? I called you like fifty times."

"I know. I'm sorry. We needed the time alone."

She studied me for a moment. "If you came in here to tell me you guys are splitting up, I swear to God I'll let the rats out of that cage and command them to go straight for your eyeballs."

"We're not splitting up. Just the opposite, in fact."

"You'd better mean it."

"I mean it."

"Good. Some good news for a change." She turned once again to her grading.

"Hey. Are you mad at me?"

"A little," she said, refusing to look up. "He *meant* something to me, in case you forgot."

"Who?"

"Father Mike. Who do you think? He left us, too, you know. My mother, my little brothers. We loved him. And now he gets miraculously resurrected from the dead, and we're full of questions, and you pick that exact time to disappear for three days."

I pulled up a stool. The lab table was pocked with acid burns from experiments gone awry. Mariette's marking pen moved furiously over some luckless student's quiz. "My mother drove me nuts all weekend long with questions," she said, "but what did I know? And Paulie's pestering me to go back and see the kitty, see the kitty, see the kitty, and in the meantime I'm picturing you on your way to Mexico or South Dakota or the North Pole for the big reunion without a word to the people who might give a damn."

I reached out to still her pen, but she resisted my advances.

"People ask me how you are," she said, "and I tell them I haven't the faintest idea." Now she looked at me. "I don't know anything about you."

"Mariette, you know *everything* about me."

"For all I know you've found him already and forgot to tell me."

"I haven't even started to look."

This seemed to surprise her. "Why not?"

I thought it over. "Why haven't you looked for your father once in all these years?"

"Because some people are better off gone. You spare yourself their excuses. What could my father possibly have to say to me? He left my mother with three kids and half a job." She marked a quiz and turned it over. "The world is full of missing fathers, Lizzy. They don't deserve to see us again."

Cowed by her anger, I got up and wandered toward a big sign that read DO NOT FEED THE RATS. THEY ARE SERVING A CAUSE FAR NOBLER THAN YOUR MISGUIDED, KNEE-JERK, BUNNY-HUGGING "POLITICS." The junk-food rats looked pretty good, considering; except for slightly greasy coats they seemed as unfazed by Mariette's culinary gulag as the rat-food rats.

"There's a carrot in the junk-food cage," I said.

"Some bleeding-heart keeps slipping them a lifeline." She set the quizzes down. "Tell me something. Anything." Her eyes welled. "I don't even miss you anymore, that's how long it's been."

A few students had begun to drift into the lab ahead of first bell. Mariette's homeroom roster comprised fifteen freshly armored sophomores: lipstick newly applied, jackets zipped exactly halfway, caps pulled low over foreheads. Toting a flapping shoulder bag, Andrea Harmon muscled through the door, her neck so mutilated by violet hickeys that she appeared to have survived a hanging. She looked more sullen than usual, shooting me a look I couldn't quite read. She sat roughly an arm's length from the junk-food rats, who, incriminatingly, rose on their haunches at the first creak of her jacket against the chair back.

"Okay, I'll tell you something," I said softly. "I met the bad Samaritan."

Mariette's mouth dropped open. "What? How?"

The students were talking amongst themselves, oblivious of us. I lowered my voice anyway. "He called me here, right after school started. We kind of got to be friends."

She squinted at my forehead, as if brain damage could be seen if you stared long enough. "You 'kind of' got to be *friends?*" A couple of the kids looked up, interested. Mariette swept me out of the room and we stood amidst the din of slamming lockers. "How could you not tell me this?" she demanded. "School started over three *months* ago."

"I didn't tell anybody."

"Not even Drew?"

"Not till a few days ago."

"You used to tell me everything first. I'm the best friend. Drew's just the husband."

The bell rang. We had no choice but to surrender to the day's momentum as the corridor churned with students who, at that moment more than any before or since, felt like fellow hostages — each of us privately held, more or less humanely treated, and unlikely to be released anytime soon.

Mariette held me by the arm, articulating in the way of a person expressing a dying wish. "Is your whole life a secret?" Then she waded into her room, shouting instructions, readying for another day of cracking open the physical world. It struck me that teaching science to teenagers required enormous, fundamental reserves of hope.

The computer lab, two doors down from Mariette, was a gloomy, nearly windowless kingdom ruled by a rotating band of unqualified Ed Techs with spotty attendance. The lab was empty but for Wally Tibbetts, a persecuted sophomore whose chief distinguishing feature was a pair of amphibious, pool-blue eyes. Because of our problem keeping Ed Techs, Wally had installed himself as the unofficial *chargé d'affaires.* I'd arranged for him to take homeroom here, his sole refuge from H-S Regional's merciless pecking order. He also took lunch in here, which was strictly forbidden and yet permitted by Rick, who expected public gratitude at such time that Wally collected his Nobel for inventing a brain-chip that allowed idiots to speak instant Japanese.

"Hey, Mrs. Mitchell," he said, pausing not at all from his keyboard, which was getting quite a beating. He typed sixty-five words a minute and possessed superior peripheral vision, which is the sort of thing he thought to tell people about himself.

"I hear you're the people guy," I said, raising my voice over the morning announcements crackling through the intercom.

"That's me." He lifted one finger from the keyboard. "What can I do ya for?" Which is really how he talked, like an old-timer sitting on the dusty porch of a general store.

"I'd like to locate a relative," I said. "Family reunion coming up."

He shoved a pad of paper toward me. "Name, birth date, place of birth, Social Security number if you have it, and I'll be with you shortly."

"Be with me *now*, Wally," I said. "It's shaping up to be a long day."

Sighing, he stopped, but did not remove his fingers from the keyboard. He'd had his hair clipped in the quasi-military style the other boys favored, but on Wally it looked less hipster than regulation, as if he were under orders from Uncle Sam.

"What's the name?"

"Michael Murphy." I couldn't help thinking that Father Mike would have liked a kid like Wally, who stoutly bore the consequences of marching to his differently beating drum.

"If it was Jebediah Swartzkoff I might be able to help you," he said. "There's probably ninety thousand Michael Murphys."

"Born on the same day?"

"You'd be surprised."

I wrote a few notes on the pad, making an effort to steady my hand.

"Prince Edward Island?" Wally said. "I went there once. It's really, really green."

"He became a citizen at age sixteen," I said, recalling the story Father Mike trotted out every July Fourth — his sister, my mother, weeping over the Pledge of Allegiance as she stood in the Franklin County courthouse. "But I don't have a Social Security number."

Wally shrugged. "Nobody ever does."

"Should I wait?"

"I'm not that much of a genius." He checked his watch. "There's only six more minutes of homeroom. If you get me out of English I can do it first period."

"I can wait."

"Till fifth period? That's my study hall. If you could get me out of P.E., second period . . ."

"I can wait till fifth period, Wally."

"All-righty. Don't hold your breath, though. He's not a John Smith, but close."

"Well, I appreciate the effort."

He snapped up the paper and studied it. "No problemo. We had a family reunion once." He smiled, and it came to me that he'd had his teeth fixed over the summer. That one gray eye-tooth, which had been knocked literally dead by someone like Glen Seavey, now sparkled like the others.

The morning moved like a fast-acting salve, beginning with two parent meetings and a transcript review, and as the fifth-period bell rang Andrea Harmon stalked into my office, her raccoon eyeliner shiny-wet and poised to spill. She melted into a chair with the poignancy of a dying swan.

"Dumped," she said. "Dumped like a month-old pork chop." She dug into her purse and extracted a matted wad of Kleenex with which she endeavored to mop her eyes. "All of a sudden, like *overnight,* he's in love with Julie Dufresne. Little Miss School Spirit herself." She gave me one of her tree-felling stares. "I suppose you're happy now. I suppose you're going to get all I-told-you-so."

"Here," I said, and she allowed me to cup her face and wipe the delicate, blackened skin beneath her eyes, a task made easier by a steady flow of tears. This child who never cried turned out to be a real gusher. She sat there, face red and buckling, for a full ten minutes while I handed her tissue after tissue, marveling at the sometimes unfathomable sources of genuine grief.

Finally, she pulled herself together, lifted her tear-gummed face. "He wouldn't wash," she said. "He'd get all sweaty on purpose, disgusting sweaty, playing pick-up ball or working out on that stupid rowing machine in his parents' garage, and then he'd pick me up and ride me around somewhere and pull over and ask me to — you know — just to see if I'd still do it." A few clots of mascara clung to her cried-out lashes. "He said I was boring." She struggled mightily for composure, her face a KEEP OUT sign made of skin and bone. I offered her another tissue but she refused it.

"There's something I'd like to tell you, Andrea," I said.

"What," she said morosely. She crammed a wad of tissue into her purse.

"When I came to your house that time. You remember? Your mother said something to me that I know you heard."

She eyed me calmly. "When you were a kid, that thing that happened."

"Except," I said, "that thing didn't happen. I wasn't abused or molested or hurt."

She looked surprised, and I realized I must have been speaking louder than I intended to, so I lowered my voice. "My uncle didn't hurt me, Andrea. He was a normal, nice man with a child to raise." I paused a moment to really see her, this young woman whose sole source of genuine, unfettered affection came from a six-pound dog. "But what I want to say to you, the thing I want you to know, is this: If he *hadn't* been a normal, nice man, if he *had* done what people accused him of, if he *had* hurt me, I would have let him." I leaned closer. "If my uncle, a man I loved, had done any of those things, I would not have protested. I would not have said no. I would have allowed it, Andrea, I would have *embraced* it, because he was all I had." I touched her hand, and she let me hold it. "It was just dumb luck that my uncle was a good man. Because I would have loved a bad man just as much."

She looked away. "Are you comparing Glen to a pervert?"

"Andrea," I said. "I'm comparing you to me."

Sometimes in this business you say exactly the right thing, accidentally, at exactly the right time. She took my full measure with what I can only describe as tenderness. "Thank you," she said, her throat husky from crying. "People say all this stuff about me, you know?"

I still had her hand. She squeezed mine — faintly enough to deny it if she had to — before hauling up her things and heading back to class.

I don't know how long I sat there with my face in my hands. After composing myself, I went to the computer lab and stood at the door, wiping my damp palms on my skirt. "Mrs. Mitchell," Wally stage-whispered. "I found your guy."

"Don't ask him how," said Jenny Morton, an anorexic freshman at the adjoining terminal. "You could both get arrested." A few heads lifted, including the shaved head of Ben Wilkes, a substitute Ed Tech who had a game of solitaire on his monitor.

Wally handed me a slip of lime-green paper. "Totally legit," he said, lowering his voice. "Don't listen to her."

On the front of the paper, in a left-slanting hand, Wally had written *Michael and Frances Murphy; 24332 Oriole Street; Conlin, Ohio.* On the reverse, a phone number.

"This can't be right," I said.

With the patience of an iguana, Wally opened his notebook and showed me the checkmarks he'd made next to Michael Murphy's unique and vital statistics. "Don't even think about paying me," he said. "I sort of consider myself as a public servant."

I could barely hear him over the rushing in my head. "Thanks," I said. "My family will be thrilled."

Then Jenny chimed in. "I could've done it in half the time."

"As *if,*" Wally scoffed. I left them there, undersupervised and bickering, and it wasn't until I returned to my office and put the paper down and stared at it until my ears stopped thumping that I realized Wally Tibbetts and Jenny Morton were in love. Two overlooked creatures for whom, it would appear, love had not been designed, were in love anyway.

I creased the paper into quarters, but it began to unfold itself, like a live, waking creature. I picked up the phone and put it down again. He had been the keeper of my dreams. My knight, my shield, my sanctuary. Also, he had erased my parents. Like the men who killed St. Bart, he skinned my parents beyond recognition and replaced them in my world. Every seed pushed into the earth, every pancake burned and re-tried, every bottle of Moxie drunk on the back steps in summer, every comfort and kindness left less of them and more of him. Then he, in turn, vanished into a vast and secret nowhere in which existed a person named Frances and an Ohio address.

Filled with a yearning that preceded my conscious memory, I realized it was my parents, those fine, forgotten people who had loved me first, that I wished I could call.

I needed my husband. "I'm leaving," I said to Jane. "Tell Rick I'm taking another day."

"I'd be thrilled to," Jane said. "Where are you going?"

"Home."

I left the building as if escaping a fire with nothing but the clothes on my back.

Drew was taking pictures of babies. He didn't trade much in babies, refusing to invest in bunting or pastel backdrops or stuffed rabbits in gingham overalls. Nevertheless, he got a few requests every month, which he fulfilled by cramming them all into a single day. The pain was more intense that way, he liked to say, but he preferred it to protracted torture.

The eleven o'clock client—a pale, ovoid, bald, blue-eyed girl who looked to be about six months old and only distantly acquainted with the concept of sitting up—was propped on a rippling drapery of black velvet. Drew loved to turn babies into art; this one looked like an ostrich egg in a sixteenth-century still life.

"'Now we are engaged in a great civil war,'" he said grimly, as the camera whirred and the baby stared him down, "'testing whether that nation or any nation so conceived and so dedicated can long endure.'" The mothers, generally speaking, liked their babies to appear thrilled and cherished. Drew favored expressions of suspicion or downright disbelief, which he was getting in spades from this baby by reciting portions of the Gettysburg Address in a Rod Steiger baritone.

"Don't you have a rattle or something?" said the mother, who was sitting near the wall, a kitten-motif diaper bag laid across her lap. "I've got her shaky-bunny in my bag."

"Are you kidding?" Drew said, clicking away, "this kid's a natural."

Which made the mother smile despite herself, but I could see that Drew was not going to sell a single print of an art baby in black draping to a woman who had picked out a diaper bag adorned with pink cats.

"I could sing," said the mother. "She'd laugh her head off."

"'We are met on a great battlefield of that war,'" Drew intoned. "'We have come to dedicate a portion of that field as a final'—Hey, Lizzy." Something in the uptick of his voice, the surprise or pleasure of seeing me, made the baby smile. Me, too.

"Look! Look!" the mother said, pointing wildly. "Oh, shoot. You missed it."

Drew put down his camera and picked up the baby, who gazed at him moony-eyed, as if he were Abraham Lincoln in the flesh. "There you go," he said, handing her back. "I'll call when the proofs are ready."

The mother stood up, clutching the baby, uncertain. "But you didn't get any of her smiling. I kind of wanted to see her smiling." She frowned at her baby, who had so easily switched allegiance.

"Trust me," Drew said. "I know what I'm doing. You'll be stunned."

She would be. Mariette had a portrait of Paulie at six months, his face emerging from a severe darkness that made him look like a baby vampire staring down the dawn. It was warped and beautiful, and except for Charlie we all agreed it captured Paulie's bloodthirsty insistence on being adored.

As the mother slumped out the door, another mother was pulling into the driveway in a minivan thrumming with children.

"What are you doing home?" Drew asked, kissing me on the cheek.

"I wanted to see you."

He checked his watch. "I'm booked till five. I squeezed in my postponements from Friday."

"I figured. It's okay. I think I'll just take a nap."

The side door tumbled open, expelling a trio of baying children and their mother, who was reciting a long list of apologies in advance.

"Mrs. Case?" Drew asked.

"Yes," she sighed, as if she really wanted to say no but knew there was no point in lying.

"Who've we got here?" he asked, as I sidled out of the office and closed the door, sitting just outside in a square of sunlight that melted in through the kitchen windows. After a moment, Mr. Peachy padded in, glad to see me. He stamped all over my lap, then collapsed in a heap.

"'Fourscore and seven years ago,'" came Drew's voice from the other side. I had often imagined him at work but had never witnessed him with a client. I realized then how truly misplaced he was, and how heroically he'd figured out how to endure.

I sat through two more exchanges of vehicles in our driveway, unable to leave the sound of my husband's voice and the things I was learning, marveling at the myriad ways he managed to find a way around the obstacle of his own unwillingness. Listening to his dramatic monologues and the occasional suggestions from befuddled mothers, I recognized that he was turning the whole enterprise into a private joke. And another thing: He had a great memory. As babies came and went, he recited most of the Bill of Rights, a three-stanza poem in an Irish accent, and the introduction from the owner's manual that had come with our microwave oven. His miniature clients fell silent under this twisted spell.

He was good with children.

At five-fifteen the last mother—they were all mothers, not a single father—buckled up her brood and drove off. Drew came out, surprised to find me still sitting there. Even the cat had gotten bored and sought other rooms.

I looked up. "We're going to have to get you moved back to Boston, Drew Mitchell."

"It's not so bad. No one threw up on me today."

"You didn't hear me. We're going to have to get you moved back to Boston."

"You're serious?"

"Rick's been trying to cram a leave of absence down my throat ever since I came back. But it struck me today that I could just take it," I said. "I could just—quit." I showed him the scrap of paper bearing Father Mike's address.

He emitted a low whistle. "Is it really him?"

"I had Wally Tibbetts on the case."

"The Nobel-wannabe kid?"

I nodded.

Drew examined the paper. "He's married?"

"Looks like it."

"Did you call?"

"No. Does it take more guts to call him, or to let him be?"

He didn't say anything, just crouched down next to me and took my hand.

"There's nothing to hold me here now," I said.

"There's Mariette," he reminded me. "Charlie. Paulie. Mrs. Blanchard. All your students."

"I meant nothing invisible."

He sat down then, the two of us now sharing a square of light.

"Do the Yeats poem again," I said. "You know that part I mean?"

He pressed my hand to his knee, but we didn't look at each other, we looked straight ahead, into a kitchen overstuffed with our conjoined possessions. "'But one man loved the pilgrim soul in you . . .'" he recited, turning my hand palm up, "'. . . and loved the sorrows of your changing face.'"

I swooned against his shoulder; I'd been raised for romance. Father Mike used to quote Yeats, too, teasing me to sleep: *Brown penny, brown penny, brown penny! I am looped in the loops of her hair . . .*

"What are we going to do, Lizzy?" He meant packing up, picking up, moving away, being married for many decades. Maybe he even meant our future children. I said, "Let's just stay here a minute. I like this spot."

He put his arm around me and there we stayed, on the white tiles of linoleum, above us a counter that housed forty frayed potholders and a cappuccino machine still in the box.

Mariette's car pulled up a while later. "Am I interrupting something?" she asked, finding us on the floor.

I'm leaving you, I thought, staring up at her. *Forgive me.*

"*Maman* wants to see us," she said.

Drew started to get up.

She said, "Just me and Lizzy."

"What's going on?" Drew asked.

"He was her best friend." She turned to me. "She's having a little trouble believing this."

I showed Mariette the square of lime-green paper.

"Oh, my God," she said, turning it over. Then she was coaxing me up, pulling on my hand, her own hands so strong and capable, like her mother's. "Come show her, Lizzy."

Because Mariette was *my* best friend, my oldest and in most ways my only friend, and because I was leaving her and she did not yet know this, I let her pull me up, embrace me briefly, and lead me back.

VESPERS

TWENTY-SEVEN

From *The Liturgy of the Hours:*
He is not a God of the dead, but a God of the living:
for to Him all things are alive.

Back at the beginning, in that first harrowing year of nonstop driving, he paused in Minnesota for a single day, arriving at dawn, penetrating the small city of Bryce Crossing in a car he bought from a lot in Boise. The car made too much noise as he passed the prudish cloister of Sacred Heart School for Girls. He parked across the road from the stone wall on which a plaque extolled the Lord's munificence and the school's ideals. He saw not a soul all day. Perhaps school was out of session—a spring vacation, or a national holiday; he had lost his notions of time. By nightfall, a city cop stopped to ask what he was doing.

Resting, he said. I'm just resting.

In front of a girls' school? Move along, friend, before I start asking questions you don't wanna answer.

Fueled by humiliation, he fled the city, the state, driving bleary-eyed, stopping one night here, one night there, landing in a place called Holmes, Illinois, where he worked for three months breaking down boxes in a food-canning plant and living in a car with a leaky fuel tank. From there he lurched from city to city, loading fish into refrigerator trucks, making computer chips in a cold, echoey room, running the cash register at a hardware store, cutting lengths of cotton twill at a fabric shop, living alone in dark apartments, refusing himself the most basic pleasures: music, books, a kitchen table, a cat. His Breviary was his sole comfort, its leather casings decomposing over the piled-up years. He read surreptitiously during a shift at a Burger King or in a clamorous tenth-grade classroom where he substituted for the history teacher. He had been pronounced dead, after all — a pronouncement he deserved — and this twilight life settled upon him as an imitation of death. The one light, weak indeed, came in through his daily offices. During the Invitatory he asked, *Let her forget me.* Or: *Let her thrive.* Which, he understood, was the same request.

Her birthdays arrived as an annual aching in his body — something like the smell of snow coming usually triggered it — until it came to him that his child was about to turn ten, thirteen, seventeen, twenty. He posted cards to Vivienne from each new address, afraid to disappear entirely from the world, calling her only on his most insupportable days, though she asked him not to. In time, her voice lost the power to destroy him. In his layman's life he learned the layman's lesson: passion fades.

He discovered, also, that the human spirit is not built for endless despair. He took up books again, found movie houses or art galleries to sustain him through the thing that appeared more and more to be his actual life. He settled in East Cleveland, in a derelict apartment near the Good Deeds shelter where he worked a seventy-five-hour week. At the corner diner they welcomed him as a certain type of regular—friendly enough, but close-lipped.

He was sitting near the door in his usual booth, cherry-red vinyl left over from the forties. It was year twelve of his exile. Idly he watched a harried woman in a boiled-wool jacket fidgeting in the takeout line—her name would turn out to be Frannie—but he was thinking of Lizzy, whose twenty-first birthday had just passed. "Emancipation" was the legal term. There was no authority Celie could now enlist who would have the least interest in a twenty-one-year-old woman. So. He was thinking about resurrection.

Oh, ho, a resurrection, is it? We're Jesus Christ himself now, are we?

This was Jack Derocher, his former confessor, the only person he ever talked to frankly, if only in his head. People looked at him sometimes; he wondered if his lips moved.

Let me rephrase.

Please do.

Reconnection. I've been thinking about reconnection.

Much better. You sound human, at least.

How do I reconnect a cord so irrevocably severed?

What's with the passive voice?

Fine. How do I reconnect a cord that I—I myself, Jack—so irrevocably severed?

Easy. You go back.

For a moment he suspended his disbelief and it seemed easy: go back.

Then, if she doesn't die of shock, you explain that you accepted twelve years of exile to save her from those fanged beasts at DHS.

Why so snide? It's the truth.

As far as it goes. You've had twelve years to simplify your story.

You're hard on me, Jack.

Damn straight. You thought you could have it all, Mike. Did having a child spoil you for making choices?

What are you talking about?

Thou shalt not covet thy neighbor's wife. You walked straight into the big trap of the Ninth Commandment. And I've gotta tell you, it was hard to watch, the pillar of strength throwing himself at temptation just to prove he could resist. You think I couldn't hear between the lines, Mike, all those casual conversations, my neighbor this, my neighbor that?

I did resist. What would you know about it? I passed the test, Jack. Give me credit for something.

Sure. You passed the test of temptation, over and over, to be perfectly fair. I'm glad to give you that. But in the meantime you let a jackass like Ray Blanchard get away with his macho bullshit just so you could look like a hero by contrast. Father Wonderful. Friend and confessor. Only you didn't court confession from her, did you, Mike? You courted adoration. And boy oh boy, did you ever do the job. When she needed a hero she knew just where to come running.

She needed a priest, Jack. When she came running, she needed a priest.

Mike. She needed a guy who could keep a secret.

His life had become a badly sutured wound that occasionally seeped, and today was a seeping day that made him want impossible things.

The kid's twenty-one, Mike. She did okay without you. Leave it.

Jack Derocher was more compassionate in real life. It hurt to hear him talk this way. But how could he, or anyone, know what it is to be accused? How could he, or anyone, understand what happens afterward? How you look back with spoiled eyes, second-guessing. Weighing everything. Reconsidering. Once somebody believes your intentions to be impure, it changes how you see yourself, the accusation flies around and then lands like a crow on your shoulder. You can't shake it off. You wonder what made your love so desperate and gushing. What impelled you to admire her child's body in the bath, the seal-slick purity of it, the strength it seemed to be acquiring, its miraculous shape-shifting? You wonder why you loved her sweaty socks, her smell as you tucked her in, her breath after she ate a plum. How can you help but wonder? You could not pass her in a room without touching your hand to her head, your thumb to her chin. What did all that mean? Tainted, all of it, your dearest memories stained for good. How can you be the same kind of father after that?

Leave resurrection to Jesus, Mike, and salvage what you can. Those cracked souls at the shelter could use your help. It's not too late to do some good in this world.

He looked up, bereft, to find the woman in boiled wool pawing through a tote bag, hands quaking. She looked his age, though he would find out later that she was younger by eight years, exhausted from tending her husband's cancer. That she had a little boy named David. That she had been driving around the city for an hour, a temporary respite far from her neighborhood in Conlin. That she passed the diner with its incongruous gingham curtains and filagreed OPEN sign and suddenly craved a glazed doughnut. That her reserves ran out entirely while waiting in the takeout line; that the room tilted as she wheeled toward him, the cherry-red seat making a soft groan as she landed, sitting up, facing him. That his face looked so lifeless she thought he was the Angel of Death come to tell her that Alfred had expired the second she left the house, her punishment for wanting a doughnut.

She stared at him rudely, as if he were the one who had taken the wrong seat.

—Excuse me but I can't stand up, she said. All I wanted was an hour of peace.

He set down his cup, taking in the sweet, blanched apple of her face.

—I'm a priest, he told her. The words emerged strangled, for the priesthood felt like another child he abandoned.

He corrected himself:

—I used to be a priest.

—I used to be a Catholic, she said. And began to weep. The timbre of her voice reminded him of Vivienne, but the way she wiped her eyes with the back of her hand looked more like Lizzy. He surrendered his handkerchief, aware of a faint dislodging, a frail internal forward motion that he only dimly recognized as hope.

This moment returns to him as he pulls into Conlin from his all-night journey. Oriole Street swings into sight, identical trash cans silhouetted at the ends of identical driveways. Frannie—the kind, solid soul who married him—will be waiting, wanting to know how his niece fared after her accident, this niece she has never heard of, this niece whose name has not once crossed his lips. And he will have to go inside his clean, warm, predictable house to tell his wife the truth of where he has been.

After anointing her, after fleeting through the corridors and down the ziggurat of hospital stairways, he stands in the middle-of-the-night quiet, recovering his breath. He is still holding the angel, her gown aglitter in the parking-lot lights. Benumbed, he staggers to the car, praying for her. All those bandages! Those poor, spindly, encased limbs. That awful contraption, his little lamb on a spit.

He left his pills in the motel. What day is this? Has he been gone one day, or two? He puts the car into gear, intending to drive south as fast as he can without getting stopped.

North he goes. As he knew he would.

Approaching the valley, he recognizes the ridge along Route 9, a service station he always favored, a nursing home he once visited regularly. A field that used to be filled with cows is now filled with driveways. Breathing in concert with the up-and-down road, he senses river, melting field, thawing ground. He looks for the shoe shop on the banks, the lights from third shift, and then remembers it has turned itself into a school.

God feels like a part of him that has been gutted and left to rot.

The town, as he rounds the long bend of the river, looks tucked into the glowering dark, innocent as a postcard. The diner abides, and Hinton Variety. Who would know him now, his hair so thin and gray, his face so thin and gray, thick, thumbprinted eyeglasses that express the mire of middle age?

Ears ringing with anxiety, he crosses the bridge into Stanton and creeps toward her address. Her silhouette, unmistakable, faces out from a lighted window, as if she has been waiting, exactly there, since the phone call. He gets out, looks up, strains to see through the tunnel of dark. She has become old, too: a softening at the shoulders, a rumpling in her once-starched frame; but her face still burns in that old way, he knows it even in this blackness. He can tell from here. They lock eyes—in the dark, even at a distance, they sense each other, two stranded souls in God's stranded universe. Her head swivels slightly, an exhausted *no*. He retakes the wheel and eases away.

How still, this town that no longer knows him. He heads upriver, a tremor of disquiet working steadily through his body. He slows at the second bend, aware of the volume of his own breathing. The sign has been painted afresh. He cuts the headlights and inches down the curve of driveway, past the parish hall, past the church, stopping just before the clearing. He can just make out the tattered remains of the moon garden. It is only March. It is possible that someone has kept it up, that come May the candytuft will pop through, then the white tulips, after that the first of the astilbes. He longs to inspect it for signs of survival but he is too afraid.

In the turnaround squats an overweight American sedan, a classic priest car. A light burns in the upstairs hallway — possibly the same night-light he installed for Lizzy, a square of glass depicting a family of bears eating porridge. But probably not. In the agony of those first weeks of aftermath, he tortured himself with visions of the place being stripped of her — of them — her clothing, her crayon marks, their cookie toolkit, her socks in the mudroom, the porridge-eating bears that shaped the light.

Between the trees he catches a glint of river. That's the spot, he thinks, suddenly knowing: the spot where the river is no longer only river, where ocean, just a few drops of it, begins.

He skulks along the perimeter, sheltered by the pines and a shocking growth of maple, poplar, and a single imperial oak, until he reaches the grown-over break in the trees. The shape of the shortcut survives amongst an undergrowth of maple suckers and brush. The farmhouse still stands. She no longer lives there but her presence does. He smells her: sumac and river, pine and earth.

Adjusting to the dark, he can just make out the roofline, the east-facing eaves, and if his eye travels down, steady, there it is: the back door, the little railing, a few flagstones that pass for a patio. He tracks the path to her house, stopping here. Here. Then here.

Then: here.

The tree limbs seem to point. The ground sinks a little. The needles gather more thickly here, or so he imagines. Then — as if God himself is watching, a bystander with nothing better to do than give directions — the clouds part and the moon makes a white connection from the middle of the sky straight to the unmarked grave of Raymond Blanchard.

When she unlatches the back door that night twenty-one years ago, he thinks it's a dream, for he has fallen asleep in the blue parlor chair and startles awake, confused. The day has been long with priestly duties and constant, engulfing thoughts of Vivienne in her lovely white dress with the red snowflakes. He finds himself in his chair, rabat and collar and jacket still on, Breviary collapsed on his lap.

Someone rattles the kitchen door and barrels into the parlor. *What*—? he cries, adrenalin already spilling. Vivienne. Her blouse oddly wet, her arms oddly blemished. Her face is somebody else's face, everything shrinking around the stung eyes of a wild creature.

Father, hear my confession! She throws herself at his feet, like Eve after eating the apple, looking nothing like the woman he held in his arms just an evening ago, his vows on the verge of breaking.

What's happened? he says. *Vivienne, get up.*

Say you will hear my confession!

Frightened, he blesses her, inclines his head. He will hear her.

It's Ray, she chokes.

Ray is at sea. Has Ray been lost at sea?

Father—

He barely hears the rest. A few wild words and she gets off her knees, breathless, leaving a stain on the floor. *Hurry up, Father! Bring the sacrament!* She pulls him out of the chair, into the kitchen, *Hurry up! Hurry up!* as he reaches for the small leather case. She seizes his hand and pulls him out the door and over the steps and into the yard toward the part in the trees. *He came back,* she gasps, running ahead of him now, flinging the words back over her sweat-soaked shoulder. *He came back, Father! I didn't mean it, I couldn't help it!*

Why is she calling him Father? Already he disbelieves what she has confessed to him. He expects to find anything at the end of this path, anything but the thing she has told him to expect. He expects Ray. Ray at the ready. This will be the man-to-man he has so often dreaded. Ray Blanchard swaggering out of the house. With a shotgun? A broken bottle? One of those hooks that go on a boat?

Running behind her, eyes fixed on the sweaty trailing wisps of her hair, God forgive him, he chooses. Running, disoriented, running into the lane in the middle of the night only because she has commanded him to, he chooses her.

The Blanchards' lights are out but the moonlight bears in. Ray Blanchard lies face down in the dirt at the edge of the moon garden, limbs splayed. He looks like a starfish that might have washed up on one of his stinking decks, some untouchable, dead thing.

What happened? Vivienne! What happened?

Quiet! she yips. *Parle pas si fort! Someone will hear you!* She glances at her dark windows, then clutches at her shirt front as if she means to rip it off. She does the same to her hair; he has never witnessed such a quaking; it reminds him of the religious ecstasy he has long envied but only read about.

He is quaking, too. He reaches down, says something to Ray: drunk, he tells himself, smelling alcohol and piss, Ray Blanchard drunk again, he tells himself, willing the thing in front of his eyes to become something other than what it so obviously is. The shovel thrown sideways like a spent bullet. The viscous puddle beneath Ray Blanchard's cursed skull.

What in God's name?

Father, give him the sacrament.

The flowers in her moon garden, identical to his but profuse even in autumn, do not sway. Their cupped white faces watch him.

He turns the man over: ruined face, nose bloodied and flattened from a hard fall forward. He examines the mashed jaw, slides his hand along the neck where nothing pulses.

Please, Father, she says. Her crying recalls the winnowing of birds in flight. *I require you to make the prayers.* She sounds more French, farther away, with each uttered word, like a fresh immigrant unfamiliar with the ways of her new home.

He unzips the leather case, removes the vial of oil. He anoints Ray Blanchard's caked forehead, speaking in Latin, his voice no more substantial than a flittering candle. From the case he takes a tiny book, *The Golden Key of Heaven,* given to him at seminary by an old priest who saw the potential of vocation in a young, eager man. The book is a relic, obsolete even when it was first given to him, but he opens it now, thumbing blood onto the onionskin pages. He finds his place and unleashes a torrent of Latin, reading by the unrelenting moonlight.

How did she do this, a woman no bigger than a bird? He scrambles to his feet and vomits into the white, white flowers.

She wipes his mouth with her hand, and he smells blood. *Help me, Father.*

Her body turns into a trick of the eye, changing under scrutiny. Her arms, no bigger around than young branches, are finely strung with muscle; her hands, used to shoemaking and hot water, knot with power as her fists close. *Help me.*

She picks up the shovel by its bloody head. *Take this.*

For God's sake, Vivienne. Call the police.

They'll take my children, she hisses. *They'll put me in jail.*

Vivienne. Take hold of yourself.

I didn't mean it, Father. He missed his boarding. He came back. He tried to pee on my flowers.

Still she is calling him Father.

The police will understand, he says. *Everyone will understand, Vivienne. Everyone knows about Ray. You have nothing to be afraid of.*

A lie. He knows this is a lie. Here is Ray, eyes milky and half open. Caught from behind and hit. And hit. And hit and hit and hit and hit and hit. His wife's blouse puckers with blood.

She holds up the shovel. He avoids her eyes, tucking his little book and leather case into his breast pocket. She places the shovel between his hands, curls his fingers around the handle, and he follows her into the woods a few yards off the path, an untamed spot strewn with sticks and branches.

Nothing holds. The night is too bright; there is both a stillness and a pulsing that alters his senses, makes walking feel like swimming, speaking feel like thinking. He forgets that Ray is dead, then remembers. Then forgets. He is holding a shovel, shocked, perhaps *in* shock, but not sorry. An unfamiliar emotion buzzes through his buzzing head, like an insect that has been present for a very long time but is just now making itself known. He does not know what this feeling is, only what it is not.

This feeling is not sorrow.

I'm begging you. Father, I'm begging you.

He clears a spot and begins to dig, reciting the Burial Absolution. This he knows by heart. *Requiem aeternam dona ei, Domine, et lux perpetua luceat ei . . . Eternal rest grant unto him, O Lord, and let perpetual light shine upon him.* He whispers, digging, trying to stay the boiling in his head.

This feeling is not pity.

His muscles remember the work of the farm, a boy's pride in helping his father and uncle dig by hand the furrows of his mother's vegetable patch, the foundation for the new root cellar. The smell of turned earth fills him, now, as then, with a confusing wistfulness, a nostalgia for something that has not yet happened. He bends down and up, down and up, each short breath slicking back at the end in a half-fulfilled cry.

Kyrie eleison, he says, remembering again: Ray is dead. He is breathing hard, wiping his hair with his wrist, flicking dirt — mercifully dry and reeking of earth — from his thighs and knees. *Make the response, Vivienne.*

Christe eleison, she gasps. The shoveling sounds soft, sickening, as if he were digging into living flesh.

Kyrie eleison, he says.

Christe eleison, she responds, calmer now.

This feeling is not regret.

Such slow going. His back burns. Vivienne disappears, returning with a short-handled garden spade they have both used for transplanting lilies. She digs beside him, mute and focused. They breathe in tandem, wet with effort. Again, he forgets. He digs and digs, becoming nothing but a body in motion, a body at work, a body physically engaged, a body being used, a feeling he has not encountered in a very long time and it is not, even under these circumstances, an unwelcome feeling, for he keeps forgetting why this hole is being dug, the present moment keeps slipping, the woman sweating beside him keeps fading from view, he keeps believing himself elsewhere, transported moment to moment to different times and places in the way of a complicated dream that begs to be told next morning to the first willing ear.

He digs and digs, this hole becoming other holes: holes for outhouses, holes for irises, holes for animals — his mother's beloved work horse, Charles Laughton; the dogs and cats, dozens of them it seems — holes of different depths and widths and always that suggestive smell of earth. A hole for a hawk he found inexplicably dead in the field, russet breast ablaze in the sun-buttered morning, talons relaxed and unsuspecting. He goes back there, admiring again that lovely raptor, its eyes dull but still beautiful.

Heaven might smell like this. He is knee high in the earth — a narrow hole, this one, more like a short trench, something for battle — knee high, then waist high, and then he startles awake, Vivienne abruptly and unspeakably *here,* in *this* hole, exhausted and panting, asking to get out, so he drops his shovel — he is here now, in *this* hole — and helps her to higher ground, his hands sliding down her sweat-slicked calves. She crouches above him, up there on earth. For a moment — a single, nauseating second — he expects her to fill the hole with him in it.

Vivienne, he says, coming to. *Think what we're doing.* But she won't. Staring down, she blocks the moonlight.

Eventually he scuttles out, roachlike, head throbbing, the hole smelling of worms and beetles and not the earthen perfume he wants to remember.

It's too late, she says, sweeping her arm over the hole, the night so bright she makes shadows.

This feeling is not revulsion.

He follows her back to the dooryard, where they retrieve Ray's leaking body — muscles burled but horridly pliant beneath a filthy layer of shirt — and roll it into the hole like a carpet being dropped at the dump.

In nomini Patri . . . He is crying now, drowning.

She strips off her spattered blouse, cleans her hands with the sleeves, and throws it into the hole. Then her skirt, and her shoes, a pair of moccasins she stitched with her own hands, the leather spackled with blood. She regards him, alert and urgent, her skin sheening, then reaches to unhook his rabat, his collar. She tears them from him, holds them over the hole in the earth, and lets them drop.

He looks down at their mingled clothes and vomits again.

This feeling is not disbelief.

She begins to scratch the earth with the tip of her spade, raking pine needles and spent leaves over their sin. But he is the one who knows how to fill a grave. This hole, again, becomes other holes; he fills and tamps, fills and tamps, places rocks to discourage animals, fills again, tamps again, then strews the ground again with broken branches.

That's all, she says. The moon has moved. He steals a glance at her half-naked body, dismayed to find the polished stone of her back clotted with healed-over scrapes, fading bruises.

At one time he could have shamed Ray Blanchard, threatened him, compassioned him into changing his ways. He had the power: God on his side. Or, God on one side; on the other, his own jealousy. And fear.

He did nothing then. Now, he helps her.

She floats across the shimmering ground, slips into the house, and returns wearing a housecoat and a clean pair of moccasins. In his shirtsleeves he misses the weight of his rabat and collar. Then it is over, the shovels washed under the outside spigot and brought to the shed; the ground hosed down and raked over.

This feeling is not surprise.

He wipes his face with his hands, glancing at the upstairs windows, and finds a fleeting shape there. He hopes it is Ray, forgetting again that Ray is dead. If Ray came downstairs it would be a relief. If Ray came downstairs and beat him senseless, it would be a relief. If Ray came downstairs, he would beat him in turn, one whack for every dent in Vivienne's narrow back. If Ray came downstairs he would do the job himself and dig the hole again and it is shame he feels, shame for his friend's scraped back, for not choosing to see until now.

This feeling is shame.

We have to get rid of the truck, Vivienne says.

When she puts the keys into his hands their skin slides together; it feels like blood, though it is only the water they have used to wash off the blood. She tells him where to take the truck, where exactly, her mind working quick and merciless. It's a place he knows only vaguely, thick with ticks and bramble, a path down to the quarry and then a steep dropoff to freezing water. Three teenagers drowned there decades ago, before the mills stopped dumping and the river rejuvenated itself. Local children swim in the river now, the quarry a forbidden and forbidding place. She tells how to go to this place no one goes.

She starts down the path to the rectory. *I'll wait in the kitchen,* she says. *In case Lizzy wakes up.*

What about—

My children sleep like the dead.

The truck smells of oil and fish and alcohol and other, far worse things that he probably only imagines. He vomits again on the way to the quarry, slowing down, veering the truck as he aims the stream on the passenger-side floor. Twice he swerves against the wooded shoulder and fishtails back toward the yellow line. The floor moves weirdly with things he recognizes: empty bottles, a rattling can of W D - 4 0, a rag that used to be a shirt; and things he doesn't: stout hexagonal bolts that attach to equipment he wouldn't know how to run, a heap of stray wire that looks too heavy to manipulate by hand. By the time Chummy Foster spots him, he not only drives like Ray Blanchard, he feels like Ray Blanchard, entombed in the cab of a truck that reeks of all form of human futility and contains a welter of unreadable objects.

He drives the sixteen miles to the place she has marked in his mind. A yellow property stake, a turnoff to a road that is no longer a road. He gets stuck once, twice, pushes the truck out of a shallow divot and then meets a deeper one in the gummy terrain, pushing with all his will and crying out, then simply crying, unable to believe he has found himself at this unimaginable moment.

The truck won't budge. Ten feet from the plummeting edge of the quarry, the truck stalls willfully in place. He feels watched, senses Ray smirking just beyond sight in the murk of trees, arms folded high on his packed chest, a genie released from a bottle.

He pushes again, feeling hairless, thin and mincing, ineffectual as a girl. The growl that comes from him then sounds both ancient and freshly ignited, wholly foreign; out it comes, aimed at the truck of Ray Blanchard, this immovable object, this stinking hunk of chrome and sheet metal with its clanking unreadable cargo, this infuriating machine whose every crack and rattle has for years existed as background sound and half-glimpsed motion, its throaty, gunning, gravel-spitting arrivals and departures enduring and everpresent, a scornful counterpoint to his own spinsterish comings and goings. Shame gives way to fury. He roars from low, low in his throat, drops his shoulder into the ass end of this clattering heap, and pushes hard enough to hear a muscle tear, but it moves, the thing moves, and his hatred moves with it, to the edge of the quarry, over the lip, into the dark and voiceless water.

His rage subsides and sickness sets in. His child slumbers back at the rectory, amongst his doilies and padding cats, believing herself safe. He prays that tonight will not be a night of a nightmare, that she will not fling herself down the stairs and find him gone and Vivienne sitting in the parlor like a zombie in a clean housecoat and blood drying in her hair.

It is not until he walks out to the road and faces the star-filled sky that he wonders how to walk the sixteen miles back to the rectory. Surely he will be seen. He can't think, mired in the present tense as if in the throes of prayer, or sexual communion.

Slow headlights appear down the road; he ducks into the trees. The car creeps to a stop and the lights flash, on and off, on and off. Pauline, in her red Firebird. He steps into the road, half hoping to be run over. They don't speak until she pulls into the Blanchards' driveway.

She did the world a favor, Pauline says. Then she gets out and disappears into the house.

He goes around back, where the dooryard appears unravaged, a puddle beneath the water spigot the only sign. He heads down the lane, holding his breath as he passes the new grave, then enters his own kitchen.

They face each other. He is filthy and sweating. He can smell himself.

We can't—, she begins. *We can't ever be—*

She looks scraped out and ruined.

People would put the two and two together, she says. *They would make the assumptions.*

He blinks at her, trying to find her former face.

She says: *They would think I killed Ray for you.*

He watches her go, her hand on the latch, her foot at the floor, her body moving through space that vanishes the instant she enters it. In his kitchen, all around him, signs of beginning: the shiny bookbag packed with Lizzy's first homework of fourth grade, her school shoes neatly placed beneath a folded sweater.

He takes in these things, then blunders outside and slips down the path and stands vigil on the ground near the grave. Blood rushing, he explains to his heavenly Father.

He makes his case: bad man. Bad husband.

He must add: human being. Child of God.

He makes his prayer for the dead.

Weeks stutter by. The dead man ransacks his dreams, poisons his appetite, loots his daily Mass. The stony rage he felt at the quarry is gone, and remorse moves in. He is sick with it.

Every day safely passed drops another stitch from his life. He feels unmasked, unclothed, unable to look the children in the eye.

His conscience becomes a live and writhing thing, and he braces for punishment. He will take what he deserves.

It is believed that Ray Blanchard left for parts unknown after leaving Gus Fournier's boat crew a man short. He'll come back when he's good and ready, which may be never, and good riddance anyway. Nothing changes; Ray's absence goes largely unremarked. Except among the children. They want to know where their papa has gone. Why does he stay away so long? If he is not at sea, then where? They cry all the time.

Lizzy, too, cries now, so sorry for her friend. She recalls Ray's dancing. He was a good dancer, Father, remember how he danced?

The children whimper in his dreams. All night long.

He stops eating now, begins instead to be eaten.

She comes to him in the privacy of the confessional.

Bless me, Father, she says. *For I have sinned.*

Through the trees, he has been watching her moving around in her dooryard. She avoids the woods but otherwise appears to move freely, a winglike lift to her step.

It has been one week since my last confession.

She has told the children to keep out of the woods. No playing there. I sprayed something on the weeds.

These are my sins: I committed murder. I love you.

Once a week, here in this vessel of oiled wood, he grants absolution again, as he must.

A cold noontime, mid-November, he taps on the farmhouse door to fetch Lizzy for lunch. Pauline says: *Chummy Foster saw Ray's truck.*

The air dampens with panic. Can the children feel it? He packs the children off, sends them down the lane to Mrs. Hanson.

Tell me. His face goes hot and clammy. Across the white Formica are strewn the remains of Lizzy and Mariette's game of Sorry, a tin of color pencils, a box of paper dolls. This evidence of innocence quells his terror.

It's not you he saw, Vivienne says, her color rising. *Who would ever think it was you?*

Never in a million years, agrees Pauline. *No one.*

He stands up, his cassock grazing his polished shoes, his collar chafing.

Even if they find the truck, Pauline says.

They won't, Vivienne reminds her. *The quarry is filled with old trucks. Old stoves, old everything.*

But even if they did, they'll think it was Ray anyway. Who would suspect the priest?

He doesn't like the way Pauline says *the priest,* as if her sister's woes can be laid entirely at his feet. As if her sister killed at his behest.

His stomach pitches. Where is the woman who came to him with the brushed hair, the lovely dress? She is all tapping fingers now, and bitten lips, nothing but nervous darting.

Still, he believes Pauline. Who would think of Father Murphy driving Ray Blanchard's truck in the middle of the night?

They breathe easier, one by one by one.

His cassock feels papered on, paper clothes on a paper man.

I'm sorry, Vivienne says.

He turns, once, before pushing open the door.

Tell God, he says. *Tell Ray.*

A day later, he asks for a transfer. Which is denied.

Tuesday night, another week gone, the children abed, he knocks again at Vivienne's door. A glint of alarm flares in her eyes, but also the old longing that, despite everything, fills him.

Something's happened, Vivienne. He looks at her now, straight at her; he needs her.

Of course she thinks it's about Ray, now past two months in the ground. He reads her fear.

Have the police —— ? Have you told —— ?

Not that, he says. *Something worse.*

Her hand goes to her throat. What could be worse?

I've been accused —— He can't bring himself to say it.

Again, she's thinking: Ray.

Not Ray, he says. *Lizzy.*

He scratches the slanderous words on Vivienne's grocery list. A word, and another, beneath the words *milk, potatoes, Pop Tarts.* By the time she puts it together, he is weeping.

Don't cry, she says. *Oh, don't.*

He clings to her bony shoulders, fingers dug in.

Ida Hanson must be crazy, she says. *Who would believe such a thing?*

It's so difficult to meet her eyes. Something different has been born in her face, a savage clarity around the mouth, a vulpine cast to her once temperate features. Is this his own reflection? It's so difficult to look.

She saw you in my bed, Vivienne, he says, eyes averted. *She thought you were Lizzy.*

What? she cries. *That's impossible.*

In your beautiful white dress with the red snowflakes. She mistook you for a child.

Her face flushes briefly. What comes to him is the buckled skull of Ray Blanchard, the collapsed and glutinous mess of it.

My dress—?

It looks like a nightgown, he tells her. Lizzy has one with red dots.

Now she gets up, pacing, hugging herself. *Don't tell, please don't tell. The two of us together that way, and then Ray disappears. They will guess.*

We'll have to chance it, he says.

She turns around, and he receives her face in its newly brutal beauty, its capacity to surprise. *No chances, Michael. I won't.*

We have to, he whispers.

They will put the two and two together!

You're not listening, Vivienne. I stand accused with no witness but you.

He lies there, Michael, she whispers bitterly, thrusting an incriminating finger toward the window as if Ray buried himself in the ground. *He lies right there under our feet! The police will know. They will ask the children, and the children will tell where we forbid them to play.*

We is the word she uses. *We.* Tears now, dear God, copious, rivering tears. *They will know.*

Self-defense, he pleads. *You tell them it was self-defense.*

He could not see me coming. They can tell. Her face horrifies him, the way its lovely contours shift slightly, then lock. *He thought I would always be afraid.*

Listen to me.

No, Michael, she says. *You listen.* Her face—merciful God, who is she?—lifts to him. *You dug a hole and put him in it. If you tell, we will both lose our children. Spare me, Father. Please, Father.* She is very close to him now, closer than she has been in weeks, her breath warm and clean, her lips warm and clean, but she is leaving him, this very minute she is leaving, and it feels like strips of skin being torn away.

He pleads but she won't listen. *Nothing will happen,* she insists. *Nobody will believe that stupid woman. Nobody will believe you could desire to hurt Lizzy.*

But what if they do?

They won't. Trust God.

I can't trust God! God can't be trusted!

Her body holds fast to the place it takes. *Then trust me,* she whispers, taking him into her arms. The physical fact of her feels like destination.

Nothing will happen, she croons, guiding him to the blue chair. She fits herself there with him. *Nothing will happen.*

He closes his eyes, listening to her.

Michael.

He still loves his name when she speaks it.

Spare me, Michael. Let one of us keep what is ours.

In his head runs their history in an endless loop, all those days with the children in their sun-brightened yards, all those cook-outs and sled rides and the small conversations at her table or his, all his missteps turned graceful through the eye of his neighbor and friend. *She has all her life for people who put their foot down. You go ahead.*

Her arms tense around him. *Promise me you'll never tell.*

I do. I promise.

Be merciful. Promise.

I do, he says, resting now, choosing her anew. How many feverish nights she has cut short his prayers. How many more to come.

COMPLINE

TWENTY-EIGHT

Although Mrs. Blanchard had not lived in the farmhouse since Buddy, her youngest, left for college, her apartment retained the faintest scent of leather. Perhaps the years of piecework had settled onto her clothes and dishes, or perhaps my accident—which had altered my physiology in unknowable ways—had added to my memory the sense of smell. In either case, her apartment made me think of unstitched shoes.

She lived in one of the new complexes in Stanton with her basset hound, Pierre, the reincarnation of Major right down to a fear of cats and a knack for opening doors. Except for the dog, the new place betrayed no outward sign of our shared past. It was small and tidy, like her. No jam jars left open on the sideboard, no recipes stashed behind the blender, certainly no skeins of rawhide laid out, no pouches full of needles. After the shoe shop closed she'd taken a job at ShopRite as a cashier, where she still worked five nights a week, leaving daytime for babysitting Paulie. Nearing sixty, Mrs. Blanchard was still lovely; her eyelashes retained their inky darkness and her lips were still full. But the radiance she had once possessed was gone, in its place a statuelike sheath, a structural beauty that gave the viewer nothing but surface.

Charlie met us at the door with Paulie hoisted against his chest. "I was summoned," he said. He looked flushed and harried in his McDonald's-owner costume, a Ronald McDonald tie floating out the front of his half-zipped jacket.

"Hi, Fluffy," I said to Paulie, which normally made him laugh, but he'd been torn from a nap and squashed his face into his father's collar.

Mariette exchanged a look with Charlie as he passed us. "Something's up," he said. "She asked me to clear the deck, so that's what I'm doing."

Nothing looked right. She kept the place eerily clean, the counters clear, the chairs pushed in, like a stage set tended by prop masters. The Mrs. Blanchard of my childhood had always seemed nestled, at one with her surroundings; now she lived in rooms designed to make normal human activity seem like acting. We found her waiting for us in the living room, which despite the daily presence of Paulie and a fifty-pound dog looked freshly swept.

"Sit, girls," she said. "I require you to sit."

We sat.

"Maman," Mariette said, "what is it?"

Her mother did not smile or sigh. She held me in her sights. "You plan to find him?"

I glanced at Mariette, then nodded uncertainly.

Mrs. Blanchard's eyes closed. "Then I have a story."

Bad news usually arrives ugly. A jangling telephone, ugly in the evening quiet. A doctor's voice in a bright and ugly room. There is no elegance in bad news. It thumps you on the forehead, causes physical pain, hurts your ears.

Mrs. Blanchard's news did not sound like that. With her supple throat and Franco accent, she released her kept secrets like a flight of doves, a steady, gradual rushing. Her voice, though grave, possessed a natural music that let the story she told us arrive in waves, the impact of the words landing just behind the words, a time-delay that made for a confusion of the senses. *What?* we asked, over and over, our comprehension arriving late by several beats.

Mariette and I were wedged together on a loveseat, mouths partly opened, coats still on, positioned an arm's length from the stuffed chair in which her mother sat with her ankles crossed, head erect, full mouth moving, words winging out. *What?* we kept saying, but she repeated nothing, moving on in the same undulating tones that had once animated our bedtime stories.

She reached for an unreachable man and was mistaken for a child. She felled her husband with the nearest weapon, a shovel for digging up gardens. She called on the man she loved to dig a grave and save her.

What?

I groped for Mariette's hand; our fingers twined. Her mother was explaining, calmly and without apparent apology, that the vessel we'd been sailing twenty-one years ago had capsized and that she'd claimed the only seat in the lifeboat.

I turned to Mariette, either to offer comfort, or receive it. She stood up, her mouth slack and foundering.

Mrs. Blanchard regarded us wanly, her eyes wounded but dry. "You girls don't know what it is to live with a man who owns you."

The dog, who had been sitting next to his mistress in a fog of inattention, suddenly took note of a barometric drop in emotional pressure and headed for a corner of the den. Mariette sprang up and spun toward the door, then slumped into a different chair, then stood up and began to move again, like an animal zigzagging to confuse its predator. It was hard to watch. Remorse washed over me. If not for me and my voices from the dead, my friend would never have had to know this. Ray Blanchard could have roamed her world alive for as long as she cared to accommodate him. She shook her head, slowly, beseechingly, side to side to side, eyes wide and fixed, trying to un-know. Overwhelmed and out of options, she fell still, hands covering her mouth, the rest of her face a puckered mess.

"My only girl," her mother said. "I'm sorry."

Mariette groaned, a bone-deep guttering. She lunged into the kitchen and her mother followed, lamenting in a soft, rapid French. Mariette banged the door open, and vanished down the stairs.

Mrs. Blanchard clutched the fridge for balance. She lifted her head, slow as a dying animal, until her gaze rested on me.

"I don't believe you," I said to her. "I won't believe he helped you."

"I wish I could say it was a lie."

"You see this?" I pulled the scrap of paper from my pocket. "He lives in Ohio. I have his phone number right here. I could ask him myself."

"He is married," she said evenly. "Her name is Frannie. She has a son, twelve years old. He works in a place for men more broken than he is."

The concussion of words hurt my face, and I squinted against it. "Is that true?"

She nodded, her face finally taking on the vividness of a living thing.

"You knew he was out there? The whole time?"

She nodded again. "He was in your hospital room. You were not wrong."

"Then it was you who called him?"

"He brought you the sacrament," she said. "Drew would not send for a priest."

"Why would Drew send for a priest? I hadn't been to church in years."

Her eyes were such a deep fallish brown, the color of crushable leaves; I could imagine my uncle falling in love with her. "You regret that he came?" she asked.

"No." My head boiled with news. "Were you in touch? All these years?"

"More, at first. But then only on big days. When you finished at your little school. When you graduated from the college. When you girls came back to Hinton. The day after your marriage ceremony. Then the last time, after the accident."

Her body seemed old to me all of a sudden, a certain eroded quality in her stance that I hadn't noticed before, as if she'd been defying a hard tide, each crash of wave making off with a cell or two until finally the difference showed in her bearing.

"He's married?" I asked woodenly.

"Five years." She tried to smile and failed. "Just like you."

Mrs. Blanchard's kitchen felt like a place afloat. Weirdly, I braced myself for the bad news I had already received. Maybe she would tell the story again, adjusting the details in minute ways — a shift in chronology, words dropped from dialogue — microscopic changes to make the story hold.

I waited. The story stood, unamended. I was thinking of the packages she sent to me at Sacred Heart — soft things: molasses cookies, hand-knitted mittens — once monthly, without fail.

"I don't know," I stammered, "I don't know how you could do this to me. You let Celie drive in there and take me. You were standing right there in the yard." I reached out and cradled her face with one hand. "You knew the truth and said nothing. He did *nothing* to me and you knew it. *This* face was the last face I saw." I squeezed as hard as I could, surprised by her unyielding bones, her tightly gritted teeth. "I was one of your little chickens, remember?"

She winced but did not resist me. I let go, confused to find the same Mrs. Blanchard, the same graying, doe-eyed Mrs. Blanchard, Mariette's mother then and now, her hands still leathered from that long-ago stitching. "And how do I give away the truth, Lizzy?" she said, her voice beginning to unravel. "How do I explain? It was not a child in his bed, it was me, and I love him, and such a coincidence that my husband has disappeared from the face of this Earth?" Her eyes went flat now, and her face, too — flat with all those stifled years. "No, I did not take that chance."

"And neither did he."

"He would lose you if I gave away the truth, and he would lose you if I kept it for myself." She sounded as vacant as a winter field. "How would they let you stay with him if they know that he buried a man and threw his truck in the water?" She knotted her hands together. "So I kept the truth to myself. I chose my children."

"And he chose you." The shock of this stole my breath. Her arms lifted — the most embedded motherly gesture — but I made another sound, and she flinched from me. "You killed your children's father," I said. "He should have exposed you no matter what he had to lose. Was he that much in love?"

In her scoured kitchen my friend's mother stared like a trapped rabbit — or like the owl sweeping down for the kill, it was hard to say which. "He was a priest, Lizzy," she said slowly. "I made my confession."

I let this sink in. "Of course you did."

She said nothing.

"So," I said. "Absolution. In the privacy of the sacrament." I remembered First Fridays, confessing to Father Mike — *I lied once; I disobeyed twice* — and how he handed out my penance of three Hail Marys, pretending not to recognize me. I looked at Mrs. Blanchard. "What was your penance?"

"This," she said. She was crying now, noiseless and delicate.

"And his?" I demanded. Blood sludged through my limbs, thick and logy, as if my body were slowing to a stop from the inside out. Soon I would lose the power of speech.

"His? Oh, Lizzy. He nearly died of missing you." She swiped at her eyes. "When you see him," she said, "I hope you will be kind." A moment passed. "You were so young. We hoped time would erase him."

"Then you underestimated both me, and time."

When she spoke again I could barely hear her. "I would have taken you myself, Lizzy. I offered to those people, let me take her. But they said no, you had to go with family."

When I didn't — couldn't — answer, she said, "Mariette needs you, Lizzy. Go to your friend."

I obeyed, leaving her — in slow motion, it seemed, down the steps one at a time, every movement reminiscent of the aftermath of accident. Mariette sat crumpled on the curb, crying. When she saw me she shot up, seemed to come to, then began frantically looking around, checking her car, then mine, *where's Paulie where's Paulie where's Paulie oh my God some-one's taken Paulie,* as I drew her toward me, *he's okay, Charlie took him, he's fine, he's safe, get in Mariette get in* and she got in, her tongue so garbled by grief it was impossible to understand anything she was saying until she threw back her head, sucked up all her breath, and released one perfectly intelligible word: "Home."

I knew what she meant, and took her there.

A hundred yards straight in. Past the parish hall, past the church. Into the turnaround, where I parked a few feet from the rectory porch. Mariette sprang from the car and thundered down the grown-over shortcut, crashing through the underbrush and shying at the end where the farmhouse came into full view.

Another family lived there now. Somebody else's clothes on the line, drawers stuffed with somebody else's mismatched spoons and half-burned candles. No one appeared to be home. Two children's bicycles had been stashed on the porch. The tire swing Father Mike put up — with Ray Blanchard, one blistering August morning, when Mariette and I were four years old — looked like the aftermath of a hanging, nothing left but a tatter of rope flapping from the limb of an exhausted maple.

"Here," Mariette said when I caught up with her. She was off the path, kicking away needles and rotting leaves — her father was here somewhere. I glanced around at the barely discernible spots where we'd impersonated dying Indians, the boulder where we played King of the Hill. Mariette knelt down and ran her hands over the damp, cold ground. "Here," she said, out of breath. "Has to be. Where she told us not to play, remember?" I experienced a frisson of presence, realizing that far beneath us the ground was still warm.

She pointed to her old house, her old bedroom window. "I was up there," she said. "They were in the dooryard. I thought they were tending the moon garden. But something seemed off. They were hugging. It was something secret."

I crouched next to her, keeping one hand on her back. "I didn't see Papa," she said. "Just them. Together in the moonlight." She paused for a few moments, getting her breath. "The way they were looking at each other, I knew I wasn't supposed to see. He was pleading, or praying. She was in her housecoat. Then he looked up, and I ran back to my bed. Papa never came back, but Lizzy, how would I ever make such a connection? How in a million years? After a while it started to seem like something I dreamed."

I petted her back. "She must have been so afraid of him."

"I wasn't afraid of him at all." She pressed her forehead reverently to the ground. "She's my mother, Lizzy. What am I supposed to do now?"

"Ladies?" came a voice from behind us. The priest — the same priest whose Mass Drew and I had attended only a day earlier — stood in the path. He leaned down as if to hear our confession. "Is something wrong?"

"Yes, Father," I said, helping Mariette up.

"Can I — can I help you then?"

"I don't think so," I told him, but I went with him anyway. Taking Mariette with me, I followed him into the rectory. I touched the door post, the coat rack, the deacon's bench that once served as a repository for our winter hats. I touched everything I could reach as the nervous priest led us into the parlor, which still held my mother's breakfront, unchanged. Same beloved books on the lower shelves, same bric-a-brac on the higher ones. My mother's silver jam server, a commemorative plate from Ste. Anne de Beaupré in Quebec, six crystal champagne flutes, a set of pink teacups, a deck of playing cards with PRINCE EDWARD ISLAND printed on their backs. The glass doors had been shut for two decades, the key buried somewhere along Interstate 9 5, where I flung it from the back seat of Celie's car on the day I was taken away. No one had since mustered the imagination to pry open the doors. Our things had simply waited here, unmoved, part of the parcel of house and land checked into and out of every few years by a new priest with no taste. The furniture, though much of it had been replaced, occupied exactly the same space on the blueprint — chair where a chair was, sofa where a sofa was, different pictures hanging in the same places. I checked to see if Mariette had taken note, but her eyes had gone distant and glassy. She crossed her arms over her middle and stared at the floor.

"Her father died," I explained, herding her to a chair. Not the same chair we had, a different chair, some godawful

Marden's close-out in mud brown. This priest lacked imagination even in the most elementary matters, and I hated him for it.

"Oh, I'm very sorry," the priest said. "When?"

I was going to say, *Twenty-one years ago,* but Mariette answered, "Just now."

"What can I do?" the priest asked. He laid his hand on his heart, and I thought, You poor, incompetent man.

Then Mariette — strong, level-headed Mariette, Mariette who always played the store owner, the army officer, the head Indian, Mariette whose favorite saint was Joan of Arc — said, sliding off the chair, "I think I'm going to faint," and did.

She came to as she hit the floor, and lay there awhile, blinking up at a ceiling we had once tried to paint with colored water in squirt guns. The priest headed for the phone, but I called after him, "Don't. She's fine," and he turned around reluctantly. He would have to be the expert here. The person in charge. He looked like a man unhappily acquainted with his own limitations.

"What's going on?" he said, helping Mariette back into the chair.

"We used to live here," I told him.

He looked at me. "Oh," he said, remembering the story, but I could see him thinking, *There were two of them? Two little girls? My God.*

"That's my mother's breakfront," I said.

He looked worried. "Would you like to have it back?"

"Yes," I said, and I did. "But I think I'd better get her home."

Mariette was slumped in the ugly chair, limp as an over-loved ragdoll. "This house used to be pretty," I said to the priest as I helped my friend. "It had pizzazz."

I gentled Mariette to her feet, accepting her weight against me. It was as if she had fallen into a freshly dug hole herself and couldn't quite find her feet after the shock of climbing out. The priest escorted us to the car but gave us wide berth, his lips moving—interceding, no doubt, on our behalf, or apologizing for his performance. Despite his appeal to Heaven I felt wholly of this world, moving slowly, Mariette's arm mantled across my shoulders.

"Just a few more steps," I said to her.

"Lizzy," she murmured. "I don't want to know this."

"We're almost there," I said, "here we go." But as I inched her closer to the car door, I began to slow, profoundly aware that our friendship was turning—for better or worse, I did not know. I knew only that we would look back at this day as the point where another Before became another After. I tried to receive the hastening moment in all its bitter sweetness, to appreciate, for once, what I was losing at the time of its being lost.

TWENTY-NINE

That night, Charlie arrived. "I gotta talk to you guys." Cold wafted off his clothes; he helped Paulie out of his jacket and released him into our kitchen.

"Where's the kitty, where's the kitty, where's the kitty?"

Drew swung Paulie up and gave him a nuzzle. "Hiding, my man. He's hip to your jive."

As Paulie trotted off in search of the cat, Charlie dropped into a chair and pushed away a supper plate. "I'm dying, here," he said, running his hands through the filmy remains of his hair.

"She told you everything?" I said.

"I sure the hell hope so. Unless there's another body buried someplace." We observed an awkward moment of silence at the mention of Ray Blanchard, his bones now commingled with the ground where his children once played.

"I don't know what to do, you guys," Charlie said. "I wanted to at least call her brothers. She threw me out of the house."

"Should I —?"

"She won't see anyone, Lizzy. Not even you." He groaned, stiff and wall-eyed. "Please, you guys, Jesus God, help me out here." When Drew put a hand on Charlie's shoulder, Charlie shuddered like a building about to collapse. "The guy's got two other kids," he said. "Don't the boys deserve to know?"

I pictured Buddy reading in a carrel at the Franklin Pierce Law Library, Bernard leading his geology students through abandoned mines in Wyoming. Two kids who had never really known a father, but they'd done all right, they'd turned out responsible, upright, passionate. Holidays they arrived toting likeable girlfriends, full of stories.

"He's got family in Canada, right?" Charlie asked. "St. John?"

"Shediac. Brothers, I think," I said, my stomach bunching. There was Ray Blanchard, summoned from down the years, step-dancing to Acadian fiddle music one summer's evening, drunk and jolly, his feet pounding so hard the record skipped with him. Now he was irretrievably dead; I suppose I'd always thought I would see him again.

"I mean, Mother of God," Charlie persisted. "I'd sure want my son to know if it was me. I'd want my brothers to know where to dig me up."

Paulie toddled in just then, lugging the cat. "Hey look, hey look, hey look," he crooned, "look who *loves* me."

"What do we do?" Drew said, freeing the cat and drawing Paulie onto his lap.

Paulie echoed, "What do we do?"

Charlie looked at us with a face as broad and earnest as a scrubbed potato. "My wife seems to think this — *knowledge,* as she puts it — is something you just kind of live with."

"Where's the kitty?" Paulie said, scrambling down for a second pursuit.

Charlie sighed. "I have to get him to bed."

"Let him sleep here," I said. "We can stay up and talk as long as you want."

Before Paulie was born, the four of us, newly wed, had sat around this very table on countless evenings, playing hearts or poker for M&M's. More often than not, Mrs. Blanchard would stop by with one of her sisters (not Pauline, our once favorite, who had moved to New Hampshire for reasons that now seemed clear). Mrs. Blanchard brought little gifts — dish towels, a chocolate cake, basil seedlings in plastic pots. I had come to depend on her face, the passionate focus I took for affection, the melancholy I traced to widowhood.

"How do I deliver my son to her every morning, after this?" Charlie said. "I'm really asking. Mariette talks to her twice a day. She comes for supper every Sunday. How do we keep doing that?"

As Charlie talked — as much to himself as to us — I feared that Drew and I might be witnessing the beginning of the end of Charlie and Mariette's marriage. Drew slid his hand over, and I latched on.

For another hour we divined ways to live with what Charlie kept referring to as "the knowledge." Paulie fell asleep in the double chair, Drew carried him upstairs, then Charlie called Mariette and talked awhile. We moved into the living room with some beer and a box of Oreos, and suddenly our home looked like a parody of old times, three friends minus one preparing to talk long into the night.

"It's not like I don't think she had reasons," Charlie said at one point. "You don't do something like that over nothing."

"He could be scary," I said. "Mariette doesn't remember that."

"Course she remembers," Charlie said. "Why else would she have married a marshmallow like me?"

"Because you're a beautiful guy, Charlie," I said.

He shook his head. "I love my wife, you guys. More than anything. But I'm not the kind of person who can live the rest of my life with a body buried in the backyard."

He was lying on the couch at this point, his forearm draped over his face, and with his arm serving as a screen he mumbled, "Even if the guy was a bastard who got exactly what he asked for, doesn't he deserve a Christian burial? This is my son's grandfather we're talking about. It's not right that he's just down there, decomposing. Unmarked."

"What are you suggesting, Charlie?" I asked uneasily, thinking of Ray Blanchard's twenty-one-year-old corpse, well weathered and gone to ash.

"I'm a Catholic. The guy's my family." He took a rattling breath. "Mariette's bawling her eyes out because her mother's in trouble and she thinks it's up to her to decide what to do about it, okay? But she's also crying because she plain loved the guy." He paused. "There's a family plot at Calvary cemetery. It's got room."

Drew set down his beer. "Don't even think it."

"Ground's still workable. There wouldn't be much left to him after this much time, would there? Dust to dust. It's not like he'd *weigh* anything."

I covered my mouth. "I think I'm going to be sick."

Charlie groaned, sitting up. "I'm sorry, I don't know what I'm saying. Crazy things."

"If you mean exhuming a corpse under cover of darkness," Drew said, "then yeah, crazy things. You okay, Lizzy?"

I nodded, thinking, I *am* the sort of person who could live with the body in the yard, and I started running down the list. Mariette: could. Charlie: couldn't. Drew: could. I knew these things about the ones I loved, and it was a heartless way to divide them, but it told me something. Father Mike: couldn't. But he had done it anyway.

"I don't know if I want Paulie in her house," Charlie said. "God help me," he added, and it wasn't just an expression; he was praying.

"She'd never hurt Paulie," I said.

"It's not like we're talking about a murderer," Drew offered, then fell silent, because, of course, we *were* talking about a murderer.

Charlie's voice — that hearty, gladhanding cascade — had dropped to a grasshopper's whisper. "She hit him from behind. She had a plan for the truck. She had a guy next door, a *priest,* thank you very much, who kissed the ground she walked on. It's just that it doesn't seem completely spontaneous. I can't believe she didn't have another choice." His mouth buckled. "The woman's been a second mother to me, you guys. She's Mariette's be-all and end-all, she lights Paulie's world. I love her."

And around he went. At one-thirty I made coffee. At two, Drew said, "I won't tell."

Ah, I thought. I knew it.

I said, "I won't tell, either."

Charlie gave me a look. "Of course you won't. Your uncle's not exactly an innocent bystander."

"I'm not protecting him," I said, stung. "Mariette's the one I'm thinking of."

"People live with all kinds of things," Charlie said. He looked at us long and longingly. Ray Blanchard would soon become the thing that both bound us and broke us. Our parting had already begun.

We dozed off, the three of us, somewhere around four. At five-thirty I woke to find Charlie carrying Paulie out to the car.

I watched them from the window, Paulie's legs dangling from the bearlike shelter of his father's body. After a time I heard Drew get up, then felt his arms around me. "Charlie got the worst of it," I said. I leaned against him. My body relaxed, a sudden exhaustion overtaking my bones.

"I would have done what your uncle did," Drew murmured. "For you, I mean, at the beginning. I would have done that for you, if you'd asked." Charlie was backing out of our driveway now, into the dim light of morning. "Back then, I'd have given up everything."

Back then. When we were two drowning people exchanging life rafts. But it struck me that he *had* given up everything: Boston, his real photography, his imagined future.

We lingered at the window. "This was home," I said. I could sense the river beyond the rooftops, its inexorable forward motion toward the sea.

At six our alarm went off upstairs, and because it was Tuesday morning and we had landed in a life where people awaited us, we scurried around our bedroom and bathroom, the cat prowling underfoot, the day arriving whether we asked it to or not. Every gush of water, every flush and gargle and slid-shut drawer announced my present life, with its most fundamental architecture — a man and a woman — still holding after a few dozen unexpected heaves of the earth.

Within a matter of hours, Charlie broke. Charlie, who granted bonuses to his employees with every uptick in sales, who changed the oil for the fries twice as often as required, who confessed full sales tax on his IRS forms. Charlie Pelletier, spectacularly ill-equipped to live with "knowledge," called the police.

Charlie and Mariette hired a trial lawyer from Portland, a silk-suit type with notorious courtroom smarts, but in the airless weeks that followed, the case would become a low-key affair, legally speaking. No public trial, just a manslaughter charge and a dragged-out cycle of meetings convened for the purpose of detangling the State of Maine criminal code. I took the sick leave I had so long resisted, and Mariette, too, stayed out of school, emerging from her house only when necessary, the way people do during ice storms. We spoke on the phone, our conversations afflicted by unbearable pauses. Because her mother had been excised from the complicated infrastructure of our friendship, our footing shifted fatally. Our past had been altered without warning and no longer held. We could no longer speak easily about that which most defined us.

In the local news, the case unfolded more theatrically, fascinating if you didn't know the players and soul-crushing if you did. A son-in-law's sensational report. A body exhumed near a Catholic church, a backhoe piercing the half-frozen ground. Dry-eyed confession from the widow—nicest woman, you'd never guess. A few rotted threads of clothing in the grave. A body decomposed beyond its ability to speak. A host of legal ambiguities. In short, a protracted mess that produced a welter of "facts."

Good guy. Drinker. Fisherman. Layabout. Wife-beater. Churchgoer.

All the usual flapping jaws. How did she manage it? A woman that size? A hole that deep? A truck that heavy? But then, a witness. The statute of limitations expired long ago on accessory, obstruction. He's coming back anyway.

Confessor. Friend. Accomplice. Lover. A dead man bent on living again.

Wait, wait, isn't that the same guy, the priest who—?

The facts don't square.

Nothing rings entirely true. Because nothing is.

The night after Charlie made the call that would set into motion the mud-stuck wheels of justice, he returned to our house to tell Drew and me what he had done. "Mariette can't stop crying," he said wearily. "In a couple of days it'll hit the papers." He rested his blunt brown eyes on me. "I'm sorry about all this, Lizzy."

It took me a second to realize he was referring to my own impending discomfort in town, my old story about to rise from the mire. He propped his meaty hands on our table and pushed himself to standing. All at once he seemed to require extra shoring for the simplest movements, his bulk no longer able to take itself for granted.

"So. That's it," he said. "Come on, Paulie-boy."

Paulie, who was in the living room making spit-drawings on the window, caught sight of his coat dangling from his father's hand and hotfooted up the stairs to the nether reaches of the house. Charlie sighed. "I haven't got the juice to go after him."

"Leave him here," Drew said. "We'll take him home when he winds down."

Too worn out to entertain other options, Charlie consented. Drew went after Paulie to keep him from our dresser drawers, and I walked Charlie to the door. "She still loves me, right?" he asked. The door made a wintry cracking as he opened it.

"She'd be a fool not to, Charlie."

He took this in without comment. After a moment, he said, "I'll have to sell the business. I don't see how we can stay here now."

For Charlie, moving would mean leaving his parents and brothers, his customers and employees, the streets and river and hills he had been born into. He'd planned to run for selectman when he reached thirty-five and turn himself into the guardian of the law, custodian of the town hall, friend to the people. Now he was going to be part of a story these same people told at parties.

The yard sheened with fresh snowfall, the kind that stayed. "It's hard to imagine this place could even exist without all of us here," I said.

But we would find, soon enough, that it could. The shape of the hills and the course of the river would not vary. We could scatter like fall leaves — Drew and I to Boston;

Mariette and Charlie to northern Maine, where they would make room for Mrs. Blanchard after her three months served — and our town would abide unchanged. But at this moment, in the silence of a lasting snow, I preferred to believe things otherwise.

Charlie made a move toward the driveway. I called after him, "Kiss your wife for me."

"Lizzy," he said, turning around, "they'll be taking statements right away. Mariette wanted you to know."

I hugged myself against the encroaching cold. "Why would they want to talk to me?"

"Not you. Your uncle. He'll be contacted before week's end." We locked eyes a moment, but there wasn't a thing to say. Charlie lurched back toward me, gave me a squeeze, then hiked up his collar and went home.

The square of lime-green paper lay on my kitchen windowsill, after two days already soft from overhandling, lifting a little whenever we opened or closed the nearby door. I had been waiting, returning to that fluttering scrap as if it were a page in a prayer book, and it struck me now that my waiting felt the way religion once had — the promise of a perfect reunion that lay perpetually in the future. Even as a child saying my nightly prayers, I dreaded Heaven, afraid my own parents might not recognize me after so long.

After supper Drew shuttled Paulie back home. The paper rustled as the door swung shut. Father Mike's name, joined with a woman's, looked like a piece of code. An odd humming began in the back of my throat, and I caught myself at something I hadn't done in twenty-one years. A single line from the Prayer to St. Bartholomew came winging back, unaltered: "Keep us ever guileless, and innocent as doves."

It rang twice. A child answered.

MATINS

THIRTY

I saw a one-hundred-fifteen-year-old woman on television once, one of those balding, toothless Russians who surface every so often to recommend yogurt or vodka as the secret to long life. Instead, she reminisced about her baby brother, who fell through the ice and drowned when she was eight years old and he was five. *He had the prettiest hair,* she said to the translator, *it was the color of yellow and smelled like the hay in the barn.* This creaky, spotted woman with a face so old it had all but melted off her skull remembered a smell from one hundred and seven years past. I thought, I know what you mean. One hundred and seven years is nothing.

He arrived in the afternoon, under a bleached winter sunlight. His wife came with him, and her son, a serious child named David who stared at me in undisguised wonder the whole time he spent in my house. I served cranberry muffins that I made myself, some milk for the child, and coffee that I'd made with crushed eggshells, though I did not tell. Also, I pretended not to remember that he took his coffee black. I did not wish to wound him with echoes of intimacy.

On the phone he had said, Can you forgive me?

And I said, I'm afraid not.

Then I opened my door and saw what a penance such as his could do to the mortal flesh. Most of the color had bled from his eyes and his once-ruddy cheeks. His copper-threaded hair had gone a lifeless gray. He was gaunt, and shorter than I remembered. His glasses tilted weakly. His sole remaining beauty was an essential kindness that still showed in the particular way the bones met in his face. Otherwise, he seemed crumbled before his time, intentionally so, as if fixed on decomposing along with the man he had buried.

He was hard to look at if you'd had something else in mind all this time. I didn't know what to call him.

He beheld me with a sorrowful calm that made me calm in turn. I was aware of my own changed, adult face, which he kissed just above the scar. His parched lips burned me.

"Lizzy," he said, his voice cracking.

He put out his hands and I took them, forgiving him already. His hands felt dry and ridged, not at all how I remembered them, except for the tattered nails. Once, I had known his step before it landed. I had drifted into sleep on the tide of his voice. I had not wholly understood where he left off and I began.

"This is my husband," I said, as Drew put out his hand. These moments seemed glimpsed and tottering; I was trying to recall them even as I lived them.

They shook hands: the man who left, and the man who stayed.

His wife, Frannie — middle-aged, short-haired, puppy-faced — said, "Hello, hello." I liked her button earrings, her homely purse. Everyone stepped inside.

"What are we?" the boy asked, as we milled in the entryway. He was twelve but looked younger. Pale and dartlike in his narrow blue jacket.

"What do you mean?" I said. Father Mike put a hand on his stepson's shoulder, a gesture that had often marshaled my own courage, as it did now for the boy's.

The boy said, "Are we relatives?"

"Sure," I told him, looking into his elfin face. "I guess we'd be cousins."

This seemed to satisfy him. He believed me. Then he glanced up at his new father, just to make sure.

❧ ❧

Frannie seemed glad to be in my house, to meet my husband and see my things. She, too, had been living with a ghost; perhaps my presence gave him form. I served the muffins and poured the coffee. Daylight carpeted through the windows as if in search of us.

We talked about the recent snow. The drive from Ohio. The changes in town. When Mr. Peachy sidled into the room and hopped onto Father Mike's empty lap, my uncle chuckled in a way that startled me.

I thought, *That sounds just like my uncle.* I began to see him then, his latter-day self bleeding through the veneer of his present-day self, like a painting beneath a painting.

"He loves cats," I said to Frannie.

"Oh, yes, I know," she said. "I'm allergic, unfortunately." She put up her hand. "It's okay, don't move him. For short periods, it's fine. I can't *live* with cats, that's all."

"Dogs either," the boy said morosely.

With forced brightness, Frannie told him, "Life's full of sacrifices."

Drew rescued the ensuing silence by offering to show the boy his studio. Frannie got up, too. She watched us for just a moment — with an alertness that made me feel benevolently memorized — before leaving us there alone.

❧   ❧

"He seems like a sweet boy," I said to Father Mike. His eyes seemed to lurch behind his glasses in the way I felt my own eyes doing. Trying to see, then see harder.

"He is. He's a sweet boy."

"What happened to his father?"

"Cancer." He reminded me of a held-back dam.

"I guess it must have been hard on him."

"It was. Frannie, too. They lost a good man."

What followed felt like the opposite of silence.

"Did you ever think of me?" I asked.

His face was fully emerging now; this was surely the man, I could see it, who used to be my young and dashing uncle. I half expected to hear his younger voice, those round and doting tones, but all he managed was a graveled "yes" that sounded like the groan of a long-tethered dog.

❧   ❧

He used to say *I beg your pardon* after a sneeze. He used to hide presents inside other presents, a doll inside a new pillowcase, a bike horn inside a new lunch box. There remained always more magic in the magic trick of our existence. Everything I shook rattled with possibility.

"Have you seen her yet?" I asked after some moments.

He regarded me in that seeing-harder way. "I saw the district attorney's people. It looks as if they'll go easy, especially after all this time." He paused. "Ray had a history. You children didn't know."

"I remember a bag of peas." I didn't elaborate, preferring to let Ray Blanchard rest in peace.

Other memories arrived instead. The brushed fedora Father Mike sacrificed to a snowman that took seven weeks to melt. How he kept his eyes open when saying yes, closed when saying no. A church picnic, not my first but the first I remember well, the croquet game set up, the races and whistles, the tables dragged up from the parish hall and set with flapping paper tablecloths. The grand prize was a sugary, hill-shaped blueberry pie. We formed our team of two and won everything — the three-legged race, the horseshoe tournament, the balloon toss. They let him win because he was Father. I knew this and he didn't. He thought we won because I was irresistible to the judges — parish ladies all, mothers with soft hands. After that fragile day of favor we lugged back to the house, spent and happy, and gorged ourselves on our prize.

"Her sister made a statement, too," he said. "You remember Pauline?"

"Of course I remember Pauline," I said. "I remember everything."

And this — this very moment — would compose part of that everything. His pressed blue shirt, the pleated skin at the base of his neck, the thin and glinting rims of his glasses, all of this was mine.

"I have a thousand memories," I said.

He whispered, "Good ones, Lizzy, I hope." His hands opened, a priestly gesture of praise, or offering, or submission. His palms were the color of unlighted candles.

"Father," I said. "How could it be otherwise?"

As he wiped his eyes I caught sight of his ring, the flash of cat that my mother had found so enchanting. It came over me then — almost before I fully registered that he was sitting in a stuffed chair, drinking coffee that had been ground with eggshells, petting a cat that drowsed on his lap, a living tableau from the frozen past—that I was happy to see him. Desperately, bloomingly happy.

He rested his drained eyes upon me. "Do you remember the caseworker who came to the house, Lizzy?"

I nodded. "It was quite a while before I put it together."

His face rushed with color. "I wanted," he said, "at the very least, to protect your innocence."

We fell silent at the word "innocence." For my part, I conjured a painted kitchen chair with a white sticker reading *la chaise*.

"Mrs. Blanchard told me I was your penance," I said. "Is that true?"

He set the cat down as if it were a piece of crockery he was being careful not to break, then dropped his face into his hands and wept. My first memory reeled in—my only uncle, asking my permission to cry. I slid off the chair and sheltered him into my arms. He was shockingly slight, his spine a beaded line, though possibly the sensation of smallness was only that I had grown while he had not. How could he be this small? I rested my cheek on the eroding rack of his shoulder and found some comfort there.

"I'm so happy to see you," I whispered. "You can't imagine."

He clutched me with the fervency of the dying, and I felt like the single thing tethering him to Earth. From the reach of childhood there washed through me an old surprise, an intimate, potent, and all but forgotten sensation: power.

He prayed then, in his old way — *our* old way — asking for the simple mercy of God. I believe we received it. The room had lost its bright afternoon light, and my worldly goods — my chairs and lamps and curtain rods and drapes — had taken on the color-lessness of early dusk and an aspect of steadfast waiting that I associated with convalescence. I helped him up, or he helped me.

He asked me again to forgive him, and this time I said yes.

When Drew and Frannie and her son joined us again they were chatting — easily, it seemed to me — the boy atwitter with discovery after seeing Drew's darkroom, all those chemicals and attendant paraphernalia. He had a voice like a cricket, though I guessed in a year's time he would begin to sound more like a man. Father Mike and I had seated ourselves again, facing each other in a soft silence, preparing ourselves, I understand now, for a journey we have yet to complete, though it looks to me as though we will. The five of us reassembled, snapping lamps on, mustering our most romantic hopes for connection, in the way we would continue to, like all willing but scattered families.

"She looks like her mother," Father Mike said to Frannie.

Everyone turned to me. I think I smiled, as my mother would have. The moment seemed to call for a toast, so I took my husband's hand, lifted my cup, and recited the only one I knew.

"All joy, all love, all good wishes to you," I said.

And my uncle said, "In God's good name."

After that, I asked for a story about my parents.

We begin there.

ACKNOWLEDGMENTS

I am indebted, first and always, to Gail Hochman, not only for her expertise as an agent but for her sharp editorial eye; and to the incomparable Jay Schaefer, my editor for six years now, which in the book business is a *very* long time. I appreciate my Chronicle Books family, especially Steve Mockus; and my paperback champions at Ballantine, especially Allison Dickens. For enhancing my understanding of the priesthood, thanks to Eddie Hurley. For guidance on French Canadian language and culture, *gros bisous* to Theresa Vaillancourt and Denise Vaillancourt. For help with certain plot points, thanks to Geoff Rushlau and Don Marsh. Much appreciation, also, to my readers: Dan Abbott, Anne Wood, Monty Leitch, Paul Doiron, and Jessica Roy; and my listener, Mary Jane Johnson.

ANY

Bitter

THING

MONICA WOOD

A Reader's Guide

A Conversation with Monica Wood

Monica Wood was interviewed by her sister, Catherine WoodBrooks.
The sisters grew up, one year apart in age, in Mexico, Maine,
with three other siblings. Catherine is vice president for student
affairs at Assumption College in Worcester, Massachusetts,
and remains her sister's biggest fan.
This interview took place at Catherine and her husband's camp
on East Grand Lake in northern Maine during the family's annual
"sisters only, no boys allowed" week. The interview was punctuated
(and often halted altogether) by familiar laughter.

Catherine WoodBrooks: I got a big kick out of seeing all the names we grew up with in *Any Bitter Thing*—Blanchard, Levesque, Derocher . . . I even noticed a minor character named after my mother-in-law. So my first questions is: How come you've never named a character after me?

Monica Wood: Hah! Cat, I could never do you justice. Besides, I'd never hear the end of it if I gave you, say, blue eyes instead of green.

CW: Hazel. Speaking of real life intruding on fiction, the obvious connection I made was our real-life uncle, Father Bob, who reminded me of Father Mike.

MW: One of the great pleasures of writing this novel, especially in the early stages, was revisiting some of our favorite childhood memories.

CW: I loved the scene where Lizzy and Mariette are playing "shoe store." I could picture us in Mum's bedroom, with all of the shoes laid out on the bed. You really captured Father Bob's great sense of humor. It would have been just like him to come into our imaginary shoe store and ask for something as outlandish as "a badger." I could see us collapsing in laughter just as Lizzy and Mariette did. It was as if you plucked a chunk of our childhood and dropped it into this book.

MW: I'm so glad you feel that way. The relationship between Father Mike and Lizzy is so critical to this story. I tried to capture the essence of what we had with Father Bob—that feeling of utter comfort and joy, that sense of being totally recognized and loved. I wanted my readers to understand what Lizzy loses when she loses him.

CW: Is it a coincidence that Lizzy loses Father Mike at exactly the same age you were when we lost Dad?

MW: Whoa. That's an interesting question. So many of these connections occur to me only after a book is finished. But you're right: a big loss at age nine, probably not a coincidence. But it was a subconscious choice on my part.

CW: I loved that Father Mike comes across as a real priest, too, not just a fun and doting uncle. I remember Father Bob telling us when it was time to read his Breviary. It seemed like hours, and we actually had to entertain ourselves for a little while.

MW: Did I ever tell you that the epigraphs that precede each of the Father Mike chapters came directly from the places he marked in his own Breviary?

CW: How could you read anything? His handwriting was illegible!

MW: No, no. I mean those silk bookmarks—remember those? When I inherited the Breviary, I just left the bookmarks where they were, and then picked something from the pages he'd left marked. But there were also a few little personal prayers written throughout, in his terrible handwriting. I left those private.

CW: How did the character of Father Mike evolve in your mind?

MW: All I knew at the beginning of this thing was that Lizzy had been in an accident, and that someone had both helped her at the side of the road and also left her there to die. It wasn't until I began to explore her background that I realized her priest-uncle had raised her. From there, after the building process that evolved from my early memories of Father Bob, Father Mike began to take over. He became his own person. And the big irony of this book for me is that despite the fact that I was guided in a sense by my memories of Father Bob— and in a more practical sense by his Breviary—I could never have written this book if he were still alive.

CW (laughing): I can't imagine Father Bob reading all the swear words, for one thing.

MW: And he'd be outraged by some of Father Mike's decisions. On so many levels he couldn't have read this book. He was such a devout, by-the-book priest above all else.

CW: Remember how he used to refer to the guys who left?

MW: "Jumping the league." They "jumped the league." That's in the book. But despite all those little real-life notes, the two people—Father Mike and Father Bob—parted company for me very early in the writing of this book.

CW: When I read the first chapter, even though I didn't know much about Lizzy, I sensed this was going to be a story about a broken woman. She was running, for one thing. You sense her gaping loneliness right off the bat. If I were to define a theme here—and I know how you hate this—was it about abandonment?

MW: Theme—as I've told you a million times—comes afterward, something you recognize after your story gets laid down. I think abandonment is accurate, though—specifically between fathers and daughters. Mariette and Lizzy have that in common. But abandonment shows up in more subtle ways, too. One of the most interesting relationships in the book, for me, is the one between Father Mike and God. Talk about abandonment! And Vivienne—not to give too much away here—works her own form of abandonment later on. Lizzy herself, feeling abandoned by Drew and Mariette, abandons them in turn by seeking out Harry Griggs.

CW: Speaking of abandonment . . . do you remember the *Patty Duke Show,* which we used to watch once a week—

MW (laughing): Till Mum made us give it up for Lent.

CW: Yeah, that was a tough one, but a good lesson actually. She wanted us to understand the concept of sacrifice. Anyway, I'm thinking of the episode where Patty decides to be a novelist and ends up weeping in her garret over thousands of pages, and when her father asks what's wrong she says—

MW: She says, "I just killed Reginald!"

CW: That's how I felt finishing your novel. I was so sad that I would never see these people again.

MW: That's how I always feel, too, except my sadness is tinged with relief. By the time I'm done writing the novel, they've given me so much trouble for so long that I'm kind of glad to say good-bye. Thrilled, to be honest.

CW: Let's talk a little about the complexity of these characters without giving away the story. You get so far below the surface of your characters. I could easily describe each character's traits and flaws. How do you fully develop these people? Is this a stupid question?

MW: No, but hard to answer. I live with my characters for quite a while—three to five years, usually—before I finally understand what they're doing and why they're doing it. It takes almost as long to get to know a fictional person as it does a real person. Harry Griggs is a great example. For the first year of this novel, his name was William Austin, and he was an art dealer from New York City who lived in one of those fancy condos on the Portland wharf.

CW: So how did you get from Mr. Fancy Pants to Harry Griggs?

MW: Mr. Fancy Pants began to bore me silly, is what happened initially. His white apartment, his wet bar, his view of the water, his everything. I never did get much below his surface, because I didn't understand him. I've succeeded in the past with characters that I don't understand, but they were interesting enough to me for me to take the trouble to crack their code. One day I just got sick enough of William Austin that I changed his name—to Billy Austin. That alone altered him profoundly. Have you ever heard of an art dealer named Billy Austin? Then I moved him from the Portland Wharf down to Hanover Street—a far more colorful neighborhood—and he became Harry Griggs, a barely functioning alcoholic for whom I had nothing but empathy. The whole book got easier after that.

CW: So you're telling me that this novel was originally about Harry Griggs?

MW: It was about a woman named Lizzy, and the man who hit her in his car. That was William/Harry. For about two years, Harry was the actual hit-and-run guy. But then it became more interesting to have him do a good deed that wasn't, strictly speaking, a good deed.

CW: Right, the "bad Samaritan." One thing I love about this book is that nobody is just one thing.

MW: It wouldn't be very much fun to write otherwise.

CW: The book is so full of surprises. Did you plan them all out?

MW: I followed my characters into a huge yarn-ball of plot, and then spent about three years figuring out how to unravel it.

CW: I'm sorry, but I just do NOT understand how you do that. And I think most people can't imagine how hard this process must be. But having you as a sister, I have to chuckle when I hear someone say they would like to take a year off to write a book. It's amazing how many people think they could do what you do if they just had a spare year.

MW: Do you remember the time we were in a grocery line, and you took a magazine off the rack that had a story of mine in it, and showed it to the grocery clerk? She looked at it and said, "I'd be a writer if I had the time."

CW (laughing): I resisted the urge to strangle her.

MW: I know! I thought: Be my guest, Toots. See how you like it. I'm lucky if I get a page a week.

CW: Enough about you and your writing process. Let's talk about what was so familiar to *me*. That scene where they're sewing shoes!

MW: Did I remember that right?

CW: Right down to the scent of the leather softening in the water, waxing the thread—should we say something about our neighbors?

MW: I guess we should. Our wonderful neighbor used to have her girls and us help her with her piecework.

CW: She got two dollars for a case of shoes—I think there were thirty in a case.

MW: That was a lot of work for two bucks. But don't you remember it as the most fun thing we ever did?

CW: We've done a lot of fun things, Mon.

MW: I'll put those in the next book, okay?

Reading Group Questions and Topics for Discussion

Warning: Some of these discussion questions reveal certain plot turns. If you prefer to be surprised, read the book first.

1. As the novel opens, Lizzy says, "I tell this with the authority of memory." A page later, she says of the girl who hit her, "She tells the cop she thought she hit a deer. She tells her parents she thought she hit a deer. She tells the judge she thought she hit a deer. Eventually, I guess, she thought she hit a deer." Shortly after that, she observes, "The human craving is for story, not truth. Memory, I believe, embraces its errors, until what is, and what is remembered, become one." What is the author implying about the nature of memory, and the nature of this novel?

2. This novel is, in part, the story of a marriage. What do you see as the turning points in Drew and Lizzy's marriage? Do you think Lizzy and Drew are well matched?

3. Father Mike was both a father, small "f," and a Father, capital "F." How well do you believe he fulfilled both these roles? How did one role enhance the other, or diminish the other?

4. Vivienne tells Father Mike, "Faith has nothing to do with the Church." Is this true? Does Father Mike's faith fail him, or save him? What about the Catholic Church—does it fail or save Father Mike?

5. Would you describe Lizzy as an emotionally guarded woman or emotionally generous?

6. What do you think is the essence of Lizzy's bond with Harry Griggs? Why does she turn to him instead of to her husband or friend? Is he more than just a stranger who will listen? Why did Lizzy defend Harry to his daughter, Elaine?

7. Is Vivienne a good woman or a bad woman? Do you blame her for her crime? Was her behavior in the aftermath merely an instinct for self-preservation, or more than that? Has she paid enough of a penance?

8. Is Mrs. Hanson a villain? What would you have done if you had seen what she saw?

9. One of the most moving passages in the book is Father Mike's lament about being an accused person: "You wonder what made your love so desperate and gushing. What impelled you to admire her child's body in the bath, the seal-slick purity of it, the strength it seemed to be acquiring, its miraculous shape-shifting? You wonder why you loved her sweaty socks, her smell as you tucked her in, her breath after she ate a plum. How can you help but wonder? You could not pass her in a room without touching your hand to her head, your thumb to her chin. What did all that mean? Tainted, all of it, your dearest memories stained for good." Are Father Mike's

parental feelings every parent's feelings, or do his unusual circumstances make for unusual feelings?

10. When Father Mike refers to Lizzie's calloused hands as "the working girl's stigmata," how does this colorful phrase suggest several layers of pride? A similarly layered observation comes at the end, when Lizzy begins to see Father Mike's "latter-day self bleeding through the veneer of his present-day self, like a painting beneath a painting." Do you think Lizzy is beginning to heal in this moment, or is she merely connecting to a time when she felt the most safe, the most loved?

11. Lizzy and Father Mike are, in one sense, innocent victims of circumstance. But how does Father Mike bring about his own downfall? After Vivienne's confession, he has no choices. But could he have made choices long beforehand that could have prevented his undoing—a choice to listen to Vivienne when she "wishes to talk about Ray," for example, or a choice to confront Ray rather than turn a blind eye?

12. What does Lizzy see in Andrea that makes her a favorite student? Do you think they are much alike?

13. What will become of Lizzy and Mariette's friendship now that they understand the full truth of the people they loved? Is a shared childhood enough to sustain a friendship for life? Is there really such a thing as unconditional love?

MONICA WOOD is the author of the novels *My Only Story* and *Secret Language* and the story collection, *Ernie's Ark*. Her fiction has appeared in numerous magazines and anthologies and she has been awarded a Pushcart Prize for the title story of *Ernie's Ark*. She lives in Maine.

Don't miss these touching books by MONICA WOOD

Join the Reader's Circle
to enhance your book club or
personal reading experience.

Our FREE monthly e-newsletter gives you:

• Sneak-peak excerpts from our newest titles

• Exclusive interviews with your favorite authors

• Fun ideas to spice up your book club meetings:
creative activities, outings, and discussion topics

• Opportunities to invite an author to your next
book club meeting

• Anecdotes and pearls of wisdom from other book group
members . . . and the opportunity to share your own!

• Special offers and promotions giving you access to
advance copies of books, our Reader's Circle catalog,
and much more

To sign up, visit our website at
www.thereaderscircle.com
or send a blank e-mail to
sub_rc@info.randomhouse.com

**When you see this seal on the outside,
there's a great book club read inside.**